He watched his body's hands reach out to touch Lancelot on chest and brow. Letting his eyes unfocus, the bard saw a slim, silver thread stretching from the prince's mouth into ... he could not see the other end, or even where it pointed, as if Lancelot's shade had fled somewhere not of this world. The cord was tight, pulled to the breaking point.

He took hold of the cord, and climbed hand over hand. Lancelot's soul-cord led into a tunnel that grew narrower with height. The bard climbed and climbed, squeezing his soul tighter and tighter. At last he could climb no further. He was stuck, leagues and leagues of Lancelot's soulstuff still above him.

He fought paralyzing dread with the coin of valor and drew the sword of reason with his right hand. "We need you yet, Prince. Come back down with me." Then, reaching up as high as he could, he cut the silver cord with his phantom sword.

The bard dropped—losing the sword, the cord, even up and down. . . .

Other AvoNova Books by
Dafydd ab Hugh

ARTHUR WAR LORD

ARTHUR WAR LORD

BOOK TWO

FAR BEYOND THE WAVE

DAFYDD AB HUGH

AVONOVA

AVON BOOKS • NEW YORK

ARTHUR WAR LORD BOOK TWO: FAR BEYOND THE WAVE is an
original publication of Avon Books. This work has never before appeared
in book form. This work is a novel. Any similarity to actual persons or
events is purely coincidental.

AVON BOOKS
A division of
The Hearst Corporation
1350 Avenue of the Americas
New York, New York 10019

First AvoNova Printing: September 1994

AVONOVA TRADEMARK REG. U.S. PAT. OFF. AND IN OTHER COUNTRIES, MARCA
REGISTRADA, HECHO EN U.S.A.

Printed in the U.S.A.

RA   10 9 8 7 6 5 4 3 2 1

Synopsis of Arthur War Lord
(Book 1)

MAJOR PETER SMYTHE, OF THE 22-SAS ANTI-TERRORIST unit, is sent by Colonel Cooper to investigate rumors of IRA infiltration of a bizarre science project: Henry Willks and his team claim to be building a time machine.

When Peter arrives, posing as a Royal Marine adviser, he discovers they are much farther along than they reported; they actually have a working model. Peter meets the young, upper-class physicist Mark Blundell—an amiable chap, if a bit naive about the IRA. Peter gains Blundell's trust by pretending to be a fellow Freemason; in fact, Peter has simply studied some of the "secret" signs and code phrases.

Also working on the project is a known Republican symp, Selly Corwin. In a pub that evening, she makes a coy reference to Peter's unit, which he misses. But that night, he sits bolt upright out of a sound sleep—the marble has dropped; he realizes both that Selly must be IRA and that she has "made" him.

Before he can nab her, she escapes . . . to A.D. 450 and the court of the historical "King" Arthur: Artus *Dux Bellorum*, Arthur "War Leader," a civilized gent who speaks Latin, wears a toga, and fancies himself the successor to the Romans, who withdrew from Britain fifty years back.

Meanwhile, at that very moment (but fifteen centuries earlier), Cors Cant Ewin, a bard in the court of Artus, moons over a new, hot babe who's floated into Caer Camlann (Camelot). He has no idea that the object of his affection, Anlawdd of Harlech, is actually a princess slumming as a seamstress for Artus's wife, Gwynhwfyr.

1

Anlawdd was sent to Camlann on a mission by her father, Prince Gormant: She is supposed to *assassinate Artus himself.* Gormant wants Harlech to be a free city once again, dominated neither by Saxons nor by Romanesque generals like Artus.

Fifteen hundred years later, Peter Smythe begins seeing a strange "forest world" superimposed over the laboratory, an alternative time line—undoubtedly caused by Selly Corwin's tinkering with history. The gal has done *something;* but what?

They try to bring her back, but she resists, leaving only one alternative: Peter must pursue her back in time.

The problem is that the machine doesn't send back physical bodies . . . it "cogniports" the mind. Thus, Selly's mind and personality lurk inside the body of somebody already in Camelot; and so, too, will Peter's mind when he follows her.

But something goes wrong, and Peter's body is nearly killed as the machine shorts out. It clings to life by a thread, the connection with Peter's consciousness nearly severed.

"Peter," himself, is cast back through the ages, landing in the body of the illiterate, semi-barbaric Prince General Legate Lancelot, an exile under sentence of death from his native Sicambria for having tried to murder the former governor, now king: Merovius Rex, King Merovee.

As luck would have it, that very same King Merovee arrives in Camlann to sign a secret treaty with Artus.

Peter meets Merovee and instantly falls under his spell. Merovee is charming, forgiving, awe-inspiring, a natural leader. The "blood royal" courses through Merovee's veins. They shake hands, and Peter jumps when Merovee slips him a Masonic handshake . . . twelve hundred years before Freemasonry supposedly began!

Gwynhwyfr arrives and tries to sit in Peter's lap while he's standing up; she and "Lancelot" appear to be involved in a lusty affair . . . which Artus knows about and makes no effort to stop, so long as they're discreet.

Peter also meets Cors Cant and decides to pump the

bard for information about the court . . . and in particular, about anybody who has suddenly begun acting strange, somebody who might actually be Selly Corwin, 20th century IRA terrorist.

His suspicions center upon Anlawdd: First, she arrived at Camlann only a few weeks earlier; second, Peter instantly realizes that she's "political." The hard, auburn-haired seamstress with a malapropos warrior's heart hides some deep, sinister secret.

Returning the favor, Anlawdd and Cors Cant realize that something has *changed* about Prince General Legate Lancelot—mostly for the better. He's more thoughtful, not as bloodthirsty. And strangest of all, he now appears to be literate. Previously, Lancelot's disdain for Artus's Roman trappings included a refusal to learn to read or write.

Anlawdd has so far refused to yield to her heart's desire for the young bard; but at last, despite knowing the duties of war, she can resist no longer. She knows the love is doomed, for when she slays Artus, she will, in effect, slay the love between her and Cors Cant, tantamount to killing all three of them with a single dagger-blow.

Alas, Anlawdd is unwilling to admit the feeling, while Cors Cant's protestations of love are too glib; neither is yet prepared for such commitment.

Meanwhile, Peter has overheard Merovee and Artus plotting: Now that the Roman Empire has withdrawn from both Britain and Sicambria, they fear the long night will come; civilization will be battered to death beneath the cloven hooves of barbarian Saxons, Jutes, and Huns. They have a plan to stave off the night and keep bright the flame of civilized knowledge.

Peter uses modern police interviewing techniques to trick Cors Cant into spilling the beans: Artus and Merovee plan to join and form a British-Sicambrian Roman Empire, one based not on the worship of the Catholic Church, as is the current Roman Empire, but upon the true divinity of Jesus through his twin brother, James.

Peter is confused: There never was any such British-Sicambrian Roman Empire; has Selly changed history already?

The Church is understandably upset by this position, and it has sent spies to stir up anti-Merovee sentiment among Artus's generals ... in particular, Prince Cei and Prince Bedwyr.

Cei, the porter of Caer Camlann and a legate of two legions, braces Peter: Cei, Bedwyr, and Lancelot have been plotting against Merovee ever since they discovered the "Long-Haired King" was coming to Camlann. Now, Cei even broaches the idea of a split from Artus, as well; Cei points out that with his two legions plus Lancelot's two, they together would have a force superior to the Praetorian Guard, who are personally loyal to Artus.

Peter is nonplussed. Should he join with Cei and turn traitor against England's first great "king," Artus *Dux Bellorum?* Or should he refuse the offer and draw suspicion upon himself? Where does his loyalty lie ... and which path will lead him to discover Selly Corwin and stop her from doing whatever she did to replace twentieth century England with virgin forest?

Peter discovers he's expected to fight a match in three days with the Saxon Cutha, son of King Caedwin of Wessex. Cutha is allegedly on a diplomatic mission to Camlann, but Cors Cant is convinced he's a spy sent to break up the Artus-Merovee alliance; the boy wants Lancelot to "accidentally" slay Cutha during the fight

Anlawdd, too, wants Lancelot to kill the Saxon: Then, when Artus is discovered slain, everyone will assume the Saxons did it for revenge, and she might salvage her love with Cors Cant (assuming he *never* finds out who really killed the *Dux Bellorum).*

Yet another player enters the political picture: Queen Morgawse, mother of Medraut (Mordred), summons Peter to warn him *not* to kill Cutha. The diplomatic repercussions would rip Camlann apart. Trying to be suave, Peter accidentally makes Queen Morgawse believe that his price for not killing the Saxon is a night with her; reluctantly, she agrees. When Peter realizes the miscommunication, he cannot think of a graceful way to back out.

Peter frets about his upcoming fight with Cutha—he's

not worried about whether or not to kill the Saxon . . . he's worried about whether the Saxon will kill *him*. He sets up a practice session with Medraut, both to learn what he can of fifth century fighting techniques and also to keep his eye on one of the prime suspects, Mordred. History paints Mordred as a treasonous plotter who slew Arthur; thus, Peter thinks the boy is a natural candidate to attract Selly's consciousness back through the ages.

But the boy belies his historical rap: He's young, eager, and worships Lancelot almost as a god.

Anlawdd has a crisis of conscience. She never wanted the job of assassin; she had recommended instead that Gormant make common cause with his brother-in-law, her Uncle Leary, the Archking of Ireland. But Gormant, ever jealous of Leary, preferred villainy to diplomacy; and Anlawdd, bound by her princessly honor, had to accept the charge.

She was eager to leave Harlech in any event, if only to get away from her brother, Canastyr the "Hundred Handed," who had molested her repeatedly after her mother died when Anlawdd was six years old. Ten years later, Uncle Leary initiated her into a secret society, the Builders of the Temple (founded by King Merovee); and now, four years after initiation, Anlawdd is caught in a terrible moral quandry: either she disobeys her father and sovereign and betrays her honor as a princess, or she obeys Gormant, murders Artus, and betrays the ideals of her higher soul and her honor as a Builder.

In the midst of this dichotomy is her growing love for Cors Cant, which is rising out of all proportion until it threatens to overwhelm both her other selves, princess and Builder. Perversely, rather than crushing the unwanted personal sentiments, she invites the bard for a ride . . . but she has a secret plan.

(Fifteen hundred years later, Mark Blundell has also begun seeing the forest world; he realizes this means he will eventually end up journeying back in time himself. In the meantime, the group tries to bring Peter's consciousness back but breaks off the attempt when his body nearly dies. Just as they shut down the machine, Colonel Cooper shows up, wondering where his crack anti-terrorist has gone.)

Peter spars with Medraut and gets his posterior kicked; at the last moment, he reacts without thinking, using modern martial-arts techniques to unhorse Medraut and send the lad flying. The SAS major realizes he has the power to defeat Cutha ... but should he tip his hand in front of so many people, one of whom might be Selly Corwin?

Cors Cant and Anlawdd ride forth from Camlann; the princess slips the bard some hallucinogenic mushrooms to prepare him for her surprise.

However, the real surprise is when Canastyr materializes with a pair of Saxon goons, ostensibly to check the progress of her "mission" but in fact to resume where he left off fourteen years ago. Anlawdd proves her mettle, slaying one Saxon, wounding the other, and unhorsing Canastyr ... whereupon her brother's own pain-maddened horse tramples him to death.

But Cors Cant heard her call Canastyr "brother" ... and heard him call her *"princess."*

She leads Cors Cant to a hidden, crystal cave and there initiates him as an Entered Apprentice in the Builders; he reveals that he knows she's a princess, but Anlawdd warns him to keep that information to himself. Rank matters little among Builders, but it does to the outside world. Bards cannot marry princesses ... at least, if anyone knows they're princesses.

She does give the bard permission to *try to win her,* however.

Coming back from practice, Peter meets Myrddin, or Merlin, an old fraud of a mummer who warns Peter to beware Medraut's treachery. Peter dismisses the annoying crank.

Harder to dismiss are his suspicions of Anlawdd when she and the boy return, telling a wild tale of being attacked by three barbarians and driving them away. Cutha makes his entrance, railing about three Saxons who were slain. Cors Cant and Anlawdd do a fast fade, but the bard later comes to Peter and tells him what really happened. Still, for some reason, Anlawdd doesn't seem to fit the IRA terrorist profile: She's too much a part of her world.

Pondering, Anlawdd remembers where she saw Cutha before: in Harlech Hall, hobnobbing with Gormant himself! Does her father know Cutha is a Saxon, or does he think Cutha is a neutral Jute? Are the Jutes allied with the Saxons now?

The next day, Peter nearly loses the match and perhaps his life, but Cors Cant intervenes as marshall. Peter casts aside his weapons and defeats the Saxon with a spinning backkick. Cors Cant sees a vision of Artus bathed in blood as well as blood on the hands of Lancelot and Gwynhwfyr.

When Peter and Gwynhwfyr find themselves in a passionate and very public embrace, it's too much for Artus, who decides to send "Lancelot" abroad until the Sicambrian cools off. Prince Gormant of Harlech has sent word: Jutes stampeding, send Lancelot, Cei, and Bedwyr. Peter worries about what Selly might do in his absence—so he decides to take as many of the suspects with him as he can, to keep an eye on them. Artus won't allow Gwynhwfyr to go, of course, but agrees to most of the rest: Cors Cant, Anlawdd, Cei, Bedwyr, Medraut, and even Merovee, if the king will likewise agree. Peter decides to ask Merovee "for the Widow's son," a Masonic code phrase.

That afternoon, Cors Cant spots Bedwyr sneaking into Lancelot's room. When Bedwyr leaves, the bard blackbags the place, discovering a bottle of poisoned wine. Just then, Lancelot returns, and Cors Cant must dangle from the window sill to avoid detection. He nearly falls but is saved by a vision of a sword, which he clutches to pull himself back to the wall. A "fate"-full choice, to reach for the sword!

Ireland's Leary arrives at Camlann—he wants to join the alliance between Artus and Merovee. Anlawdd dives under cover until the Harlech expedition, to avoid Leary seeing her and blowing the gig.

Peter finds he cannot resist Gwynhwfyr; he is drawn to her as a moth to a flame, despite the destruction, the long

Dark Ages he knows the affair will cause. He beds her, but his emotions are so intense he becomes frightened. Peter has never really been in love before.

The night before they are to leave, Anlawdd climbs to the roof, lowers a rope, and slips into Artus's apartments. Robed and hooded, she lays in wait, dagger in hand. Artus returns and begins his prayers, and Anlawdd makes to strike: She hopes that way, he'll die in a state of grace. But she repents, her hand drops, and she simply cannot do it.

Anlawdd is a warrior, but she is not a murderer.

Lancelot and Cors Cant spot her, and she barely escapes with her life. She prays that neither recognized her beneath the hood.

The next morn, the expedition to Harlech begins, as Peter silently exults that he stopped "Selly Corwin" from killing Artus the night before.

After a march to the Severn, they take ship on the *Blodewwedd.* Peter sets each suspect to spy on the others. But he finds himself disturbingly attracted to Anlawdd ... undoubtedly because he has no emotional feelings toward her; his dangerous love for Gwynhwfyr displaces to a safe lust for the auburn-haired seamstress, Cors Cant's girl.

But all desires fade when they arrive at Harlech to find the city engulfed by a holocaust: The marauding Jutes have sacked and pillaged Anlawdd's home town!

A millennium and a half later, back in Willks's laboratory, the team secretly powers-up to send Mark Blundell back after Peter, whose body cannot stand another attempt to yank back his consciousness. But Cooper realizes what's up and arrives in time to stop Blundell. The Colonel forces them to try to drag Peter back.

Blundell's worst nightmare comes true: Peter's body convulses and dies in the process. There is now no way for the major ever to return to his own time ... and somebody must still go back and tell him.

Back on the *Blodewwedd,* during the night, Anlawdd secretly flashes a message to shore by lamplight. She thinks she is talking to her father's men, and she tells them that she failed: Artus is alive, Canastyr dead. But Anlawdd discovers she has actually been talking to the Jutes; she has betrayed the expedition to their enemies.

Peter reveals his plan: They will drive toward shore, roll off the side of the trireme into the water, then regroup on the shore. Anlawdd says nothing about the impending ambush.

Nervous, Cors Cant walks the deck, meeting Merovee. The bard has another vision, this time of a shrouded body and the queer, Latin words *et in Arcadia ego*—and in Arcadia, I. The meaningless letters begin to anagram, getting as far as *"I tego ar—"* before the vision fades ... but not before a dream-Anlawdd gives the bard a potion labeled "drink me."

At last, Cors Cant finds Anlawdd watching the flames of Harlech. Oddly, she makes him promise he'll believe she's a princess, no matter what he may hear. Then she reveals that it was indeed she in the *Dux Bellorum's* room, come to slay him. When she faltered, she lost faith in herself as a warrior. Now she doesn't know what she is.

She once gave Cors Cant permission to try to win her; now it is she who must try to win his love and trust back.

The bard is shaken by the revelation. Is the world redeemed from Anlawdd's act of murder only by her love for him? That is a fundamentally wrong reason for a person like Artus *Dux Bellorum* to live or die.

Cors Cant falls into a fitful sleep of night cries and torments, then is rudely shaken awake just before dawn.

The counterattack on Harlech has begun.

CHAPTER 1

NOT TODAY, THOUGHT CORS CANT EWIN; I'LL NOT THINK about betrayal today. . . .

The *Blodewwedd* caught a swell, cut it and shot skyward, then dropped as if the hull had fallen into Pluto's Underdwell. Cors Cant clawed madly uphill, then slid on his backside down the wet, slippery, wooden slope. A wash of spray stormed the deck, struck him full in the face. He choked on the briny water, pressed forward.

Lancelot, Cei, and the captain crowded the bow, stared toward the city. Cors Cant joined them, remembering Cei's suggestion to stick by the champion.

"There," said the porter quietly, pointed at a black speck upon the water. "See it? A galley, I'd stake my right hand."

"Two," said Captain Naw, then immediately corrected himself, pointing leftward. "Three. Another half a mile nor'eas'."

"How the hell did they know we were coming?" demanded Lancelot, pounding the deck rail. "No running lights. Bloody hell, we're blown. They're turning toward us. Evasive action, immediately!"

Naw turned and ran past Cors Cant, nearly bowling him over, shouted, "Right, veer hard *right,* damn yer eyes!" More men crowded the bow, swore angrily, but the captain ordered them back to their posts.

At the stern, a handful of sailors threw their weight against the tiller. The ship rolled, dipping the left side deck clear beneath the waves.

Cors Cant grabbed for the rail, felt his feet slide from

under him so that he dangled by his handhold. Horrified, he watched, unable to help, as one of Cacamwri's soldiers washed overboard. The man screamed, barely audible above the tumult, and sank immediately in the turbulent wake.

Cors Cant was buffeted so wildly he barely saw the two Jutic war galleys upwind of the *Blodewwedd*. Naw drove directly toward them, riding both wind and oars. The ship swerved again as it hit another huge swell, nearly capsizing. Cors Cant lost his precarious hold.

He slipped across the crazily angled deck, rolled twice, and scraped along slick wood, scrabbling madly for a hold. His feet fell over the edge of the deck, and he knew he was dead.

But someone seized his hair, jerked him to a halt. He grabbed a rigging line, stared up at a furious Anlawdd, her clothes soaked clear through by ocean salt, hair brown in the false dawn.

"Trying to make a liar out of me so soon, Cors Cant? I should have known a bard couldn't resist a glorious death!"

Too terrified to contradict, he clutched the thick rope while she maintained her death grip on his hair, her legs wrapped around part of the railing. She reeled him in as he climbed back, hand over hand.

"It's all fallen to pieces," she shouted. "How did they know we were coming? We were betrayed, that's how, and sure but I know by whom!"

Oh Lord, thought Cors Cant—*I know, too!* He remembered the Saxon prince, Cutha, standing at the gunwale with a fetish, fire lit inside. The burning candle was an offering, the Saxon said. But it could as easily have been a signal lantern.

She let go his hair. He lay on the rolling deck, gasping for air. His chest felt squeezed, as if by a blacksmith's vise. The *Blodewwedd* wallowed in her own turbulence for a moment as her luffing sails sought the wind, then leapt forward like a startled buck, due south toward the nearest Jute.

As they cut parallel to the shore, the ship rolled rather than pitched as it cut the swells. Cors Cant and Anlawdd crawled to the foremast and gripped it tight, ignoring the sailors who shouted at them to go somewhere else.

Harlech still burned fitfully, reflected a frothy sky, red as blood soup. An arch of arrows sprang from the Jutic galley, fell short.

"Hold tight when we ram," warned Anlawdd. "It's a shock like nothing you've ever felt!" He looped his right hand in a dangling line, gripped the harp tight with the other. *My sword! I should check to see if it's still by my side.* But that would involve letting go one or the other, and Cors Cant really did not care that much about the blade.

"Load the catapult!" bellowed Captain Naw. He stood, astern, gladius in hand, howling like a *bean-sidhe* and taking the teetering deck in stride. "Filth and foam, ram the bastards!"

"Why don't they fire the catapult?" asked the bard.

"It slows the boat, and we need the speed to ram. We'll fire at the other one, I promise. Make fast, here it is!"

Cors Cant stared in shock as the Jutic galley loomed like a Roman fort that had found legs to charge. She had cut across the *Blodewwedd*'s path, now desperately tried to turn her own ram to bear.

It was a terrible miscalculation. For an instant, war and wave stood still. Cors Cant read the name *Stinging Wolf* painted in yellow on a hull the color of dying embers.

The *Blodewwedd* struck near the bow. Cors Cant was flung to his face by the hammer blow, the mast torn from his grasp as a toy torn from a child. Anlawdd slammed into him, grabbed the bard by the waist. They rolled together on the slippery boards for an instant, Anlawdd howling some exultant battle cry about Jerusalem.

The *Blodewwedd* still drove forward, and Cos Cant was astonished. It sheared off the *Stinging Wolf*'s bow, retaining some of its momentum.

A stream of fire erupted from the sinking ship, caught the stern of Lancelot's warship. The prince shouted

"Greek fire," and marines rushed to make a futile try at dousing the flames. Cors Cant stared; he had never seen such magic before. The fire quickly spread to the aft cabins, and the sailors fled forward, screaming in panic.

Anlawdd staggered to her feet, pulling Cors Cant up, and shouted, "Get to the bow, the *Blodewwedd* is lost! We'll have to board the next galley." They dodged forward, Anlawdd dragging the bard, Cors Cant dragging his harp. He looked back; everything aft of the mainmast was aflame.

Sky and sea reflected sunrise red. Belowdecks, the oarsmen screamed in agony as they were caught and burned.

Soldier and sailor, everyone crowded forward. The *Blodewwedd* had barely regained half her speed after ramming the *Stinging Wolf,* and the other galley approached fast. Unlike her sister, she turned expertly, drove directly toward Lancelot's ship. Leeward, Cors Cant saw the third ship flicker through black smoke. The *Blodewwedd* was trapped between hammer and anvil, a burning bier.

Lancelot shoved through the massed bodies in the bow, using ratlines to keep his balance. A smoky hood of wild, black hair surrounded his head. "On Cei's mark, over the side—on Cei's mark, over the side!" he repeated again and again.

"Into the *sea?*" shouted Cors Cant. *My harp!*

"Onto the beach!" corrected Anlawdd, pointed landward. "Look, it's but a half mile. Cors! You can swim, can't you?" The sudden note of fright was the first emotion she had shown during the botched attack.

"Of course," he answered, neglecting to mention he had never swum a half mile in a choppy sea naked, let alone in clothes and boots, dragged down by a sword and a waterlogged harp.

Together, he and the princess stumbled forward like tumblers on plank-and-ball, balancing left and right as the galley rolled vigorously.

A momentary crash knocked Cors Cant to his knees.

Anlawdd fell across him. The galley shuddered, continued noticeably slower. "We struck bottom!" yelled the boy.

"Sandbar," said Anlawdd, "myriad sandbars. Someday we simply *must* have this harbor dredged. . . ." Again the ship impacted against a submerged bar. The unmanned oars flailed in every direction, snapped with thunder-crashes as they caught the sandy bottom. The strong, morning wind still raced them toward the Jutic galley at three-quarters speed, though they were little more than a fast-moving fireball.

"HIR EIDDYL'S MEN, OVER THE SIDE!" bellowed Cei, battle-trained voice cutting through crackling flames and splintering wood. The ship shuddered as the catapult discharged from the bow fort, raining dozens of head-sized stone balls at the galley directly before them. Most over-shot; a few struck the bridge. The Jute's tiller swung free, cleared by the great (or lucky) shot.

"Are we Hir Eiddyl's?" asked Cors Cant, panicked. No one answered, but Anlawdd did not move, held him down.

A dozen marines crawled up the dragon-prow, tumbled over the port side into the boiling ocean. It glowed like coals in the false dawn, opened its maw to swallow them whole. Cors Cant was too busy hanging onto Anlawdd to see where they surfaced.

"SUGYN'S MEN, OVER THE SIDE!" ordered Cei.

"That's us!" cried Anlawdd, yanked Cors Cant forward. They joined the knot of men as they surged forward, Horse-Sergeant Sugyn ap Sugnedydd at the tail.

Cors Cant shinnied along the ram in turn, desperately wishing he could surrender. Better to take his chances with the Jutes than mad Llyr, god of the sea! He crawled far-ther, yelped in surprise as the sharp blade of the ram sliced his palm.

He dropped his harp to his side, grabbed his left hand, and stared at the widening blood line. Where had he seen that before? It was Anlawdd's cut, sharing her blood, the Builders of the Temple. . . .

The ship danced again along the swells, now so close to shore they were breakers. Off-balance, Cors Cant rolled upside down, dangled momentarily by the crook of his knees. The wrapped harp swung on its cord, smacked him in the face.

Anlawdd dived headfirst behind him, arms wrapped tight around her axe. "My love!" he cried, lost his grip, and followed her into the icy sea.

The ocean pounded like the kick of a war-horse, knocked his breath loose. He rolled, tumbled in the eerily lit water, swallowed salt and silt. *Up! Swim up, up to air!* But which way *was* up? In the ink black chaos, he could not tell one direction from another.

Cors Cant struck out with his hands, touched nothing but water. He thrashed about, terrified that he might be swimming deeper. He blinked his eyes, and a half memory stirred, something Myrddin once told him.

He blew out a breath, watched the faint sparkle of the bubbles. They fled straight sideways. Ignoring his crazy sense of up and down, the bard followed the bubbles.

After two strong strokes, his head broke the surface as a wave trough passed across him. The wave covered him in an instant, breaking over his head, but he realized how close he was to the beach.

Cors Cant lost his breath, inhaled a lungful of water. He clamped his teeth, desperate not to cough and inhale even more. The chaos passed as the ship vanished. The sea still surged in the wake, but only up and down, and it soon subsided. He was caught directly where the waves broke, however, the roughest place to swim.

He labored back to the surface, lungs heaving against teeth and lips. His sword and harp weighed him down, but not as much as the armor the others wore. What of Cacamwri, Cei, and Bedwyr, with their Roman breastplates? *Forget them!* said the voice. *Save yourself, then find Anlawdd!*

Thunder crashed, deafened the bard. He took a quick look as he topped a swell. The *Blodewwedd,* now fully engulfed, had impacted against the second Jutic galley. The two ships were locked in a fiery death kiss. Men dived into the sea from both.

Cors Cant choked, vomited seawater. Wearily, he rolled on his back, struck out for shore. He breathed raggedly, coughed again.

After an endless swim, something tugged at his dangling harp. Too sick to care what monster grabbed him from below, he ignored it. Then he tumbled into a trough and nearly broke his wrist as his hand struck the sandy floor. A turbulent wave rumbled across his face, stunned him awake.

He rolled to his knees, half crawled, half walked up the sloping shelf onto the rocky shore.

A hundred yards away, a longboat beached. Fresh, undrenched Jutes leapt out onto the rocks, charged the exhausted Britons.

Cors Cant stood, drew his sword, and waved it hesitantly. He choked violently, belched seawater. A shadow loomed over his head.

A Jute. Why is he moving so slowly? Interesting, I'm going to die. Cors Cant felt nothing. Time slowed. His attention focused on the huge Jute's hacking axe with such intensity it was a wonder the weapon did not melt. Cors Cant, like everything else on the beach, stood frozen, immobile.

The Jute's face contorted in berserker rage, his short, red beard speckled with saliva. He howled something unintelligible, breaking the spell, and struck.

He was overzealous, swung too hard. Cors Cant collapsed backward, slipped the blow.

A mystery force seized the bard's arm, raised his sword point first. Afterward, he would swear the sword thrust itself, dragging his arm along as an afterthought.

Unable to check his momentum, the Jute stumbled, drove himself onto the blade, and Cors Cant Ewin scored his first battle kill.

The dead man fell heavily, pinning the boy to the ground and covering him completely. A tangled knot of Jutes, Britons, and Sicambrians surged past, swinging sword and axe in exhausted combat. Cors Cant caught glimpses through the tangle of his late opponent, flashes of red and gold, splashes of white light, like sun-flickers off seacaps through patchy clouds.

The gaggle swirled right across Cors Cant, missing him beneath the dead Jute. When they passed, and all was temporarily calm, the bard struggled the body aside, rose to unsteady knees.

An island of solitude in an ocean of battles. He stared wildly, unable to comprehend the tide of battle. Who won? Who died? Bodies lay strewn, ten or a hundred, he could not tell. Was one of them Anlawdd?

For the first time since crawling from the sea, emotion broke through the bewilderment. Terror welled up his throat; he tasted it, bitter and burning. *Oh gods, does she live? Where did she land?* He looked seaward.

The third galley had never caught the *Blodewwedd.* It stood dead in the water, rolled to one side, beached on the sandbar that the smaller, Roman *trireme* skimmed. The Jutic galley swarmed with warriors, who streamed into the longboats and made for shore. Farther south, the burning hulk of the *Blodewwedd* groaned like a birthing mother, rolled gently and sank, sacrificing herself to Llyr.

Behind Cors Cant, up the beach, a crazed sailor shouted "Artehe! Artehe and a Merovee!"

The bard turned dully; a pair of pipes blew across the narrow strip of land between foam and forest, chanters of the *Dux Bellorum* calling them together. Knots of battling men broke into rough lines, streamed apart. *God, I never want to do this again.* Cors Cant limped toward the aching sound, harp in one hand, sword in the other.

A small, slender figure materialized before him. Panicked at the thought of being cut off, Cors Cant threw himself sideways and slashed at the figure's gut.

Anlawdd yelped, swirled a sword in a short arc to meet the bard's blade. "Cors Cant Ewin, when I said win me I didn't mean with a pigsticker!"

"Anlawdd!" Cors Cant froze. He stared at this bloody sword, dropped it into the sand as if it were a snake about to bite him.

"No harm, no judgment," she declared, picking up his

blade. "I dropped it in the ocean, what do you think? Come on, we're rallying!"

"Anlawdd ... where'd you get that sword? You had an axe!"

"I dropped it when we dived in the ocean. I couldn't very well swim with a heavy axe in one hand and a shield in the other, now could I? Use your common sense; I'm sure it's bardic." She seemed untouched, unbloodied, covered with sand. "Yes, before you ask, I'm fine; I've been ducking and dodging. Can't very well fight with nothing but skin and sword, can I? Come, hear the pipes? We're rallying!"

She grabbed him by the sword arm, perhaps to prevent further blind attack, and raised her *gladius* overhead. "A Merovee, a Merovee!"

"A-Artus!" managed Cors Cant.

Gold rays of morning sun turned her hair to fire, washed out her freckles in thin, pale light. One sleeve of her tunic was torn away, revealing her right arm from shoulder to fingertips, muscles flexing beneath alabaster skin. Cors Cant's breath caught in his throat as she dragged him along. "Athena!" He breathed, mistaking one goddess for another.

Bees buzzed in his ears. His hands trembled violently. He shook his head, dazed. Was he growing taller? He looked down on Anlawdd from a height, down on her and the young bard both.

Two tiny figures on a beach, one of them himself, while ants swarmed and swirled, fought meaningless combat over anthills built too close together. He drifted higher.

A princess's voice, far below, unimportant. From this height, he saw Harlech, the fortress, the forest that extended from sea to snowcapped mountains in the North.

Someone shouted a warning, spoiled his pleasure at the view. The voice was urgent, an annoying distraction: "Cors Cant Ewin, you come down here this minute!"

Concentration shaken, he fell like the dragon of his poem so long ago on Merovee's arrival day, shattered into pieces by a great rocking. He blinked twice. The princess had one of his ears in each hand and was shaking vigorously.

"You're coming back now," she said, voice oddly calm and quiet for the middle of a battle. "Back into your body. You're standing on the beach. The battle rages around you. Return, be calm. Don't exteriorize now, we need you here! You're not going to die. Come back to your body."

"Where am I? On the beach, still?" The bees buzzed more violently than ever, and his head pounded as if Bedwyr beat each side with a soup ladle.

She sighed in relief. "Almost lost you there, Cors Cant. Leary always said there were many ways to reach the oversphere, including the imminence of death."

"Leary? When, I mean *what* are you talking about?"

"Why, when he visited me in Harlech, of course. Or my father, actually, but he always found a way to sneak from the hall and give me lessons. You know, Cors Cant, I think you're about ready for the next Builder degree, which teaches soul-flight and how to control it."

"Soul-fight? I don't know what that is."

"Soul-*flight*. You've just experienced it, silly!" She resumed her progress, trotting toward a clump of soldiers that the bard now recognized as Lancelot and his expedition. The Jutes had withdrawn for the moment, perhaps surprised by the ferocity of the British response.

"I thought I already *was* a Builder," Cors Cant gasped, panting from the exertion. Anlawdd seemed unbothered.

"Just an Entered Apprentice," she explained. "That's the first degree. There are many, many levels above your head, Cors Cant!"

They slowed to a walk, caught their breaths. "Then— then what—are you?"

She smiled enigmatically. "My mother's daughter," she answered, "and student of a snake."

He was trembling again, watching the ugly mob of Jutes only a few hundred yards distant, howling and shaking their bloody weapons. *This is no dream, no song. The bastards really intend to cut us down! Cut me down, and Anlawdd too, Lancelot, all of us!*

Cors Cant began to weep, fear and shame taking hold. He was no soldier, no warrior. He depended on a woman to protect him, a woman far above his station. Unattainable. "I . . . I don't know, Your Highness. What if I'm . . . not ready?" He looked away, unable to face her eyes. "Princess, I almost didn't want to come back. From *there,* you know, back to *here.* Not even for—for you."

"But you did."

"You brought me back."

"I *called,* Cors Cant Ewin; you answered. Anyway, you wouldn't want to spend the rest of your life as an Entered Apprentice, would you? That's like reading the first verse of a poem over and over."

She stopped, took his shoulders, and rotated him to face her. "Cors Cant, it's perfectly normal to be caught in rapture when you rediscover one of the ancient gifts of King Pwyll's line. The first time I exteriorized, I stayed 'up' for three days! Uncle Leary thought I was never coming back. He told Father I had a fever, but the only thing elevated was my spirit."

Cors Cant said nothing; she continued. "If it never happened, you'd never miss it. But now that it has, you'd better learn to control it, else it will happen again and again and scare you to death, which would be quite a shame, Cors Cant."

He stared at the ground, unable to meet her gaze.

"Something else?" she asked. "You're probably feeling a little like a horse tied behind a cart, neither pulling nor pushing but struggling to keep up."

He looked up, startled. It was the exact image that had just formed in his mind. Something was odd behind those grey-green eyes, a force not merely human, a force that had raised a dagger, ready to plunge it into the *Dux Bellorum.* He swallowed, pushed the thought back down his throat.

"Cors Cant, I'm not Merovius. I don't have the blood royal, and I certainly can't look into tomorrow. But I *can* see you've got one life in your left hand and another in your right."

He stared down at his harp, his sword.

Anlawdd continued. "I can't choose for you. I already chose for *me,* and that should be enough for any girl, wouldn't you say? Merovee says it's coming, whatever *it* is, and coming soon. No life will be the same afterward, he says."

She gently raised Cors Cant's head, stared into his face, and would not let him turn away. Her lower lip trembled slightly, and she bit it. Anlawdd blinked rapidly, as if her eyes stung. "I really hope you'll try, Cors Cant Ewin, because I—well, for many reasons."

He felt hollow, cavernous. "I don't know," he said at last. "I just don't. Aren't I supposed to study in a quiet place for years, learn from an archdruid, some kind of master? I'm stumbling from one act to another, skipping half the scenes."

A brilliant spark appeared atop the mountains. The sun rose, washed pale the red sky. Anlawdd looked at it for a moment, sunfire turning her eyes as clear as glass. She dragged him along toward Lancelot again.

"You're right, Cors Cant. It's not supposed to happen this way. But it's more practical to sing the verse we're given, rather than denounce the author in the public square, which is generally a waste of time. Especially with *this* song! If you can write a better poem, do it. But don't criticize Merovee's, at least until you've heard the last verse."

They rejoined Lancelot, Cei, Bedwyr, and Merovee as the war-leaders took stock of who was left.

Still carefully watching the Jutes, Cors Cant unwrapped the layers from his harp and inspected it. It was quite wet; the oilcloth, intended to guard against rain, had done little to protect it from the sea. He wrung out the bottom of his leine and wiped what water he could from the wood and strings, praying they would not warp or snap as they dried. But the harp would never sound the same. He retied the instrument to his belt.

A grassy sward flowed from the forest and nearly touched the ocean, marking the division between the two battle lines. Behind this strip, Cei ordered the British troops into a Roman square. In the center stood Lancelot, with Cutha and the Saxons next to him.

Cei pushed the bard and the princess-seamstress to the center of the square. Cors Cant edged away from Cutha, remembering the "fetish" signal lantern. *The damned Jutes knew our position, our plans. . . .*

Behind, in supposed reserve, Merovee lined his Sicambrians. "Not supposed to fight," muttered Anlawdd in Cors Cant's ear. "I wonder if that plan has changed?" She, too, stared at the Jutes, and Cors Cant realized she was counting them, estimating troop size and deployment.

But Lancelot watched *her. He knows!* thought the bard, panicked. *He recognizes her from his brief glimpse of the assassin in Artus's room!* But the legate said nothing.

The bard struggled, but had forgotten what little he had read about battlefield tactics of famous generals—Caesar, Octavius, Artemisia, Boudicca. Even to his untrained eye, it was clear the Jutes wildly outnumbered Lancelot's little band, even counting the Sicambrians.

He consciously relaxed, breathing as Myrddin had taught, a technique that frees the mind from the chains of flesh, lets it soar through airy memory. Abruptly, an image flashed before Cors Cant: Cutha standing at the rail, heavily cloaked, holding a burning idol up to the leeward side of the galley, a fetish lantern to Donner. The Saxon worried, he said, that his men would think him fearful and superstitious if they found out.

Cors Cant's cheeks flushed as he remembered further: another hasty promise, his word of honor too quickly given to Cutha—"I'll tell no one I saw you here," the bard had sworn—just as he had given his word to Lancelot to answer all of his questions.

O Christ, Macha. It's my fault. The whole thing is all my fault! Stunned, Cors Cant realized that had he not kept his foolish promise, had he told Lancelot or Cei about the Saxon's suspicious "disability," they would have been warned of the treachery. They would have landed safely somewhere else. Lives would have been spared.

"A LANGUEDOC!" cried Anlawdd, good-humoredly. She waved her sword like a dragonfly's wings, gripped his shoulder to reassure him.

Cors Cant looked down at the sand, ashamed to join her cry.

Lancelot strode up and down his lines, remarkably unruffled, readying his troops for battle.

CHAPTER 2

NOBODY SPOKE. MARK HEARD THE SQUEAL OF THE WHEELS as the firemen rolled the gurney to the stairs, kicked the legs closed, clumped up the stairway.

Helpless, Blundell saw the litter of plastic bags, hypodermic needle caps, pull tabs from bags of mystery fluid to be squeezed into Peter Smythe's arm via an IV needle. He avoided looking at Peter's dead body being lugged up the stairs.

They would resume pumping his chest as soon as they gained the ground floor. Futile; they pumped only to ward off a possible lawsuit.

Cooper left with the ambulance. The rest sat disconsolately; Hamilton wept softly. Willks prodded the machine with a pencil, as if poking a dead dog by the road.

Blundell stared at Willks until he caught the man's attention. "I've got to, Hank."

Willks said nothing, seemed to understand.

"There's nothing wrong with the machine." Still the old man refused to respond, perhaps could not. Blundell cleared his throat. "The p-p-problem was Peter. He resisted. His connection was tenuous anyway, never should have . . ."

Blundell closed his mouth, determined not to rake anyone over the coals. Bad form. Decidedly not cricket. Rather. *You spineless bastards.*

"I'm going," he said with finality.

No one argued, objected. Mark swallowed, aware he had just committed himself more deeply than an oath of enlistment. He was a soldier now, a time trooper. Honor compelled him to see the job through.

"I'm going. Henry, fire it up."

The old man moved mechanically to Blundell's order, volition burned away. The techs and scientists watched, stunned. One by one, they drifted to their positions, trapped in a collective nightmare that stripped conscious will, propelling each dreamer through choreographed steps, jig-dancing at the end of a string.

No one gets a vote, not even me, thought Blundell as he jerked and shuffled to the energy console.

In silence they worked, suffused in the wicked, blue glow from the doughnut, beckoning like Stromboli the puppeteer, yanking their strings from creation to collapse. The crew exchanged the bare necessity of words: 'power 100% . . . field focused . . . microleakage negative." *I can't back out,* thought Blundell. *I can't stop. I can't say no. I am dragged back to 48.851.164.817,00 by Calvinist predestination.* Numb, he rose from the console at the appropriate moment, walked to the doughnut, his shoes making faint noise on the cement, though each step startled him like cannon fire. He stripped off his clothes.

The field tingled, then stung as he crawled among the coils, laid him down to sleep at its center.

I should say something. Last words, as it were.

"Push the button, Max," quoted Mark Blundell, and gritted his teeth for temporal transfer.

The planet spun on its axis, swirled around the sun, careened wildly about the galactic center, rushed away from everything else in the universe at redshift relative velocity. Then it slowed, collapsed upon itself to eventual nought-volume point-mass.

His stomach twisted, wrung like a gymnasium towel. Mark was the Hanged Man, the world turned upside down.

Cold ... frigid! He fell, screamed. Not a sound; he choked on a lungful of seawater.

Blundell floundered, dragged to the bottom of a bottomless, black, churning ocean, pulled down by great weights clamped about his body. Armor, knightly armor pulling him into the vasty deep.

Swimming would have been a useful talent to learn when I was a boy, he thought dispassionately. Then his feet touched bottom and he stood in the choppy sea.

All about him men pushed and streamed toward the shore. Dead bodies tumbled in the breakers, the ocean foamed red. Confused, Mark splashed after them for the beach, wondering what hell he had flung himself into.

CHAPTER 3

PETER PROCESSED THE SITUATION. AS HIS TENTH DAY DAWNED in fifth century Camelot, the police action was not exactly proceeding as planned. In fact, it was botched as thoroughly as Londonderry. (*Sergeant Donovan, back to the car, blown apart like a red paint balloon dropped from the roof. Or was it Donohue? Damn it, why can't I remember?*)

He shuddered, dismissed the image. It was more important to see how many "Selly Corwins" had survived drowning and melee.

Cei and Bedwyr shouted their troops around; Cors Cant and Anlawdd shivered in the wet chill, centered within the Roman square Cei had ordered. King Merovee survived, but looked shaken at the death by drowning of six of his

Sicambrians. Thirteen Britons had gone missing, including Medraut. Except perhaps for Medraut, none of the prime suspects had died.

But some could be eliminated straight off, for they did not fit the quick glimpse he had had of Selly when she tried to murder Artus: Cei and Bedwyr, for instance, were much too stout.

Unless they're accomplices, thought Peter. Or worse, what if the assassin was not Selly, but somebody else dressed in black, creeping into the *Dux Bellorum*'s apartment? Peter shook his head; the speculation was too wildly coincidental to even consider.

For the looming battle with the Jutes, Peter had thirty-six Britons and fourteen possibly noncombatant Sicambrians. Alas, Cutha and three of his bodyguards had struggled from the waves.

"Medraut," said Cei, pointing. Peter turned. The young man limped from the sea, sword still sheathed. He looked dazed and confused, stared at the assembled company as if he had never seen them before.

Damn. Not a single suspect died. "Medraut," called Peter. "Hunh?"

"We need sergeants."

"Sare . . . jants?"

Peter realized the word had sounded alien. It was probably Sicambrian, and Medraut, despite the affectation of his name, did not speak the language.

He was also quite lithe and slender, just like . . . Peter tried to imagine Medraut dressed all in black; the boy certainly seemed the right size.

"Foot captains. Um, you've never actually led troops in battle before, right?"

"What? No, never!" Medraut's eyes widened at the thought. The lad had lost all his bravado in the face of a real fight. Either that, or "he" was Selly and was afraid Peter had spotted "him."

"No matter. No bad habits to unlearn," Peter lied. "You're now a foot captain, take orders from . . ."

"Centurion Cacamwri," supplied Cei under his breath.

"Cacamwri," concluded Peter.

"Oh, uh, yes sir." Medraut wandered off toward a clump of soldiers without even saluting. *Going to be a definite problem,* thought Peter, watching Medraut's departing back.

Many Jutes still lay on the beach, dead or wounded. The enemy were bloodied, but still heavily outnumbered Peter's forces.

"We're not too bad off, boys," he said when the lines were formed. "We had half a century; now we've thirty-six."

Merovee spoke up. "You still have half a century, General." Peter raised his brows, hoping the king meant what it seemed he meant. "Yes," continued Merovee, "we did not pursue the war, but it seems the war pursued us. I should have known it was useless trying to remain neutral with Lancelot of the Languedoc in the party! Sicambria joins against the butchers of Harlech." He smiled, and Peter could not help grinning back.

A ragged cheer erupted from the remaining Britons. At that moment, the Jutes finally massed and charged the survivors at the water's edge. No battle line, no reserves; they simply mobbed together and ran toward the square.

Artus's men reacted before a single order could be given, spacing themselves tightly. Waterlogged and sputtery pipes droned a low tone like a French horn, their leather windbags still dripping salt water. Peter drew his axe and braced himself.

The Jutes broke against the square, waves against a seawall. The swordsmen up front performed the maneuver Cei had drilled on the deck of the *Blodewwedd,* locking shields, raising and stabbing the man on their right.

It was bloody and effective. Occasionally, a tall axeman reached over the top of the front line and popped a Jute in the face with the sharp tip of his axe. Cei and Cacamwri ran behind the line, shouting orders to the piper.

Peter stayed in the center, giving Cei technical orders. Then the Jutes made a critical mistake, massing on the left to try to push through Medraut's position.

Peter grabbed Cei on the fly, shouted in his ear, "Turn 'em leftwards!"

The piper blew a different tune, and the left flank fell back, as if driven by the Jutic onslaught. Simultaneously, the right hooked around. Within moments, the lines had reversed. Now the Jutes had their backs to the sea. The Britons pushed forward in a wedge.

Cutha stayed close to Peter—hid behind him would have been a better description. "Urtowulf," yelled the Saxon in Peter's ear, pointed at the Jutic general. "Son of King Hrundal, an iron hand over his troops he wields, but stupid."

"Pull 'em back from the left!" ordered Peter, ignoring Cutha's distracting commentary. The befuddled Medraut stared, not comprehending the orders. Fortunately, Hir Amren pulled his own men back, and the rest got the idea.

Urtowulf saw the supposed opening, whipping his men into the breach. They stumbled through soggy sand, burst through the lines, jubilant in apparent victory.

Then Merovee's Sicambrian reserves, still fresh, fell upon the exhausted Jutes like a whirlwind. The fish-scaled soldiers sustained a few casualties, but they slaughtered Jutes like terriers among rats.

The invaders scattered, routed. "On, after them—but maintain formation!" urged Peter.

He stayed close by Cei, watched as many of the suspects as he could. *Somewhere, somehow, she has got to make a mistake,* he knew. Selly Corwin was many things, but not a battle-hardened soldier. If she were, the SAS would have had a file on her.

Anlawdd stayed just behind the lines of soldiers, occasionally striking a blow when a rattled Jute managed to crawl past the shield wall. She was joyous in the melee, unbothered by the blood and screams of the dying. She moved with an acrobatic grace—just as the assassin had dived for the line outside the *Dux Bellorum*'s window.

Cors Cant stuck to her like Velcro. The boy looked sick, frightened . . . like someone who had never been in battle before. He also looked guilty; *I've got a bellyful of secrets* showed plainly on his face.

"Selly Corwin" or not, Anlawdd was clearly a trained soldier. Who in this ancient age would train a woman to fight wars? Even in Peter's day, that was rare everywhere but in America. And why on earth did she pretend to be a *seamstress?* She was hiding something, and Cors Cant would be no help spying against her.

Medraut, too, seemed lost on the field, a failed experiment, unlike his practice encounter with Peter some days ago; he struck not a single blow for the cause. Hir Amren took over the lad's men without being asked. The troops followed gladly, grateful for a firm, experienced hand.

Everyone else fought with gusto and abandon; either Selly was a lot more cold-blooded than Peter imagined, or none of them was she.

The lines dissolved into clumps, predators and prey; they leapt through bloody foam and sprinted across the coarse sand, utterly forgetting about Roman discipline and battle orders.

Peter grabbed Cei's shoulder. "Recall!" he cried. Cei shouted the order to the piper, who sprayed an insistent, watery bellow. Reluctantly, the troops broke off the pursuit and returned.

"But Prince, we can finish them!" complained Bedwyr.

"*If* they have no reserves," said Cei, "and *if* we're willing to expose our own center when the line breaks. Which we're not." His weary tone suggested it was not uncommon to have to explain elementary strategy to Bedwyr.

Far in the distance, Peter saw the Jutes clump together. They did not look happy. The Jutic captains herded their men back until they could barely be seen. Meanwhile, a hospital brigade slithered onto the field, dragged away those casualties who seemed as if they might live.

Cei gestured toward their own fallen, and a two-man crew inspected the crippled, wounded, and maimed. "Don't think they expected that much resistance," he mused. "Sure we gave 'em a damn good thrashing. They'll not be sticking their heads up soon."

"Bollocks," said Peter. "They're stalling for reinforcements."

Peter surveyed the damage: five more Britons and three Sicambrians struck down; three were brought back as salvageable. But the Jutes had lost fifteen or more.

The wounded men whimpered in pain. Sword and spear had bitten deep. *Jesus God, what do I do with them?* Without medics, airlifts, an offshore hospital ship, the men must live or die on their own. Their mates bound their wounds as best they could.

"Stand them down," ordered Peter. The men gratefully fell to the sand, gasping and panting.

A small knot led by Bedwyr volunteered to "examine" the Jutic casualties. Peter had a sick feeling he knew what they meant, but a confrontation might jeopardize the operation and seem "out of character" for the bloodthirsty Lancelot. He turned his head, studied the ship while Bedwyr's ghouls stripped the bodies (and perhaps worse).

Cei and a dozen others waded into the waves to retrieve what they could from the beached, burned, and capsized galley. They passed some surviving sailors, who ventured forth from the water only now that the Jutes were driven off.

"So what do we do with all the bodies?" wondered Peter. He sat upon a mussel-covered rock, inspected the carnage.

"Sacrifice them to Llyr?" suggested Cors Cant, joining him on the rock. The boy was shaken, covered in blood from brown hair to grey boots. None was his own, so far as Peter could tell; he had emerged unscathed. He hugged his harp like an Andy Panda doll.

"Llyr?" asked Peter.

"Our god of the sea. Float them out to sea in thanks to Llyr. He chose not to drown us."

"Is this customary?" It sounded barbaric. *Different cultures, different customs,* he warned himself.

Cors Cant shrugged, seemed younger, unsure of himself. He shivered in the brisk breeze off the ocean, his still-damp tunic clinging to his flesh like cobwebs. "I don't know, it just seemed like a good idea. Odysseus's men were given to Poseidon as punishment for eating the cattle of Helios. Artus would love it, it's so *classical.*" He lowered his gaze, picked small shells off the rock, and threw them in the water.

"Surreal, isn't it?" asked Peter. "Ever seen people killed before?" Cors Cant's skin was paler than usual, and he shook slightly. Peter had seen exactly those symptoms in a hundred young boys in their first firefights. *Keep the lad talking, don't let him dwell. Don't want him going into shock.*

Cors Cant turned a peculiar look on the Sicambrian. "You know I have," he answered warily. "My father, mother, sister, aunt, and uncle. Don't you remember when the Saxons overran Londinium? You commanded the force that retook it." His voice turned harsher, older. "Sire, forgive the question, but *who are you?*"

Peter felt his skin flush, adrenaline pumped through his veins. *He knows!* Dry mouthed, he decided to bluff it out. After all, Cors Cant could not be sure.

"I know who *I* am, boy. Lancelot of the Languedoc. Who the hell is *she?*" Kill him quick before he *talks!* Lancelot's hand crept to his axe, undid the bond. He started to draw the weapon, end the life of this beastly singer. Then Peter froze, realized it *was* Lancelot's hand on the axe . . . not Peter's.

Lord God and His only son! What am I doing? Too casual by half, Peter continued his reach around his side, tugged on a breastplate strap as if adjusting it. *That's strange, too,* he thought; *I meant to ask the boy, "Who the hell are* you."

Had Cors Cant seen the sudden threat? The bard shifted uncomfortably, swallowed, and stared seaward.

Peter bit his lip, using the pain to wake himself up, push bloody Lancelot below the surface again. The Sicambrian pushed insistently, like sea pressure on the air lock in Peter's mind. *He'll break through at last,* he thought. *Only a matter of time. Time and an innocent victim.*

Cors Cant spoke softly. It took Peter a moment to remember the bard was responding to a question—two questions, in fact: stated and silent. "She's my heart, and I'm just a cup who pours lies," said Cors Cant, staring at King Merovee.

"You mean lays. Poems and such."

"Sorry. Lays."

So that's the size of it. He knows I know he knows. But neither of us can speak it out loud.

"We were betrayed," said Cors Cant.

"Says who?"

"Prin—Anlawdd said."

"She's probably right. Saw you wandering the deck last night; see anyone suspicious?"

"I saw—" The bard stopped abruptly, struggled against an invisible wall. He raised both hands, rubbed his eyes. "Damn my tongue!"

"Cors Cant, whom did you see? Spit it out."

"I saw someone, but I'm honor-bound to silence."

Christ, not again! What is it with this lad and his honor? Cors Cant wore integrity like a white suit in a muddy pigpen. "You had better unbuckle your honor and loose that tongue. Unless you'd prefer a court-martial."

"Would you make me *oathbreaker?*" Cors Cant's eyes widened at the thought. "Once, I told *you* a secret of the *Dux Bellorum,* because I'd given my word. You didn't complain then!" He buried face in fists. "Three oaths a day, and faith betray," he quoted.

Peter looked angrily back over his shoulder, tried to calm himself. Back on the rocky beach, the wounded men had been gathered together, surrounded by Merovee's troops. The Britons in turn silently encircled the Sicambrians.

The king himself stood at the center of the concentric circles. He knelt, disappeared from view. Peter turned back to the stone-faced Cors Cant.

He'll tell me. He's a boy; he'll not be able to keep silence. I only have to outwait his Celtic stubbornness. Peter decided to try a bit of psychology, saying, "No, don't tell me. I don't want to know."

"You don't?" The bard looked suspiciously at him.

"Nope. I couldn't care less. Just keep your secret.

Maybe next time, your betrayer will betray Anlawdd. With your help."

The boy's face reddened. He pressed his lips together tightly, trying to trap the irresistible pressure to spill his guts. *Like Sergeant Conroy, McDonnell, O'Conner, why can't I remember his bloody, bloody name?*

"Lancelot!" cried Cei from behind them. "Found something in the wreck you'll be interested in."

Peter stood, crunched through the sand to the surf's edge, left Cors Cant on the rock alone, thinking. "What did you find?" Peter asked.

Cei leaned close, dripping seawater on Peter's boots. "Of all things," whispered Cei, "look what survived fire, rocks, and roiling sea!" He pulled a bottle from under his cloak. *The* bottle.

"I swore I lost that back at Camlann." Peter stared at the bottle as if it would shortly grow wings and fly up the beach.

"You did. It accidentally fell into a rubbish basket in the main hall, but I rescued it and brought it along." Cei smiled nastily, obviously aware the bottle had not "accidentally" fallen anywhere. "Just think," he added, "when we're toasting our victory on the walls of Harlech, we'll have something to serve that damned, Long-Haired King! And you'll not be losing a chance to demonstrate your loyalty to Britain and the old ways . . . *Legate.*" In Cei's mouth, the Roman title, commander of a legion, sounded like a criminal indictment.

A sudden exclamation caught Peter's attention. The crowd around the wounded men parted suddenly, quickly backed away. Sicambrians fell to their knees, touched heads to the ground.

One of the wounded lay perfectly still, clearly dead. Another lay on his side, breathing raggedly. *He'll be gone in five minutes,* Peter knew.

The third man sat up slowly, shaken but alive. He put his hand beneath his leather cuirass, drew it out, and stared at the blood.

Merovee rose, long, black locks tied in a four-strand

braid down his back. "His wounds were not as serious as
we feared," said the king smoothly, laying his hand on the
patient's head. The man stood, a punch-drunk boxer.

Merovee led him to a rock, one shoulder under the
man's arm. Cei let out a faint whistle, clicked his tongue.

"Fortune smiles upon us," said Peter.

"Fortune my ass," rejoined Cei. "That son of a bitch
was pierced. *Through the lung.* But now his wounds are
'not as serious as we feared.' "

Peter turned to Cei. "What did he do? Wish the wound
closed? What are you saying?"

Cei shrugged. "Maybe we should serve Merovee the wine
now. Before the bastard raises someone from the dead."
Without another word, the porter strolled back along the
rocks and slipped the bottle into a rescued field pack.

⟪HAPTER 4

I DANCED ABOUT ON THE SAND, WHICH FELT LIKE MYRIAD
sharp needles—which makes sense, in a way, since I'm a
"seamstress" now. I watched That Boy conversing with
Lancelot, and I was so anxious I nearly went over and
rudely joined them, despite the fact that they might have
been talking about me.

So what would I do if That Boy ratted me out at his first
opportunity, as he seemed to be doing? Not much, I
supposed . . . as soon as the prince knew I had caused the
carnage of our abortive assault, he would probably keel-
haul me right there on the beach . . . well, you know what
I mean.

But it just didn't seem in character for That Boy to spill
the broth in Lancelot's lap like that; after all, he had kept

the *Dux Bellorum*'s secrets for ten years without telling anyone! In any case, I decided to act as natural as possible around Lancelot, assuming that whatever secrets That Boy whispered to the legate were harmless tales of Gwyn and the horses in the stable that one night or Gwynhwfyr's peccadilloes.

But as I shivered in the ocean breeze, staring across the sand at the huddled, angry Jutes, I realized I simply couldn't keep my secret bottled up any longer; the pressure built inside me like fizzie juice that has fermented and strains to burst the jar apart. I had to tell *someone!*

Eyes bored into my back, bleeding me like a surgeon. I turned, stared back at Merovee.

Almost without thinking, I walked toward him, my feet slipping in the beach sand; I was pulled by those eyes, hooks that reeled me closer. I licked my lips nervously, while the Sicambrians who had surrounded him faded into the tangy, morning air, leaving us alone.

Merovee mentally undressed me, removing my tunic, chemise, skin, muscles, and bone, stripping me down to my heart and brain. Then he averted his eyes from my naked soul, raised his hand to form a comforting, artificial wall.

How did he know I so desperately needed to confess?

"I really messed it this time, Sire," I began. I opened my mouth to tell him about my father, about my charge, what I had nearly done in the *Dux Bellorum*'s chamber—but the words simply would not come.

I kept opening and closing my mouth like a bass, sucking in breaths and blowing them out, just as That Boy had done the night before. I suddenly understood my problem: I knew I had to confess, but I didn't know which action was my sin!

Was it by accepting my father's charge to slay Artus? At the time, I barely knew the *Dux Bellorum* or what he meant to the world (and to That Boy in particular), but my father was my father. That would be the sin of bestialism, mindlessly following orders.

Or perhaps I sinned when I faltered, when my hand

dropped to my side, nerveless, unable to strike that magnificent figure while it prayed, fearing for my own soul if
God chose to take revenge. Cowardice?

How about disobedience, refusing my father's charge at
the end? Or even the cardinal and usually fatal sin of inaction, not being able to make up my mind which sin was
the greater!

Merovee waited; I had to force out something; so I con-
fessed the first thing that popped into my head: "Lord, forgive me, but I ... I love That Boy. Cors Cant Ewin, I
mean."

The instant I said those words, I wished I could grab
them and shove them back into my mouth. It wasn't true!
I couldn't possibly love ... *him!*

Merovee chuckled, and my face flushed crimson. "Sister, you cannot confess love as a sin," he said. "Love is a
feeling; you can confess only actions or intents. Feelings,
especially those as deep as love, are planted as seeds by
the Great Architect. Do you plan to dishonor yourself and
the boy by fornication?"

"No! I mean, we nearly did once, but we pulled back.
It just didn't seem right. Not that I think there's anything
wrong with for-for-fornication, Sire ... I'm a Builder, not
a Roman. But it was wrong for us at that moment."

"Sister, the Builders define fornication a bit differently
than would, for example, my dear friend Artus. Whenever
the animalistic aspect of rutting seizes control from the
conscious, human mind, so that what should be a holy act
that elevates the spirit instead becomes a grunting, groaning, uncontrollable groping, then the spirit has been lost,
and that is, indeed, the sin of fornication.

"But really, Anlawdd; are you confessing that you *didn't*
give in to the beast?"

"Doesn't make sense?"

"Hardly."

I sighed. He had caught me, and he knew it; but I
wasn't ready to confess my sin yet ... not until I clarified
in my own mind which was the sin. I felt like the gold-
smith in the puzzle who has eight sacks of true gold and

one sack of counterfeit and gets only three weighings to
determine which is which.

"Come to me when you are ready to embrace your own
spirit, renouncing your animal nature, Sister. In the meantime, speaking now as a father rather than a Father—" The
king grinned; I clearly heard the distinction. "Until you
learn to love yourself, Anlawdd, you cannot love another . . . not even him."

This time, however, I couldn't quite catch which he had
said: him, or Him.

Did it matter? I don't know; I guess not. Maybe they're
the same, sometimes. I sighed, returned to Lancelot, who
had dropped That Boy and was now engaged in earnest
conversation with his porter, Cei.

CHAPTER 5

PETER SIGHED, SHOOK HIS HEAD. "WE HAVE A MORE PRESSING
task, Cei. An unpleasant one, I'm afraid. Bring me
Medraut."

A smile flickered across Cei's lips, almost too fast to
see. "I was afraid you missed his performance in the heat
of battle."

"I saw."

"I didn't want to conduct the inquiry myself."

"Neither do I. But it must be done, for the boys." Peter
nodded, and Cei stepped to Hir Amren, spoke quietly. Peter continued up the beach, waved Anlawdd to his side.

"Young lady, you're born in Harlech?"

She stiffened. Peter made a mental note not to call her
"young lady" again.

"I am, or I'm a young man," she answered.

"Know this area?" He indicated the beach.

"Of course. This is Redsand Beach, called that because of the time along back before I was born when a cask of red dye fell overboard from a Roman merchant's galley and spilled—"

Peter interjected quickly, before she got started in an interminable digression. "No time, no time . . . we need a place to run where the Jutes won't follow, so we can regroup and decide what to do next. Suggestions?"

"Up the forest there's a hill, and behind it a glade about as big as two Camlann *stadia* side by side."

"Perfect. Lead us to it, Anlawdd."

She nodded, trotted to the forest's edge. The trees grew nearly up to the sand, gnarled and bent so close to the ocean breeze. Peter instructed his troops to follow the girl quietly, no pipes or shouted orders.

The Jutes were far enough away that they could not see clearly where they went, save that it was forestward. *If luck holds,* Peter thought, *they'll decide discretion is the better part and wait for reinforcements before chasing after us.*

The forest was sparse at first, grew denser as they penetrated deeper. Oak, linden, a typical wood; but within half a mile, Smythe was completely turned around. The troops huddled nervously, looked around and over their shoulders. The branches, mostly bare this late in the year, nevertheless managed to screen the sun so often that when it did appear, it was always in an unexpected quarter.

Peter sniffed: raw and fresh, a forest scent he had not smelled for many years in his own time, his own England . . . at least, not until the same virgin forest began to superimpose itself over the real world back in Willks's laboratory.

I wonder what murmuring pines and hemlocks smell like? Peter shook himself, concentrated on Anlawdd's back as she ran forward, stopped, stared in puzzlement for a moment, then ran on. Presumably, whatever ant trail she followed was difficult even for her.

Either that, or she isn't really Anlawdd.

They climbed a steep hill, higher than Peter expected to find around Harlech, easily fifteen miles south of Mount Snowdon, which strangely enough was snow-covered. The ground crumbled beneath his boots, like slogging through clay. His half century straggled behind, maintaining contact, but just barely.

Then Anlawdd disappeared from sight entirely. Annoyed, Peter held up his hand to stop the troops, then continued alone around an earthen shoulder. He found himself standing in a field that sloped sharply upward to his right. It was overgrown with wild grass and what looked like leeks or onions. Anlawdd stood in the center, facing him, hands tucked in her belt behind her.

"I'd not be forgetting my own backyard, now would I be? That's as silly as forgetting how to untie your own front door. I said I'd get you here, and did I now?"

Peter nodded. "This will do. Thank you—thank you, Anlawdd." *What was I about to say? Thank you, love?*

She had exaggerated the size. It was as wide as two *stadia,* but only two-thirds as long. It would do for its grim purpose, however: a quick field court-martial for poor Medraut. He returned to his troops, gestured them forward.

They gathered around. Bedwyr, who had apparently talked to Cei, arranged them in a semicircle facing the high side, where Peter stood. Cei joined Peter, and after some discussion, so did Merovee, representing the interests of the Sicambrians.

Medraut looked scared, but stepped forward of his own will.

"No formalities, son," said Peter, hoping to put him as much at his ease as was possible in the circumstances. "What happened out there?"

Medraut looked back into the crowd, found no friendly face. He turned back to Peter, still trying to formulate an answer. But what answer could there be?

He doesn't understand the purpose of this, Peter thought. *I wonder if the lad thinks he's going to be whipped, or executed?*

If he is *just a "lad."* When he had first met Medraut, the boy was cocky, sure of himself and his position, not very bright but a quick study. Suddenly, in the midst of the beach combat, Medraut underwent a sea change, became confused, spun-around, almost as if he had jumped into the middle of a chapter without the preceding pages.

Perhaps he was just out of his element in his first real war. Perhaps he was a twentieth century terrorist who suddenly appeared in the midst of a fifth century engagement.

Blundell said I could appear before or after Selly by as much as a few days. Peter chewed his lip as he studied the boy, wondered how he could tell. *If this is Selly, and she's just appeared, now is the time to shake her up, when she's already disoriented.*

But if so, then who *was* the black-clad assassin back in Camlann?

"No excuse, sir," said Medraut, answering the question at last.

"I didn't ask whether you had an excuse. I asked what happened."

"I don't know, sir. I . . ."

"Yes?"

"I became disoriented. Didn't know what was going on."

"Disoriented?"

"Yes, sir."

"All of a sudden?"

"Yes, sir. I don't know what happened, sir."

"What is the first duty of a commander?"

Medraut stood silent.

"How about, at the least," suggested Peter, "he ought to know as much about what's going on as any man in his command?"

"Yes, sir."

Peter looked at Medraut, used his eyes as weapons to pierce Medraut's armor. Medraut stared rigidly forward at attention, as if he had been trained in a modern army.

Now let's see what you do when faced with "the Lady or the Tiger."

Peter drew his combat knife in one quick move. Shorter

than a *gladius,* longer than a British commando knife. Without warning, he snapped it into the ground at Medraut's feet. Medraut twitched, but did not otherwise break attention. *But would* Medraut *have such control, or a trained killer?*

"Do you have the killer instinct, boy?"

"Yes, sir," said Medraut forcefully.

"Show me."

"Sorry? Sorry, sir?"

"Pick the knife up."

Medraut hesitated only an instant, stopped and plucked it from the ground, not taking his eyes off Peter.

"Now use it. On the gentleman to my right."

Cei looked at Peter, raised his brows. Medraut's cheeks lost some color, eyes flicked from Peter to Cei and back. "U-use it on, ah, General Cei, sir?" asked Medraut.

She could have heard the name at any time during the battle. "Kill Cei. For me. For Artus."

Medraut gritted his teeth, breathing much too quickly. His knuckles were white on the hilt of the dagger.

Peter glanced at Cei. The porter smiled faintly, watching Medraut with too much contempt. *Are you so sure, so sure it's only a teenage boy, my friend?* Peter knew he would be faster than Selly, being "halfway out the blocks"; but there was always a risk.

"Kill General Cei. That is an order, Medraut . . . if you want to travel in *my* company, you'll obey me without question, without thought, without conscience or pity." The IRA way . . . or so Peter had always been taught. They certainly seemed to show no pity. But Peter was uncomfortably aware that an IRA Provie might believe the same about the SAS.

And she'd be right. I would obey that order. But I'm not a teenage prince on my first command in King Arthur's court . . . and neither is Selly.

Maybe.

Medraut stared at the ground. His cheeks, once drained of color, now flushed deep vermilion.

When the explosion came, it was so sudden Peter almost threw himself in front of Cei, which would have spoiled the illusion. Medraut hurled the knife into the ground at his own feet, where it stuck deep. Peter stifled his reaction, stood motionless as an unrippled pond.

"No, *sir!*" said Medraut, almost a shout of anger.

As quickly as the illusion of "Selly" had waxed, it waned. How silly. Medraut, a twentieth century IRA murderer transported fifteen centuries back and dropped into the ocean?

Besides, Selly had already struck at Artus, days ago, long before the transformation of Medraut.

Peter nearly smiled with relief but maintained his solemnity. "So it seems the cockerel can make a decision for himself. Won't have to hang him after all."

Medraut did not answer. But his face lost the certainty with which he had rejected the order. He looked blank, nonplussed by both the original situation and the sudden reversal.

I still have the original problem, an officer who stood like King Log as his troops died around him. I cannot forget my duty as a commanding officer, even when playing cop. He's vulnerable, ready to understand . . . strike now, or strike never! Peter continued rapidly. "Nine-tenths of the time, all it takes is a decision, boy. *Any* decision. Do it right, do it wrong, but *do* it. Don't wait for complete clarification; you won't get it. Don't wait to be told; I want you to tell the men. Don't make me pull your strings . . . I want a war-horse, not a pack mule."

Do they even have mules yet? Peter wondered. But Medraut seemed to understand.

"You know you can act, can make a decision and carry it through, willing to suffer the consequences. You proved that when you chucked that knife into the dirt. And you've seen your men in combat and know they can take it.

"I expect great things from you, lad. Great things. Let's try to stay ahead of the eight ball, shall we?" *Whoops . . .* Peter bit his tongue, prayed that if Selly were among the crew, somewhere, she had not picked up on the faux pas. "Stay on top of things."

The mock trial had almost ended, but the hardest moment loomed. The complex drama just played would impact Medraut; from a single day spent sparring, Peter knew the lad to be motivated and committed. But the troops might not understand anything that had occurred, might even think Medraut had failed again.

And they had a great deal of undischarged anger. Suntzu taught in the *Art of War* that punishments must be swift, severe, proportional to the crime, and could not be withheld for politics or other unjust reasons. Justice must be done, and it must be *seen* to be done. Justice is judged by the standards of the victim.

Peter swallowed, stepped over the edge of the abyss.

"The court-martial is prepared to pass sentence." Medraut returned to attention, held his breath. "We sentence you," intoned Peter as gravely as he could manage, "to one blow from each man you imperiled by your indecision and confusion, to be executed immediately. Hir Amren!"

"Sir." The sergeant of foot stepped forward cautiously.

"Assemble a gantlet with your men."

"A . . . gantlet?"

"Two lines, facing each other."

Hir Amren got the idea. The men were lined up, looking nervous. When it was ready, Peter stepped close to Medraut so only the lad could hear. "Courage; I don't think they'll hurt you too badly. But watch them closely, and *remember* any man who strikes too hard a blow. We'll deal with him later."

Taking a breath, Medraut began a slow walk down the gantlet, pausing between each step long enough to receive the love taps of the men on either side.

The men used only their fists, and one or two put everything they could manage into their single blow, staggering the boy and on one occasion knocking him to one knee. Peter noted which men, in case Medraut forgot.

But the farther he progressed along the lines, the weaker fell the blows, so that by the end the men were doing nothing more than a *pro forma* touch of face or shoulder with their fists, rather than actual punches.

When he reached the end—still on his feet—the men cheered and crowded around him, supporting him back to a log where he could sit. Hir Amren himself brought cool water and a cloth, cleaned the blood from Medraut's face.

Cei seemed mollified. He slapped Peter's back, returned to the rest of the troops to inspect wounds and assess fighting strength.

Merovee spoke from close behind Peter. "Lancelot would never have thought of that, sir. In some ways, you are a distinct improvement." He leaned around to speak into Peter's other ear. "But there is a *time* and *place* for everyone . . . and this place"—he squeezed Peter's shoulder—"is Lancelot's."

Peter turned to ask Merovee whether he had done the right thing, handled the Medraut problem properly. The king was already gone, back with his Sicambrians.

Instead, Peter approached Medraut. The men surrounding the boy melted away like the snows from Snowdon, left them alone.

"How do you feel?" asked Peter.

Medraut did not speak, stoically nodded.

"Take your time. Collect yourself. I'm going to send Anlawdd out to scout around. We have three hours left before we move."

At the word "hours," Medraut blinked, glanced at his left wrist. Though he tried to conceal the horrific mistake, turn it into a movement to rub his sore shoulder, Peter knew what he had seen.

Smythe's face grew clammy, chilled. He felt dizzy for a moment. Only years in clandestine antiterrorist work allowed him to continue chatting with no outward sign he had noticed that good old Medraut *had tried to look at his watch.*

Peter did not remember what he had been saying, but apparently it was innocuous enough that "Medraut" did not realize that he had been "made." Peter rose, thanked the "lad" courteously for accepting the judgment, and strolled away.

Peter's mind was already plotting how to do Selly in without rousing the whole army.

CHAPTER 6

CORS CANT SHIVERED, THOUGH THE SUN SHONE HIGH ON THE yellowing field. He followed the trial, understood its purpose. But no clearer evidence could there be that this Lancelot was not Lancelot of the Languedoc, who would have quickly slain Medraut, along with any soldier who dared strike an officer, whatever the provocation.

Cei might well have thought up the "gantlet," and certainly Artus. Never Lancelot, the Sicambrian war demon.

Neither Cors Cant nor Anlawdd had participated in the gantlet. The princess stood at the other end of the clearing, staring north with the intensity of a wolf at a badger hole. A plume of smoke was visible in that direction, rising from the remains of Harlech.

"What next, my lady?" he asked. "Do we attack the city?"

She spoke without turning her head. "Not unless Lancelot is another Gormant, who always strikes when the iron is lukewarm. Where would we strike? Which gate? How many Jutes roam her streets, man her battlements? Answer these questions and you can ask the truly important one: how do we make thirty-five soldiers into three and a half centuries?"

"To answer those questions, wouldn't we have to actually enter Harlech itself? Either that or fly over it like eagles."

Anlawdd turned. "Can your Druid magic turn us into eagles, Cors Cant Ewin?"

He shook his head. "Maybe Myrddin, were he here. Though I admit I've often heard him talk about flying, never seen him do it."

She looked disappointed. "Afraid I'll have to turn into a snake, then, instead of an eagle."

Cors Cant waited, but she did not elaborate. *If she's not after telling me, I'll not ask,* he thought, irked at her cryptic prediction. "So we enter Harlech as spies, then."

"We?"

His ears flushed. "You mean—you'd enter alone, without me?"

"I don't want to, Cors Cant. I'd sooner swim in a cesspool with a Roman breastplate. But somebody must, which translates into *Anlawdd* must—it's my city! Though I don't see how I could get you along, and it would violate my oath to protect you, anyway, not that I care at all about you (and I'm still not speaking to you, by the way)."

Breast! She said breast.... Unable to stop the juvenile thought, Cors Cant flushed slightly, hoped she could not really read his thoughts.

She wet her finger, held it up as if checking wind. "No, I expect the spies to comprise Lancelot, for he wants information only his eyes can see; Cei and Bedwyr because they're attached to him at the wrists; and, of course, me, for who else knows Harlech?

"But what—now don't take this wrong, for I love Druid bards; a definite improvement over soldiers and seamstresses!—but what, exactly, would you *bring* to the expedition?"

Cors Cant's stomach tightened. "I . . . I could cast a Druid blessing on the rest of you."

She nodded, still watching the skies. "Which you could do as well before we left."

"What if you got into a terrible fix and needed Druid magic to extricate yourself?"

Anlawdd smiled. "Sure and you can't even turn yourself into an eagle. Perhaps Myrddin, were he here!

"But as you say, I've seen my share of cups and balls and headless doves, mechanical marvels, and magnetized princesses who think they're chickens, and don't you think I mean myself, for I would *never* lend myself to a show like that, and anyway, you weren't even there to see how I kept my royal dignity.

"But when has even the greatest Druid made armed men invisible, save in that story of Caswallawn you sing so well?"

"Wasn't a Druid," corrected Cors Cant, peeved. "It was a magic mantle."

Anlawdd shrugged. "Well, there you are, wherever that is."

"I could go along to make sure you forbore to stick a dagger—"

He stopped, stricken. He had never meant to say that, intending, in fact, to forget what she had almost done.

Anlawdd flushed crimson, setting off her auburn hair. She closed her eyes wearily. "I've lost the right to object to such dagger wounds as that, Cors Cant Ewin, and besides, it's true; yet even so, is it a thrust calculated to smooth our road, or a golden apple of discord to cast between us?"

The bard continued. He could not let the subject go. "My lady—"

"Call me *Anlawdd,* Cors Cant Ewin."

"My lady Anlawdd, I don't know why, but something between heart and head tells me I *must* go."

The words tumbled out. "I don't know why, but it's more important for me than for any of you, as mad as that sounds. If I stay behind, though you win the battle of Harlech, *you shall lose* the final war, lose the great empire that Artus and Merovee build, an empire not of stone and steel, but of blood—the Blood Royal!"

She stood silent, considering his words. Then she stepped close, stared into Cors Cant's eyes.

Her eyes grew wide, expanded until they filled his vision—big as saucers, big as millstones, grey pools that washed his soul, flowed like the freezing ocean, half a day, half a millennium ago. He felt Anlawdd about him, inside him, enveloping his spirit.

Were it anyone but she, Cors Cant would have savagely resisted the mental invasion. But Anlawdd felt *right*.

Then she stepped back shaking her head, broke contact. "I don't know how you know, or even if you're right. But you're not lying. You believe what you say; I'm sure of that." She tugged at her lip. "We'd better talk to Merovee, for he can actually *see* within, while I can only feel." She touched his cheek. "Will you come?"

Cors Cant nodded.

"You may find more than you negotiated."

"So may you. My Princess."

She smiled. "An ugly thought. Probably true. The sky spins like a top that you've bet your last *solidus* on!"

They threaded across the field, found Merovee at the heart of his men. He contemplated a shard of crystal, banded at both ends by silver, one end attached to a silver chain. "I expected you," he said. "Come and follow; I need witnesses."

The king rose and pushed east into the thickest part of the forest that surrounded the glade, never glancing back. Anlawdd and Cors Cant followed at a discreet distance. When Merovee stopped, they were surrounded by tall oaks, which grew angled out of the side of the hill, bent upward toward the sky.

A cold autumn breeze moaned among the sere trees, caught at Cors Cant's shirt, and pressed up beneath it. He looked up at the middle branches of the surrounding oaks; each tree sported a clump of mistletoe. "Good omen for us," he said, pointing.

"Bad omen for the trees, though," said Anlawdd, reasonably. The mistletoe would eventually choke the tree to death.

"What is the question?" asked King Merovee.

Anlawdd pointed at Cors Cant. "He wants to go. On the spy mission. I say forget it, he'll get killed."

Merovee smiled. "Hm. That question I did not expect." He held up the crystal. "Here."

Anlawdd shook her head. "I'm not going to be magnetized into thinking I'm a chicken again! I've got to get ready to crack that Harlech walnut."

"Not you," grinned the king. "I. You shall speak the cantrip." Half a smile flickered across his lips.

Anlawdd stared for a long moment, shocked. "Me?" She reached out, hesitantly plucked the crystal from Merovee's fingers, and let it drop the full length of its chain. It dangled at the end, spinning first deosil then widdershins.

Merovee gestured, and Anlawdd raised the amulet. The king knelt, stared into the crystal as it caught the end rays of the sun, splintered the light into a thousand rainbow jewels. He rocked slowly fore and aft, never losing eye contact.

Anlawdd tried to speak, her voice a hoarse whisper. She swallowed, started over. "Look . . . within, o Lord. Find a—a sphere. It glows with bl—with red light. It pulses."

The choppy words smoothed as she grew comfortable with phrases only heard before, never spoken. Cors Cant was as entranced as Merovee, but he watched Anlawdd, not the crystal. She sounded like a young bard at the Druid College, stuttering her way through first-year expositions.

"Let the sphere surround, take you. O Lord, it consumes you, fills you red with redmost light. You fall, the ball surrounds you as a pool of blackred water.

"Now it changes as it falls, bright red now. Your stomach lifts, falling off the forever cliff. Now the ball is orange, and the orange grows bright. Sunbright as she sinks, and yellowing now. Yellow is the sphere, yellow through heart, head, hands, and feet."

Cors Cant craned his head, saw that Anlawdd's eyes were as yellow as the sun sphere she conjured. Her hand was rigid as a beam, yet the crystal rotated in slow circles, winding all the way up, all the way down. It seemed to catch only some of the sun's rays, glowed distinctly orange-yellow.

"Green is the color the master makes the grass, green is

the treetop, green the moss. Green the sphere that falls faster, fast the fall that darks the green to blue."

Her voice dropped steadily, a whisper now. "Blue is the sky, deep blue as the sun sinks. Deep, dark, farther down the forever face. Dark, purple sky, night sky. Not a star, only the sphere, deep violet that pulls you down and deep, down and deep, down and deep."

She stood silent a long time. Cors Cant hardly dared to breathe. As she spoke, Apollo sank and reddened. Anlawdd's eyes were shadowed, blue-black like the magical sphere that enfolded them all in Cors Cant's mind.

"Speak, then," she commanded. "Speak what you see as you consider this question: does Cors Cant enter Harlech with us?"

The bard stared expectantly at Merovee. The king of Sicambria still swayed gently, eyes closed, but not still: behind the lids, his gaze darted left and right as if following a scattering flock of doves.

Impulse gripped Cors Cant, irresistible and irrational. He began to sing the lay of "Orpheus in the Underground." He had sung it at Camlann's last feast, at the feet of the *Dux Bellorum* he might never see again.

Silhouetted against the dying, splintered light, Merovee spoke. His solid voice contrasted starkly with the brittle, keen night wind that whipped dead leaves across sere branches. Smoke from the razed city to the north tasted tangy in the bard's mouth, sharpening the king's prophecy and making Cors Cant shiver.

"I see sparrow and hawk. They fly beside. I see Mouse and Badger. They burrow beneath.

"Mouse finds a great crack, tumbles into the abyss. The badger at his heels is no warning, no blame. Mouse passes an old woman on the road, gaunt and bones. She stretches a bony hand, no touch.

"Mouse meets the mother of all mousers, miser of all mothers. Mousy skin peeled from bones, grey blood left behind with his voice. But bones float on a great stream, and Mouse is born as a man from God's loins . . . and yet has the sun to rise."

He fell silent. Anlawdd chewed her lip, pressed her nails into her palms in frustration. It broke the spell that bound Cors Cant, and his song faltered.

Merovee did not see, his eyes still tightly shut. But he suddenly looked at Anlawdd from behind closed lids, raised his voice once more.

"Badger dies.

"A shade through the underground, wraith chasing Orpheus, Shadowbadge creeps through night, murders the yellow sun! Shadowbadge finds Hades on her own feet, finds the deepest black-dark shadow and vanishes.

"Reborn to taste a hero's soul, at last plays Mouse to the Man to save her litter's litter . . . and yet has the sun to rise."

Many heartbeats passed as Cors Cant and Anlawdd waited for the king to say more. The bard realized that during the prophecy, he had moved close to Anlawdd and taken her hand, or she his; but he had no memory of doing so.

He held it now, though, and would never have let go had their quest not been so urgent.

"I guess he's through," said Anlawdd. She did not drop his hand. "That sybil talk was as clear as Harlech Bay when the current stirs up the mud!"

"Um, maybe you should bring him back? My lady."

She turned toward Cors Cant, made a face, and cast his hand aside. "Just Anlawdd will do, Cors Cant Ewin. But I guess even a bard can be right now and then, if the moon turns blood and roosters lay eggs."

But before she could say a word, the king spoke a third time: "The fool and the emperor drink a toast to Death, and the bigger fool drops his cup. The king of the Gauls goes hunting, loses his path, and finds himself in Scots-Land. And in Arcadia, I—"

He stopped, opened his eyes sheepishly. They were unfocused.

After a long wait, Anlawdd whispered, "I'd better bring him back, now. Watching him is like staring into a mirror while wearing Caswallawn's cloak of invisibility."

She spoke quickly, reversed the original cantrip. The sphere rose through the rainbow the opposite direction, violet to red, and when it reached a red too dark to see, Anlawdd dissolved it with a word.

The incantation was so vivid, Cors Cant actually saw the globe for an instant. He clutched at it, but it vanished into his mind's eye before his fingers could touch.

Merovee woke, blinked his eyes rapidly, and shook his head clear. He smiled candidly. "I hold a fervent hope that one of you wrote down whatever I said, for I haven't a word of it!"

"Wrote down?" asked Cors Cant. "You and Artus, you're so Roman." He took a breath, repeated Merovee's exact words in a close approximation of the king's voice, pausing where Merovee paused, even pronouncing the words with a trace of a Sicambrian accent.

It surprised both king and princess, but was trivial compared to the first-level bardic exam: a thousand lines to recite from memory, chosen from among thirty poems by the Druid bardmaster. *Of course I didn't quite pass that test,* he remembered, shuddering.

"Well, I think we know who the sparrow and hawk are, and the same for Mouse and Badger," mused Merovee.

"Me and Cors Cant?" asked Anlawdd. This was not her element.

"Vice versa," said the king.

"That's what I meant!"

"So Cors Cant falls into the abyss, passes the old crone, Death, on the road; but she misses the touch. He meets the mother of all, is stripped of flesh, blood, and voice, and carried away by a great river. But he is reborn from the loins of a god. Is that a bit clearer?"

"As a foggy night in Blackheart Fen."

"But the badger, that is you, Autumn-Hair—for you incessantly badger me for knowledge you're not ready for, and you badger your father and uncle for arms you cannot bear—you will become a shade, murder the yellow sun, descend upon your own feet to the depths of Hades, plumb

the furthestmost pit of despair, only to crawl at last before
your love to save your children's children."

Cors Cant mused. "I just had an epiphany. Don't Saxons
and Jutes call themselves Sun Children and dismiss us is-
landers as Moonborn? Perhaps you murder a Jute."

"An army, no doubt," added Merovee, eyes crinkling at
the corners.

Anlawdd turned a glare of ice first upon Merovee, then
Cors Cant. She smiled, but the curl of her lip was no comfort. "Well, that part is true at least. So there is something
in this prophecy after all. Though I still wonder about your
stories of seven fat cows and a floating finger, Your Highness." She pulled at her lip. It was a Lancelot mannerism.

Cors Cant felt a sudden chill. *I wish she wouldn't take
after him so.*

The princess continued. "But what about that last bit,
drinking a toast to Death? Who are the emperor and the
fool?"

Merovee shook his head. "I am too personally involved,
my child, for the last prophecy was meant for me. The
king of the Gauls, that is, I get lost while hunting and find
myself in Scots-Land . . . it's the beginning of a mighty
Builder tale that even I do not fully understand, though I
know we use the image of the land north of Hadrian's wall
as metaphor for the confusion of moving to the next stage.

"Do not worry about it today," he concluded. "It will
make itself clear when we gather for the toast."

"In any event," decided Anlawdd, "with a prophecy like
that, as clear as a church window, there is no way above
or below the Earth that Cors Cant is going to go right if
I go left or up if I go down. He travels with me, where I
can keep an eye out for pits, abysses, and old crones, and
that"—she stamped her foot—"is final! So you'd best stop
complaining and get used to the idea, Cors Cant Ewin."

The bard opened his mouth to protest, thought better of
it. *A wise man knows when to win the loss,* said Myrddin
in such circumstances. Cors Cant meekly followed
Anlawdd and Merovee back to the meadow.

CHAPTER 7

*THAT SON OF A BITCH WAS PIERCED THROUGH THE LUNG.
Medraut is Selly Corwin—either that, or he isn't. Lancelot pounds at my head, head, HEAD like Jesus at the gates of Hell! The bloody bastard was "perced to the roote," and now he's up and aboot like Banquo at the banquet. . . .*

Peter drifted closer to King Merovee. *I should be frightened,* he thought. *If Cei speaks truth, I've just witnessed Jesus healing the lepers.* Instead, a flutter in his stomach uplifted his spirit, gave him hope.

Why does he affect me so? Why do I want to open myself as I never did to the priest in the confessional?

Merovee approached, smiling eyes at Peter. Peter felt flustered, as if meeting his own queen (*Gwynhwfyr or Elizabeth?* Peter could not yet say).

Cei tugged at Peter's arm, but the general felt nothing. Dimly aware they should move out of range of the Jutes as quickly as possible, Peter's feet sprouted roots into the sand instead.

He "heard" the words clearly, so real, so near he flinched: *I am your ally.* Was it Lancelot of Merovee?

Phantom voices in his ears, tiny "hand puppet" voices:

> *Initiation never ends—
> From now on, we're your only friends!*

The king's gaze penetrated Peter like a hot needle. Truth! To those grey eyes, Peter could speak only truth.

But what is truth? asked the voice. *Not until you be-*

come as a little child, not until the male becomes female and the female male shall you know truth. Not until you die: *mors ultima ratio.*

Death is the final accounting.

"Bloody voices in my head!" swore Peter, teeth tight. A strange compulsion gripped him; suddenly, he could stop his tongue no longer. "Forgive me," he begged. He glanced around; they were alone among the trees. He did not remember walking.

"Confess," commanded Merovee, head bowed and eyes averted.

It's not real. It's not a real confession, not unless Merovee is a pr—

"I'm not really who I . . ." *Good Lord, Smythe, what the hell are you doing?* It was Colonel Cooper's voice. *How'd you like to sing me a few choruses of "John Barleycorn," explain exactly how the hell you came to blow your own cover?*

Please . . . please, I need the peace of confession to wash away the sin of playacting, deceiving the whole world my whole life!

Acta est fabula. The play is over.

But it was not, could not be while Selly Bloody Corwin stalked Camelot, assassin's dagger in hand. Peter speed-shifted gears to a different sin, a "safe" sin. "Merovee, there is a plot to kill you. Beware the wine we offer."

In wine there is truth.

Merovee put his hand on Peter's shoulder. A much larger, invisible hand wrenched Smythe's face toward the king. Not as painful as he feared, Merovee's eyes. They soothed. They understood.

"My son," said the king, "you cannot confess the crimes of another."

"Confess? You're no pr—pr—" That word again; it stuck in Peter's throat.

"You know better."

Eyes. Not painful, burning, dreadful.

His face, whiter than lamb's wool. *His* hair, Bible black; his trust, brittle and dry as the wafer. A pale hand touched

Peter's brow, the fingers cooler than the rock that the faith was built upon. *Blood is blood,* said the voice, *and a rock but a rock.*

The Big One hurled forth without mercy, ripped Peter's chest open to expose his bleeding, sacred heart. "I killed my friend, my comrade, my sergeant! I didn't stop and check the sec-second cart, and Mary save me, *I can't even remember his damned name!*"

Merovee's hand stroked Peter's brow. "A sin of omission, or commission?"

"Omission, Father. Terrible, terrible omission. The second cart . . . they usually plant *two.*" Peter paused, confused; he could visualize the plastic explosive, but could not think of the word for it.

Because there isn't *a word for it yet, not for a thousand and five hundred years. And it's not a cart, it moves by mechanical power, trucks vegetables to the market. Damn, what the hell are they called?*

They usually plant two: the first explodes, draws a crowd, including soldiers. Then the second explodes a few minutes later.

Merovee considered Peter's sin, kept his eyes averted from the sinner. "You failed to protect your man," he pronounced. "You failed in your duty. Guilt weighs upon your head like an iron crown." Merovee raised the heavy hand from Peter's head; Peter gasped, actually feeling a physical weight, a crown, lift from his head.

My God . . . Gunny Conway didn't check that bloody lorry either!

Peter blinked in astonishment. Conway, that was the name! It leapt back into his head the moment Merovee removed the "iron crown of guilt." Along with the name came the obvious realization:

Gunnery Sergeant Conway was as much to blame for his own messy death as Peter Smythe. Both men were too shaken to check the other vehicles on the Londonderry street. Both men failed—it was just dumb luck that Conway happened to be standing directly between Peter and the explosion. The blood that had stained Peter's

hands since Londonderry was finally washed away by another's blood.

*Lorries, Semtex. Where do words go when they fly from
my head?*

"Go," said Merovee, "sin no more."

The compulsion to confess drained like a thrown switch,
left Peter limp.

Merovee pressed forth his hand, and they shook. The
king offered a Masonic sign. Peter bit his lip, his chest
squeezed like the end of a toothpaste tube. *You may run on
and on,* ran the old song, *but great God A'mighty's gonna
pull you down....* He did not return the sign; to those
eyes, he could speak only truth.

CHAPTER 8

*THE PROBLEM: HOW TO SIFT A BODY TO FIND AN ALIEN SOUL?
How to drive her from the boy without killing them
both?*

"We'd need an army to lift this occupation," said Cei.

"An army? Consider: three or four days back to Cam-
lann, a couple of days to raise the troops, then back again.
A week and a half. Think the Jutes will still be here then?
If they are, think they'll still be sunk in swinish revelry?"
No time, thought Peter. *It's us or no one.*

Cei sniffed. "Perhaps. They are Jutes, after all."

*If I kill Medraut, what happens? Selly probably reap-
pears in her own body in real time. When she does, they'll
surely take her into custody. Cooper will be there by now.
She disappears into the Maze or the Crum, and nobody
has to answer any embarrassing questions.*

"We'll find either ghost ruins or a well-fortified city-state," said Peter. "We must strike *now*, before they're ready. *Carpe diem*—seize the day."

Cei turned an exasperated look on his general, black beard glistening in the red sunlight. *"Cave canem.* What do we do, throw ourselves upon their blades and die for honor? *Mors ultima ratio?"*

Peter smiled. "Simple. Right up my alley. We can't wrest Harlech from their grasp, but we can at least burn their bloody hands."

"Hurt them," said a small girl's voice. Peter turned at the interruption.

Anlawdd appeared as quietly as she had vanished earlier. No longer the soldier, she had transubstantiated into a simple teenage girl, her home gutted by a man-made holocaust.

"Hurt the bastards. Make them scream as they hold the burning coal of Harlech." She clenched her fists. But to Peter's eyes, she exuded not rage but guilt. Anlawdd may as well have said "hurt *me;* make me scream."

Cors Cant stood beside her, almost put his hand on her shoulder. But he looked away, dropped his hand instead.

Peter nodded. "She has it right. They want one of *our* cities? Fair enough, but Jesus and Mary, they'll not take it cheaply."

Maybe Medraut can die in an "accident." Another accident. God, does it never end?

Peter snuck a glance at the pale beauty: Anlawdd, Cors Cant's best girl. Her face drawn, frightened, usual banter ringing like a brittle cymbal, a thin drumhead stretched across a hollow gulf. Whatever secret she hid, she concealed even from her bard, and it ate at her innards.

Begone! I conceal the secrets of God. The phrase popped into Peter's head. He looked suspiciously at Merovee, but the king concentrated on Anlawdd.

Peter followed Merovee's gaze. *Lord, but she's a piece.* Peter bit his lip. Much as his heart belonged to Gwynhwyfr, he could not help wondering what Anlawdd would look like without the dirt, the leather, the scrounged sword, the tunic. . . .

Get a grip, man! She can't be even twenty yet. And besides, she's the boy's, and he is hers.

But his unruly mind stripped the powder blue tunic, the off-white chemise: Anlawdd stood naked in red-haired glory on dead, brown grass. He looked away, sighed.

"Get on the bloody hump," he ordered, voice tired. The sergeants ordered the troops, and the company moved deeper into what would someday become Snowdonia Forest and National Park.

Retaliation would be easier than Cei thought. The Jutes presumably had no experience with guerilla warfare, knew nothing of Vietnam, Afghanistan, thirty years of continuous warfare against the IRA. What did Jutes, Romans, or even Artus *Dux Bellorum* know of infiltration, terrorism, fear, and confusion springing up within the ranks like garden weeds?

Imprisoned Lancelot howled with laughter at Peter's *hubris,* called forth image after bloody image of an endless campaign against the Germanic tribes, years earlier. Lancelot and Merovee fought together then under the Eagle and *Pan-Draconis* standards.

Peter stumbled over a root, banged his head on a tree. It was hard to navigate with his brain flooded with visions of German bodies stuck on pikes for mile after mile along the road, a giant's pinwheels carefully planted. The two Sicambrians, soldiers of civilization against barbarity, burned villages, hewed down old men, women, young boys. They burned crops, slaughtered stock, and left their flesh to the carrion crows.

They sealed village gates, allowing consumption, smallpox, and red plague to rampage inside, leaving no survivors.

Oh, we know of your terror, chuckled the chilly voice. *We know. You've nothing on me, my demon brother. . . .*

Smythe shivered. Surely there were some modern terror tactics the Jutes had not yet seen. His plan depended on the Jutes being panicked into irrationality by a few, well-placed blows chosen for "maximum savagery." *In other*

*words, exactly what the Afghanis did to the Soviets, the
PLO did to the Israelis, and what the IRA does to us.*

The sun had long set, shadows indistinguishable in grey
twilight. *Thus endeth Day-Ten,* thought Peter. Far off in
the woods, away from curious eyes, he jotted notes in his
investigative log, starting at every snapping twig or rus-
tling pine.

He reread his notes by the full moon's light—it was the
only way Peter could ever organize his thoughts.

The men rested from many hours marching, straggling
single file along an animal track, surrounded by dense pine
forest, lost to everyone but Anlawdd. Peter prayed she
knew the land as well as she claimed.

After finishing his suspicions of Medraut, Peter slipped
the pages inside his shirt, returned to the troops. He found
Cei, explained the plan to him.

"Fear, confusion. Let them think we're ten times as
many as we are. We strike and kill, move quickly before
the survivors can pinpoint our location or number."

Cei nodded. "But before we strike a single blow, Sire,
we need solid intelligence."

"Bring the seamstress, Anlawdd."

Cei conveyed the order, and Anlawdd padded close,
looking as "lean and hungry" as Cassius.

"We didn't seem this far from Harlech, Anlawdd," said
Peter. Did she actually know where she was going, or was
she just lining bees?

"Not as the eagle flies, Prince Lancelot, but we're not
eagles, which I guess I don't have to tell you."

"We're following a circuitous route?" That worried him
even more. What if they got lost?

"Like a snake entering a garden, Lord. We've circled
Harlech from south to northeast, for it lies now in that direction." She pointed directly where the sun had set;
southwest, as Peter reckoned it.

"We need a way into the city without being spotted."

"Yes, Lord."

"Something no one would expect, something un-
guarded. Is there such a path?"

"Yes, Lord." Her mind drifted in private horrors. "A pass, a badger hole winds through the woods, snakes up to the city wall. It's where I've been leading you. We can sneak in there, if the Jutes haven't discovered the passage, which I'm sure they haven't because most men of Harlech don't even know it's there, including the man who calls himself prince. That is our destination, isn't it?"

"Harlech? Yes, I told you."

"Then we *are* going to liberate the city." Her glittering, intense eyes betrayed interest for the first time since they had bailed off the *Blodewwedd.* Peter's groin stirred.

"Anlwadd, you saw it from the boat. There isn't much we can do." Her face reddened, but she said nothing.

Peter continued. "Forget liberation. Put it from your mind. Think of revenge, an eye for an eye. Think of destroying the village in order to save it. Maybe the Jutes won't come any further into Prydein."

She lowered her cold, hard gaze. "So we're to die for the honor of Artus."

"Die? No! Why do you people keep saying that?"

"But—if we attack, knowing we cannot win . . ."

"Damn it, there are many kinds of victory conditions. I have no intention of leading a suicide brigade!

"I said we can't count on *liberating* Harlech. Not today. But we can sure as hell strike a blow for the cause, even if this battle is lost. And maybe, *maybe* the Jutes will think better of this whole adventure and withdraw, bloodied and cowed, before Artus himself can arrive, leading an expedition."

Merovee spoke in the silence that followed Peter's speech. "Such an easy victory must surely have surprised the Jutes. They probably thought to harass good Prince Gormant and leave. Artus has never before lost even a single city.

"But our brother Gormant panicked and fell, or hesitated in fright—I know not. The Jutes are stunned, already uneasy."

"He was betrayed," interrupted Anlawdd, quietly. "That's all I have to say about that. Gormant's a bastard, but no coward. Why, it's like adding new door bolts, then finding the jewelry missing; you suspect an inside job."

Merovee held his hand up to quiet Anlawdd. "Betrayed by his men or himself, what matters is that the Jutes hold a vicious eagle in their arms and they're desperate to let it go."

Cors Cant moved closer to Anlawdd, took her hand. She let him.

"All right," declared Peter Smythe, "let's give them a way to let go. Anlawdd, get us as close as you can without being seen. If they see us . . . well, I needn't tell you how we'd fare in a pitched battle."

She looked up the hill, where the sky was only slightly more purple than black with the sunset's afterimage. The ground sloped gently upward as the forest grew denser. The smoke plumes were not as thick as the night before, but clearly visible.

Peter asked, "Can we get close enough to spy? Close enough to find your secret entrance without being seen?"

"If they don't have pickets," she said. "Scouts," she added, looking at Cors Cant.

Peter nodded. "Good point. Anlawdd, sneak through this damned forest and spy out the Jutic positions. We'll wait here and decide the best plan when you return. Cei, have the men fall out, have a smoke if they want."

"Have a what?"

Damn, I did it again. "Never mind."

CHAPTER 9

CORS CANT WIPED THE SWEAT FROM HIS FACE, STARED IN DIS-may at the city wall, a steep mound of packed soil braced by weather-hardened logs that surrounded the entirety of Harlech. The moon, hovering low in the east, two days past full, clearly illuminated their predicament.

"Impregnable," he breathed.

"That's what the boy usually says to the girl," said Anlawdd from behind him. "Not that I would ever fall for a line like that, and I don't mean to imply that you would use it. It just struck me." She had the words, but the tune was not the normal Anlawdd song. She was subdued.

"*I* should strike you." A halfhearted, *pro forma* sally.

"Now *that* sounds interesting. Perhaps one day in our future, that is if we have a future, which is still not decided, Cors Cant Ewin."

The main gate was visible through the trees. The wall itself was ancient, a great, nearly vertical mound of dirt. The gate alone looked Roman-built: straight, thick, wooden wall ten feet high with a peculiar scaffold above the gate itself.

Anlawdd slapped an insect on her check, reminding Cors Cant of his own recent flea bites, which began to itch on cue. "Won't get the soldiers over that fence," said Anlawdd. "Not in one piece anyway. It was built when this was a fort, back in the days of Augustus. Come on, Cors Cant, follow me."

"Where are we going?" He clenched his fist, tried not to scratch the bites.

"Back to Lancelot, of course. If we storm that wall, we'll end up fighting Jutes at twenty-to-one odds while the reserves loll back and make side bets. I wouldn't want to imply that Jutes are a match for true men of Harlech, but they'd still cut us into mutton chops. Besides, there's a better way. For a few of us, at least."

"Your secret passage." He licked his palm, moistened the bite on his elbow. The cool, evaporating saliva soothed it for a moment.

She briskly threaded a twisty path among the trees. Cors Cant struggled to keep up. The path, never wider than a footfall, faded to nothing and reappeared past a grove of pine trees. They walked upon a cushion of brittle linden leaves and spongy pine needles, skirted a heap of blue-gray boulders, tossed upon the ground like dice thrown by the Fir Bolg, the Irish giants. Moonshadow painted many false caves that were only hollowed-out depressions in the rocks.

"How by God did you ever find this sheep track?" he asked.

Anlawdd did not answer, caught Cors Cant's arm, and dragged him off the path into a solid line of trees. He let himself drift with the irresistible tide, praying it might turn into another chance such as he lost back in Anlawdd's room a thousand years ago.

Instead, she pulled him around the shoulder of a cliff that loomed above them, and the vast, western ocean burst into view.

Cors Cant gasped, voice caught in his throat. The blue mountain fell precipitously from his feet to the sea; a misstep would plunge him into the phosphorescent deep. From the height, the world stretched out before him, round as a ball. Never before had he stood atop a mountain and stared across the endless sea. *Jesus, Mary, Rhiannon, would that this hill were the height of the great peak five leagues north!*

The moon spilled silver light upon the water, caught the whitecaps in eerie glitter. The illuminated waves nearly outshone the brilliant, starry sky itself.

Anlawdd laid her hand on his shoulder. His tongue clove to the roof of his mouth, could not even mutter "Your Highness" or "my goddess." Gentle lips touched the back of his neck. Cors Cant's breath caught, transfixed by the arrow of desire.

"Betwixt sky and sea," breathed Anlawdd, "do we not stand together at one height?"

Gnosis crawled up his spine like quicksilver, piercing his brain. *She loves me, I love her—and she meant to murder the* Dux Bellorum. *All else is accident. . . .*

Cold wind pricked his skin, blew up his leine and tightened his groin. He felt the chill of a great sadness blow across Anlawdd. He turned; silver tears gleamed in her eyes, caught the moon, and hurled Her back to the sky.

Anlawdd's voice was so soft, so feminine that Cors Cant could barely hear. "But we live not in sky or sea, nor even on Harlech Hill, but in a stonewall barrow, the court of Caer Camlann. I'm afraid they'll find out what I begged you conceal. I'm afraid they'll place me *here,* cast you down *there,* and hands outstretched shall not grasp one the other. I'm afraid they'll discover where I was, what awful charge I almost filled, and kill me or cast me out like a dog who bites the new babe. I'm afraid, Cors Cant. I've never been afraid before; it's not princessy to shiver."

She smiled sardonically, wiped her eyes. "Weep no more. Let us return, hand in hand like sister and brother. For a while, at least. Take my hand."

Fingers interlaced, palms together, they withdrew from the high place, found the track, and wove back to the encamped martial company.

She led the bard to Lancelot, told her tale. Merovee, Cei, and Bedwyr crowded close, but the other troops kept distance, including Cutha and Medraut. Lancelot kept glancing at Medraut with a dour, suspicious eye.

"You said there was another way over the walls," reminded Lancelot when she finished.

"Under. Not over. And for a few, not sixty."

He plucked at his mustache. A strand pulled out, and Cors Cant winced in sympathy. "A tunnel?" asked the legate. "How many can march abreast?"

"Barely one, and you wouldn't be marching so much as crawling, that is if you could even fit. Big as you are, you or Cei would have a hard time, but I think you could make it. And by the way, the other end of the tunnel is quite public . . . not that the Jutes are likely to be hanging around there."

"Where?"

"The old baths. Plenty of room to assemble, maneuver, and slay as many Jutes as sands on the beach before they bring us down."

"Anlawdd," said Lancelot, peeved, "that's not what—"

"I know, I know, you're not leading a suicide mission. If you were, I'd not insist Cors Cant join the expedition."

"What?" demanded Lancelot. He repeated himself, "What what what?"

She continued. "King Ricca restored the baths when Artus returned from Rome. When there's peace, you'll find lots of my—my fellow citizens baking in the sauna or splashing in the cold plunge. Day or night, as I used to enjoy doing myself."

"This King Ricca," Lancelot asked. "Would he rise and help us?"

Anlawdd stared at Lancelot for a long moment, face cryptic. Lancelot looked from face to astonished face, his own cheeks turning apple red.

He doesn't know! thought the bard. *How could he not know?* King Ricca had died defending Lancelot's own left flank at the last battle of Mons Badonicus, misunderstanding a complicated maneuver designed by Artus to deny the line to surging Saxons. Lancelot raged about it for months, called Ricca a "badger-brained, slope-browed, Barbary ape with a tinned-copper cup on his head."

"Um, not from the funeral bier he won't rise," said Cors Cant. "Not even Myrddin could raise a body after four years."

"I knew that," said Lancelot with suavity.

Another lie. A creep ran across Cors Cant's spine. Who was this new Lancelot, so different? A demon prisoned within the general's body?

"What of Prince Gormant?" the boy asked Anlawdd. "They say he's the *Dux Bellorum*'s half brother." Bedwyr's face contorted angrily, and the bard quickly appended, "B-but no one believes that base lie!"

Anlawdd's eyes fired a warning bowshot at Cors Cant. Dangerous territory, but the bard had no intention of violating the oath taken in his princess's crystal cave.

"That son of a bachelor," she said. "He's a—he's a—I wish I could say what he is! *He* won't help. Probably feasting the Saxons, or Jutes, I should say, even as we speak, with taxes ripped from little babies' mouths! Well, you know what I mean."

"A vengeful, Harlech mob would only get in the way anyway," Lancelot added.

After a moment, he continued. "All right, here's the plan. You lot"—he indicated the entire company, his own men and Merovee's Sicambrians—"are going back to the shore to find a boat. There's got to be something at the harbor."

Captain Naw stepped forward, face showing the first sign of awakening since the *Blodewwedd* sank. "I'll be takin' that detail, General."

Lancelot nodded absently. "Filch the biggest thing you can find. Take your cues from His Highness, King Merovee, though he's not in your chain of command."

"I'm glad you did not suggest I crawl through the tunnel, Lance," said the king. "I fear my best tunnel-crawling days are long past."

Lancelot announced his volunteers: "Cei, Bedwyr, Anlawdd, and Medraut. The rest of you follow Centurion Cacamwri. Captain Naw, take point."

"Medraut?" demanded Cei and Bedwyr, simultaneously.

"Yes, why the boy?" asked Anlawdd.

Lancelot seemed at a loss for a reason. "Well . . . he could—or he could guard . . ."

"Need I remind you," said Cei, "That you are sworn to protect the boy? I hardly think it appropriate to drag an inexperienced lad on such a dangerous expedition."

Anlawdd looked significantly at Cors Cant, but he refused to meet her eyes. The bard *had* to go; Merovee had prophesied it.

Lancelot conceded with a grumble. "All right, Medraut goes with Merovee. That leaves Cei, Bedwyr, Anlawdd, and myself."

Cors Cant waited; after a long pause, Anlawdd finally said what she had agreed to say. "Five against five centuries. It *is* a suicide mission."

"Five?" asked Lancelot, brow raised. "I count four. Who else is coming, the cook?"

"Don't be silly, she's not even on this campaign, thank the Savior." Anlawdd counted off on her gloved hand: "Let's see. There's you, Cei, Bedwyr, Cors Cant—"

"Why *Cors Cant?*" demanded Lancelot, a bit too testily.

The boy stiffened. "Well, why *not* Cors Cant? I can climb a tunnel as well as the next man!"

Cei interjected, "Any objections I have to Medraut go double for the bard."

Anlawdd defended him, but Cors Cant could tell she did so reluctantly. "We need him to read my map. It's in Greek, which is—"

"All Greek to you?" asked Lancelot, sarcastically.

"Which language I've forgotten more than I ever knew. We'll have to sneak into Caer Harlech by back alleys I've never been through."

"Let me see the map. Maybe I can read it for you."

"I told you, it's in Greek!"

"Even if it's in Greek," snapped Lancelot, "I'm sure I can read a bloody map!"

She fished inside her chemise, plucked out a rolled piece of vellum. She untied it, spread it flat against the bushes. It was a page of densely written text.

Cors Cant leaned close, translated aloud: "three doors . . . past bakery . . . stables are. Through them one . . . can pass, divesting onto . . . Street of Tragedies."

"That's a map?" asked Lancelot.

"Well, a traveler's journal, actually," admitted Anlawdd. "But it was written only forty years ago and describes Old Harlech that surrounds the fort, right where we need to go."

Lancelot accepted defeat gracelessly, and for a moment, Cors Cant's fears about the Sicambrian were allayed. Ill humor was thoroughly Lancelotian.

"How long a journey?" he grumbled.

"Breaking out, that is, descending from Harlech to the entrance over Blue Cliff, I entered the tunnel at sunrise and exited by starlight. Nineeeen or twenty hours. It's a long road, my lord."

The general savagely chewed his mustache as if he were

not used to it. "Start at midnight, should arrive somewhat after darkfall. I hope we'll depart Harlech in greater glory."

Anlawdd nodded. "Like the Christian martyrs," she said cheerfully.

He glared. "If we're successful, the Jutes will be in such disarray that we can take the overland route. How long? I mean to get to the tunnel mouth."

The princess shrugged. "Half a day, or rather half a night. Can't run too fast in darkness, even with this moon, for there are plenty of opportunities to take a header into the deep, like Icarus. Is that whom I'm thinking of, Cors Cant?"

The bard nodded. "Flew too close to the sun, crashed into the ocean."

"Midnight's passed," said Cei. "The moon is veering west."

"Away with you," said Lancelot to Cacamwri and Naw.

Anlawdd grabbed Cor Cant's arm, led him into the blue-black hills. The three great warriors stumbled after them, tripping over roots and scraping through the brambles.

CHAPTER 10

A QUESTION NAGGED CORS CANT. "ANLAWDD," HE WHISpered, unwilling to disturb the cool, aloof pines, "if you're really a princess, you grew up at the fort. Why would you need *any* map?"

"Are you always this suspicious?" she asked. "Because I sure wouldn't want to spend the rest of my life with someone who doubted my every statement. Not that I admit I'll spend any part of my life with you, you under-

stand. Besides, I led a sheltered life." She tossed her belt
knife, caught it on the third flip, began again at one rota-
tion.

"I'm sure that I want to spend the rest of my life, *et cetera.*"

"*Et cetera?* Cors Cant, why must you always qualify
simple, sincere statements with annoying affectations? In
any case, we'll need to interpret this map. It's out of date."
She squinted at the scrawled characters, difficult to make
out in the moonlight. "For instance, this bit about Lion
Fine Garments is wrong. It's been a scribner's shop as
long as I can remember."

"Well it's the same building, isn't it? I mean, we can
still use it as a map."

"Of course. That's why I brought it. It would have been
remarkably silly if the buildings were changed 'round!"
Anlawdd smiled, and the sight of her laughing face sent a
warm wave to lap around his heart.

"May I borrow the map?" he asked, still floating.

"You aren't going to lose it? Here, I trust you." She
handed him the document, and he quickly read it through
twice, as if it were an epic for the Druid Examination. He
handed it back with thanks.

The germ of a thought tingled just behind his eyes. After a moment, it sprouted, and he plucked at Anlawdd's
chemise sleeve. "Wait . . . how did *you* know it said Lion
Fine Garments? You *can* read Greek!"

She stared at him as if he had turned into a Saxon. "And
when did I ever say I couldn't?" She extracted her arm,
quickly squeezed his shoulder. Had he blinked, he would
have missed it.

After several moments of silence, Cors Cant let his
breath out. In the dark, no one saw the happy, red flush
spread across his face, nor the immediate splash of guilt
that followed.

CHAPTER 11

WE HAD SOME TIME BEFORE LANCELOT WANTED TO LEAVE, so I shooed That Boy away and sat in the dark, quietly thinking. Ever since Canastyr and his Saxon friends had waylaid That Boy and me along the road, I could not force the image of my brother's horrible death from my brain: whenever I closed my eyes, I saw his terrified, white form, arms cast up in useless protection, as his pain-maddened horse trampled his face and body into bloody remnants barely recognizable as human.

Each time I brutally trampled the vision itself down, like the horse trampled Canastyr. But this time, I determined to dwell upon it, examine the death and life of Canastyr the worm, though my heart galloped in fright. *It's very unwarriorlike,* I told myself, *to flee a vision just because it scares you.*

I forced myself to see the scene again and again, and my conviction of my own guilt in the murder began to fade. I had wounded his horse, sure—but did *I* know the beast would throw Canastyr and slay him? And even if I had murdered him myself with a heavy rock, wouldn't I have had provocation enough, considering what Canastyr had done to me so many nighttimes as we grew up, betimes in my own bedchamber?

The bastard deserved to die as he had, and I had earned the right to be the blade. I finally understood that what I regretted most was that I could not rightly claim his death upon my hands, for the same reason I had raised earlier in my defense! I had *not known* that his untrained mount would react so violently.

71

Oh Lord, I asked, *were these guilt feelings really an undeserved boast at the death of an enemy?* Alas, that sort of question was beyond me, best saved for Uncle Leary someday, who constantly asks and answers questions such as "If the gods created us, who created them?" or "If two people truly love each other more than life itself, and one of them has to be sacrificed, is it more selfish to live, or to die and cause grief to the loved one?"

For the moment, at least, my mind was clear. I followed the pages of Canastyr's life backward and had another blinding revelation: it was the earthworm who must have introduced Cutha to my father in the first place!

For the first time in a long while, I could think clearly: was he really such a worm? Did Canastyr fear to wipe his arse without Father's permission?

They certainly acted that play . . . but the thought struck me that it *was* nought but a play for their own amusement, to fool the others, including me. Neither had ever liked me much, and if the rumors of my parentage were true, I understood why. Canastyr, at least, was Gormant's, even if he weren't Mother's.

If it were really Canastyr who controlled Father, instead of the other way 'round, many things fell into place, not the least of which was why Father allowed Canastyr to torment me for so long . . . and why Canastyr himself came all the way to Caer Camlann to make sure I carried out my charge and slew Artus: *it was Canastyr's plan from the beginning, not Gormant's.*

Maybe Father really didn't know about—the nighttimes; or knowing, maybe he was powerless against the earthworm. Mayhap I've tried and judged him too harshly.

(Another horrible thought occurred: did Mother *really* die in childbirth? Or was the earthworm even more possessed and perverse than I imagined, evil enough to . . . ? I shook my head. I couldn't imagine even Canastyr being so brutish as to slay his own mother.

(Of course, she wasn't *really* his mother . . . did he know that?)

My skin began to creep most uncomfortably, and Lance-

lot and crew began to stir about in a decisive manner. I
stood, brushed twigs and stones from my rear, and shook
out my auburn hair, turned mousy brown in moonlight.
The most direct approach, I lectured myself, *is simply to
ask the blackguard when we rescue him from his own
Jutes: how did you come to be in such a predicament?*

CHAPTER 12

ANLAWDD LED THE STRIKE TEAM ALONG A TRAIL UNTROD IN
ages, overgrown by roots, blocked by fallen pine
branches and a single sapling torn from the ground and
cast aside. *Bear,* thought Smythe, *or a raging man.* The
girl and her bard hopped lightly over all obstacles. Peter,
Cei, and Bedwyr, wearing armor, climbed more ponder-
ously.

The ground was soft and springy, but not muddy; the
rains had held off for many days. Peter stared hungrily at
Anlawdd's pale, moonlit hair, the rise of her breast beneath her thin chemise, until he caught himself. *Not her;
not now.*

The air was sullen. The hills were not tall enough to
catch the frigid breeze off the Irish Sea. Instead, in this
surreal interpretation of Harlech, the cold air swept up toward Snowdonia and her mountain sisters, trapping heat in
an inversion layer. Peter sweated, wished he had followed
Anlawdd's example and shed both armor and outer layers
of clothing.

She turned abruptly, charged directly up a trackless hill
until she found a second, hidden path that began from a
tall, deciduous tree, ruddy but not yet golden (frost had not
yet triggered the turning).

"There's no one path following a single direction from tunnel to sea," she explained, "or sea to tunnel, for that matter, as the one usually means the other."

It took another hour, Peter reckoned, finally to reach the tunnel mouth, artfully hidden within what resembled a wicked thistle bush, but was actually passable. The moon was past overhead, perhaps midnight or twelve-thirty, considering the moon phase.

Peter ordered Cei and Bedwyr to lift the heavy, stone cover carefully. Anlawdd handed a lit torch to Peter; he had not seen her light it. He realized uncomfortably that he had no idea how to do so; his days and nights as "Lancelot of the Languedoc" were all spent in the palace or among a troop of soldier "Boy Scouts." He had not yet found occasion to coax fire from flint and tinder himself.

He lowered the torch into the opening as far as he could reach. The tunnel was barely more than a crawl space, branching off a dry, crumbled wall, angling left, and rising slightly. Outside in the direction of the tunnel, he could see no city, just more hills.

"I think I better go first," said Peter. "Intersections?"

"A few. I'll be right behind you. Of course it would certainly make more sense for *me* to go first, so if you get tired, let me know."

He smiled. "You'll be the first I tell. Cors Can, Cei, Bedwyr, follow in that order." Peter thought for a moment: what about ventilation? And what would the Jutes think to see three armed soldiers emerge from a public bath? He made a quick decision: "Men, drop everything, axes, swords, armor. Take only your knives."

Bedwyr cried out as if jabbed by an electric cattle prod, but Cei obeyed without argument, glaring at Bedwyr until he, too, complied. Anlawdd and Cors Cant carried no armor and no weapons but knives.

"Anlawdd," said Smythe, "you knew the tightness of this passage. You might saved us the trouble of hauling this bloody pile out here and told us to leave it at camp."

"I told you you'd barely fit and with your armor you'd be like a bear in a barrel, and if you would just listen once in a while to a woman, you might save yourself trouble left and right!"

Cors Cant looked troubled. He had no axe or sword, but he clutched his harp to his chest as if it were a life preserver and he a drowning boy.

"Leave it, son," said Peter, his voice deep and, he hoped, fatherly. "I know what it means to you, but ... Well, we can come back for it later, sometime."

The bard's face was pale, though it might have been a moon trick. His eyes found a horizon beyond the hills that should have concealed it. "I know I must cast it aside," he whispered, "but now is not the time. The time comes."

"You're going to drag that bloody thing all night and half the day through a tunnel?"

He blinked, returned from wherever his spirit had wandered. "Sire? Oh, yes. I must! I cannot leave it here."

"Why not? You said yourself you'll have to cast it aside."

"But not *here!*"

"Why not?"

Cors Cant shrugged, and Anlawdd rested her hand on his shoulder. "He's a Druid bard, you know, and they sometimes get these feelings, like when a woman knows her you-know-what is about to come." But she, too, watched him curiously.

Peter changed tacks. "When?"

"I'll know the time. Very soon, and I dread the moment. But for now, I must sling it, tunnel or no."

"All right. It's your weight. Let's go." He handed the torch back to the girl.

Peter sat on the edge of the hole, lowered himself until he could set his feet on the lip of the tunnel. He stretched his hand, caught the underside of the tunnel ceiling, pulled himself inside.

Cei swung beside him, unlit torch tucked under his arm, and caught Peter's hand. While Anlawdd, Cors Cant, and Bedwyr lowered themselves into the hole, Cei made a tiny pile of his tinder. As Peter watched intently, the porter crouched over it, struck sparks with his flint. One caught.

Cei gently breathed it into a flame. He held the sticky torch above the slight flame. It caught slowly, but burned bright and with less smoke than Peter feared.

Smythe crouched, squirmed along the tunnel. Anlawdd kept her hand on his belt, and the tunnel train chugged along. The passage bent slowly to the left. Within minutes the entrance was lost.

The air smelled like a crypt, despite a blowing wind that carried the stinging torch smoke back toward the mouth. The walls were moist, cold. Peter heard no sound but the scrape of their own boots, their labored breaths.

His legs quickly cramped from the unnatural posture. He heard groans behind him. Every so often they stopped while one of the team worked out a locked knee and the rest greedily swallowed water. Peter clenched his teeth, urged them onward.

Hours passed unseen in the black-dark womb. "How far?" he gasped. The slope had turned sharply up, now at a twenty-five-degree angle.

"We'll come—to an underground—stream that is— directly beneath the wall," said Anlawdd. She sounded weary, depressed, panted for air. "Still a long—way ahead—if you don't drown—in the dripping water— another—long crawl—to the baths. Two candles, three, maybe. Not sure."

"Three candles!" exclaimed Bedwyr.

Anlawdd caught her wind, turned indignant. "Oh stop complaining. I've crawled the whole distance—a hundred times if I've done it once! Honestly—you men make such an expense of—everything!" Cors Cant, who had been panting in anguish, abruptly silenced himself.

Peter worried about another danger: the air circulation had changed, blowing the smoke forward, announcing their approach to anyone with a nose. Nor were they silent to those with ears.

After resting as much as possible beneath the oppressive weight of earth, they moved out. The passage narrowed, barely wide enough for Peter's broad shoulders to pass. Had he been armored, he would have stuck fast. *What a nightmare to get the whole company along here!* he thought. Anlawdd was right.

Even Peter began to get claustrophobic under the hill. He could not shake the memory of lying at the bottom of a pile of rubble, covered in the blood of Sergeant Conway. He curled his lip, blinked stinging sweat from his eyes.

A day passed, another day; a week fled. Soon, years tumbled down the tunnel like stones down a drainpipe. At last, Peter smelled the overpowering odor of rot. As they closed on the underground stream, the stench intensified. Peter tried breathing through his mouth, gagged immediately.

"Wet a kerchief, hold it before your nose," suggested Anlawdd. "Doesn't make the smell any better, but it makes you think it does, which is almost the same thing."

They paused, sacrificed precious water to wet cloth "gas masks."

Water dropped onto Peter's brow, then again, a stream of diseased, viscous liquid trickling onto his head. Water fell from the ceiling as gobbets of chalky mud, full of lime, copper, and other toxic, corrosive metals and minerals.

"I wouldn't sip this water, if I were you," added Anlawdd unnecessarily. Peter would sooner have sipped the River Ganges, where Indians float their dead ancestors.

The ceiling lowered again, and they were forced to belly-crawl through the sucking mud. "Good God, you've crawled through *this* a hundred times?" he asked.

"Well, perhaps not a hundred," admitted the girl. "I actually crawled it, oh, let me add them up. . . ." She was silent for a long moment. "Twice," she concluded. "Once when I was six, and last year when I escaped. I mean left."

He stopped, turned back to the harpy, her hair turned brown by the torchlight. "Only *twice?*"

"Well, I did say if I've crawled it a hundred times, I've crawled it once. It's logically true, since I've done neither." She was too tired even to smirk.

After an interminable period of squirming and belly-crawling, which reminded Peter of his first month at

Sandhurst, the tunnel suddenly filled with torch smoke. He choked, thrust out his hand. Groping fingers found the obstruction before the torchlight picked it up: a collapse of dirt.

A sudden moment of panic: the tunnel could collapse, bury them alive! Then his training reasserted itself; he fought the terror down.

It's not real, just a dream, he told himself sternly. *Discorporate, drift high, look down at that body crawling through the mire. You do it most of your life.*

Many years, too many campaigns. They seemed ethereal now, a manufactured past. Blurred, overlapped: who was he *really?* . . . Knight of the Table Round, ersatz Mason, Special Air Serviceman?

He lay still, dug one-handed at the dirt. No one talked; they choked on the smoke, lay on their bellies to find what air they could below the hot fumes of wood and pitch.

Jesus and Mary, I've forgotten which is cover and which the real career! A frightening thought, mirrors bent around so that he saw only the back of his head—*is that me? Why this mission into Harlech, to seek a renegade Irishwoman or avenge the butchery of a city I don't even know in a time I don't really believe existed?*

His hands wormed into the packed dirt, nails pulled, fingertips sore. How far did the blockage extend? He could only find out by digging. "Prince, we can spell you," called Cei from Somewhere Back There. A pious thought, but useless. There was no way Cei could crawl over Bedwyr, Cors Cant, Anlawdd. The girl *might* be able to lend a hand, however.

"Can I help?" she asked, as if she read his thought. Peter flexed aching hands, readily agreed.

She squirmed forward. He squeezed as far to one side as he could, but even so, her body rubbed along his as she inched forward.

In her own way, Anlawdd was as beautiful as Gwynhwyfr. Not a Page-Three girl; she did not exude raw sexuality, the combination virgin-harlot that Peter's ex-wife always said men wanted. But Anlawdd was self-possessed, aggressive, determined. And her body was still a first-water gem, if not the Blue Carbuncle.

Peter felt a tightening in his groin, against his will, despite sticky mud and collapsing soil. After a moment, Anlawdd stopped digging, looked at him. She felt it too; how could she not, pressed so close? In her eyes he saw ... trepidation? excitement? Unquestionably some desire.

She flicked her eyes briefly toward Cors Cant, imperceptibly shook her head. He could not tell whether she meant "later" or "never." She returned to the dirt pile. But she *had* felt something. Perhaps only in her head, not in the thigh that pressed so close.

Too close.

Nervously, Peter said, "My turn, I believe."

She stopped, lay silently against him. "I'll get out of your way." Her voice was uncharacteristically soft. Anlawdd squirmed back, making no attempt to avoid contact.

It took another hour to clear the rest of the dirt away, perhaps longer. Without sun, stars, watch, or even conversation to mark time, it could have been any duration. At last the passage was clear enough to wriggle through.

Not too soon for Peter. The air had gotten so bad from torch smoke and their own carbon dioxide that he nearly passed out.

The drops ceased directly they crossed the threshold. "We're on the other side of the city wall," explained Anlawdd, still subdued. "A dug river runs along outside the city. It's that canal we just passed."

"Anlawdd," asked Peter, "what did you mean, escape?"

"Escape?"

"You told me the second time you passed through here was when you escaped."

"I'm sure I don't know *what* you're talking about. I didn't say escape."

"You did."

"Didn't. I said I left."

He dropped the issue. The point carried; but what point

exactly? *Suspicious-er and suspicious-er,* he thought. On the other hand, would Selly Corwin concoct such an intricate, easily broken lie? Was Anlawdd's dark secret a previous incarnation as a twentieth century terrorist? No, it was too complicated.

Unless that's exactly what she wants *me to think . . .* Peter shook his head, dismissed the speculation. A classic disinformation matrix: each new datum muddied rather than cleared the water. The only defense was to arbitrarily stop the cycle of doubt-believe-doubt. Besides, the boy, so suspicious even of the new Lancelot, would surely have noticed if the girl he loved became another person.

First there is a mountain, said Lao-tzu in the Tao, the Way, *then there is no mountain, then there is.* Was the pop singer Donovan—another Irishman!—a double agent for the Chinese?

He crawled faster, now on the "downhill" side mentally. The long underground was unhealthy for mental stability.

The tunnel turned sharply upward. They laboriously climbed a crumbled, moist ramp of mud, weaving ropes of sand.

Ropes of sand. An investigation where *everybody* was a suspect, a player. "Remember," said instructor Hyatt on the first day of Peter's Criminal Investigations ("Terror 101") class, "in a true conspiracy, *all players are pawns,* regardless of their rank."

"Quiet now," commanded Anlawdd, *sotto voce.* "The baths adjoin the gate guards' privy, where they pass a lot of time doing their business and handing around Greek scrolls with drawings of naked women. Like that deck you have, Cei. Goodness, but you men make such a mystery of it!"

"Naked women?" asked Cors Cant.

"Where does this tunnel come out?" whispered the Sicambrian.

"That's the best part, Prince. We're going to get *very* hot, but I guarantee the Saxons will never find the entrance."

"Jutes," corrected Peter, faintly annoyed. *Blast her,* I'm *a Saxon!*

"We've arrived. Let me up front, Lancelot."

He ignored the familiarity. The passage was wider; this time he made certain there was no contact as she wriggled past.

They stopped below a trapdoor in the ceiling. "There's one tiny problem I forgot to mention," she said.

He waited, said nothing.

"If they're running both sides of the *hypocaust* . . ." she began, trailed off. She pulled her glove off, reached out, and very gingerly touched the trapdoor. She yanked her fingers away as if from a hot stove, then touched it a few more times before laying her hand flat against the copper.

She smiled. "They've raked the fire back to the firewood door, the lazy, unwashed badgers. Why exert themselves keeping the entire *hypocaust* lit when they won't use the baths anyway?"

"So? What does that mean, Anlawdd?"

"We can pass without getting baked like loaves of bread. You must have a luckstone, General, or perhaps it's the luck of having a bard along. Now aren't you glad you didn't leave Cors Cant behind?" She snapped back the bolt, pushed against the trap with her shoulder.

Peter climbed up after her, found himself in a low-ceilinged room with scores of piled-stone pillars supporting the roof. Away to the left, the room was afire! His face instantly flushed at the heat, and he gasped for air, then realized it was a walk-in furnace. The ceiling was poked with holes, allowing the heat to propagate upward.

He understood Anlawdd's comment about luck. If the entire furnace were lit, the tunnel would open into an inferno . . . another excellent defense against an enemy using Harlech's own tricks against her.

"We're directly beneath the *caldarium,*" whispered the girl. "Quiet! Flues lead up to the floor above. We'll be heard if we're noisy."

Cors Cant was next, followed by Bedwyr and Cei. They crouched under the ceiling tiles. Anlawdd pointed at fif-

teen huge piles of cordwood stacked against the walls, surrounded by brick-cut stones. "If Jutes ever bathed, we'd be
baked like pork roast."

She pointed toward the far wall. Carved into the concrete were indentations for climbing. A second trap
loomed above their heads.

This time, the soldier-seamstress opened the door very
slowly, put her face up to peer into the *caldarium. Whatever that is,* thought Peter. "Go," she whispered, opened
the door, and bolted up through it.

The *caldarium* turned out to be a Turkish steam bath,
currently neither steamy nor occupied, though well lit.
*Even under occupation, the oil-lamp fillers continue busi-
ness as usual,* thought Peter.

The floor was covered with an intricate mosaic of
painted tiles, a geometric design of squares, circles, and
curlicues in red and purple. Wooden and concrete benches
lined the walls, and the floor contained holes through
which steam would rise when water was poured over rocks
heated by the *hypocaust* below.

When Anlawdd saw the baths were indeed empty, she
collapsed onto the nearest wooden bench, began to hyper-
ventilate. The boy knelt beside her, held her hand while
she put her head between her knees.

She was terrified! realized Peter with a shock. Was it
the tunnel, or fear that there would be Jutes at the other
end? He moved forward awkwardly, was stopped by a
hand on his arm.

"Let the boy handle it," said Cei. "I wouldn't mind sitting quietly here a few moments myself, calming my own
pulse."

Peter grunted, sat down on a bench across the room. He
turned away, felt an absolute cad. *What right have I to fan-
tasize about this girl? What she and the boy have is truly
love. I only want what's between her legs!* Disgusted with
himself, he brooded on the next phase of the mission.

"Prince?" asked Cei when some time had elapsed. He
leaned over, spoke for Peter's ears only. "What's it to be?"

"Search and destroy," said Peter automatically. "Welcome to Terror 101. We're going to introduce King Hrundal to a whole new concept in your basic art of warfare."

CHAPTER 13

ANLAWDD LEANED CLOSE TO CORS CANT, WHISPERED IN HIS ear. His breath caught, she was *very* close. "Cors, you don't have to do this. Asking a bard to search and destroy is like asking a lark to hunt rabbits."

"What is search and destroy?" he asked, listless and exhausted from the tunnel-crawl. "It sounds so horrible and bloody. You should excel at it."

She touched his shoulder. He twitched, as if starting at a sudden noise. In a pained voice, she said "Cors Cant Ewin, you must think me a monster. I'm not surprised, hacking and chopping as I've done more than once this week. And—well, you know. But that isn't me, not me!"

"Anlawdd, does it matter whether it's the first time or the hundredth time?"

"What? Cors Cant, do you know, or do you care if you do know, that when I slew my brother Canastyr and those Saxons a few days ago, it was the first time I'd actually killed someone? My first blood, first time. Just as when we started to—you know—in the princess's room, it would have been the first . . . I mean, if we had done what we might have done it would have been the first time I did—that."

"First or hundredth time, what's it matter? Blood soaks your hands like wine soaks Myrddin's." He lowered his head, voice faltering. "I'm sorry, my—my Princess. I *don't* think you're a monster. I think you're . . ." She waited. Cors Cant found his word: "wondrous."

Technically true; Anlawdd inspired wonder in the bard. But his cheeks flushed, for he knew what he meant her to understand, and it was a lie. Wonder, awe . . . it was not love. Not at that moment. Too much anger for him to love her, anger and even fear.

All gods and goddesses, am I afraid *of Anlawdd, afraid of my own heart,* mo chroi?

"Wondrous? Really? Cors Cant, that's like—that's as good as . . ." She trailed off, speechless for once, but pensive rather than happy. Anlawdd entwined her fingers among his, put her other hand over both. Yet her eyes flickered momentarily to Lancelot. She did not smile.

"Anlawdd, I—"

"It's so different, training and the real thing." She looked over his shoulder, at the wall, the ceiling, anywhere but in his eyes. "For a while, my stomach crumbled into a ball the size of a walnut and about as hard. It was all I could do to continue our ritual after such an oracle. But I think I did a good job of keeping it out of my face and voice, didn't I?" She finally looked at him, eyes pleading.

Cors Cant stared. The news that she was so terribly affected by the killings shook him. "Yes, you did." *Jesus and Mithras, her own brother! Yet she was so calm immediately after.*

Anlawdd closed her green eyes, bowed her head. Wisps of auburn covered her face. "I say, Saxons, who cares whether they live or die? Beasts. It helps me live with what I did to the worm and what I almost did to the world."

She wrapped her arms around herself. "I can still see that awful horse trampling him, like pressing the juice out of very, very red wine-grapes. I wasn't even there! Not me, not who I am. Something else in my body. Maybe a demon."

She was wrong. Cors Cant knew it was she. Even in the heat of battle, her "Anlawddness" was unmistakable. *But it comforts her to think it was a demon,* he thought, and said nothing to contradict.

I've never seen this side of you, my love. Maybe no one has. He stretched an awkward hand, brushed the hair from her face. She pulled away. He pulled his hand back, but in an eye blink she caught it, held it once again to her cheek.

"That's part of winning me," she said, watched him impassively. "Or rather, me winning you back." Anlawdd was once again in control. "I'll tell you now, Cors Cant Ewin, and I hope you remember because it's important and I can't keep telling you. You have to break through what you see right now to find Anlawdd, like eating an oyster. Let's go."

She stood, dropped his hand with finality. His throat tightened again. Fear, confusion, tore him in half. *It's not supposed to be like this.*

Cors Cant hung back as she combed her hair with her fingers. Autumn red had become rust and filth. Her damp tunic clung to back and legs alluringly, but he feared he might never get any closer than that moment. *Look thou but touch not. . . .*

Lancelot gestured them forward. Only one door led out of the *caldarium.* Rather than pass through it, the Sicambrian edged toward the crack, peeked in both directions carefully. They still had no idea of the hour, seeing only enclosed rooms lit by lamps.

Lancelot preceded them all into a smaller room. *"Tepidarium,"* explained Anlawdd, proud of her few Latin words. "The men take off their clothes in one room, jump into a cold bath in the *fri—frigidarium,* then warm up here before entering the steam room."

"What about the women?" asked Lancelot.

"Oh, we have our own bathhouse. Romans have such a quaint sense of propriety. There's a third bath outside the walls, for the regular citizens; it's hardly as stuffy, I could add."

"Regular citizens?"

Anlawdd scowled at Lancelot for a moment. "Those below the rank of knight, of course. *Prince.*"

Cors Cant stared at the Sicambrian giant as well. Superficially, he still looked like Lancelot, prince and legate, champion of Caer Camlann. Yet unlike Anlawdd, the bard had hard, empirical evidence that Lancelot was possessed: all the little slips, the personality change; but most convincing, the prince could suddenly *read.* If the others suspected demonic possession, they kept it from Cors Cant, not surprisingly.

"So, ah, how did you find out about this secret passage in the *men's* bathhouse?" Lancelot smiled feebly, trying to mask his lacuna with another jest.

"Goodness, you sound like Cei questioning a blacksmith's bill! I did a lot of, um, exploring when I was a little girl," She nodded, sincere. Lancelot turned away, clearly unconvinced.

That makes at least two of us who think your oyster shell hides too much, thought Cors Cant.

The *tepidarium* was much smaller than the *caldarium,* only a few seats. The floor tiles were yellow white in dawnlight that filtered through slits in the roof. Hanging curtains were painted on the walls. *At least we know the time now,* thought Cors Cant. *It's the wee, sma' hours in the morn, as an Eirelander would say.*

Lancelot led them into the *frigidarium,* Anlawdd close by his side. Too close. The bard bit his lip.

The *frigidarium* was colder than the first two rooms, illuminated by cocklight but no lamps or lanterns. Cors Cant shivered. Sharp, cold scenes were marked on the whitewashed walls—a snow scene, probably in Hannibal's Alps. An attacking army rode a herd of improbable, cyclopean creatures that might have been Cei's elephants. It was hard to distinguish the dim, ancient drawings by dawntwilight.

Sunrise is close, thought the bard. He shivered, either from the chill or the thought of having crawled a night and a half through the bowels of Pluto's demesnes.

They passed through an open doorway into the last room, the changing room, *apodyterium,* a word Anlawdd seemed not to know, though any civilized Roman would.

This far from the center of the world, in far-flung Prydein, Britain, how civilized were they really? *Do we fool ourselves, playact at civilization like children playing Antony, Octavius, and Caesar?*

Cors Cant felt the first flutter of fear. Even if the impossible happened, if no one found out about the difference in their rank, could he and Anlawdd, the wild *Cymric* princess-assassin, ever live under one roof? Cors Cant had necessarily tasted pagan ways since Princess Gwynhwfyr graced the court, but they frightened him. He was not at all sure he could handle the savage practices of Harlech, the barbaric North, where the people (they said) were born with dagger in hand. *I am too Roman, too civilized. I fear hell and the wrath of the Roman Christ should I sink into pagan ways.*

He sat down, leaned his head back, thought of Caer Camlann. Princess Gwynhwfyr swam from bed to bed, unworried about reputation, dignity, even her husband, the *Dux Bellorum.* "Guest-Right," she called it, offering herself to every petty king of every microcosmic kingdom or cantref in all Britain.

She danced naked in the moonlight, sometimes in the sunlight! She cared nothing for learning, study, discipline, only the sensuous worship of Aphrodite, or as Gwynhwfyr called Her, Brigit.

Was Gwynhwfyr a sorceress, as some did charge? Preposterous, she had no patience whatsoever! The bard would lay long odds that she had never memorized a single epic, knew nothing of Homer or Vergilius, barely remembered her own legends: Pwyll and Pryderi, Rhiannon, the marriage of Branwen, the terrible war between the islands, the feast of Bran's head.

Cors Cant jerked awake, realized he had dozed. Some time had passed, yet they had not left the baths. *Probably waiting until daybreak,* he thought.

Lancelot stealthily entered the disrobing room, gestured them against the wall. The front door was thick wood, warped so it no longer fitted properly. The Sicambrian slowly pulled it back, as Cors Cant crowded close to Anlawdd for his first glimpse of occupied Harlech.

The bard stared in astonishment, blinking in the long, red shades of sunrise. *Mithras, I did sleep!*

In the shadow of fire-gutted buildings, the brave defenders of Harlech scurried about their normal business. They barely glanced at the cold ashes of an apartment building directly across from the bathhouse, hurried past as if the burned remains were nothing more than an overturned applecart.

"Lady save us," whispered the bard in sudden stillness. "Your people are bewitched!"

Beneath his hand, he felt Anlawdd's muscles jerk. She was an inflated air bladder, ready to burst in all directions. She spoke coldly, deliberately: "The motherless bastards should have fought."

"Perhaps they did," rumbled Lancelot, watched Anlawdd carefully; *Lancelot worries she might lose control, fly among them madly with her knife,* thought the bard. Nervous, he watched the princess himself.

"Are we ready?" asked Cei, looking at Anlawdd.

Anlawdd took a deep breath, let it out slowly. She unlaced her pale blue chemise, pulled out the map wrapped in oilcloth. A brief glimpse of breasts—Cors Cant's breath caught as he stared hungrily at what he could not have. She laced up the leather thongs, unaware of the raging emotions she had stirred, or unconcerned about them.

She flashed a grim-lipped, business-as-usual smile. The fury had passed, or been buried. She pointed at a phrase in the map. "This says Senators' Apartments, I think. Doesn't it? There they are, or there they used to be. So I'd start reading from here. If I could read Greek." She gestured at the smoldering ruins across the street.

Cors Cant translated from memory, staring at the blackened walls. He spoke haltingly at first, then with increased certainty as he caught the rhythm of the travelogue. "The streets . . . surrounding the bathhouse . . . are narrow and twisted, full of beggars whose maimings and disgusting deformities ... are clearly the diabolical work of gentile and heathen rituals."

"Cors, you're not even looking at the map!" Anlawdd read slowly to herself, moving her lips. Her face reddened. "But you're perfectly right. How can you read without looking at it?"

"Read it? I already read it."

"When?"

"When I borrowed it. Last night."

Anlawdd put her hands on hips, lowered her brows threateningly. "You only had the map for a few moments! How could you memorize ... ?"

Cors Cant spoke slowly, wondering whether it was a trick question. "Well, being a Druid, we memorize about a thousand poems and texts of various—"

"Never mind, just forget I even asked, Cors Cant Ewin." Annoyed, she shoved the map back between her breasts. "Continue, show-off."

"Full of beggars whose maimings and disgusting deformities ... are clearly the diabolical work of gentile and heathen rituals. These godless pagans do rend and—"

"Skip to the next building," suggested Lancelot.

"Hey, it was getting interesting," objected Bedwyr.

Lancelot made a gesture like a cart wheel rolling. Cors Cant mentally skimmed until he found more descriptography. "Two are the streets that branch from the bath, a narrow street of artisans that wends toward the fisheries, and a horseshoe-bent alley between the millhouse and an apartment frequented by well-to-do corn merchants that leads to the main way, ah, Eighth Street."

"Eighth Street?" demanded both Anlawdd and Lancelot, simultaneously.

"He shifts into Latin sometimes. *Vicus Octavus,* he wrote. Eighth Street."

She shook her head, scowled. "No, must be a mistake. There's no numbered streets in Harlech. Whoever heard of such a stupid name for a street? Where are the other seven?"

"Maybe it should've been Vicus Octavius?" suggested the bard. "Street of Octavius?"

"Ah, that's what we want!"

"You're sure?" asked Lancelot.

She nodded. "It leads to the old fort, where I'm sure the Saxons are holed up. I mean Jutes. Horseshoe-bent alley it is."

Lancelot nodded, ducked out of the bath.

They slid into the street, frigid in the morning mist. Cors Cant smelled urine, burning wood, a long-dead animal.

The travelogue author was right about the beggars. Despite the hour, several score mendicants and hand-in-caps crouched in doorways and alleys, lay in gutters, hid between buildings.

Rags and hoods ill-concealed their deformities: stumps where limbs once grew, melon-sized goiters. Some wounds even appeared self-inflicted.

Two who sat near the bath particularly disturbed the boy. Where should have been arms and legs were only clawlike flippers that clutched and squeezed, the hands and feet of a newborn babe.

> *Snips and scrapes, cuttings, ends,*
> *From now on we're your only friends. . . .*

Lancelot scanned the tumble of buildings. "There's the mill, I suppose."

"Are those corn merchant apartments?" asked Cei.

"A prison," corrected Anlawdd bitterly, pointed at the iron door, barred window through which lonely hands protruded. "Many changes were made when Ricca died, which is one of the reasons I left so hurriedly. You can't go home again, they say, and sometimes they come along and take your home right out from under your feet when you *do* go home."

"Well that *has* to be the horseshoe alley," said Lancelot, pointing between the two buildings. Anlawdd nodded.

They pushed through the mob, and Cors Cant tried not to look at the surrounding beggars.

A man bumped into the bard. Cors Cant stared, swallowed heavily. The beggar had two mouths, lips and all, in his throat. "Millie?" he croaked through the top mouth.

Cors Cant stood entranced, unable to move. "I ... I have no money," he gasped at last. True; he gave his last coin to Anlawdd in her crystal cave, when she initiated him and bared her soul.

Another man pressed against his back, two more surrounded him. Cors Cant had become the hub of a wagon wheel, with beggars like spokes holding him fast. He tried to peer over their heads, catch sight of Anlawdd and the others; but he was too short, the spokes too many.

Frightened, he shrank inward, reflexively grabbed his harp, wrapped his arms around it. *My harp!* He had intentionally not played it since it was drenched, allowing the strings to dry. Would it even pluck properly? A tune, a tune to turn their hearts to peace!

Blank! Bloody hell I can't think of a thrice-damned thing! At once, a cool, comforting, shepherd's song from the pastures of Lludd-Dun, Londinium, popped into his head, a song his mother used to sing as she skinned a ewe for lamb stew. Before the burning time, the sack of Londinium by Vortigern, the coming of Lancelot and Artus. Shaking, Cors Cant began to play.

His fingers slipped on the strings, plucked a wrong note. A pair of hands splayed like hooves grabbed his arms, caught his leine. A hook-bent woman seized his leg, nearly yanked him to the ground. Frightened, he almost screamed for help.

Then a soothing voice spoke within. "Find your cup, find it within. It is *there*." Like a burst aqueduct, the shepherd's song exploded from his gut. His fingers found the strings, plucked them better than he had ever played at a Druid examination.

The harp voice raced like a mountain stream, burst from white rocks high above a verdant plain to sweep among the lindens, broom, the heather bells. Unstoppable as water, it laughed across a black-rock streambed, cascaded down a deep, green, mossy pool as frogs croaked in chorus. Stream water swirled, gently flooded the grassland, sweet as new-mown hay.

Sheep grazed, lay in the water to cool. Wolfhounds ran left, right, harried the flock and rounded them together. The hounds were led by shrill whistles from the shepherds high on the cliff . . . the very cliff, now seen from below, where the stream and the music had begun.

Cors Cant plucked the last note, brought the song full circle from cliff to grass and back to shepherds on the cliff. Looking up, he found himself still in Harlech, still plucking his harp in the shadow of a prison, surrounded by a mob of tormented beggars.

They wept. Some stared at the ground, saddened by the futile journey of the waters of life. Others cried at the beauty they saw in their own hearts. Two-Mouths spoke. "Right fine that was, good lad. Righteous as a standing stone. Worth a *milliarense,* a gold triple *solidus* if 'twere owed."

He stretched forth a hand missing two fingers, touched Cors Cant on the top of his head. The bard did not flinch. This beggar understood the song more deeply than anyone in Caer Camlann had. He had once played it to thunderous silence in Camlann's *triclinium.*

The water is my life, flows from high to low; it sinks at last, sluggish and spent, into tomorrow's inert mud. But all is guided by shepherds on the high cliff who rise above the sheep and dogs.

That is the part of you that is a Builder of the Temple, said the echo of a thought. His own? Or Anlawdd's? Cors Cant let the harp drop slowly to his side, tethered by the ship's line dangling around his neck.

The beggars stepped back, drifted to their lairs and holes. Cors Cant looked full at each, separate and unique in the light of day-begins. When they had all left, he saw Anlawdd and the rest of the company. They waited for him.

"You were in no danger, boy," said Lancelot. "We wouldn't have allowed you harm."

"They meant none," said Cors Cant. "Just wanted a *milliarense.*"

Anlawdd lowered her brows, perhaps remembering where his last coin had gone. "Did you pay them?"

"No complaints."

She watched him with a half smile. *Did she hear the song?* It was one of the "noncanonical" tunes he had mentioned to Merovee.

He hurried to join the others. As he passed Anlawdd, she smiled cryptically. "Every princess needs a bard, of course," she said for his ears alone.

She led the company through alleys and cracks, streets of hammered dirt, half-buried cobbles, even to Wobble Way, built of wood boards nailed together, lined with wooden buildings painted yellow with mysterious, Arabic writings that Cors Cant could not translate. Everywhere, beggars surrounded, pressed in. But the raiders moved too fast to be surrounded. No Jutes marked their journey; in fact, they saw only the exhausted nightwatch, half-asleep and half-drunk, dangling closed lanterns against their sides as they lumbered toward a guardhouse. Neither saw they any sign of armed resistance. The citizens of Harlech accepted their conquest unconcernedly, scurried after their money-ways.

Cors Cant translated from the Greek travelogue, and Anlawdd interpreted. Lancelot said nary a word, and Cei and Bedwyr took their cue from him.

Where they paused, the buildings were built so close together the street was in complete shadow, though midday had passed. Anlawdd squinted at the top of a tall tower, four flights, its top brilliantly illuminated by winter white sunlight.

"Whither now?" asked Cors Cant. "The Greek turned here, strolled along Vicus Ludibrium. But the fort lies yonder." He pointed at the ancient Roman fort.

Lancelot looked at Anlawdd, raised one brow. "Harlech battlements?" he asked. She nodded.

The fort was nearly as large as Caer Camlann, a large central building with a long, L-shaped extension. But where Camlann was built primarily for comfort, a villa rather than a fortress, Caer Harlech was a siege artifact, built to resist invading barbarians. That it fell so quickly to but a few thousand marauding Jutes was a criminal indictment of Prince Gormant's unpreparedness.

Two huge outbuildings sat next to the main hall. Both had red-tiled roofs, both made of white concrete surrounding solid oak construction. Battlements, sharp wooden stakes—all classically Roman.

The north face of Caer Harlech was painted with many symbols of Cymru, including the red dragon of Artus *Pan-Draconis.* Judging by its poor execution, it was a recent addition after civilization fled Britain half a century before. A garden wall of whitewashed wood circled the enclosure; its top was a geometric wood carving of stylized knotwork, another recent add-on.

Harlech fortress! The thought thrilled and frightened Cors Cant. Now what? What would four warriors and a song-spinner do against an army of Jutes? Lancelot gestured them together, backs against a barricaded building.

"Once a candle shop," said Anlawdd, "seized by Greedy Gormant for nonpayment of taxes."

"What can three soldiers, a girl, and a bard do against the Jutes?" asked the legate. Cors Cant jumped; could this Lancelot-demon read his thoughts?

It was a rhetorical question, for Lancelot continued. "Back in—in Sicambria, we developed methods for striking against a vastly superior enemy.

"Our greatest weapon is invisibility, our tool is fear. The edge of this fear is a silent attack from darkness, by shadow soldiers . . . by us."

"What do you mean, in-visible?" asked Bedwyr. He scratched his head, puzzled.

"Like Caswallawn," reminded Cors Cant, "who threw a magic mantle about his shoulders so that none could see him kill the six men of Caradawg, son of Blessed Bran."

Lancelot continued, as if he had heard neither Bedwyr nor Cors Cant. "Sabbah's assassins left flame-daggers in the pillows of princes and slew one man among three in a bedroll without waking the other two.

"We strike in blackness while the enemy sleeps. We don't allow him to see who we are or how many. We leave bodies where they're sure to be found."

Bedwyr rose to full height, aghast. "No! I am a general in the imperial army of Artus *Dux Bellorum,* not a murdering Saxon."

"Silence, brother," said Cei to Bedwyr, cutting through the argument like a razor. "You think murder is uncivilized? Remember Nero!"

"Your *brother?*" asked Lancelot.

Cors Cant smiled. He had guessed long ago, but it was the first time Cei had slipped in public.

Cei's face flushed. "Ah, Sire, please do not tell the *Dux Bellorum.* You know how he feels about . . . about you-know."

"Incest?" suggested Anlawdd.

"Nepotism, you foul-minded harlot!"

After a long, embarrassed silence, during which Cei and Bedwyr each pretended the other had vanished into the Summerland, Lancelot coughed noisily. "Well, to quote Anlawdd, let's do it." The princess nodded in determined agreement.

Lancelot peeked around the corner of the candle shop, studied the fortress. Cei crouched behind him, thought out loud. "We're not strolling in the front gate. Guards seem drunk and half-asleep, but not completely blind. I suppose we could ambush Jutes for their clothes and sneak in, but that seems overly complex. Any ideas, oh Great Prince?"

"I can get us in," said Anlawdd.

"You're right," said Lancelot. "Too much danger we'd be spotted. I don't want to jump Jutes anyway; they're well-armed. There isn't a lot of traffic in and out . . . are there really only ten gate guards, Cei? Do you count more?"

"I know how to get us in, and I'm sure Cors Cant will back me up on that."

"Yes, I'm sure you do, Anlawdd," said Lancelot. "I know you grew up here, but you didn't live in the palace, did you? Just let us handle this."

"Well actually," said the bard, "she *did* live—" Anlawdd's elbow caught his solar plexus. He squeaked like a kicked puppy, gasped for a breath.

"Eleven, General. Where are the rest?" Cei shook his head, astonished at an occupying army that worried so little about a counterattack. "They must think we fled back to Cardiff."

Cors Cant glared balefully at Anlawdd, who scowled back. He swallowed, forced himself to breathe. He cleared his throat, prepared to tell some lie about her having worked in the fort. But Anlawdd beat him off the starting line, rose, and voted with her feet.

She sauntered around Lancelot and Cei, hands behind her back. The west side of the fortress overlooked a steep hill, the shore, the ocean. Anlawdd walked through the candle shop archway, crossed the fifty paces to the cracked, whitewashed wall that surround the fort.

Lancelot stared, demanded, "What in God's name is she doing?" She had passed the men before any of them knew what she intended, was now across the vacant lot upon which the wall sat.

Anlawdd looked quickly in both directions, pressed her fingers deeply into a crack in the fence. She pulled hard on something, leaned into the wood with her other hand. A concealed door opened slightly, just enough for her to squeeze through. It looked unused in years. She vanished behind the wooden fence.

"Mithras!" breathed Cei, astonished and admiring.

A pearl white hand snaked from around the door. A single finger gestured them forward, then the hand vanished again.

Annoyed by her teasing, Lancelot ordered them forward at a languid pace, slow enough not to arouse attention. Just padding down the street for an ale, for all the guards could tell.

Cors Cant was first to follow her through the secret gate into a tiny courtyard overgrown by ivy and weeds. Anlawdd slid her knife blade into the door crack, lifted the inner latch. She pulled the door open with a dreadful squeak, squirmed through the opening into blackness.

The bard scurried after his red goddess, pushed through the dilapidated door into a smoky corridor, lit only by slivers of daylight from the hanging door. The arched ceiling was blackened from centuries of torch smoke, obscuring what once had been a brilliantly colored mosaic of a hooded man, sere branches growing out of his head like antlers. Faint cracks of light shone through the plaster, merged with the doorlight; but most of the room was in shadow.

Anlawdd stood against a wall, the sunslice bisecting her body from breasts to shoulder, picking out scarlet highlights in her locks. Her eyes were turned away from Cors Cant as he entered. She stared down the sinister, black corridor, trembling slightly.

In a *very* quiet voice, she said, "Down the hall, turn right at the oaken door, then across the courtyard. That's the main hall, where by all rights these swine of Helios will be sunk in drunken stupors."

Lancelot leaned head then shoulders into the room. He inspected left and right, gestured the others forward. They squeezed past, assembled in the corridor, streaks of light illuminating Lancelot's grey eyes, Cei's breastplate, Bedwyr's mailed fist.

"We've got to move fast," Lancelot decided, rumbling voice so soft it was nearly inarticulate. "Before they wake. Where are we?"

"This wing was abandoned when I was ... um, about ten summers younger, when the ancient roof collapsed. Caer Harlech is very old, and it sits on an even older building that was surely here even before we became civilized, before the divine Julius set foot here, or at least his legions."

Anlawdd noticed she was illuminated, moved to stand in deeper darkness. "Look, Caer Harlech is like a square piecrust, hollowed in the center." She drew a square in the air with her fingers, barely visible. "We're directly across from the hall," she continued. "We can either cut straight across the *level* courtyard, or putter around the *square* perimeter."

Lancelot's brows raised momentarily, as if she had conveyed some secret message. Cors Cant felt a twinge of unreasonable jealousy. *What the hell do I care if she sends secret signals to that barbaric Sicambrian general that all the women throw themselves at?*

"Well we can't just sit here like *widows*," said Lancelot. "Let's move out, find a place to hole up till late night."

Widows . . . a reference to the widow's son? Is Lancelot a Builder? What in Mithras's name are they saying to each other? Are they arranging something? He clenched his fists, nails pressed sharply against his palms.

Level, square, she had said. Cors Cant felt his stomach tighten; he remembered the weird Latin that Lancelot had "transcribed" from the conversation between Merovee and Artus a week and a half ago: *we meet on the level . . . my table is round, not square.*

If Anlawdd needed help, needed a confidant, why did she not ask me? Cors Cant stepped into shadow himself, wondering how much of what he saw and heard was truly real, how much a strange song within his own head.

"I'll lead you to them," whispered Anlawdd. "But beyond the veil of Caswallan, I have no idea where we shall ever hide."

She moved from dark into light, but for a moment stood against a crack. Sunlight reflected from a whitewashed wall, silhouetting her perfectly.

Cors Cant's eyes widened; Anlawdd stood exactly as she had at the *Dux Bellorum*'s window.

The bard glanced quickly at Lancelot. The Sicambrian stared, raised his brows for an instant in recognition; then just as quickly, Lancelot glanced away.

But Cors Cant knew that in that moment, the champion saw and understood.

CHAPTER 14

ANLAWDD FOUND AN ABANDONED STOREROOM WHERE THEY waited upon "the reign of Chaos and old Night." *Thus passeth mine eleventh day,* thought Peter, *and now I have two assassins where only one stood before.*

At last, the distant sound of revelry faded, ceased. Peter let another hour pass, then roused his *Einsatzgruppe.*

Silent as Old Nick 'round a barrow, they eased back into the hallway, followed it through the building toward the inner courtyard. Anlawdd pointed out the door, hand white as the dead flesh of a grave ghoul . . . the same hand that, a few days past, had held a dagger aloft over Artus.

Peter eased it open, led the party across the shadow lane, hugging tree and hedgerow, to a sword-scarred door, black in the moonlight. *What are the odds of a burly bouncer just inside, holding an axe or a 12-gauge shotgun?* Bold and giddy with fear, Peter yanked it open.

A hundred souls snored through the Land of Nod: a fluid, phlegmy cough, an unintelligible murmur of sleeptalker, a cry in the night. They paused outside the hall.

Peter gestured them close. He unrolled his cloak over his shoulders, pulled the hood tight around his head and face like a veil. The others followed his lead. He drew his workmanlike, triangular dagger with nary a scrape, crouched low, crept into the room. He rolled each footstep, avoided the clop-clop of "horse hooves."

As his eyes adjusted to the dim illumination, he made

out a few score candles that flickered through swirls of dust. He scanned the room: about one hundred men. Some wore necklaces and crowns of gold and silver, uncut precious stones, pieces of battle armor. Most were drunk, asleep, half-naked to Peter's blade.

Two richly dressed gentleman sprawled stuporous across the nearest table, overturned wine jar between them. Peter approached in silence, though he could have ridden one of Hannibal's elephants and fired a cannon for all the winos would hear.

Eyes upon him. His men watched, held their breath in anticipation.

Peter stretched his blade hand forward. Steady: his iron will quelled the palsy. He had never cut a throat open before, only given the order to "open fire" and squeezed the trigger in his Mac-10.

Gently, Peter touched the blade against the white throat of the nearest Jute, ice line across the jugular, clamped his other hand over the Enemy's mouth and nose. Just a little pressure—

Steel froze his heart. *No, not a man! Just an exercise, just a training run. No more—no less. It's a wax dummy. No more.*

The Jute stiffened, woke. Pushing thought, fear, his immortal soul aside, Peter pressed hard on the blade, quickly slid the knife backward and down, feeling the tension relax as the sharp blade bit deep. *Just like carving a Christmas roast.*

For an instant, his vision flickered: the man beneath his blade was not a Jute, not an Enemy, but Artus *Pan-Draconis* himself. *Jesus and Mary,* he thought; *now I'm seeing through Anlawdd's eyes!* Peter shut his eyes tight, trying not to think of slitting the *Dux Bellorum*'s throat.

Peter's stomach seized tight. He clenched his teeth, swayed as his vision dimmed, greyed. He had to put a hand to the table to avoid falling; but he covered his reaction well. In the dark, no one would know how close he had come to disgracing himself and the regiment by collapsing because of a stupid hallucination. Artus, indeed!

The Jute's eyelids fluttered. A thin, red blood line formed, widened. Blood spurted for a moment, oozed from the death wound. Peter squeezed his throat shut, fighting down the bile. *It's for the* Dux ... *the* Dux Bel—

Life ebbed. Young, the lad was twenty-three at the oldest! The Jute turned his eyes, saw his slayer. Opened his mouth. Spittle rolled down his cheek. His eyelids drooped, one eye turned to the left. The boy died, quiet as snow on Snowdon.

Sleep no more, commanded Peter; *MacSmythe hath murdered sleep.*

He turned back to the squad, urged them on with a silent, savage clenched fist.

Peter, Cei, Bedwyr, Anlawdd swept the hall, fell upon the Jutes like mad hounds. *Bloody devils!* Knives flickered like sugarplum scalpels, caught the candlelight as tiny stars, mirrors into their black souls. The Jutes fell without waking.

Only the bard, Cors Cant, cut no throats. He stayed close to Anlawdd, ashen faced. Once, he made to reach out with his own knife, but she stopped him. Anlawdd looked at the bard, and to Peter's eyes it seemed she desperately implored Cors Cant to hold tight some measure of innocence. Then emotion drained from her face, and she continued the Caswallawn butchery.

At last, a half-armored Jute with a gold torque, perhaps an officer, felt a disturbance. He staggered up, still tipsy and but half-awake. Peter seized him from behind, arm around throat, drove his dagger to the hilt in the man's back, but not before Gold Torque screamed something inarticulate, but loud.

It was alarm enough. A new cry arose, far behind, screams of horror. Peter and the band had killed about ten men, each among other untouched. *Let the rest know terror!*

Up-down, up-down, chopping like Old Leather Apron himself, *fee fi fo fun, spill their blood like an Englishmun!* Peter's accursed blade found its own targets, slit throats of its own choosing, punctured hearts without the major's conscious control. Blood bathed his arm, chest, face. He slipped in the sticky stuff, rolled across a table laden with food and riches to butcher stuporous revelers just staggering awake, blind drunk, blind with panic.

More ghastly cries, a few words. Peter spoke no Jutish, could almost translate anyway. "Go!" he cried, the first word he had spoken. Cei paused, realized it was a command, and grabbed his brother Bedwyr. They sprinted for the door, followed by the bard.

But Anlawdd did not hear. She transferred her knife to her left hand, grabbed an axe from a slain Jute.

She turned viciously upon the waking wounded like Lizzie Borden, axe aloft. The blade sliced a spinal cord, embedded in a chest. Her mad eyes saw nothing but blood, Banquo's ghost taking revenge for every bloody deed ever suffered by the girl at the hands of Jute, Roman, Saxon, or Brit.

Cors Cant was halfway to the door when he realized she was not with him. He skidded to a halt, slipped to one knee in spilt blood, and scrambled back to his love. He seized her from behind, pulled her back.

Anlawdd brought her elbow back high into his face, decked the lad. She turned upon him, berserker blind, raised her knife over the bard. Cors Cant lay perfectly calm, chin raised to offer his throat.

Peter froze, too far to intercept. He knew what he must see next. The woman was battle-mad, saw no one and nothing but enemies. He had seen it in Ulster among his own command—seen it in Anlawdd herself in the *Dux Bellorum*'s apartment!

"Princess," cried Peter, *"strike not the widow's son!"*

She gasped. The magic words checked her blood fury. For an instant she hesitated, then shook her head, realized where she was. The spell broken, Peter sprinted across the room, grabbed Anlawdd's arm, pulled her off the bard. Darkness and drink saved their lives; the Jutes still plucked pieces of sleep from their eyes.

Peter shoved Anlawdd and Cors Cant towards the door,

where Cei and Bedwyr waited impatiently, propping open the heavy wood.

They fled the hall, across the courtyard. The Jutes did not immediately follow and lost the trail.

Princess? Princess Anlawdd? Peter grabbed her arm, dragged her to a stop. "Where?" he demanded. *Where did I get that "princess' cognition?*

"Gaol!" she cried. " 'Tis where my father is surely held, along with the fighting men of Harlech who still live!" She turned sharply left toward a newer wing, ducked under an archway. She jogged along the passageway, turned and battered upon a wooden door. Cei and Bedwyr joined her. Together, the three broke it in.

The room was ancient, much older than the rest of the fortress. It did not even look Roman: stones laid with no plaster, no concrete, not a single tile or drop of paint.

"Would any still be alive?" asked Peter.

"Of course," said Cei. "Their ransom would be worth more than all the treasure of the fortress, for each man has a family and each family will pay dearly for his return."

In the center of the room was a black, gaping hole. Long, railless stairs wound into the gloom, their bottom lost in blackness. Anlawdd tucked her stolen axe in her belt, charged down the stairs like the French cavalry at Agincourt. Down a few steps, she abruptly stopped, looked back to the rest of the company.

"Come, unless you'd care to stay behind and discuss Aristotle with the entire Jutic nation, which I'm sure is even now searching this whole crumbling fortress room by room!"

CHAPTER 15

CORS CANT FOLLOWED, FIVE STEPS AT A TIME. ANLAWDD WAS barely visible below.

The steps narrowed; the wall scraped his arm. The bard edged away from the stone and his left foot slipped off the stair. He teetered for a moment, then lurched sideways, regaining his balance. Shaken, he descended more slowly.

A hand touched his shoulder. "Gently," whispered Cei. "We know nothing of where she leads, what's down here."

"Anlawdd is down here," answered Cors Cant.

"Very helpful you'd be, plunged over the side! Easy, now. Mind the crumbles."

Cors Cant pushed against the cold, rough wall, continued like Orpheus into the cenotaph. A dank smell assailed his nostrils, must and rot. He heard moans, piteous cries from far below. A woman sobbed—not Anlawdd.

The bard's next sandalstep trod upon the back of a monster rat. It squealed and bit his ankle. Cors Cant clapped a hand over his mouth to stifle a yelp. The rat squirmed free, and Cors Cant's foot shifted, rolled into empty space.

He grabbed frantically for Cei's grasping hand, missed, and slid over the edge of the stair, scraped his leg open. For a sickening moment he plummeted, caromed off the next stair loop, spun through the air again.

Anlawdd's cry of "Cors!" was the last he heard.

Cors Cant blinked, slowly regained consciousness. He lay on a stack of rotten sheets, his mind blank. Dazed, aware that time had passed, he lay still, hoping memory would return. What was he doing in the musty dark? For that matter, who was he?

First a trickle, then a flood of thought. *Cors Cant, bard, Harlech, Jutes!* The next instant, his skull split open, an axe of pain buried deep in his forehead.

The pain flowed to a spike of agony, then ebbed in moments. He gripped his head, gasping for air.

When Cors Cant could breathe again, he struggled to sit upright, leaned back against cold, wet stone. He kept silent, listening as Myrddin taught: the scrabble of rats in the corner, the buzz of a fly. His own heartbeat. He was alone, frightened.

Leg is numb. What did she say? Built on top of older ruins. Older than civilization in Britain. He trembled in the dark, fumbled in his sleeve pocket for tinderbox and candle end.

Where the hell are Anlawdd, Lancelot, Cei? Why don't they come get me? The obvious solution made a shiver ripple across his skin: *because they can't. Because there's no way down save the route I took.*

Still shaking, Cors Cant struck a spark, lit the wick. When the candle flared, he inspected his prison. It was a tiny room that once had a thatch ceiling, now gone. He looked up. The walls were lost in the gloom; he could not see the stairs above. He started to stand, but his head gave two enormous throbs, and he collapsed back against the sheets. Now his back and leg began to pulse, discordant, like the wrong strings plucked together.

My harp! It had torn loose in the fall, lay like a frightened bird along one wall. Cors Cant stretched his arm, was unable to grasp it. He leaned over, groaning as his back shifted, and crawled to the instrument.

He grabbed it, held the candle close. It seemed all right, though a string had broken. He plucked the others. Other than needing to be tightened, they had survived.

Panting, he inspected himself and his wounds. The scrape along his leg looked bad, but he could walk, if his back allowed. He licked his palm, rubbed as much of the dirt out of the wound as possible.

He stood, excruciatingly slowly. With every breath, his back bit like a dire wolf. Twisting his torso was unthinkable. But if he kept his back rigid like a Roman soldier, he could walk, albeit at half speed.

The room had only one door, slightly ajar. He tugged it open the rest of the way, squeezing another stab of pain along his spine; the wood protested, yielded after a fight. Cors Cant limped through, leg and back competing to see which could debilitate him faster.

As he dropped the tiny, brass tinderbox back in his sleeve, he felt something smooth and round. He pulled out a vial, could not for his own life remember having put it there.

The stoppered vial was labeled. *BIBE ME,* it said; Latin for "drink me." He strained his memory, finally remembered the dream-vision on the *Blodewwedd.* A shrouded corpse, Princess Anlawdd dripping blood, invading his dream. She gave him a potion. *But that was a dream!* he thought.

"No," he said aloud, trying to persuade himself. "It's left over, it's the one she gave me before I was initiated. It must be!"

What did she say? *Alone in the womb, wounded, afraid, drink this something something to the light.* His mouth was dry, his palms wet. He bit his cheek, realized he was grinding his teeth.

Well, I'm alone in the womb of the Earthmother, wounded, and shaking in my sandals. So do I trust her or not? He licked his lips, unstoppered the vial, and brought it to his mouth. He gingerly tasted the liquid; it was not the same potion she had given him before.

This is stupid. Either drink it or don't! If you don't even trust her, how can you love her?

Quickly, while he still had his nerve, Cors Cant upended the vial over his mouth. It tasted vile, spoiled milk and seawater. He made a face, forced himself to swallow. The fluid burned his throat, like heavy wine drunk too fast.

Now what? No choice. Only one exit.

He crept along the silent corridor, hand shielding candle, teeth clenching with every back-jarring step. No doors; the passage seemed interminable until at last he came to a blank, brown, brick wall.

He touched it gingerly. The brickwork was ancient, dried mud, no longer smooth but broken. There was no concrete, no mortar; it undoubtedly predated the coming of Roman civilization, four centuries earlier, as Anlawdd claimed.

Individual bricks jutted and cracked. Cors Cant grabbed one, twisted hard; the brick pulled loose, crumbled in his hand. He worked the remaining piece left and right, pried it loose at last. Holding the candle end behind him, Cors Cant put his eye to the hole.

It was a tunnel, barely illumined by the candle that flickered in his hand, mostly shadowed by his own head. The shaft was bare, curiously void of dust. *Has it been recently swept?* Cors Cant knew it had not been, knew that no feet had trodden the corridor in hundreds of years. *No human feet,* he corrected.

He stuck his hand through the hole, worked more bricks loose. After an hour's work, an hour's agony of his back, he had an opening large enough to crawl through.

The tunnel was wide at the mouth, where the ancient wall had protected it. But the farther it traveled, the more it narrowed, like a spear tip.

"Great. Now what?" He risked a look back, was rewarded by a stabbing pain and the same lack of alternative choices as before. Resigned, the bard walked, crawled, finally wriggled down the tunnel, head and arms scraping dirt from the sides, trying to ignore the pain.

He choked on the sand, frightened as he looked forward, afraid to look back. Dread began to grip his mind, some *thing* might be behind him, something so horrific that if he saw it, he would fall dead, like the baleful eye of the Fomorian giant Balor.

If he had to die, Cors Cant desperately wanted it to be anywhere but in that hole. His spirit might never find its way back to the surface.

Another strange question, he thought. *Why no bones of travelers before me? Surely I'm not the first to misplace a foot on those treacherous stairs.* With every step, the weight of his own inadequacy crushed him lower into the dirt, until he slithered along his stomach like a snake. The tunnel was bare; no remains cluttered his path, not even a tooth or a knucklebone.

No one has ever been as useless as you, quoth a malevolent shade in Cors Cant's head. *Love a princess? You can't even navigate a stairway without falling into a pit! You deserve to crawl on your belly in the dirt.*

Despair grew with every foot forward. Cors Cant's labored breathing echoed like the North Wind.

He wept, ashamed to be worthless, ashamed of his presumptuous love of a princess, ashamed even of the tears themselves. *You're not even a real bard,* accused the evil doubter.

Why stop at weeping just for me? he thought. Cors Cant shuddered, wept for every *one,* every *thing* he had ever known: people, dogs, ducks, pigs, flowers, ships, swords, cups; they all crowded down the tunnel with him, wailing and gnashing their teeth in despair.

Cors Cant reached back, felt the comfort of his harp. *No, don't weep, Pachys the penis-head. It's all where it should be. Remember what She told you: there are known links between the stones of the earth and the stars on their spheres. When you crawl through the earth, you journey through the heavens. What's above is below. Silly boy!*

Despair left as suddenly, as artificially as it had arrived. He was glad no one had seen him lose control. "The cantrip," he said, voice muffled in the dirt tunnel. "It's Anlawdd's potion that affects me so. Drink me! Never again, Princess—never again."

Ahead was a bulk, a shape. It was a box, chiseled stone, oddly shaped, much longer than wide or deep. A box for a body. Cors Cant realized it was a coffin such as the Christ worshipers used, but much bigger than it should be.

Now fear assumed palpable shape, fingers clutched around him, ready to crush. This time, however, he recognized the emotion as foreign, descending upon him like a shroud thrown from above, fear instead of despair. *Some-*

thing or someone tries to drive me back, keep me from this box.

For a moment, panic welled up Cors Cant's throat. But knowing the source deflated the fear to the false terror one experiences in a dream. The bard closed his eyes, breathed as the Druids taught.

A poem—a hero! He silently recited the tale of Pwyll and his trip into Anwfyn, the Shadowland. Pwyll confronted Arawn, Lord of the Underdwell, just as Orpheus confronted Hades.

Pwyll's courage calmed the bard, filled him with pride that drove fear before it, channeled it like a teamster harnessed a team of horses, sweeping away the mental cobwebs.

Cors Cant opened his eyes, resolved not to be driven off.

His candle was nearly burned, but he held the last bit of wax up to the box, illuminated it well enough to see. An image in *bas-relief* was chiseled into the lid, a young boy (or girl?) clutching a stone scroll to his or her chest. Four stone mourners surrounded the supine image. They wore pre-Roman Sicambrian armor as Lancelot still did, but with unadorned Christian crosses on their shields.

The stone boy's hair was long as King Merovee's.

What did it signify when the candidate crawled through the narrow passageway into this temple?

"He was born once again," croaked the bard. He blinked. Where had that answer come from? His own throat, but surely not his own mind, own memory, own prophecy!

"And who was *he*, Cors Cant Ewin?" Anlawdd's muffled voice, calling from inside the coffin. He felt nauseated. A splash of bile heaved up his throat, burned like fire. *It couldn't possibly be her. It couldn't be anything— it's my own mind, playing tricks!* He made a second resolution: ignore all phantom voices while journeying so far beneath the world of men.

The candle sputtered. Quickly, Cors Cant held it up to the stone-carved characters. Most were in Hebrew, which not even the Druid College in Londinium taught. But one pseudo-Latin phrase circled the boy's head like a crown:

I TEGO ARCANA DEI

It was not quite as illiterate as Lancelot's Latin mangling, but it still made little sense. The closest Cors Cant could come in translation was "Begone I conceal God's secrets."

In his mind, the letters burned, flickered in the air. They began to rearrange themselves, moving with stately grace, a pair at a time, like a Roman dance:

I tEgo arcana dei
et iGo arcaNa dei
et in oarcaGa Dei
et in Oarcada geI
et in arcadia GEo
Et In Arcadia Ego

The familiar, vaguely disquieting phrase that had haunted Cors Cant for days: *Et in Arcadia Ego. And in Arcadia, I.*

An old trick of the Greek numerologists, making up anagrams. In the same dream he saw a shroud covering a person he knew and loved, slain by the Most Beloved Apostle.

What in Anufyn did the phrase *mean,* and why did it keep turning up like a bad *denarius?* First from Merovee (filtered through Lancelot), now carved on the tomb to which a dream of Anlawdd led him! Cors Cant leaned close, crouched over the box. His candle died before he could make out any more words.

"I can't see *anything,*" he said, beginning to feel fear again. "It's dark."

"No one can see in the dark." Another voice from the blackness; Anlawdd again, but not-Anlawdd as well.

The bard shivered, somebody's foot treading upon his deathsite. "I'm not listening," he promised, hummed an old Druid tune. He realized it was a funeral dirge, and fell silent.

Snuff out the candle, don't blow. Never use one element to quench another! Don't never ever slap Branwen! Cave canem, *beware of the dog.*

Frightened, Cors Cant's heart raced like a shaggy highland pony. The stone vault terrified him, though surely it must contain nothing more than dust by now. *It can't be as old as Julius. It's a hundred years younger, young as the Church. Who put it here? why bury it so deep?* He reached out, misjudged the distance in the dark, and scraped his knuckles on the stone. *Oh Mother, did it just move closer? Gods, I don't remember it being so close to my face!*

"The wand of intuition led you here. Let the *solidus* of valor support you now. You know what you must do."

"Yes! First, I must stop hearing voices where there is only silence."

But whom do you trust?

I trust only myself! he shouted, defiant. *No, that's a lie. I don't trust anybody, not even me. Wait, I trust my mother. I trust the elements to bury, drown, blow, and burn. I trust—*

"What must I do?" he asked aloud. "This is *madness!*"

No it isn't, answered his deepest part. *I trust you all. I know what to do.*

The inner sanctum of his mind spoke truth: he *did* know, though he did not know how he knew. Cors Cant put out his hands in the blackness, felt slowly along the stone seam of the coffin lid until he found a crack. He wedged his fingers in, tried not to think of the walls and ceiling collapsing, crumbling around him, burying him forever beneath Caer Harlech.

He worked by touch alone at the facing side of the sarcophagus, trying to slide the heavy lid back. At first nothing happened—*too much weight.* Then it shifted, creaking ominously.

Buoyed by success, Cors Cant heaved vigorously. Back screaming in anguish, he strained in the black-dark, moved the stone slab another handwidth, just enough that he could snake his hand and arm inside the coffin.

It was occupied by a small body, a young girl or boy like the picture. But this body was only a few weeks dead. The head lay toward Cors Cant, face and hair intact, taut as the day the child died, though shrunken. Cors Cant pressed against the child's brow, trying to determine how old it might have been at death.

He yelped, yanked his hand back as the skull crumbled like the bricks in the ancient wall at the tunnel mouth. Weeks dead? Centuries, more like. The body had been preserved by some means, but by whom, how, and how long ago, he could not possibly say.

Beneath his still fingers, the head moved.

It slowly rotated against his hand. Cors Cant was paralyzed, unable to pull his hand free. *His hand will reach out,* he thought dully, *and when it finds my own, I shall fall to the floor dead.*

He waited, breathless, for the climax. *Control the air, it is always the key.* Then the head rolled off its neck into the corner of the granite coffin.

It was still dead. The bard giggled in hysteria, relieved that he was not, quite yet, mad. *Nothing there,* he thought, *just mummified remains. I have the sword of reason and the coin of valor—I will not be fooled.* He took a long, deep Druid breath of musty air, pulled back his leine sleeve and thrust his arm deeper.

He grunted involuntarily as his hand slid down the front of the corpse's tunic. He felt a scroll of parchment, just as depicted on the lid, and tried to draw it from the coffin.

The child would not let go. It held the parchment tight. Angry, Cors Cant yanked harder. He heard a crack like dried twigs, and the scroll flew from the coffin into his lap. Something was attached; Cors Cant inspected it by touch, discovered that a dead, mummified hand still gripped the scroll, tightfisted even in death.

He fought dry heaves, broke off the fingers one at a time until he could work the document free. He placed the hand and fingers carefully back inside the vault. As he leaned over the coffin, Cors Cant smelled decaying flowers, cloying and sickening.

The roll felt like vellum, fine lambskin beaten to thin parchment. He dropped it down his leine sleeve to look at when he had light.

You found what you sought, Cors Cant Ewin. This time, the "Anlawdd" voice sounded clearly from within his head. *Now it is time for the candidate to come again into the light!* "she" continued. *You cannot go back. You can never go back. For,* it croaked, *initiation never ends.*

She was right. There was no way back: backward led only to the stairless room into which he had fallen as if from the crystal spheres of the stars. But could he possibly go forward?

Nerving himself, Cors Cant crawled atop the sarcophagus, holding his harp out of the way lest it crack against the stone. He squirmed between its top and the dirt ceiling, tunneling like a worm to the other side. There, the tunnel continued, still pitch-black. The only good news was that his back seemed better, only twinging occasionally.

He was just about to crawl on his way when his conscience tugged.

Hooves and horns, he'll be so cold in that box!

Cors Cant wrestled with the thought and lost. He wriggled back atop the coffin, struggled the slab of a lid back into place. At last, he crawled on, turning his back on the dead boy (or girl).

A new voice spoke inside his head, thoughts of a different tone: *Sword, wand, pentacle, and now the cup of sympathy. You have all the tools to find your way out of the Temple of Solomon . . . pray that you lose none of them.* Cors Cant shuddered, belly-crawled through the black. The voice sounded rather like Merovee that time.

Again, not quite, but a close counterfeit.

CHAPTER 16

PETER OUTDISTANCED CEI, BUT ANLAWDD BEAT THEM BOTH, recklessly leaping down the stairs five at a time. Suddenly, she leaned back and her feet flew from beneath her. She fell heavily on her rear and began to slide.

She tumbled over the side, clutched at the stairs to stop her own plunge. Her eyes were wide and white as Peter finally caught up. He darted a hand out, grabbed her hair.

A half turn ahead was a fire-scorched landing. Three steps below the landing, the stairs ended abruptly, the wooden scaffolding charred and collapsed. Anlawdd had barely stopped in time.

Peter reeled her in, both of them shaken. "You plan to follow him, arse over teakettle down that hole?"

"Let *go* of—!" She fell silent, stared down the aborted stairway. "The stairs to the crypt are gone," she marveled, noticing consciously what her subconscious had spotted several seconds earlier.

"No. *Really?*"

"Really! Can't you see? They end right after—"

"I know the damned stairs are gone! You know this place? You said crypt. Is there another way down?"

"Of course I know this place, and no, not that I know of. Get me a rope, I'm going after him!" She stared in anguish down the pit.

"No rope," muttered Cei.

"Then I'll jump! If Cors Cant survived, surely I would!"

Peter wrapped his arm around her, pulled her away from the edge. She did not struggle; neither did she look away from the blackness. "No, Anlawdd. He might be hurt, might need you. Lot of use you'd be with a broken spine yourself. And what if he *didn't* survive?"

She said nothing. A tear wet her cheek, but of anger, not grief.

For long moments they shouted the bard's name but heard no answer, not even a groan. Peter ground his teeth. His next order was the hardest he had ever given. "I'm sorry, Anlawdd. We can't take the time to go after him. They'll tear this place apart to find us, the Jutes will. All we can do is pray he's okay and continue to the gaol cells to rescue Gormant and your father."

"Then what?" Her voice was thick, strangled.

Peter bit his lip, felt a complete fraud. What right had he to assume any kind of command, after what happened to Sergeant Conway because of Peter's incompetence? "Then I guess we can look for Cors Cant, after we free the Harlech soldiers."

Even in torchlight he saw her stricken face. "No," she pleaded.

"Maybe he's all right. Maybe he'll find his way out. There must be another way." Peter let Anlawdd loose.

She sat upon the landing, still staring. "No. There's no other way. He can't get out." She drew her knees up, folded arms across them. Slowly, she lowered her face onto her arms. "He'll die in there," she predicted.

> *I throw myself upon the luckless Jute*
> *With no regret, bloody axe in hand,*
> *Revenge my love with murder swift and mute,*
> *A guard to line the road to Summerland.*

Peter let her weep for a few moments, then took an elbow and pulled her toward the doorway leading from the landing. She resisted, but he outmassed her by thirty kilograms. "Take us to Prince Gormant," he suggested. "Is your father in the same place?"

"No!" Anlawdd struggled against him, did not want to leave. Moonlight filtered down the hole from the upper room, reflected from her wet eyes. "He's all right, I know he is. He's a Druid bard. He must have some magic to protect him. And you're just going to leave him down there like a puppy at the bottom of a well!"

She furiously pushed past him, shoved the blackened, wooden door aside without a thought for the noise it might make. The door collapsed with a crash. Peter jumped, looked up the stairs for signs of pursuit.

The corridor down which she led them was narrow, nearly straight. It bent slightly, and the pit passed from view. Anlawdd paused twice, gently touched the wall, but never looked back. Her steps had lost all spring; she plodded like a cart horse.

She stopped before a cell door, dark wood with a small, barred window opening. Her stony face was white as the Dover cliffs. "I don't have a key," she said, untalkative for the first time in Peter's memory.

"Cei," said Peter, nodded at the door.

The porter looked through the tiny window. "Another door," he said, subdued.

"Cells," explained Anlawdd.

"Pop it."

Cei nodded, jammed his dagger into the crack between the jamb and the door. He pounded it home with a single, open-hand blow that tore the latch from the jamb. They yanked the door open.

The other door had a sliding bolt on their side. Behind it was a long corridor of doors, each bolted and tied with cords. There were no locks. A single, weary guard sat on a stool.

He rose, said something in a guttural language Peter did not recognize. The guard squinted, realized they were not Jutes. He fell back and fumbled for a spear propped in a corner.

Anlawdd charged, caught him reaching. She tackled him from behind, arm locked around his throat, and buried her knife in his back as Peter had done in the feast hall—a very modern combat move.

All of Peter's alarm bells rang at once: did she learn it just by watching him the one time? Or perhaps in a *train-*

ing camp in Belfast? But no—I have my man, or woman: Medraut is Selly; Anlawdd is just an "ordinary" psychopathic murderer. Must not lose sight of that, let myself doubt my eyes. Medraut tried to look at his watch!

The Jute soundlessly opened his mouth, rolled his glazed eyes upward. He died in her arms. She flung the body aside like a mannequin. *Like I must do to Medraut when I can lure him away from the mob.* But the seed of doubt had already sprouted, and Peter wondered whether he could ever do it: kill someone he knew; look into the eyes of a young lad and close them with a knife thrust.

Startled faces appeared at the cell window holes. "Which is the prince?" asked Peter. He watched the girl warily, did not allow her to get behind him.

Anlawdd scanned the room, approached a cell. "This is Prince Gormant," she said. She approached the cell. "This is Lancelot of the Languedoc, sent by Artus to liberate you and restore the throne of Harlech."

A forty- or forty-five-year-old man peeked out of his cell at the assembled multitude. "Great warriors," he breathed in a thick Welsh accent, "Praise be to God and His Prophet Jesus that you've come! By Jesus and my bloody axe, we'll drive these Godless pigs from the city, by the Lord!"

Peter studied him dubiously. Strong in spirit, he looked a physical wreck, sick from captivity, like Terry Anderson when he finally got out of Iran. How long had it been? A few weeks? Cei cut the cord that bound the bolt, and giant Bedwyr pulled the door open.

Gormant tried to walk out of his cell with stately grace, but his knees collapsed beneath him. He clearly had not eaten in days. "Let us release the men," he wheezed, as Cei and Bedwyr helped him up.

Peter did not shift his attention from the seamstress-princess-assassin-whatever-else she was.

While the others helped the prince, Anlawdd cut cords and threw back bolts. The rest of the fine fighting men of Harlech were equally debilitated. Nearly a hundred crowded the corridor, the majority still backed up in their cells. None looked strong enough to roll a drunk.

Anlawdd returned to Gormant, spoke quietly but urgently. "Father, *I didn't tell them.* You understand?"

Peter drew back. *What did she call him? And what didn't she tell to whom?*

He looked her up and down. "I owe you my life, by God and Jesus and Mary. If ever I may serve, do not hesitate to call my aid. Just one question I would ask." He turned his face from the girl, voice thick with suppressed emotion. "I don't know you. Why do you call me father?"

CHAPTER 17

PAST THE TOMB, CORS CANT CRAWLED SO LONG HE LOST track of time. He saw a pinprick of light. It was a hole in another brick wall. The tunnel narrowed to nearly a point before the wall, so tight that, when he stretched his arm, he could not touch the crumbled brickwork. He was trapped.

Cors Cant wriggled his shoulders until they throbbed with pain, pressed forward. Something caught. *My sandals! They're snagged on something!*

He reached back, could not find the obstruction. With a resigned sigh, he unlaced them from his calves, squeezed on barefooted.

Another item caught, this time his knife. Without conscious thought, he unbuckled his belt, left knife and pouch behind as he crawled forward. He felt dizzy, confused. *Still Anlawdd's potion,* he decided.

Yet the greedy earth would not let him pass. He had but one possession left, gripped surely in his left hand.

No!

He tugged, but the harp, too, was stuck fast in the bottleneck, still looped by a strong cord to the belt left behind. By stretching his right arm to its limit, nearly dislocating his shoulder, he barely brushed the bricks that could free him.

But the harp, given him by Myrddin for his first bardic examination, now held him back from complete freedom.

No . . . ! Cors Cant closed his eyes, looked away from the spark of light. *Don't be a stubborn jackass,* said a voice—his own, he knew. *It's just a harp. Myrddin has scores in his crystal caverns, tucked in boxes and trunks.*

But it is mine! I can untie the cord. . . .

The bard was thoroughly stuck, right arm pressed forward to the bricks, to freedom, left arm pulled back as far as it could go, the harp at the ends of his fingertips. He tried to worm backward, but he could not move. His elbow scraped the tunnel roof, and a mound of dirt cascaded upon him, nearly burying him.

He could barely feel the harp, did not even have hold of it anymore. He could only touch it. Cors Cant understood: if he tried to go back, the rest of the roof would cave in, and he would be entombed forever as the eternal bodyguard of the child in the stone sarcophagus.

Damn your stubborn pride, it's nought but a possession! It weighs you down. It nearly drowned you, nearly got you killed for a milliarense *outside the baths. Leave it!*

For several moments he did not move. More dirt fell upon him. What had Myrddin told him once? Not making a decision *is* making a decision—the decision to do nothing.

No, he finally decided, *I cannot! It's too much a part of me, everything I've worked for, since I was too young to have a name.*

He stretched again, touched again the rough brickwork. It would take but a few sharp blows, and he would be free. But he was still a few feet out of range.

Tears rolled along Cors Cant's cheeks. Quickly, before he could change his mind, he slid his left hand forward.

The precious instrument was lost forever beneath falling dirt.

So long, old friend, he thought sadly. *But I have to move on. To the light.*

Wearing nothing but his leine-shirt, he dug his bare feet into the dirt, pushed himself forward far enough to strike the brickwork.

Cors Cant tapped again and again, feeling a sharp pain in his knuckles. *Probably broken,* he thought morosely. *Is freedom really worth the price of never playing my music again?*

No options. The rest of the ceiling collapsed upon him even as he worked, burying him in choking blackness. His final blow cracked the wall, just enough for his bloody fingers to work through. Weeping again, this time in pain, he pried first one brick, then another from the wall. At last, he had a hole big enough to squirm out into another corridor and fall upon the floor.

A great cloud of dust puffed up, blinded him. When it settled, he looked back into the hole he had just escaped. Neither shoes, belt, knife, nor harp could be seen. The hole had sealed behind him.

So too is my life sealed behind, he thought; *I am bard no longer.* Another part stood outside his head, critically accusing the rest of him. *You sound like an overdramatic Greek tragedian; shall we summon the slave to commit suicide in your place? Or would you prefer to do it yourself?*

He realized his spirit had once again drifted up from his body as it had on the beach, bumping against the ceiling. He looked down upon all his myriad selves: the frightened, little boy who had almost been killed by a cave-in; the cynical critic, dismissing every noble thought as pretense; the bard-to-be, rewriting the adventure even as he sat and shivered, searching for a classical, dramatic twist that would hold the audience; the dispassionate observer, floating up by the ceiling to look down upon the other selves; and within them all, the laughing Druid, who realized that every self, including IT-self, was but a tiny piece

of the whole that contained them all and 9,995 more
"selves."

Even the whole was a part, the smallest part, since it
could be perceived by each of the other points of view.
*The world contains me, but I contain the world. It is all
within my mind. Macrocosm mirrors microcosm; that
above, so also below. Goddess Anlawdd, how can I describe this without sounding like Myrddin, that pretentious
mountebank?*

Cors Cant shivered in a drafty hallway, could not help
laughing. The stone floor shifted, rolled beneath his bare
feet, grumbling like Taranis Thunderer.

He sneezed, tried to shake off the grogginess as he staggered, still giggling, down the rock passageway. The floor
tilted alarmingly.

At times it was primitive, rough-hewn rock, a cave.
Then it flickered, became a rug-strewn corridor in Caer
Camlann with wooden walls and hideous masks that leered
from alcoves. Then, back to ancient stone. But always the
floor rolled, languid waves across Harlech Bay.

*Yes yes yes, I remember it now. Your potion, goddin-
princess, like drinking rainbow colors and hearing them
spill down my chin.*

Dizzy, hard to think straight. He looked at his hands:
were they always tinted green? He looked back at a bend
in the corridor where the floor bowed like Iris's Woof (another rainbow) beneath his feet. Bard stood always at the
bow-bottom, no matter how far he walked. The air was
tangy, a monstrous storm about to burst.

Cors Cant rubbed his eyes: something funny something
in the wine—but *what* wine? Turtles peeked from under
dark curtains, green boys chuckled, exposing sandaled
feet. *See? See? It straps on like wisdom!* But the seabard's
feet were webbed bare.

A pointy-eared chap stared at Cors Cant, caught in pe-
ripheral vision. His toes curled upward. *One of the Tuatha
de Danaan?* wondered the boy.

"That's what you're *spores* to think!" shriggled the
gnome. Cors the Cant himself setsat, legs crossed beneath

tied in pretzel-nots, gripped head in hands and squeezed
brains out his eyesnose. "What am I doing, what damned
I hewing?"

But Cutha spit over the rail, metal clang of a lantern as
he whirled to fleece the boy. "Your whored you gave," he
wish-spurred, grippled. "Tell no one you sow me, herd
me!" Rune bowls burst from his face, curved into a circle
of late that spun like a cart wheel.

The green turtles pointed their ears, chanted, "It's a test,
a toast, a boast, another host!"

Who are you? asked Cors Cant, terrified of the great,
black shapes that bulged around him.

We're the Laughing Shibbols, they squeaked like clean
bowls. *It's another room in the House of doom! Don't you
see what is meant for thee? Do you not get the meaning
yet?*

"I don't understand!"

You hold us in the heel of your hand!

Cors Cant peeked; a green eye peered back, pupil contracted, pinpoint of black. *Many chambers has the chapel,
you wander lost, afraid: the chambers are but rooms you
made, rooms to sing and serenade. Forget the gold! Look
for the silver apple!*

"Stop!" he cried, tried to hide, stuck his head his arms
inside.

"Initiation!"

"It's all right!" (The Shibbols squeaked—one left, one
right.)

"Initiation *never* ends. . . ."

"From now on, *we're* your only friends!"

CHAPTER 18

ANLAWDD SAT IN A CORNER, HEAD IN HANDS. PETER WATCHED her, worried. *Is she? She can't be. Selly would never be so stupid as to fall in love. Can she help falling in love? No that's foolish, they don't even have the capacity for love, the murdering IRA bastards.*

She looked at Gormant. Her pallid face flickered pumpkin orange in the candlelight, lips full. She took his breath away. For a moment he imagined, then brutally crushed the fantasy. *Cad! Her boy lies at the bottom of a pit, broken and bleeding! And you've your own bird to think about, waiting back at the castle.*

Peter swallowed, remembered what the love of Lancelot and Guinevere had cost.

No one else spoke. They sensed the tension. Gormant would not meet Anlawdd's eyes. Or was that just a trick of Peter's imagination?

No, it's not, he realized. *In fact, none of the freed prisoners would look at her.*

She stood, shouldered her way past the men of Harlech. One fell over, but the rest followed Anlawdd. Peter, Cei, and Bedwyr made up the rear guard.

"Gormant," said Peter, "follow us to the docks. Merovee and the Sicambrians may have been able to free a ship. We can take you to safety."

"Merovius?" asked Gormant, face lit with hope. "Merovius Rex comes to free Harlech, praise God!"

"No, the boat! We've no force to fight a battalion!"

"Gain the surface, storm the hall, by God!" shouted the prince, ignoring Peter's suggestion. "Storm the gates, by

God we'll sweep Caesar Causeway free of vile Jutes, by
the Lord! Let us by God and Jesus take back this city, burn
those who dare invade, as they'll burn in hell when the
Lord comes to judge, for they know not the Savior!"
Gormant waved his arms, nearly stumbled again.

"For the widow's son," said Anlawdd, uninflected,
weary. She rolled her eyes, disgusted.

"For Merovee!" answered the prince of Harlech. "Merovius, True King of Jerusalem, fish against the Rock, by God
and Mary!"

Jerusalem? But Peter had no time to ask. He was swept
along by the tide of desperate hope.

CHAPTER 19

THAT BASTARD! THAT RIGHT BASTARD! I TOOK BACK EVERY
nice thing I ever thought about Father—forever just
"Gormant" now, as he's chosen his destiny: to hell with
deciding whether he led Canastyr or Canastyr led
Gormant ... they're two pumpkins in a patch.

I followed behind the idiots as they surged toward
doom, fuming inside. Damn them all! Damn Lancelot and
That Boy, damn especially me. Imagine, allowing myself
to feel hope about Gormant and me, eager expectation that
everything would change when I rescued him from his
fate.

Did I think a lifetime of hatred would be washed away,
like when you dip a soiled chemise in soapy water?

I traveled in good company, behind those whooping,
hollering, damned souls. I was just as much a ninny as
they, bore just as much false hope.

Gormant had surely discovered Canastyr's death long

before I signaled from the *Blodewwedd,* undoubtedly through Cutha, who he thought was a Jute. What a fool I was to think I would finally beat out the earthworm, even in death, in Gormant's heart!

The dolt still thought to keep his city, to hold Harlech; he thought that an act of foolish bravado would erase his own treason in Artus's mind. Gormant dared not openly accuse me of Canastyr's murder, for what I knew about Gormant's own treason would drive nails through his hands and feet on a rebel's cross. So instead he shunned me, decided to shut me forever out of his life.

Well, to Hell with him, and me too, I decided. Let us all be damned to Shadowland!

I cast my spirit aside, charging forward in animal lust to kill, to die. Only one part of Anlawdd was left, the lonely niece of Archking Leary, asking *is this what Merovee warned me about? Is this* fornication *to a Builder?*

CHAPTER 20

CORS CANT SAT ON HIS KNEES, ARMS OVER HEAD, CRADLING his mind like Llyr Sealord rocked the island Earth. *Can't let them stop me can't let it get me.* Far away he heard Anlawdd call. Was it really she? His own yearning?

At least the nursery rhymes are gone. Scant help; he had never felt more alone in the world.

She doesn't care. What does she want from me, fall down and worship at her feet? She's a princess, not a goddess!

A sudden suspicion occurred: *was* she indeed a goddess? Did she wait for recognition, for Cors Cant to realize who Anlawdd really was?

An extraordinary revelation, like two of every three thoughts he had ventured lately. "It *would* explain a lot." One of the Laughing Shibbols, hand-sized now, cocked its head. Cors Cant tried to explain. "Who but a goddess, having the might of Bran or Herakles, wielding an axe like Thor's hammer, would hide behind the chemise of a seamstress? Could a mere waiting maid come unscathed through war and battle?"

Small, insignificant Cors Cant Ewin curled tighter, hugged his knees. Another revelation, they came two or three to a breath now: what cared a goddess for an unlearned half-bard? She toyed with him.

"It's not worth it," he said, flat voiced. "May as well stay right here. What use am I? She reads Greek as well as I, knows the paths of the world. I was useless from the start, a plaything!"

The Shibbols pressed against the boy, one to each side. They were fuzzy, warm, black-and-white hind flippers lost in the dark. They squeaked a few times, tried to cheer him. "We don't think you're useless!"

"Yes, we think you ought to get out of here and help your friends!"

"Thanks, guys."

He patted their heads and they squeaked again, appreciatively. Who were these furry Shibbols anyway? They obviously lived down in the catacombs. It made little difference; they comforted him, befriended him when he was alone, just as *something* had when he was a child, but he could not remember what. Something that slept with him, guarded him from demons in the dark.

"Face it," he said. "Lancelot is mighty, Cei knows the mystic flow. Bedwyr commands hundreds, they jump to obey. Anlawdd is ... well, Anlawdd is Anlawdd.

"I'm the short pony. What's left for me but singing heroic songs to drunken legionnaires? I don't even have a harp anymore."

"You missed one," said a Shibbol on the left.

"You didn't mention the king, Merovee!" said the other.

Merovee . . . the name stirred deep memory. What had he said, what about a—a chapel?

Cors Cant lay on his back, cold stone floor pulling him like a lodestone. Suspended above his head a sword, point up, bloody and notched. He gasped, jerked away. His hand overturned a chalice at his side. It was not there a moment before.

Once our Lord faced such a choice, he thought—or was it Merovee's memory? *He chose the sword. Choose you now!*

Blood and all, the suspended sword shamed all the blades of Camlann, even the dream sword Cei had given him on the ship. It was alive, sang with power! Cors Cant stretched a hand upward, touched the jeweled pommel; a globe of lightning fell from the hilt, exploded next to his face.

I know the sword! A sword saved me once from death outside Lancelot's window. Let this sword save me now!

The corridor grew silent. Even the Shibbols said nothing, crouched at Cors Cant's side and peeked through their flippers. The creepers and scurriers froze, trembled in expectation.

The little world of Corridorland waited breathlessly. *Choose, choose,* it implored.

His hand shook . . . Merovee, what did Merovee say?

What did Merovee say? It was urgent he remember before choosing!

Choose, commanded the cool Sicambrian wind; *which is most needed, sword or grail? Joseph of Aramathea caught each loving drop of the Blood Royal, the* Sang Raal, *in this very cup. But this sword cuts through the armies of the world. Choose now!*

The sword—what was the sword? Cors Cant stretched again, fingertips brushed the blade. "Oh no!" cried the Shibbols in unison. "Don't *think* it through . . . use your heart, not your head!" They squeaked in alarm.

Reason! The sword was "reason," the hairsplitter, blade of induction. What was Cors Cant's life but a constant cal-

culation, weights and measures, pro and con? What lacked
in his own soul?

But the cup; *Sympathy,* Merovee called it. Empathy,
feeling, understanding. Reason, the right hand; unbalanced
without sympathy, the left.

It was clear. Cors Cant rolled quickly as the sword
dropped. It rotated in flight, buried itself to the hilt with a
bang in the stone floor, directly where his heart had lain.
He clutched for the golden grail with a desperate cry.

But he grabbed only air, for it was gone. It faded like a
dream-creep in sunlight. The clouds faded with it, his
mind cleared. Despair, fear, self-loathing, all evaporated in
sudden mental illumination.

The Shibbols gave a final, plaintive squeak. "Don't ban-
ish us!" they cried. "Let us stay! Let us staaaaaaaay. . . ."

They fuzzed, squeaked piteously. "No!" cried the boy,
grabbed for them. He felt—*almost* felt their soft fur, sleek
bodies, heard a last squeak: ". . . fare—" they cried,
"—well. . . ."

*Let them go, you don't need them anymore. Put boyhood
behind. Forget the warm friends of your cradle. You've
chosen the harsh Inner path—now have the courage and
intuition to follow it.*

Cors Cant leapt to his feet, looked wildly about. Where
was he? The corridor was just a corridor again; the only
scurries and scampers were rats and spiders. A red glow
like a furnace lit his world. It shone beneath an ornate,
ancient door hung with faded holly wreaths. To the furnace glow, the door was queerly translucent, as if cut from
the crystals in Anlawdd's cave. Mistletoe dangled from the
handle, and Cors Cant smelled sharp charcoal smoke from
the right.

Leftward, the passage faded into darkness, mist, and red
flickers.

"I'm tired of darkness!" he decided. He pulled his hair
back, tied it behind his head with a white ribbon from his
leine sleeve, a white ribbon for winter. "I'll take a door
over darkness, today and tomorrow."

Nervous, heart beating like footsteps at his back, he approached the door. He touched the handle, hesitated. What lay beyond? He clenched his fists, took a deep breath, and knocked twice, loudly.

Wh-who-who-who-who gooo-o-oes? A voice, the wind, or just a mindshade? *F-f-f-f-friend?*

Friends? His only friends, who were they? The furry Shibbols, black-and-white, flippers and smiles. They squeaked in pleasure, loved him like puppies. And now they were gone.

He stared down at his bare feet, trackless in the deep dust. *Am I a shade too, summoned from Hades to give consultation to Odysseus?* He raised his eyes, declared himself loudly: "I am . . . *Shibbolless.*"

Enter then, in the name of the Llaw Gyffes, *the Skilled Hand.*

The handle turned. The door opened inward, all the way, pressed flat against the wall. There was no one behind it. The passage was empty. Cors Cant blinked rapidly, passed quickly through.

The door debouched into a great, square chamber, still far below ground. A single, silken woven-rag rope dangled motionless from far above, a heavy weight at the aft end, the top lost in light too bright to watch.

As the bard approached, the twisted cloth swayed slowly in a phantom breeze, as if whispering *climb me, climb and see. Plumb line,* thought Cors Cant, *used by builders to set a wall straight.*

He took two steps, caught the flimsy rope. It would break under his weight! He still felt dizzy, head spinning from Anlawdd's potion taken . . . how long ago?

It leads to Anlawdd. Cors Cant knew this as surely as he knew the world was round and strange upside-down creatures dwelt on the far side. To Anlawdd, to others, at last to Merovius the Builder.

He leaned his weight upon it, stretched it tight as he knelt, right knee on the floor. *More squares,* he thought. *My legs form a square, my left arm is bent square. The world is made of squares, tiny squares sewn together like patchwork. We part on the square—who told me that?*

The line felt solid. He began to climb into the glare.

He soon lost the ground far below. How high? He trembled, clutching the rope. Woven of rough rags, it bit his hands.

Cors Cant calmed his mind, used an old Druid song taught him by Myrddin, the "Naming of the Kings": slow, lengthy verses forced an in-hold-out breath pattern. Cors Cant unfocused his eyes, chanted the "Naming" as he climbed.

The fear left. Faster he climbed, unafraid in certainty. Who was he? Cors Cant Ewin, bard of Caer Camlann, and none other! He had won, conquered all four souls: *courage, gnosis, reason, understanding,* Cei's four suits: Pentacles, Wands, Swords, Cups. *That* was the secret, the final revelation! Truth and union!

Caution, counseled the inner voice. *Faith, hope, charity are better jewels.* The boy ignored the patient warning; it was old, he was young. *The age of youth!* he thought, felt as strong as Llud Llaw Gyffes himself.

At last, after a century of climbing, Cors Cant reached the lip of the hole, the other side of the Abyss. He had passed safely through the temple at last. He grabbed the lip and swung himself over. . . .

And stumbled to the cavern floor, the same one whence he'd come before.

Shibbols looked up, each face like a pup. They squeaked and laughed most happily. "Now you see!"

"Don't you see? From now on, *we're* your only friends!"

"Initiation *NEVER* ends! You've done us well!"

"You've done us proud!"

They cheered and whooped and hollered loud.

The bard sat up with sheepish smile, spied the stairs that rose a mile. Climb a rope? What a laugh. Fall and write his epitaph!

"How could I not have *seen* them there?" Laughing, Cors Cant climbed the stair.

CHAPTER 21

PETER HURRIED TO CATCH UP, CURSING PRINCE GORMANT OF Harlech. The old man had seized Peter's strike team, rushed them along sowing the wind. Peter's men!

Peter tried to pull them back, but the fool-killer called, reaping a harvest of blood on the whirlwind, and the men heeded him not. The prince of Harlech was seductive where Peter was rational, stirred the blood that Peter (and Artus) worked so hard to cool. Cei and Bedwyr did not even hear Peter's harsh shout to stand by, belay the order to charge.

Anlawdd heard, looked back briefly, then turned again to the force that pelted through the dungeon door. Peter could almost read the desperation on her features, the mad desire to *do something,* when the best thing to do was *nothing.* First her beloved, now her city! Can you not *do something,* Lancelot? Do *anything?* Then by God *I'll* do something!

Anlawdd threw her lot in with the fool-killer. She numbly shook her new axe abovehead and followed Cei, Bedwyr, and her father/no-father, Gormant of Harlech.

Peter was alone. With a shout of exasperation and frustration, he followed, Tail-End Charlie.

They burst through an old, warped door, bowled over an unarmed Jutish functionary. Somebody killed the poor man. *Please God, not Anlawdd.* The crowd surged on.

A small, red staircase led up. The mob mounted the steps four at a time, slipping clumsily on the slick, narrow stairs, without even the proverbial pitchforks and torches of monster–hunting villagers.

By the time they reached the surface, Peter was hoarse from shouting at them. Clouds covered the moon; he could barely see the pale, beautiful skin of the vixen ahead of him.

The Jutic soldiers took notice of Gormant's charge, scrambled suspiciously after the mob, still unsure what was happening. It would not take them long to figure it out, once they received word of the gaolbreak.

The whole damned thing is going down the loo! In desperation, Peter raised his hands, cried "Oh Lord my God, is there *no* help for the widow's son?" at peak volume. A vain hope; would Anlawdd even hear, or care if she did?

But the words stopped her like a silver chain. She slid to a halt, slowly turned back. Tears streaked her cheeks, glittered like hard diamonds in the sky, somewhere beyond the clouds.

"What? What?" she cried. Torchlight framed her hair, gave her a bloody halo. "Am I not allowed even *so* much rage?"

Nonplussed, Peter nonetheless took advantage of his temporary victory. "Anlawdd, the fools rush to their deaths. What will five hundred well-armed Jutes do to those brave eggshells of warriors?"

"Who knows." It was a statement, not a question.

"Anlawdd, you'll *die.* Is that what you want?"

"Who cares for a betrayer?"

"I care. Would that be a fitting tribute to Cors Cant?" Did she mean Gormant or herself? Peter could not tell.

She lowered her gaze, collapsed to one knee before catching herself. "Then, he is dead," she whispered. Peter almost could not hear her.

He shook his head. "You don't know that."

Still she hesitated, still not sure. "Take my hand," she pleaded. "Look me in the eye." She planted her right foot just inside his on the cobblestones.

He did as instructed. Her thumb pressure was so slight he would never have felt it if he were not expecting it. She pressed between second and third finger, pass-grip for Master Mason, or whatever they called it thirteen centuries before "masons" existed. He returned the grip firmly, same rank. If that were her rank, she would not understand a higher degree handgrip; worse, what he learned and what she learned might not match.

Her eyes narrowed, voice suspicious. "What temple?"

"Brotherhood of Amalgamated Illuminated Torys. You probably haven't heard of us; based in Whitehall. Have you attained higher rank than what you've shown?"

"Um, not yet. But I fully expect to, once I get a chance to really sit down and memorize all that—"

"Then I outrank you, so listen up! Find me another way to get to the bloody docks. We *must* get back to the docks and Merovee. Gormant won't make it two blocks along Eighth Street."

"Octavius Street," she corrected automatically. "Cors Cant would have memorized . . ." Her voice broke, and she turned away that he would not see her tears. "No, from now on I won't feel anything for anyone again. I'll do the best I can with the Greek words."

Without looking up, she pulled the map from her shirt, scrolled it past her eyes, squinting in the dark.

She painfully sounded the words. Her dead voice sent a chill along Peter's spine. "There's . . . a winding path of aleshops and tanners, Lunch Street, that leads to a temple of Augustus. Used to be a temple of Augustus, who knows what it is now. It's not that close to the gate, but it does abut the wall. From the roof, says the traveler, you can see over . . . so I guess you can climb over, too. Then it's a straight run to the docks, where Merovius waits, if Mary and Rhiannon smile on us. Will that do?"

What a fiasco. First the boy, now Cei and Bedwyr gone. Peter's first command in this new duty, and it had entirely fallen apart.

Harlech fortress hulked more than three blocks away, up a hill—an anthill they had thoroughly stirred with Peter's brilliant infiltration gambit. *Oh, Lord God, it worked well all right!*

"The temple is perfect," he agreed without enthusiasm. "Lead on, Macduff!"

"Who?"

He shook his head, waved her on.

She scanned the courtyard, began to walk toward a narrow alley.

She had not taken a dozen steps when she suddenly fell to both knees, arms locked around her belly as if she had been shot.

Peter rushed to her side. She sobbed uncontrollably, yet silently, teeth clenched, cheeks streaked with salt tears.

"Oh God, my God, he *is* dead, isn't he?" It was somebody else's voice, echoing from a thousand miles away. "I won't see him? Not even once more to tell—to tell . . ."

"You don't know that. He might be alive."

"That pit has no bottom! I've been told."

"You were told wrong. Think, Anlawdd; every pit has a bottom somewhere." Peter held her tightly, let her sob against his shoulder. He felt a tug-of-war, protective and embarrassed simultaneously. His mouth was buried in her hair, whispering words of comfort and pressing tiny kisses. Her hair was clean, he noticed absurdly.

"Then he has fallen to the bottom and died. Prince, I would know if he were alive. I would feel his heartbeat. I feel nothing. He's dead."

"Maybe it wasn't that far of a fall." *Sure,* thought Peter, *maybe he's only lying there with a broken back and a severed femoral artery. Maybe he only impaled himself on a wooden stake.* The horrible fact was that Anlawdd was undoubtedly correct: Cors Cant was dead, or as near to dead as made no difference.

But Peter had to say something, lest he lose the last member of his strike team. Something pulled at his heart, frightening feelings toward the girl.

"Anything could have happened, Anlawdd. Cors Cant could be very much alive, trying to find a way back up to you. I've seen boys survive a fall from a . . . from out of a . . ."

He paused, puzzled. He could *picture* the machine: a huge, rattling, droning beast with great arms that flew

through the sky, soldiers huddled in its belly. But for the
life of him, Peter could not remember what it was called.

"I've seen them survive tremendous falls. Anlawdd, you
must have faith. All is lost without faith. Surely you've
learned that in the—in your secret lodge."

"Faith," she muttered, unconvinced.

"Faith like a little child. 'Unless you turn and become
like children . . .' "

" 'You will not enter the kingdom of heaven,' " com-
pleted Anlawdd automatically. Peter started; had she actually read the Bible? But she continued: " 'Not until the
male becomes female and the female, male will you enter
unto the kingdom of heaven.' "

Peter's throat squeezed; his mouth was dry. What verse
was that? Where had she heard it? He stroked her hair,
calming her somewhat.

She fell silent. Her breath was so regular and deep that
for a moment Peter worried she had somehow fallen
asleep. But then she looked up at him, a faint smile
ghosting across her lips. "Perhaps dead in body, but never
in spirit so long as I have breath and mind; so unless one
of your Jutes or Saxons kills me in battle, that shall be
ever so long a time that he'll live, won't it?"

"We won't forget him. Neither of us."

"He's not dead."

"No, not dead. Not really." *He's dead, lying at the bottom of a bottomless pit, a broken rag doll like Sergeant
Conway after Londonderry. And I hold an assassin in my
arms.*

She rose. Peter held her hand, absurdly reluctant to let
go as they made for the alley she had marked earlier. They
followed Anlawdd's "map" as the sky lightened, false
dawn, Day-Twelve for Peter.

"Winding path," wrote the traveler, and it was an under-
statement. Lunch Street twisted and turned, at times so
narrow Peter and Anlawdd barely squeezed past overturned, sour-smelling applecarts, rainbow-painted, hole-in-
the-wall shops, crumbling, mosaic-tiled apartment houses.
No rhyme, no city planning; butcher shops abutted temples

and churches. Very non-Roman, Peter thought. *Don't they have zoning laws?* The stench of tanners and a small slaughterhouse invaded pub and house alike.

"There," declared Anlawdd. She pointed at a building indistinguishable from the rest, said, "There, the temple. Looks like it's been converted to a Church. Of Attis, no less . . . watch your manhood, Prince Lancelot."

Hunh? The girl sounded as if she had pulled herself together, for a time at least. Peter mulled her last remark, could not make sense of it.

They approached the temple. Behind it was a great mound of dirt, twenty feet high: the city wall. Scaffolds ran the length, left and right out of sight. Soldiers jogged northward, toward a wooden gate two hundred yards distant along the wall.

"Jesus," he whispered. At least a hundred Jutes ran broken-step toward the gate road that must be Caesar Causeway. Toward Gormant's pitiful force.

Anlawdd saw. Her lip trembled, but she was true to her word, refused to allow herself to feel. She resolutely looked away from the gate, the causeway, toward the white temple.

Peter closed his eyes, heard the faraway roar of the battle, individual voices lost in the whirlwind. He itched to follow the tumult, rescue his men.

Hell, I wouldn't mind just leading the buggers into battle! Real warfare, hand-to-hand, man-to-man, as God intended. None of the nonsense of "modern" warfare, with buttons to push, logistics, air support, surface-to-surface missiles, Stingers, Harriers, helicopters, tanks, and a thousand and one layers of command, with generals supervising colonels supervising majors supervising lieutenants supervising gunnery sergeants. And the shadow of Whitehall looming over all: vast, cool, unsympathetic intelligences from the alien planet Politicus, judging every round fired, every door kicked, every security action undertaken.

Peter felt the seductive whistle of the fool-killer wind. For a moment, he simply listened, eyes closed, trying to imagine what it could be like.

Then reality intruded. Were Cei and Bedwyr still alive? Would they survive, make it back to Camlann? And what of the boy? He opened his eyes reluctantly; Anlawdd was watching, her eyes seeing too deep.

Peter's face flushed. "Quickly," he said, gestured to the door. *Still have the girl to look after, suspects to investigate.*

The door was barred, but the bolt was weak. Two combined kicks shattered it.

They dashed into the gloomy, stone building, discovered a small circle of yellow-robed men who stared wide-eyed at the intruders. Each man had a candle in one hand, long and wickedly curved crescent-knife in the other. A naked, stuporous boy, no more than twelve, sat on a stone table, swaying slightly in the breeze. Peter and Anlawdd had apparently interrupted a sacrifice.

"Oops, pardon us, we were just leaving anyway," said the girl quickly. She did an about-turn, then froze. Without looking, Peter knew what she saw behind him. He kept his eyes on the forward ring of armed priests.

"Our prayers have been answered," chanted a bald devotee, face lost in hallucinogenic ecstasy.

CHAPTER 22

THE STAIRS WOUND UP AND UP, EACH STEP A HEAVY NIGHTmare. Cors Cant panted, wheezing like an old man. He could no longer see the Shibbols, but felt their presence. Warm, fuzzy flippers held his hand, up the forever stair. He staggered, mind still beleaguered by the madness of Anlawdd's potion.

The walls were slick with algae and green-glowing

moss. As he climbed, the cold grew more intense; he shivered in his leine.

Arms enfolding himself, nose running in the chill draft, he would have wept at his plight were it not an uncivilized mannerism fit only for women and Celts.

I am Cors Cant Ewin, a Roman through and through! Never a naked, barb'rous, grunting savage painted blue. The Shibbols giggled, worry niggled. Anlawdd filled his every thought, 'gainst his sureness fiercely fought. Not a Celt? He felt on shaky ground, Euclid's reason quite unsound.

And still they came, those tears, forced by worries, forced by fears.

But she drove him upward, up the stair, Shibbol flippers always there. Maid or murderess, princess, goddess, he did not care; only for her autumn hair, white skin snow fair. *Hurry, hurry, don't be late—one doesn't make a giddess, I mean a goddess wait!*

The scroll from the dead boy's crypt crinkled with every step. With enough illumination, he could possibly read it. "ET in Ar-CA-di-a E-go," he chanted to drive his steps. Was that chill just wind, or premonition? *And in Arcadia, I,* babble or chilling message? Anlawdd was deep; she would ken. "And if not she, Merovius, then!"

He took a step, fell forward onto his face. The stairs ended, deposited him into a circular room that contained only a still, black pool. The pool disappeared beneath a low arch in the wall.

Gingerly, Cors Cant felt the liquid. As he feared, it was icy, colder than the Alban Sea. He pulled his hand free, shook it. Whatever the pool contained, it was not water: a viscous fluid clung to his skin, coated like grease.

And She was on the other side. He knew; he could not, would not hide.

He swore by Anlawdd, stripped his leine. He shivered as the chilly wind blew across naked skin. *The only way back is down the hole, crawl through caverns like a mole. Never this, that chill abyss! I'll swim to give that pit a miss.*

Cors Cant folded his leine, held it high above his head in one hand, the vial in the other as he stepped into the fluid. He gasped involuntarily, legs instantly numb from the cold. He hesitated a long moment. At last he walked into the pool, bit off a whimper; soon he would see his goddess again.

If she's still alive . . . The thought vanished as the liquid lapped painfully at groin and belly. He clenched his teeth, danced along the bottom, arms high.

He passed under the stone arch, noticed the keystone was not cut quite square, but fit perfectly anyway. *Marvel of engineering,* he thought; *must be Roman.* At that instant, the ground dropped from beneath his extended toes.

He slid into the clingy fluid, opened his mouth to shout, and inhaled a lungful. Cors Cant flailed his arms, fought for the surface.

Much worse than the Harlech surf! Unlike water, his hands slid through the queer, black liquid without purchase, immersed him deeper, if anything.

Cloth wrapped his face. His forgotten leine tangled his arms, though he still gripped the scroll tight. The bard thrashed and squirmed, hit bottom at last, completely submerged. Desperate to cough his lungs clear, he dared not. Cors Cant pressed lips together, lungs heaved. *Not an animal—hold back, I can hold back!*

A warm, happy shape ghosted through the frigid liquid, frightened the boy. Another followed—*the Shibbols!* he realized, *Can they swim through here?*

"Of course we can, we have no fear!"

"We love the water! We're Shibbols."

"Both!" They spiraled through the clingy froth.

Save me, or my life shall end!

"We'd never toss away a friend!"

"Grab ahold the dorsal fin (the one on top), drop your leine and let us glide. Trust us, trust us!" Shibbols cried.

I cannot see! How can a bard not see his death?

"Ho! Open your eyes and take a breath!"

Cors Cant forced his eyes open, discovered he could see through the liquid as well as air. No longer small and fuzzy, the lithe, graceful Shibbols were in their element. He suddenly knew where he had seen their like. Once, fishing with Gwyn (insufferable now that he was apprenticed to Cei), the boys had stumbled across a community of Orcas who played and breached in the waves.

Terrified, Gwyn Galahadus Minor, Lancelot's son and namesake, begged Cors Cant to turn back. The bard refused, and since he alone knew the Druid magic of navigation, Gwyn was stuck. The Orcas circled and eyed them, laughed and sprayed water, bumped the boat and breached.

Cors Cant had stared, captivated. Once, he reached out a hand, ran it along the side of one of the great, black-and-white beasts. It felt smooth and slick, a toy air bladder! They sang and cried. He could almost understand them: *we will come, come again—will you swim beside us then?*

"Give me your backs," begged poor Cors Cant. Like a graceful, watery elephant each Shibbol obliged, wriggled in for him to grab its dorsal fin. *How could I think they were furry?* he wondered. *They're smooth as tanned leather.* He grasped one Shibbol firmly, could only hook his left hand around the other, for he still grasped the cylinder.

A thought seeped through his ears, down his throat, into his stomach: *why haven't I breathed? Oh gods, am I dead?*

Dead, dead and blind. What bard am I? I can neither feel nor see! I failed the examination, I'm not fit to carry that harp. Better that I left it behind than disgraced it by further pretense!

They sang a Shibbol song as they swam. Cors Cant held tight, tears washed away by the water world. Miraculously, the scroll remained undamaged by the liquid, even as Cors Cant remained undrowned.

> Shibbols play,
> Night and day,
> Waves and shimmering sea!

Their powerful tails lashed up-down, up-down, propelled the trio through invisible water, eagles through the air. *I find Anlawdd, find Lancelot, then what? Now that I know what I'm not, what am I?*

> *Feed on fish,*
> *Tasty dish!*
> *Squid and shark shall flee!*

The boy felt almost an Orca himself, powerful lord of Llyr's domain, holy emperor of the Eire Sea, Gaul, even the mighty Mediterranean, Middle Earth, the Roman lake.

"Don't make us more than we truly are," warned the right.

"That's right, we're far from Orcas or eagles," explained the left. "We're Shibbols! A *deus ex machina* deft!"

"Which is *much* better!"

"And swifter, too, for here we are."

"And here are you!" They stroked for the surface. Cors Cant, momentarily terrified, squeezed tight with hands that once caressed music. The Shibbols flew through the air, like his broken dragon dream a thousand years before.

"Don't worry," said one, "you will not drop."

"We're your friends, bottom to top."

A sad silence. "But even friends must someday part," said right-hand Shibbol, with heavy heart.

Cors Cant said nothing, truly saw his powerful friends for the first time. The eyes that glinted mirth at the liquid world melted sadly at land's pain. Mouths frozen in forever smiles, they tossed their heads and squeaked, powerful, gentle, unfathomable. Made of fuzz and fur after all, not sea-slick skin, their terrible teeth nothing more than cut cloth, hind flippers lost again in darkness. Cors Cant floated at the surface on transparent water, viewed down upon them. The Shibbols had changed the moment his eyes broke surface.

"Thank you, my friends. I owe you my life."

The Shibbols looked at each other, squeaked with laughter. "Your life! Your life? Flesh and soul?"

"Your precious harp? That crumbled scroll? In the end,

you'll pay a higher toll!" With a final leap and breach,
they squeaked happily and swam away.

Cors Cant stopped struggling, discovered he could float
after all if he remained calm. He gently swam toward a
distant light, no longer frightened, but awed by the
Shibbols' majesty and mischief.

He was naked and unadorned, save for the cold, slippery
cylinder clenched in his left hand. The water, if water it
was, had warmed considerably; but it grew cold again as
he approached the red flicker.

He rolled onto his back, backstroked toward the light.
The sky was dead black, no stars; he thought it might be
a ceiling, lost in gloom above. *Naked I was born. Perhaps
naked I'll leave, no harp, no leine, no sword, no boots.*
Cors Cant would have given even the scroll itself for the
ability to weep, for he had foolishly cast his last tears
aside in the Shibbol pool. Now he could not find even that
much life.

His stomach and nasal passages hurt. Dry mouthed, he
remembered swallowing a lot of water. *Did any of it truly
happen, or do I still lie on a cold, dirty dungeon floor,
back broken, head swollen with my traitoress's hallucina-
tions?*

His head banged against stone, a wall that dipped far
into the water. He could not see the top.

*Great. Now I float until I sink from exhaustion.
Unless . . .*

He took a breath, pulled his arms and legs tight together
to sink through crystalline liquid.

Three times his own height straight down, Cors Cant
found a gap in the wall. His ears throbbed painfully as he
swam through the hole into a black, underwater tunnel.

The change was so abrupt he almost gasped. For the
first time since the Shibbols saved his life, his chest
heaved for air.

Water—*real water!* It was cold, but not supernaturally
so.

The tunnel seemed endless. As Myrddin taught, each
time he thought he could not live without another breath,

Cors Cant exhaled a short burst of air. As the tunnel continued, he expelled nearly half the contents of his lungs.

Stretching a hand upward, he could not feel the tunnel roof. Was it ended, or just widened? His vision narrowed to its own tunnel, jack-o'-lanterns sparkled around the black edges of sight.

At once, the urge to cough returned twentyfold. Unable to stop himself, Cors Cant lost the last of his air in an explosion of bubbles. He barely stopped himself from inhaling, clawed desperately for the surface through muddy, opaque, but real water. *Please, Goddess Anlawdd, let there be a surface!* Instead, his head banged against the tunnel roof.

Sight completely gone from lack of air, Cors Cant weakly dived. His belly scraped stone. He stroked forward madly, ears pounding like ritual drums.

At long last, his head broke through the surface to cold air.

Cors Cant stood, gasping and choking. He crawled forward, rose dripping, exhausted from a shallow pool, the terminus of the underwater passage.

A mob in yellow robes stared incredulously. A crescent-shaped dagger dropped from the nerveless hand of one of the yellow men.

"He—he—he has been raised from the dead," cried a familiar voice—*Anlawdd's voice!*—"and he is going before you to Gal-Galilee." Then she fell heavily as if slain.

One of the robes pointed at Cors Cant, spoke in mingled awe and terror. "It is Attis the Boy-God, rising from his watery grave!"

Lancelot's mouth opened in horror. "Good God," he shouted, "you're alive! And *starkers!*"

CHAPTER 23

MARK BLUNDELL TRIED TO LAY THE SITUATION FLAT IN HIS head while he jolted along behind the other officers in the raggedy platoon.

First, how much damage had he done as "Medraut" by stumbling about like a drunken toreador in battle?

Probably very little, he thought; *I wouldn't have landed in Medraut's body unless there were some strong similarities in our personality and brain functioning.* Sad to say, Medraut would probably have bollixed it just as thoroughly on his own had Mark never arrived. Mark tended to panic in a crisis, lose tempo and initiative; from the reaction, he seemed to have confirmed what everyone already feared about Medraut, rather than drop totally out of character.

Second, how to repair the damage? The best plan, he decided, was to single out a benefactor, someone who could be his sponsor, his mentor. Someone willing to take on a disciple, not daunted by Mark's previous failures, and with enough status to lend some to Mark so he would stop being despised.

The choice was obvious, so the third question became how to attract Merovee's attention. In this respect, Mark had an advantage over Medraut: he had no personal stake in any of this. It was a game, albeit a serious one (for Peter, whoever he was in this world), and Mark had no ego tie-up. Thus, he decided to make a bold move, one that probably *was* somewhat out of character for Medraut; but it could not be avoided.

Mark quickened his steps, caught up with Merovee's

armored guard. From comments, Blundell knew that Merovee was a king from a far-off land called either Sicambria or Languedoc, or perhaps of a people called *the* Languedoc. A king, in any event.

"Um, sirs," he began, waited until two of the guards noticed him. The shorter one faintly inclined his head, and Mark continued. "Sirs, I beg to be allowed a word with His Majesty, King Merovee. It's very important!"

The two Sicambrians or Languedocs conferred between themselves. Then one stepped close and whispered to the king. Merovee nodded his head, and Mark was waved forward into the midst of the guard circle.

As Mark approached, he found that suddenly he *did* have a personal stake in the outcome, though he could not explain why. His mouth grew dry, mind blank. The careful words he had composed flew from his head like soup from a spinning bowl.

"Sire, I beg—I beg—beg a . . ." The boon could not escape his lips. Mark looked full in the face of the monarch, and Merovee looked back. At once Mark felt a cool, dry hand caress his soul, felt a breeze upon his cheek and love in his heart. He was not a bumbling, gawky, rash, callow, moneyed, Little Lord Fauntleroy; no, Mark Blundell was an especially loved child who knew that Merovee would accept him even when he dropped the ball or forgot his declensions.

"Sire, I beg a boon . . . I really botched my first command, and I feel like a complete penis-head."

"Others have done better," agreed the king. "Some have done worse."

"I just want . . . Your Majesty, I'd really appreciate it if you'd take me a bit under your wing, as it were, and teach me something about this battle business."

Merovee half smiled; his ancient eyes had seen everything twice over. "The world is full of strange conversions these days," said Merovee, but he did not explain the remark. "I don't know how good a teacher I can be. Is your cup empty or full?"

"I thought it was full, but I guess it all leaked out. It's empty now, I'm pretty sure."

Merovee nodded. "Good start. For right now, my men could use a good lad to supervise restringing bows, now that we've arrived at the forest's edge."

Mark saw they had returned to the beach, though they must have veered off onto a different trail than the one they followed on the way in, for they were much farther north, toward the occupied city, than they had been during the battle.

They hid in the tall grass and flowering weeds a long time, spying on the Jutic stronghold. Harlech, Merovee called it, though it was hard for Mark to see the bustling Welsh city within the burned hulk of primitive mud and wattle houses, behind a Roman mound-wall, sprawled beneath a small castle or fortress that was no longer anywhere to be found, not in the *real* timeline Mark knew.

Several score Jutes milled upon the beach before the city gates, purposeless. Some were sober, most were clearly pissed, staggering and passing pottery jars to each other. A long, light brown dock jutted from the beach; it floated upon pontoons, rather than standing on stilts above the water, down and back up . . . probably a Roman addition of the past hundred years.

Tied against the restless pier was a ship like the one that had passed close by Mark Blundell as he bobbed in the ocean immediately upon arriving in Medraut's body. Against this ship was tied another, smaller, and yet a third, so that the only way to reach the last was to climb from dock to ship to ship to ship.

"We need one," said a soft voice. Mark looked back. Merovee knelt behind him, arm resting on knee, staring at the three boats gently rising and sinking with the swells.

"A boat?"

"Just one."

Mark felt a tingle at his left. He quickly turned his head, for an instant caught Cutha the Saxon cocking his ear, listening intently. Then a sense warned the straw-haired Saxon, and he turned away, seemingly uninterested.

Mark understood little about the dynamics except that Cutha was an enemy of Merovee, Lancelot, and the men. Mark could not guess why Cutha accompanied them; from his few conversations with Selly, he remembered that the Saxons were invaders at this point. The Romans had just left, and the islands were ruled and inhabited by Celts in the north: Welsh, Scottish, Cornish, and Irish, with presumably the odd Pict here and about, and Saxons in the south.

For some reason, he felt a twinge of discomfort that Cutha had been listening.

"Medraut," said the king, "come speak with me."

Mark crept stealthily down the slight rise back into the forest, rose and jogged after Merovee. The king walked into the trees without a backward glance, then began to talk, serenely confident that Medraut had followed. "Lancelot and his squad will slay many Jutes, and perhaps free the prince if he still lives. They will leave the enemy in disarray, but it will not last. We must depart directly they join us—by sea, for we could never outmarch the mounted Jutes.

"If we succeed, we leave behind a badly demoralized, frightened army that may well even quit the city before we return. But if they catch and slay us, they will rejoice in victory and take heart. Then, even if Artus hears about the occupation, the Jutes will hold and reinforce the city against him."

"So all depends upon our stealing a boat," said Mark, trying to follow the strategy, "and making it ready for Lancelot's escape."

"But the boats are guarded, Medraut. What have your studies taught you? What is our plan?"

Mark bit his lip, stymied. The real Medraut may well have studied military tactics, but Mark Blundell had never been in any sort of combat since public school.

Clear the mind, let the words flow; don't let your Self get in the way!

"A diversion," he blurted. "We need to draw them off in the wrong direction while we seize a boat."

Merovee smiled, leaned back to stare at the treetops. His long, black, silky hair cascaded down his broad shoulders, covered his back like a cloak. "You are wise so far."

For several long moments he stood thus. Mark, ordinarily a bit hyperkinetic, discovered he was content to stand peacefully, watching the king. Something about the man soothed, calmed him.

"Yes," said Merovee at last. "The city stands north and east of the dock, nearly a mile apart; but deep forest marches all the way up to within a few hundred yards of both. We must send a force through this forest to burst forth and fall upon the Jutes at the dock from the city side.

"They will be confused, perhaps thinking the troops are their own until we close. Then they will respond, and the beach will empty as they desert their posts to meet the sudden enemy."

"And this is when we attack and grab a boat?"

"The second, smaller force will fly from cover at this instant, rush forth, and seize the first, largest boat. The others will be set adrift and fired, for we cannot risk pursuit."

"What about the first group? How will they escape?"

Merovee smiled sadly. "Theirs is a difficult job, my lad. My hope is that the Jutes will see the burning ships, panic, and run back down to the beach. If the diversionary force can win free and fade back into the forest, the Jutes may be too disarrayed to mount a pursuit.

"In this case, we can pick them up back at the rendezvous point, where we shall meet again with Lancelot."

Mark envisioned the attack in his mind: feint from northeast, then the real strike from the south. The boats are fired, the Jutes turn. . . . "Or do they?"

"Medraut?"

Mark hesitated; telling Merovee his plan might not work was unthinkable. "But, if the Jutes don't turn and run away from the diversionary force . . . then, ah, what becomes of them, Sire?"

Merovee lowered his eyes. "Theirs is a dangerous task,"

he repeated. "Some may win through to the sea. We shall pick up whom we may."

Blundell stood silent a long time, a lump like Selly's biscuits in his esophagus. "Many will die, won't they? Maybe I'll die. I suppose I must be in the diversionary force, since I'm no, ah, no Herakles, able to seize a ship single-handedly."

The king eyed Mark for a few beats. Then he smiled, knowing and amused.

"What? What's the problem?" Mark tried to sound non-chalant, but he could hear the faint edge of fear in his own voice. Had he slipped, revealed himself?

"Nothing, my lad. It's merely that you remind me of someone."

"Some friend?"

"A stranger from a far-off land. But a friend, I think, nonetheless." Merovee stepped closer, turned the corners of his mouth down. "One thing only I must warn you about, Medraut. There is one I do not trust in our party. You know to whom I refer."

"Uh, Cutha. The Saxon."

"And his guards. Say nothing to them of this plan. *Tell them nothing.*" Merovee's voice was deep and icy, penetrated through skin and muscle to reverberate around Mark's heart and abdomen. Merovee continued. "As we approached Harlech in the galley, one of our company warned the Jutes that we were coming. Alas, I fear it may have been our guest, who is not quite the ally we hoped he would be."

Warned? Mark pursed his lips, wondering what had happened. Whatever it was, it was probably responsible for Mark's materializing in a swirling ocean, instead of on the deck of a mighty galley.

"I won't breathe a word," promised Blundell. His eyes locked into the king's gaze; he could no more have refused the command than cut off his own penis.

"I charge you," said the Long-Haired King, "in the name of the widow's son."

So entranced was Blundell by the looming presence that

filled his sight that he barely noticed the Masonic reference. "The widow's son," he repeated.

Merovee took Mark's trembling hand, held it briefly. Mark felt the sign, returned it.

"We meet on the level," said Merovee.

"And p-part on the square," whispered Blundell.

"Go, and fear no more." Merovee turned Mark about and gave him a quick push toward the company.

Mark stumbled over a root, banged his head on a tree branch, and found himself in the silent company assembled. All about him, men were scurrying like busy elves at the cobbler's bench, readying their weapons and armor, all but Cutha. The Saxon watched Mark closely as he emerged from the deep trees.

Cutha smiled, open, disingenuous. Mark gazed back, curious. *Why do they all suspect you, my friend? What have you done to merit such an accusation?*

Mark had the uncomfortable feeling that it fell upon Cutha for no reason other than his race . . . a race that in real life, Mark Blundell shared.

"Well," he muttered to himself, "at the very least I can talk to the gentleman. But not a word about . . . !"

CHAPTER 24

"WOE UNTO YOU," improvised PETER, "WHO DISRESPECT the avatars of—" *What was that name?* "Of Attis! You shall be punished for this sacrilege." He waved his hand agitatedly, urging Anlawdd to jump in with both feet. "This heresy!"

Anlawdd stared, mesmerized, strands of auburn fallen unnoticed across her face. Not even a breath.

"Sacrilege," he repeated. Peter turned his stare to Cors Cant, hoping to catch his eye, praying the boy would catch the lateral and run down a goal. *How did he get here at this instant? What in God's green earth happened to his clothes?*

"Uck," said Cors Cant.

Peter held his breath. It broke the spell that bound Anlawdd; Peter felt her tense, take a breath at last, prepare to cover for the lad.

But Cors Cant found his tongue, blurted, "On your—on your knees! Apostates! Heretics!"

Anlawdd pointed furtively at the already-prostrate priests. She jumped into the *comedia*. "Attis," she declared with hauteur most convincing, "is *most displeased* with His soldiers." She got into the role. "I mean, honestly! You'd swear the lot of you are a bunch of Christians or tax collectors, sitting around on your fat posteriors all day stuffing yourself with excessively starchy foods. Useless! Who among you has made the ultimate sacrifice?"

What's she after? Who's Attis, what's the ultimate sacrifice, and why does she want to know?

Two priests raised their hands.

"Lord Attis, I have."

"I made it first."

"Balls. It was I."

"It never was! I helped you, for you had not the courage to work the shears yourself."

Ollie and Stan, Peter decided for convenience.

"Accompany us," demanded the girl. "All those two of you who raised your hands that you've rendered to Caesar, come along, that *all might know* we are the Boy-God Attis and His chosen and let us pass." She said the last slowly, nudged her head roofward.

Light dawned. Peter spoke quickly before Cors Cant could blunder into a suspicious error. "Does the, ah, Lord Attis still desire to *walk the walls* of the city and survey his domains, as he indicated earlier?"

Cors Cant looked confused, but nodded vigorously. "Yes, that sounds like a great—I mean, yes, the Great

Lord Attis will walk the walls. You who stay behind," he added, "know that ye too art blessed, touched by the holy, inef—ineffable presence of Ishtar's lover-son." The bard expanded a little, swept his hand magnanimously. Peter fidgeted. "Feel my holy power surge within you, bask in the glory of—"

"Beg pardon, Your Vegetableness," interrupted Anlawdd, fist punching thigh impatiently. "Not to rush You or anything, but hadn't we better get going while it's still today?"

"Oh yes, of course," agreed Cors Cant. "Rise and lead us forth, obey Me!"

Good Lord, the lad's going to parade the city walls in the emperor's new clothes! "Ah, perhaps the, ah, the Lord Attis should don a cloak?" Peter suggested. "Wouldn't want to ... burn out the eyes of the unpure." *Jesus and Mary, haven't these people any shame at all?*

Cors Cant shivered, seemed to feel the chill air for the first time since emerging from the fountain. "Right, don't want to burn their eyes out."

A priest doffed his cloak, a gorgeous, white fleece with foxfur lining. Cors Cant wrapped himself, and Peter breathed easier.

Lord, we men look disgusting. How do women stand it?

"Wallwards," said Cors Cant, "that all may see and know the truth—Attis is risen from the grave after three days and three nights in Death's realm."

The priests whooped and hollered themselves hoarse. Ollie unlocked a door, led the climb up a spiral stair, finally gained the scaffold catwalk that ran the length of Harlech's mound-wall. Anlawdd, Peter, and Cors Cant followed, and the other priest was "Tail-End Stanley."

From the catwalk, Peter saw Harlech spread below. Fires burned, buildings collapsed; a desolate pit; a prepubescent Dresden. Anlawdd turned her head, stared at Cors Cant's back.

The harbor lay westward, and Cors Cant led them thither. Along the wall, the ground rose and fell, like black-earth ocean swells flecked with brown-grass seafoam. Yet the Roman-built wall maintained a constant level, no more than fifteen feet above the ground at some points: a hard hop, not likely to break bones. Peter alternated watching for a jumping-off point and straining for a glimpse of Cei, Bedwyr, and the frail wraiths of Gormant.

CHAPTER 25

THE HOURS STRETCHED LONG FOR MARK BLUNDELL, SITTING beneath tree cover stringing bows and sharpening axe blades. Not sure of his ability to "supervise," he took the task himself.

The city was clearly visible from their vantage, and many pairs of eyes watched for a sign that Lancelot and his raiding party had succeeded in twitting the Jutes, pricking them like a picador, perhaps even liberating Prince Gormant.

Who was that auburn-haired woman? wondered Mark. *Could she be Selly?* The coincidence of hair color could be just that, but like minds attracted in the temporal transfer. The only woman on the expedition. *Maybe one fiery redhead calls to another? She'll bear watching. . . .*

Merovee stared, motionless, barely breathing. Perhaps he could see over the mound-wall, through the smoldering ruins that once were Harlech. Mark saw nothing.

Blundell felt a soft touch at his elbow. It was Cutha.

"How it goes?" The Saxon pointed at the axe, which still lay unsharpened in Mark's lap.

"Oh! Sorry, is this yours?" Cutha nodded, and Mark busied himself with the whetstone.

"Did you too they tell?"

"Tell?"

"We were betrayed, so they think." Cutha's voice sank to a soft, depressed tone. "By me, they think. But why? Only because a Saxon I am, and Saxons they do not like!"

Cutha's dark brows folded down; he pressed his lips together, as if trying to hold back great emotion. Mark immediately felt guilty, as he always used to whenever the Pakistanis marched through London streets for better wages and an end to racism. Guilty, guilty! Though he was not himself a racist and thought no ill of Saxons. Or Pakistanis.

"Well," suggested Mark, "you're—different. We always fear strangers among us. Goes back to primate tribes, of course."

He realized that he was babbling, and that Cutha probably had had little contact with Charles Darwin in any event. But he could not stop himself. "Monkeys attack any monkey that looks or acts different from the rest, for it tends to attract predators. But I guess this doesn't really apply here, for there are no wolves or crocodiles about."

Cutha continued as if he had not heard. "I fear. I, a Saxon, fear! A suicide attack King Merovee plans."

"Oh? Does he?" Mark squirmed. The conversation had touched uncomfortably close to what he was Not To Reveal.

"Me by the king himself, Merovee wishes to remain."

"You with him? With Merovee?" *But which group will the king join?* wondered Mark ... to himself.

Cutha nodded, sat silent, watched the city. They watched for a sign from the great man, from Lancelot du Lac. *But what if the signal comes,* thought Mark, *and we do not recognize it?* He turned his attention back to Cutha's axe and the stone, using long, careful strokes as the armorer had shown him.

"My men to part from I fear," said Cutha, after several minutes, his voice now nearly too low to hear.

"You're parting from your men?"

"Another group they join. Bigger group; part of the main attack the king says."

Ah, thought Mark, *so now we can deduce several points:*

1) Merovee would never tell Cutha the truth, believing as he did that the Saxon had betrayed them.
2) So Cutha's men had probably been assigned to the diversionary force, not the main force.
3) Therefore, Cutha and Merovee himself were assigned to the main attack on the ship.

Simple logic, Mark concluded, squirmed at the nagging feeling that he had missed an important clue.

"A trap I fear it is. But my men! Ever again shall I see?"

Mark said nothing, flushed red. *No,* he longed to say, *you won't. Your men will die when the Jutes counterattack, when everything falls apart, when the ship assault fails to turn them away from the diversionary force.*

Cutha watched Mark carefully. He seemed to understand some of Mark's inner turmoil. Cutha gently laid his hand on Mark's arm, gave it a squeeze of hope. "No problem there is. If I must, I must die. But my men, safe they shall stay? My responsibility they are, for a sword oath to their mothers before leaving I took."

Mark dropped the whetstone, said, "Oaths . . . Oaths are important. But sometimes even the best, with the best intentions, cannot . . . you know."

"I know?"

"Some oaths cannot be kept, no matter how sincere."

Cutha looked puzzled for a moment, then seemed to understand. "Ach," he whispered. His face dropped, eyes gazed at the ground. Mark snuck a glance; the Saxon's skin was pallid as a half-moon.

"But in a grand cause it is, and death in battle is rewarded. Though heavy news to their mothers it may be, to know of the son's heroic deaths they shall be comforted. And ach, the ships, the ships so desperately we need!"

"The Jutes have horses," agreed Mark. "We'd never outrun them on the land."

Cutha shook his head. "From the king, much I could learn. We all could. Strategy as a Roman of long ago he commands! As a Caesar! Not in a hundred years this would I have plotted."

"Afraid I know nothing about strategy." It was true. Mark could envision an n-dimensional manifold, but not armies crashing together.

"Two prongs," explained the Saxon, "together like hammer and anvil they strike." Cutha smacked his fists together. "Glory! A valorous death we die."

"But only one to strike," said Mark. "The other's but a useless appendage to draw the attack, then run away. If they can." He was surprised at the bitterness in his voice. A large chunk of the army was being thrown to the wolves, and it made Mark's stomach churn. *No, close yourself,* he ordered; *Say nothing! Let no one know how you feel, for they always use it against you, soon or late.*

Generally far too soon. . . .

"What?" Cutha stared, aghast. *"What?"* he thundered. Blundell fell backward, startled by the vehement protest.

"I, a mere diversion to be? By Donner in his heavens! I to *run away* they ask?" Cutha's face turned as red as Colonel Cooper's; but this time, Mark feared a sudden attack upon himself rather than a stroke in Cutha.

"No! No, your men, *they'll* be the ones to divert and run!"

"Saxons, from battle running!"

"But don't you understand?" It was important to Mark, urgent, that Cutha realize that it was not prejudice, not racism. He was not being sacrificed, his men not being humiliated.

No, sneered Mark's conscience; *his men are being sacrificed and he is being humiliated! Much better form, that.*

"That Saxons from battle do not run, that I understand."

"Cutha, we shall strike the main blow, you and the king and I. Your men are a mere diversionary force . . . they're not running away, they're drawing the Jutes after them so we can burn all the ships but the biggest, for that is the ship we shall sail."

Cutha began to speak, closed his mouth again. He seemed gradually to calm himself as he understood it was not a trick to slay or humiliate him in front of his men. "A Saxon general I am," he muttered.

"Merovee knows that," Mark soothed.

"My pride I have. A great warrior am I!"

"If you weren't, you wouldn't have been picked for the job, would you?"

"Hm." Cutha picked up his axe, hefted it. "Hm." He swung it absently, cut down a sapling in its prime. "Much to think you have given. I will retire, think." He stepped away slowly into the greening wood.

Mark sat on a stump, watched the city through the trees. A bird cawed hideously, as if struck in the throat by an arrow. *Why are they always so sensitive?* he wondered. *Nothing was meant, no insults.*

The bird cawed again. Evidently, the hypothetical arrow did not bother it.

Like a chick hatching from an egg, a tiny thought kicked and pecked its way up Mark's brain stem. *You know,* said his omnipresent conscience, *you told him an awful lot more than you intended.*

I had to! I didn't mean to. Do you really think so?

Conscience nodded vigorously. *An awful lot more. The whole plan, in fact.*

Suddenly, Mark Blundell sprang up as if stung by a bee. "You imbecile!" he cried, slapping himself with all his might across the face in frustration at his own stupidity.

"He tricked you! And you let him!"

Mark noticed he was the center of attention of a small, puzzled crowd. He flushed with embarrassment, though one cheek was already bright red from the slap.

"Um," he began, then stopped. How could he ever explain his terrible mistake?

Great, I can hear the conversation already: did he

*threaten you? No sir. Did he hypnotize you? No sir. Then
how did he drag our entire battle plan out of you?*

*He looked sad, sir, so I spilled the beans to cheer him
up!*

"I . . ." No escape; Mark had to do the right thing. He
spit the words out quickly before he could change his
mind. "I need to find K-King Merovee."

He lowered his head, dishonored. *I am a dead man,* he
thought.

CHAPTER 26

FOUR TIMES, THE "FOLLOWERS OF ATTIS" MET A THREE- OR
four-man Jutic squad on the scaffold. Each time, Ollie
and Stan shouted the same phrase, more or less in chorus,
in some Germanic language, probably Jutic. Cors Cant
translated, another unexpected talent: "Aside, aside, Attis
the virgin-born is risen. We are his chosen, and we follow."

Whenever the Jutes heard the name Attis, they shrank
away as if the priests were plague-ridden, curled their lips
in disgust. When Peter and his men had all passed, the
Jutes invariably pointed and laughed . . . derisively, Peter
thought. He shook his head, annoyed, though he did not
know why.

Anlawdd stayed close to Cors Cant; she looked as
though she wanted nothing more than to throw her arms
around him, but for some reason could not.

Wants to maintain cover, thought Peter; but he knew it
was nothing so shallow. Were they alone, he knew, she
would still hang back, hunger checked by wariness: a
starving fox staring at possibly poisoned food.

Cors Cant barely seemed to notice them. No longer the small, frightened boy who entered Harlech; now his haunted eyes held the "thousand-yard stare" of prophets and criminal lunatics.

Where is he looking? What does he see? What is that cylinder in his hand that he tries so hard to hide? Peter chewed a stray strand of mustache, watched Boy and Girl carefully, trying to anticipate the next act.

Anlawdd dropped back, whispered to Peter, "When do we dive for the ground? Should be no problem to thump these two half men, with what we know about them."

Ollie was impressive, weighed at least twenty stone. Much of it was fat, but he looked powerful nonetheless. Stan was less imposing, but tall and rangy, hardened by years of carrying sacrifices, toting idols, or whatever it was that priests of Attis did to pass time. Both looked like distinct problems indeed if they ever realized they had been humbuggered.

"What do you know about them that I don't?" asked Peter.

"Whatever do you mean? You know what I mean, the loss of essence. Prince Lancelot, are we going to make it out alive? You don't have to pull the blow because I'm a girl, you know."

"Sure, we'll make it." *Make it to a shallow grave, most likely.*

Anlawdd smiled faintly, amused but sardonic. His voice betrayed him.

Fifteen feet ahead, Peter saw a high, steep-sloped hill abutting the outside of the wall. The perfect diving spot, as Anlawdd called it. He turned to her, said quietly, "Here's where we dump the priests. Now what the hell do you mean, loss of essence?"

"Dump the priests," she said, lips drawing back from her teeth. At the word "priest," Ollie stopped and turned, puzzled. Anlawdd turned her snarl into a beatific smile, strolled up to the giant.

She gasped and pointed over his shoulder, pretending to

see something horrific. She was a terrific actress; even Peter peeked before he caught himself.

Ollie turned like a flat-footed chump. Without a moment's hesitation, the alleged seamstress doubled her fists
and swung them like a cricket bat at the base of his skull,
where the line between brown scalp hair and fine, black
neck hairs blurred.

She hit a six. His head rocketed forward, dragged his
lumbering body after. Ollie staggered against the waist-
high railing of the catwalk, belly spilling over. He stared
at the packed-soil street below, slowly tipping, unable to
right himself.

Too much weight—he rotated like a teeter-board, hands
and feet stiff, unmoving, and toppled limply to the ground.
He landed with a dull crack, lay without moving.

Stan stared, stunned by the sudden disappearance of his
chum. *Now!* screamed Peter's brain, whipping his sluggish
body; *Now, now! Don't let her show up the 22-SAS!*

Peter stepped behind Stan, drove his fist into the man's
kidney. But Stan was a rock. He stumbled to his knees,
spun and staggered up, grimacing, but ready to defend
himself.

Peter stepped forward, caught him with a boot to the
groin. The man winced, but did not otherwise react. He
jabbed. But as Peter slipped the jab, he was caught by
the priest's flashing right cross.

Peter was under water, oceans swirled his inner ear; the
blow caught him flush on the temple. *Bloody hell, you really* do *see stars.*

As Peter stood, blinking stupidly, knees wobbling, Stan
caught hold of his leg and yanked him off-balance. The
priest began an ear-piercing bellow that cut through Peter's
injured ear like an ice pick. Even without Cors Cant's
help, Peter could roughly translate the shout as the local
variant on *"'Elp! 'E keeps wallopin' me on the 'ead!"*

Cors Cant froze, stared at the tableau. He started to
move, retreated again. He did not seem frightened, just
confused.

Peter dropped to his buttocks, kicked with his free foot

at Stan's jaw, then solar plexus without effect. Then the priest's head was yanked back as Anlawdd tugged at his hair.

He let go Peter's foot to grapple with the girl—a critical mistake. Peter arched his back and delivered a powerful, double-footed kick into Stan's heart.

The priest folded like a lawn chair. Before he could recover, Peter and Anlawdd together rolled him off the catwalk like a barrel. He struck the ground knees first. Peter turned away from the sight of the man screaming in agony, cradling his powdered kneecaps; Anlawdd did not seem bothered.

She panted, exhausted by the melee. Then she gasped, "Why did—you kick—him *there,* of all places?"

"What?" snapped Peter, massaged his wrenched leg.

"I should have thought—a blow to the knee—or something, not—not between the legs! Yes, I'm fine, Cors Cant."

Cors Cant finally unstuck himself, tripped to Anlawdd's side. His face was white as the fleece cloak he wore. "Goddess! Are you hurt? Are you all right?"

Peter grumbled, still stuck on the criticism of his combat technique. "Well I expected him to react a *little* more to a groin kick."

"Yes, I'm fine, Cors Cant," Anlawdd repeated, this time waiting for the bard to ask the question. She turned back to Peter, suspicious. "Prince Lancelot, do you feel a fever coming on? We asked for those who had made the ultimate sacrifice, if I'm not wrong, which of course I rarely am unless I get so upset I add eight to twelve and get seventeen."

Peter stared at her from under Lancelot's razor-thin, black-dark eyebrows, waiting for illumination.

She spoke slowly, incredulous at his ignorance. "You *really* don't know what it means for a priest of Attis to make the ultimate sacrifice?"

He dumbly shook his head. Anlawdd pantomimed a pair of scissors with her fingers, snipped them between her legs.

Peter felt a jolt of sympathetic pain in his own groin, winced. "You mean they . . . ? Oh, Mother of God!" He gagged, envisioned a rusty pair of sheers creeping closer, closer. "Bollocks! Is it an elaborate ceremony, or do they . . . do it to *themselves?*"

A groan escaped the bard's throat. He was pale, lips pressed tight as if sick or in pain. He crouched, leaned against the wall hugging his knees, staring at his feet, shivering.

Anlawdd noticed the same time Peter did. She spoke distractedly to Peter, but watched Cors Cant with sideways eyes. "You ought to know this. You *used* to know this. The god Attis was so distressed by Ishtar's, um, unnatural lust for him that he—removed the object of her affection."

"Ishtar?"

Anlawdd was silent for a moment. Cors Cant did not seem aware of the attention he had attracted. "Ishtar, his mother. His priests, well, do the same to themselves." She raised her voice. "Isn't that right, Cors Cant? You know much more about these myth things than I, being a bard and all. And a Druid, a Druid bard. And all."

She reached a booted foot out, poked his bare leg.

Cors Cant spoke mechanically, head still bowed, as if ashamed. "Yes, thus do *they* worship *their* goddess."

He made no overt change of focus, but Peter understood that the subject had changed from priests of Attis to Cors Cant and Anlawdd. An icy creep tingled Peter's spine. *Today,* he thought, *this is* not *a healthy relationship.*

"Cors Cant," she answered, speaking past him, as if it were too uncomfortable to meet tête-à-tête, "it certainly is a grand thing those priests were as stupid as they were. They should have known you weren't Attis, with that, heh-heh, huge piece of evidence staring them right in the face."

"Evidence?" His question was lackluster; he clearly did not follow her joke.

"Lancelot had a shade of a time getting you to don that robe."

Now Peter was confused. "What are you talking about? Spit it out, girl."

She smiled, still caught up in the endless joke that no one found funny. "You were su-supposed to be Attis, but it's clear Ishtar never removed a b-bloody thing from you, don't'cha know, heh heh heh." The anemic laugh indicated that she, too, realized the humor was a nonstarter.

Peter's blood rushed to his face. He had tried mightily hard not to notice the bard's enormous endowment, found the entire subject acutely embarrassing. But Anlawdd's ill-fated joke made it impossible to ignore.

Confound that woman! Must she make a huge thing out of it? He turned and tugged vigorously at his mustache. A strand came out in his fingers.

"Um, Lancelot?" Anlawdd looked pensive, dredging up a subject she would rather let lie. "About, um, about Prince Gormant. My father. I. . . ."

She trailed off; Peter gestured for her to continue.

"Cors Cant, you remember how those Saxons recognized me? The ones we—the ones I slew out by Camlann?"

Dead silence. Anlawdd had both Peter's and the lad's complete attention.

"Well," she concluded shakily, "they recognized me because they'd seen me before. In Gormant's court." Peter waited, and she dropped the other shoe. "When they met with my father to plot alliance with the Jutes against Artus."

Peter nodded. "I guess we know how the Jutes got past the Harlech defenses, lass." *Too bad, Gormant; I could have told you about Stalin's pact with Herr Hitler. "You can't invade me, I have a piece of paper you signed!"*

But Peter knew she still was not telling the whole truth—Gormant's treachery did not explain what she, herself, was doing in the *Dux Bellorum*'s room dressed in black, knife in hand.

"Well," rumbled Peter, "we'll have to tell Artus."

"I know."

"And I don't know what will happen to you."

"I know. The waiting is torture, like proposing marriage just before leaving on a month-long campaign."

Peter reached out to pat her shoulder, but somehow missed and touched her breast. She did not move, did not pull away. Her eyes gestured to the bard, his back still turned. Much too slowly, Peter dropped his hand.

And why didn't the boy react to the tale of betrayal? wondered Peter. The answer was obvious: because Cors Cant already knew.

Peter could barely contain his fury. This time, the bard's twisted sense of honor had actually cost men their lives.

Had Lancelot escaped from Peter's prison just then, Cors Cant would have been lying dead in a lake of blood. As it was, the only thing that kept Peter himself from striking out, killing the bard in red rage, was his rationalization that all these people were already fifteen centuries dead anyway.

Cors Cant still stared over the wall, but now his eyes narrowed as he focused on something on the Harlech side.

Peter followed his gaze. At first, all he saw was the tangled web of pre-Roman, earthen streets—no rectangular blocks here! Then a narrow, white dirt lane caught his eye. It curved around the outside of the wall, intersected the single straight, Roman road that led through the gate. The two streets met at the roofless shell of a stables.

Twelve to fifteen drunken, jeering Jutes surrounded the stables, sporadically firing arrows into it. Inside, Peter saw Bedwyr crouched at the window, shooting back at the Jutes and missing badly. Cei hovered beside his brother, axe gripped in futile resistance.

Bedwyr ducked back inside as a half dozen arrows stuck into the window wall. Almost exactly a second later, they faintly heard the rapid-fire thunks. *About three hundred fifty yards,* calculated Peter by habit. The Jutes howled like hyenas.

"Mithras!" breathed Cors Cant.

"What are you two looking at?"

"Bloody hell," growled Peter, "a half an hour out and those fools managed to get pinned down in a building. How did they managed to reach a ripe age without eating poisoned mushrooms, or finding a lake, falling in, and drowning?"

"What are you two looking at? Answer me!" Anlawdd stamped her foot. She craned her neck, but could not zero in on the donnybrook.

Cors Cant pointed. "Stables, crossroads, your High . . . I mean, Fair One."

Anlawdd squinted; apparently, strong vision was not a job requirement for seamstress-warrior-princesses. "Um, a bunch of people running around a building. Should I know them?" Suddenly she "got it" and gasped. "Oh my goodness! Cei and Bedwyr!"

"Tweedle-Dum and Tweedle-Dumber." Peter held his breath as Bedwyr fired another random arrow. The shot was answered by an arc of arrows and derisive laughter. Everybody missed; the Jutes were drunk, toying with the pair.

"You know," said Anlawdd thoughtfully, "I wouldn't want to sound overconfident, but I'd bet my auburn hair—not *red*, Cors Cant, please notice—that if we fell upon them screaming like *bean-sidhes,* we could cut the buggers to Jutelets before they even dropped their wine cups! I mean, if we all pulled an oar." She drew her knife, raised an eyebrow at Peter.

"Get stuffed," he responded.

"Well for goodness's sake, you can't let your own men be hedgehogged! It's like watching a kitten being run over by a cart wheel, and not lifting a finger to shout a warning! Oh, you know what I mean."

He shook his head. "Aren't my men anymore. Remember? They told *me* to get stuffed."

But the shade of Lancelot bulged from his mental prison, frantic at the sight of his best friends under siege. *The bitch speaks true,* he rattled, dry and furious inside Peter's skull. As if driven by the omnipresent Sicambrian, Peter edged closer to the railing.

The worst part is, Lancelot is right. Peter's petty-minded pouting was unprofessional. "Yes, yes," he sighed, "I know she's right."

"What?" Anlawdd looked confused.

My brothers! Can't let them die like Saxon dogs! Lancelot was still on the warpath, forcing an answer from Peter.

"Yes, blast it, I know I can't!" *Two fallback suspects . . . except they're innocent, for Medraut is Selly. And after I kill him, Cei and Bedwyr will cut me down—I'm about to rescue my murderers.*

"What? Um, not to be rude, Prince Lancelot, but . . . who in Hades are you *talking* to? It's maddening, like hearing every other verse of a song!"

Peter paused, one leg over the railing, fighting the mad urge simply to vault to the ground and charge, screaming (as Anlawdd suggested) like a banshee.

He forced himself to stop, study the diorama: five Jutes hovered directly opposite the window, three on the left flank, one on the right. Six had bows, all had axes or swords. Four Jutes clustered behind the stables, cutting off retreat. Behind the rear guard, two young boys held six horses.

"That's thirteen combatants and two transport specialists," reported Peter.

"Transport specials?" asked Anlawdd.

"Horse holders," said Peter, pointed at the boys. "They're vulnerable behind the lines. That's the key, but I'm not sure how."

"I'm sure I don't know what's so important about the horseboys," complained Anlawdd. "Our best chance is to sneak up behind those three on the left, to widen the battle line."

Cors Cant bowed his head. *Poor lad!* thought Peter. *How humiliating this must be, when the object of your crush is a better warrior than you are! Perhaps too much of a warrior.* "Anlawdd," he said aloud, "you're thinking like a warrior, not a soldier."

She waited, palpably resenting his dismissal. Peter continued. "Miss Princess, we don't fight just for sake of fighting. We fight to *win*. Nothing else matters. Nothing!"

With effort, she swallowed her retort, looking ready to burst from the pressure. "All right, Great Prince General Legate Lancelot. You're the boss . . . if we *don't* attack, and *don't* leave them to die, what *do* we do? Throw rotten eggs and tantrums?"

"Use your head, girl. What's worth more, two unknown

victims pinned down in a ruined stable, or six war-trained horses?"

"What?" She faced him fully, lips parted, completely lost. Peter felt a stir in his bowels, an unexpected leap of his heart. It was the hair, the green eyes, the pallid, Celtic skin framed by relentless waves, now red, now amber, now gold—an auburn mix, not a solid color.

Cors Cant's round face suddenly brightened like a full moon. "Horses!" he cried, breaking the spell. "We loose the horses, and the Jutes chase after them!" The wounded expression vanished; for once, Cors Cant had understood a strategy before Anlawdd.

"Wait, wait, wait," she begged. "I get the part about horses and Jutes, I mean I'm not stupid, I know how much horses cost. But if we start grappling with the horseboys, won't the soldiers pile atop us like dogs on a fox?"

Girl is right, puffed Lancelot, still lusting after Jutic gore. *What about it?*

Peter knew what to do. *Lord knows, I've done it before, myself and a four-man squad outside a "known" pub in Londonderry.* Slowly, he drew his knife, held it between them, blade pointed up. "Anlawdd," he whispered, "we don't grapple. We 'do' them. Quickly."

And so it starts all over again, droned the morality circuit, *just as it did in Gibraltar, Belfast, Londonderry, Armagh, Paris. The long, downward spiral begins with a single decision, always "forced" upon you. Begins with an end so important, the means become negotiable.*

Both Anlawdd and Cors Cant stood silent. The girl blinked, something in her eye. She shook her head slowly.

"You swore an oath," reminded Peter. "Said you'd never feel anything again." She took a step closer to Cors Cant, but did not reach out to him. The invisible wall still stood.

"What," continued Peter, "a warrior like you, worried about a couple of Jute boys? Look around! Look, what *used to be* your city!" He gestured savagely at burned ruins, deserted, crumbled apartments and stores.

A low blow. Anlawdd refused to look, lowered her gaze
to her boots. Peter held his breath.

Then she raised her knife level with Peter's, trembling
slightly. Cors Cant did not join them; he stood silent,
swathed in the big, fleecy robe with foxfur trim, lost and
betrayed by his goddess, daughter of a traitor.

"What's it to be," Anlawdd asked, "talk it, or do it?"

Peter crouched, vaulted the wooden rail to the rooftop
below.

(HAPTER 27

I KNOW IT'S DIFFICULT, BUT TRY TO PICTURE AN ENORMOUS
bear that hasn't missed a decent meal in years. Or a big
boulder with legs and arms, covered with hair like a
Barbary ape.

I don't wish to cast aspersions on our Sicambrian brothers; after all, the Master Builder himself is of the Languedoc! But Lancelot is not exactly lithe or svelte, though he
is graceful, in a barrel-ly sort of way. And hairy. I'm glad
That Boy isn't hairy.

So when he tried to vault lithely (or sveltely) over the
railing, he caught his boot on a wooden stake instead and
squawked and rolled down the dirt mound, much like the
great, hairy boulder I asked you to envision.

I jumped after him quick as I could, but his head start
proved insurmountable, like chasing a runway wagon
wheel down a hill or a dropped apple down a spiral stair.

I kept my feet beneath me for three steps, then took a
dive and slid face first the rest of the way down. It was
worse than falling off Merillwyn! I must have looked as if
I were diving off a cliff, for That Boy leapt after me with

a yowl. Honestly, he thinks I'm a clay figurine that might break at any moment! But I was too busy to stop and be properly furious.

Lancelot hopped to his feet once; a mistake, for momentum carried him back onto his face. I didn't even try—sliding was better than tumbling.

The general collided with a yellow house. I managed to strike his boot heel with my face, knocking myself silly. That Boy arrived a moment later, frantic after my health but afraid to touch me for fear of offending my princessness with his lowly bardic fingers.

Worse ... he thinks I'm a goddess now and touching me would be blasphemy. A slippery slope: figurine to princess to goddess. And traitor from a long, dishonorable line of traitors.

Mary's blood, but I'm glad Gormant's not my birth-father.

Lancelot stood, wavering like Myrddin in his wine cellar.

"Look," I asked him, "are you *sure* you're all right?"

"Of course um sure, never better," he lied and used both hands to uncross his eyes.

"Good," said I, and pointed out the obvious. "Here come the Jutes to remonstrate and petition."

I spoke bravely for the benefit of That too-Roman Boy. But in truth, I was ready to execute a very unroyal retreat, letting Cei and Bedwyr go to the Dark King. My "noble" bloodline showing through? Never liked the twins anyway—they called me "girl" and thought I'd look better with pot and pan than axe and sword.

For a moment, the nearest Jute stared as if we'd sprouted from the ground like mushrooms. Then he recovered, shouted, and ran toward us, followed by a chum.

(An arrow arced over my head—I ducked about a day after it went by, feeling very much like the sheepish "girl" those two blackguards had called me. I tell you this only to keep the record perfectly complete.)

Lancelot bounced to his feet like a coiled spring, cool as

a well-trained hunting dog facing a bear, or in this case, two heavily armed Jutes.

But the original plan still struck me as best, so I turned and bolted for the horsekids.

It was a hundred strides to the horses, and my mind outraced my feet. Could I truly knife a pair of boys not yet twenty, only slightly older than I? I tried to rally my resolve, but the only thing that rose was my gorge.

Drunken soldiers were bad enough, but they *were* menat-arms; and what they had done to beloved Harlech! But these children?

Halfway to the boys, I crouched low, hid behind a light grey pony. *I'll frighten them off, but that's the worst,* I thought, *and that's final. If Lancelot wants to dagger them ... well, he'll have to catch them himself.*

I spared a quick glance back to make sure That Boy was safe.

He was rooted to the spot, as if Zeus had turned him into a rowan tree. He stared at the Jutes, then at Lance, then me, indecisive ... well, when we're together finally, I'll fix that. Maybe I'll mold him.

He wanted to move, it was clear. But every choice looked wrong! I became a statue myself, transfixed, as if he were Medusa and I were caught without my handy, mirrored shield. "Cors Cant!" I called, none too loud, frantically gestured him my way.

He stared at me. He ought to have sprinted up behind me, being a bard and not a warrior.

Instead, he balled his fists and stood defenseless next to the prince.

I cried in anguish. There was nothing I could do—I could never get back in time! My only choice was to carry on.

I bent double, pumped my knees up, and outraced any good Arabian stallion and half a hundred native ponies. *Please, Mother,* I prayed, *Let them value horses more than hides!*

(Not that I particularly cared what happened to That Boy, you understand. He means nothing to me. I snap my fingers at him. But it would be a shame for such a young boy to lose his life in a foolish display of typically male *fortitudo falsus.* You see, I only wish this record to be thoroughly accurate.)

I became Macha Herself, or the whole triple battle goddess, or a Gorgon, as I charged directly at the boys, fashionable black mud and white gravel in my hair, screaming like a demon from Anwfyn!

The first kid staggered back, blue eyes big as millstones, and I swear by the Blood Royal his straw hair turned bone white, curled like white coral, and he shuddered and twitched for the rest of his days. He flung himself to the ground, hands over neck, and naturally dropped his line of ponies. They took the opportunity to exercise their liberty.

But the second lad was granite compared to soapstone, even a little attractive, if you don't mind hair like a wheat field. He braced his shoulder, took my charge like a man.

Alas, being a woman has *some* disadvantages, for example, giving up fifty pounds to the next fellow. I'm not my Aunt Gwenabwy, who, I swear, lifts cows over pasture fences and picks up the house by actually picking up the house.

I caromed off the horseboy like a potato off a stone statue, but managed to hook an arm around his waist. I ended behind him, gripping him about his midriff.

I planted my insteps against his heels and yanked. We went over like a row of shields when you're trying to be quiet sneaking home at night, but you drop the first one and it knocks down the next ten or twelve.

I locked my arms and legs around his body—not much else I could do from beneath him—and grabbed for the only thing that was sticking out.

If he hadn't been in such pain, he'd have gotten the romantic thrill of his young life. He screamed some barbarous curse, while I whooped and hollered and tried to make life miserable for the stupidly placid horses. But they munched weeds contentedly, unconcerned about two lunatics thrashing in mortal combat around their hooves.

For an instant, the tangle parted and I caught a quick

glimpse of the other melee. The Jutes stood wary, obviously recognizing Lancelot. They shouted threats and brandished swords; Lancelot roared in response, shaking his fists. I thought of my cousins Bradwen and Sian, who used to have pissing contests and insisted I judge them.

That Boy stood behind the prince, which showed at least some intelligence. But both had completely forgotten about the horses. Honestly!

"Cors Cant Ewin," I bellowed, "remember the plan! Help me! Spook the horses!"

Ho! I may as well have shouted into the oven for all the good it did. Then my wrestling partner squirmed and I lost sight of That Boy.

With a shout, Cei and Bedwyr finally joined the fray as light dawned on marblehead. Two marbleheads. I could hear their battle cries but couldn't see them. I heard the four Jutes behind me, and the brothers engaged them thirstily. Bedwyr especially plunged into the fray, and his exultant cries were probably heard in Londinium.

But that still left a batch of unaccounted Jutes. Unable to disengage, I rolled my prisoner onto his face to at least look around. I finally spotted them—a huge tangle stood and *watched* the fight, like a gladiatorial combat!

Arrogance, smugness! I was amazed, but never so grateful. They refused to dishonor their fellow Jutes by ganging up!

Having located my targets between the boy's legs, I gripped them with a firmness generally reserved for cracking walnuts or juicing cherries, while the horses romped, nickered, and brazenly stuck close to see the final decision. I think they placed bets. I kicked at a stallion, missing by five leagues.

Like stones from a ballista, Cei and Bedwyr stumbled upon us, writhing on the ground. We were immediately joined by a stench of Jutes. And *finally,* Cei (bless his shrewd if treacherous heart!) realized the point of our brilliant plan.

He shoved Bedwyr forward, shouted, "Hold the bastards," and prodded the lead horse in the arse with his axe tip.

I assure you with all solemnity, I had never credited That Boy's account of Pegasus until that moment, since never before had I seen a horse fly. But this bayard, a full-sized draft horse, levitated twelve or fifteen feet without benefit of Myrddin's magic, rotated in midair, and headed back toward Wessex with all deliberate speed, o'erleaping a small building that blocked his way.

The other equines, in a burst of Athenian democracy, voted unanimously to follow. They packed their hooves and followed the bay blur.

For several moments, none of those silly Jutes realized what had happened, and I thought Lancelot's plan had gone bust.

The eight spectators were first to wake up. They shouted in surprise, turned and argued, turned back, called bootlessly (or fruitlessly) after the vanishing mounts.

Then as one entity, they sprinted after the horses, leaving their proud comrades locked in mortal combat with Lancelot, Cei, and Bedwyr.

Four Jutes realized the hopeless nature of Fortuna. They faked a charge, spun and bolted after their chums, quite fleet of foot considering their ungainly Jutic bodies.

The field grew silent. Only two Jutes were left, thrusting long, sharp, full-sized swords at—at That Boy. And at Lancelot.

I let go of my handle, rolled the lad off; he had lost all enthusiasm and willingly complied. Exhausted, I approached the ridiculous fight warily. The tableau was absurd, but whenever people brandish sharp weapons, there can be accidents.

Please Lady, I prayed, aware I was praying an awful lot this day, *I don't want to cradle That Boy's head in my arms as he bleeds to death on the streets of Harlech.*

"Ho," I interrupted, but was ignored. "You! Anybody home?"

"Anlawdd!" shouted That Boy. "Stay back!" His face white as snow, he held a wooden club he'd found, a tree branch. It rested far less comfortably in hand than the old harp he had stupidly lost.

Very resourceful, I thought. True, not much of a weapon: but like a pony that throws a caber, you don't care that he does it well—you're amazed he can do it at all!

"Cors Cant Ewin, don't you speak to me like that!" I responded, just so he would know I was happy to see him alive. I stamped my foot for good measure, and to distract everyone. "Anyway, I'm not speaking to you. I'm talking to those two fish-headed Jutes." I took a deep breath and spoke in command tone, as Merovius taught. The voice came from deep within me, but outside me as well, the Voice of God. I spoke in Saxon, near enough Jutish, I supposed.

"STOP AND LOOK AT ME."

I had their complete attention. *Great,* I thought, *now you'd better think up something interesting to say. . . .*

The Jutes surveyed the situation, for the first time realized the changed dynamics.

"Do you notice," I continued, "a sudden feeling of loneliness and desertion, like goslings left behind by an impatient mother duck?" Goose, whatever. I was excited. Battle lust, I'm sure.

As illumination dawned, the Jutes shrank together, swords out in all directions at once.

Cei grinned, stepped forward to finish the job, but Lancelot stopped him, a noble gesture that just goes to prove you never have someone as tightly versed as you think. "Cei," he commanded, "I don't think there's any call to . . ."

The porter of Camlann was not pleased with his general's transformation. Cei glared at Lancelot like a hunting dog whose master won't slip the leash. After a moment, Cei backed down, unwilling to challenge the champion. Just then, anyway.

But I marked Cei's eyes, knew Lancelot would soon be betrayed—and Artus too. I guess my—I guess Gormant and I are not the only traitors in Prydein. Cei turned back to the terrified Jutes, dismissed them savagely.

They stood not upon the order of their going, but departed nearly as fast as the horses. Upon the instant, we were alone with victory.

Victory? I didn't feel victorious. The horseboy still sobbed at my feet, hands clenched between his legs. At once, I felt sick, queer, as if something were falling out of me.

Falling, dripping, pouring. Sudden panic—did I miscount my days? I couldn't have: fullish moon tonight meant my time was still nearly two weeks away. I'm always so careful.

All the feelings were there, but I didn't know why. Blood loss, it felt—huge pieces falling from my body. I couldn't think what to do!

I mumbled an excuse, heart pounding (they didn't even notice, brainless men don't even think what it means to be a woman). Then I walked, out of sight behind the remains of the stables.

Almost running when I cleared the wall. Cheeks wet, chest tight as a drum, I thought my whole insides were sliding out between my legs. Felt sick and faint.

But when I hiked my tunic up and stuck my finger down there, and it came out dry. No blood. Of course. Fullish moon.

What is it? What is happening?

Then I remembered the betrayer, his sunken, hollow eyes. Both then, when he made the deal with the Dark King, and now, when he saw how he, himself, was betrayed to death. Was that me? Or Father?

I sank to my knees, wrapped my arms around me. He looked me right in the face and denied me, Peter that he was. Was I truly my father's daughter?

Harlech hadn't gone anywhere, not truly. Here it was, here I was.

A few buildings were gone, some people fled or dead. But here the capital was: palace, stadium, baths, fountains, even though no water ran and the baths were cold.

I was stunned that I had told Lancelot, even before I could confess it to Merovee. My second betrayal was the greater . . . when I tried to signal my father's men ashore, tell them I rejected the charge to murder Artus, tell them my brother Canastyr was dead, it was instead received by the bloody Saxons, or Jutes, rather, who already infested the town.

I felt horrible, like telling my girlfriend about a tryst with a new lover and discovering he's her husband.

I sobbed, heart in my throat, breaking my oath to Lancelot. I strained as my mother must have done to bring me into this stupid world. Nothing good came from either endeavor, for my eyes were dry and I've accomplished exactly nothing in my entire seventeen years. Half my life it is, and I've nought to show but a lad who would build me a temple but not a home, sing me war songs but never love songs.

And a traitor for a father, and a coward for my reflection in the glass. Maybe it's a lucky throw that he denied me, after all.

Another debating point struck me then: it's immortality That Boy's after having, through his songs, same as me joining the Builders, and sure but they'll both live long beyond our own deaths, songs and Builders, I mean. Are we both cheating Her, or does She laugh and reap at once?

Harlech is alive, I can see it. It will recover. But at the same time, it's dead, like Leary tells me the Godless are alive and dead at one and the same time.

It's not the marauding Jutes. We've been taken so many times they may as well use chalk instead of ink when they draw Harlech on the map!

I never understood when I lived in Harlech, but Camlann taught me. Merovee, Artus, That Boy, even Lancelot showed me how much we have lost. To them, each loss seems a gain. But I *know.*

We once were warriors; now we are *soldiers.* Once we had a King's Council; now our senate levies *tribute.* Greeks, Jews, Druids, even women and princesses used to debate philosophy on the Old Hall steps: Speak in turn, hear the truth! Now we squabble before Gormant, who betrays his *Dux Bellorum*—why not? All honor is relative!—

and can't even recognize his own children. Grandpapa governed; father merely *administers*.

What's that Builder ritual?

> *One generation passes*
> *And another comes,*
> *But earth abides forever.*

Another generation whispered suddenly, like a courtesan from the temple door. *But you know it does not,* said the seditious seducer, *for have you not felt your soul, sure as the cobbles that cut your feet, sharp and hard?*

The Fool-Killer: I know Her well. She drove me up and down to heights and depths, always ready to spur me like you spur a reluctant pony who refuses to jump a wall.

You may die, but you will yet live, just like the Godly of Merovee. For it is there—you touched it, that soul! Saw it, felt it, took it out of the box and turned it in the sunlight. That's what it means to be a Builder!

"The true gift of Merovee," I said, "what a Builder builds. That's my love present to you, Cors Cant Ewin—if ever you'll just take it."

Footsteps crunched on the crumbled, broken road. I stood quickly, but it was only That Roman Boy, hair like a wild horse's mane, fiery in sunrise.

I turned away. Dry cheeks or no, my eyes must have looked a fright. The fear was gone; I wasn't losing pieces or even bleeding. But I still felt dead inside. *Good thing he doesn't expect love,* I thought, because today he'd not get any, even if he normally did.

But faith, I wish he *did* simply offer love. That's all he'd have to do—one honest offering of love, and I'd throw myself at his feet, his to do with as he would! But I'm damned if I'll give myself to animal lust, divine awe, or "proper civilization."

"Are you safe, An—Your Grace?" he asked, looking through me so hard I felt it even with my back turned. The words sent shivers. Sometimes he knows more than any boy should! Those bard eyes look too deep for anyone's good. But grace was what I needed now, being damned like those coves in Hades, stooping to take a drink, only to have the boulder roll down the hill again.

"Harlech," I started, but faded into silence. I wasn't sure what to say, like waking up from a wonderful dream of flowers and rainbow fish, only to find the colors washed to grey and your boots too tight.

Besides, there was my promise to Lancelot. *Holy Apostle Mary, hold me now. Don't let loss sneak sorrow into my voice. I shan't feel anything ever again, even with That Boy still alive.*

He must have felt it himself then, death pressed around us like a blanket tucked too tight.

I had no right to cry. Harlech died a long time ago, before I was even ten years old, when the last, bright dragon ship sailed off to Cardiff, declaring Harlech the stuff of Rome—a dream our grandmamas told.

I heard a strange sound, turned back toward Cors Cant. He knelt before me, head bowed.

Stupid Boy! What new grief was this? "I suggest you climb back up to both feet like a bard, Cors Cant Ewin, that is if you still entertain any thoughts about winning me."

I pushed him back toward the men, toward Lancelot, Cei, and eventually Merovee and a boat home. God of true creation, how I longed to see Camlann again and forget this homeless place ever existed.

Just then, a sudden thud made me jump. We all stared as Lancelot collapsed like an armload of wet linen. I rushed to his side as soon as I touched ground again, but Cei beat me.

"Lord!" he cried, stricken. So they still meant something to each other, even after all the tensions and conflicts. The prince writhed like a snake, arms wrapped around his head.

"Too tight," he gasped, voice like a leather rope stretched way too thin.

Cors Cant grabbed my hand, and I squeezed as tight as

I could. *You stupid boy, why can't you just hold me in your arms?*

Poor Lancelot screamed in pain, as an invisible knife cut the taut strands of his soul.

CHAPTER 28

"OH CHRIST, MITHRAS. . . ." CORS CANT CRADLED LANCElot's head, checked for a pulse—nothing. The bard put his ear to the prince's mouth—not a breath stirred. "He's dead," announced the bard, astonished.

Cors Cant looked up, first to Anlawdd, then Cei, then Bedwyr. All wore masks of stone.

The porter stooped, brushed Cors Cant's hand aside and felt Lancelot's throat himself. "Kid's right," he declared. Anlawdd took the next turn, listening for a heartbeat.

"What is this?" demanded the bard. "A surgeon's convention? Didn't you all believe me? I can take a pulse as well as the next man."

Still no one grieved. Cei glanced significantly at his brother; Anlawdd unconsciously rubbed her fingers between her breasts.

"Well, what in Macha's name do we do with the body?" asked Cors Cant.

"Leave it," suggested Cei. Bedwyr grunted agreement.

Anlawdd shook her head. "We've got to haul him back. Owe him at least that, whatever our private disagreements. He died in the line of duty, for the *Dux Bellorum.*"

"There is that," agreed the porter, reluctantly.

"Artus would be furious if we dumped him," added Bedwyr.

"That, too." Cei sounded distant.

Cors Cant stepped away, across the broken cobbles, a peculiar dread squeezing his lungs. *Gods, he just dropped dead, right in front of us, and no one cares!* The bard realized his own spirit had drifted again, was viewing the scene from an arm's length directly over his own head. Superimposed on the sunlit street, the five-person tableau, the crowd of curious onlookers pressing close was the crypt of his vision aboard the *Blodewwedd:* the covered body, slain by the most beloved.

Did the prince die at Anlawdd's ill-timed revelation?

"No," whispered Cors Cant, "this is not he. This is not meant to be." Detached, he pulled on puppet strings, moved his dislocated body forward in jerky, artificial motions. As it approached Lancelot's body, Cei and Bedwyr stared, crowded away as if they sensed the supernatural hollowness of Cors Cant's empty body. Anlawdd watched, mouth open; but she did not run. Instead, her eyes searched the air above the bard's flesh, centered on the space occupied by his spirit. She squinted, trying to focus.

Cors Cant stretched his fingers, watched his body's hands reach out, touch Lancelot on chest and brow. Letting his eyes unfocus, the bard saw a slim, silver thread stretching from the prince's mouth into . . . he could not see the other end, or even where it pointed, as if Lancelot's shade had fled somewhere not of this world.

The cord was tight, pulled to the breaking point.

Ignoring the misty, blurred humans, Cors Cant reached out, took hold of the cord, and climbed hand over hand. Lancelot's soul-cord led into a tunnel that grew narrower with height. *A funnel-tunnel,* he thought.

From now on we're your only friends. . . .

The bard climbed and climbed, squeezing his soul tighter and tighter. At last, as in the underground chamber where he found the sarcophagus, he could climb no farther. He was stuck, leagues and leagues of Lancelot's soulstuff still above him.

What to do, what to do? Cors Cant was frantic, knowing he had to make a decision, not knowing which was right. *I can't do it—I'm only a boy!*

"No," said a voice. "You have all four suits of the tarot. You are a man, and this is a man's decision." Cors Cant realized the voice was his own.

He fought paralyzing dread with the coin of valor, drew the sword of reason with his right hand. "You can only go up or down, my Prince. I don't know which you'd prefer—but your destiny is not to die yet. You have a task, I'm sure of it, as sure as I have my own.

"We need you yet, Prince. Come back down with me." Reaching up as high as he could, Cors Cant cut the silver cord with his phantom sword.

The bard dropped, lost the sword, the cord, even up and down. In a moment, he landed with a sickening lurch inside his own body, which fell across Lancelot's.

Dazed, he rose to his knees. The prince gasped, turned his head, and coughed up a great blob of phlegm. Color flooded his cheeks, turning their pallor to beet red.

Cors Cant felt for Lancelot's pulse, but the legate shoved the bard's hand away from his throat. "I ... I guess you're back among the living, Sire," said the bard.

Cei, Bedwyr, even Anlawdd stared at Cors Cant in horror.

He stood, and the crowd scattered back several steps. His three companions stood their ground, but it was obvious they would have preferred to join the mob.

"Brass balls," said Bedwyr, "fucking bard's got the fucking *Touch.*"

"Sang raal," whispered Cei.

"The blood royal," Anlawdd translated.

Lancelot spoke up, annoyed. "What are you yammering about? What happened to me? Come on, let's get the bloody hell out—" He looked at Cei, scowled back at Cors Cant. "Look, what's all this, then? Why am I on the bloody deck?"

Anlawdd spoke quietly, a caricature of her normal self. "Boys, unless you want the Jutes to dine on brochette of Briton tonight, I'd suggest we follow Lancelot's suggestion and get the bloody hell out, if you'll pardon my using such language."

Cei and Bedwyr helped Lancelot to his feet, cringing a bit at the touch. The group hurried back toward the wall.

CHAPTER 29

IT TOOK MARK BLUNDELL FOUR TRIES, BUT HE FINALLY CON-fessed to Merovee that he had told Cutha the battle plan.

The king took the news well. In fact, he looked decid-edly chipper. "No harm, no blame, Medraut," he said. "I'm sure you tried as hard as you could."

Merovee's Cheshire Cat smile maddened Mark, who would have preferred any punishment, however terrible. *I let him down again. I let them all down, my mates.* He slunk to a dark tree shadow, buried his face and waited for the sudden knife thrust or arrow shot that would end his useless foray into the timestream.

Instead, the king gently touched his shoulder. "Time, Medraut. Get your men ready for the attack."

Merovee's hand comforted Mark. He looked up, a puppy who expects a rolled-up newspaper, and the king patted his head and hurried back to his men.

Mark rose and called the sergeant, Hir Amren, deter-mined to prove himself worthy of Merovee's redemption. "You have the plan?" Mark asked.

Hir Amren nodded curtly.

"Let's get the team together, then."

An hour later, nearly dawn, Mark led the diversionary company along a goat trail that he hoped would dump them out of the woods northeast of the Harlech docks. From there, they would feint, drawing the Jutes away from the ships, which Merovee's force would then seize, burn-ing all but the largest boat, a huge but clumsy, classically

Germanic galley. The other boats were sleeker, Roman vessels that had probably belonged to Harlech before the attack.

Merovee's "army" comprised nearly fifty men, of which the king assigned fourteen to Mark. Blundell's heart pounded faster than a lovestruck boy's until he saw that Hir Amren was among his men, would be his senior NCO.

As the platoon slunk through the chilly, misty forest, slipping as silently as armored men could slip from tree to bole, Mark kept getting a "phantom count" of thirty or thirty-five men. *Jesus,* he thought, *let's hope the same magnification illusion applies when the Jutes first see us.*

Mark's diversion squad would set the timing for the main attack; there was no need to coordinate. Merovee would wait until the Jutes responded to the perceived threat, then attack their rear guard.

If Mark were lucky, the Jutes would panic, turn, and allow Mark's squadron to fade back into the forest, joining the main force as reinforcements . . . and Mark Blundell would live long enough to find Major Smythe and break the news about—what happened to his body.

How do I tell him? What do I say? Whoops, Brother Smythe, we killed your body back in real time. 'Fraid you're stuck in King Arthur's court for the rest of your "life" in someone else's body.

Mark shook his head. It was going to be rough. There were no diplomatic words to grease the bearings. *I'm bringing him a death sentence. He can never come back home.*

A cold hand gripped Mark's shoulder. He almost yelped, stifled it in time.

"Legionnaires in position, Sire," whispered Hir Amren in his ear.

"Great. Now what?"

"Well, far be it from me to suggest tactics to an officer, but . . ."

"Yes?"

"Well, Sire, I wouldn't want to overstep my position. However . . ."

"Spit it out, damn you!" Mark saw the sergeant major smile, barely visible in the dim light. *The old sod enjoys making me crawl. And thank God for that.*

"I'd suggest, Prince-captain, that we wait until the sun tops those mountains in the east, then attack out of the glare. Might serve to confuse the enemy about our, ah, tiny numbers."

Mark nodded sagely.

Dawn came late in the shadow of what would someday be the Cader Idris mountain range. Mark waited impatiently, at last saw an instant of green followed by the burning sun, which quickly grew too bright to watch.

"Now?" he asked Hir Amren.

"Momentarily, Sire; let it fully rise." The sergeant major crouched, frozen in time. At last he hissed in Mark's ear: "Now, Sire!"

"Now," parroted Mark.

"Now!" cried Hir Amren, full-voiced with the official attack order.

The roar of a mob erupted all around Blundell, far more than fourteen throats. Shapes rose around him, more than twice the number that had been selected for the diversionary squadron. *I'm going mad!* he thought, stumbling after his men to lead them into battle.

Half the men charged down the hill, sprinted across a graded field, and engaged a large army of Jutes halfway toward the docks; the nonexistent other half of Blundell's men advanced in a crouch, using the charging first wave as concealment for their own maneuvers.

Mark pelted past the skulkers, catching up with the first group. *What the hell's happening? It's all bollixed, they sent too many of us!*

Worst of all, the Jutes did not respond as advertised. Rather than charge to meet the unexpected foe, they retreated and formed a shield wall. More than half their men drifted backward, toward the direction from which Merovee's men—what few he had kept—must attack. The Jutes looked over their shoulders, directly back at Merovee's position, as if watching for him.

"God in Heaven," shouted Mark to Hir Amren, as they maintained close contact with the front line, "that bastard Cutha did it again! He spilled our plan to the enemy!"

"I hope to Mithras you're right," said the old sergeant major, grinning cryptically.

The front fifteen of Mark's men drove forward, pushing back the much superior Jutic forces. It was too easy, as if the Jutes deliberately allowed themselves to be herded. They continually reinforced their rear, pulling men from the front line.

"Where the bloody hell is Merovee?" demanded Mark. At almost the same instant, he heard the wail of bagpipes, saw the silver-and-white figure of the king himself emerge from the forest . . . exactly where the Jutes were strongest.

Astounded, Mark realized that the king was surrounded by no more than ten of his Sicambrian guards.

The whoop from the Jutes chilled Mark's marrow, sounded as he had always imagined the "Rebel Yell" of the Confederates in the American Civil War. Nearly the entire Jutic army disengaged the diversionary force and ran full tilt toward the real attack, completely unfooled.

"We're dead men," said Mark, voice cold and emotionless. "They didn't buy it."

"The pig-fuckers bought every last yard of it, Sire. *Charge!*"

Hir Amren gestured savagely forward, and the entire reserve force rose from the mists, joining the forward squadron. The company, now at full strength, exploded after the Jutes. They crashed against the token line the Jutes had left, swept across it without breaking or slowing, finally impacted the rear of the main Jutic force.

The enemy were stubborn, refused to believe they had been bamboozled. They continued to chase after Merovee and his honor guard, who retreated toward the docks as fast as the Jutes advanced. More than half the Jutic army was cut down from behind before they realized their terrible mistake, tried to turn to meet the real threat.

Mark was left floundering in his own unit's wake, struggling to catch up to Hir Amren, who Mark now realized, was the real commanding officer. The advantage, Blundell realized ruefully, was that at least he did not have to chop anyone with his axe—a prospect he had dreaded. Neither did anyone get the chance to chop him.

When the Jutes finally turned to make their last stand, they must have fully appreciated their folly in trusting the word of a Saxon spy. Crowded onto the pontoon jetty, unable to keep their feet as the tramping men and surging sea caused the wharf to shimmy and roll, they were killed almost in single file, unable even to form a line. It was butchery, and after a few moments, the sight worked past Mark's practiced objectivity and nauseated him. He tried to pretend it was nought but a movie—they were all dead and buried fifteen centuries ago, Jute and Briton alike!— but he could not. The scene was too visceral.

No Jute surrendered, none taken prisoner. They were all killed or driven into the sea, where they either drowned or straggled back to the beach to run away. Mark was caught in the middle of his troops, swept by the irresistible tide aboard the largest galley. The men did not stop, hopped over the gunwales to the smaller, Roman *trireme*.

Looking back, Mark saw Hir Amren still on the bigger ship, directing a small group to start fires at strategic points along the deck. *Bloody hell, even that was a lie!* thought Blundell. *We're taking the smaller, faster boat, not the man-o'-war.*

Men caught his elbows, gently urged him forward over the next set of gunwales onto the outside boat. "Come, Sire," said a man Mark recognized as one of Merovee's Sicambrians, "we must to cast off, it is to get away quickly recommended."

Hir Amren's fire brigade retreated to the second boat and fired it as well. Mark backed away from the flames, against the outside railing. Suddenly, a hand clutched his ankle, and he yelped.

From the seaward side, a dozen men swarmed up the hull, flopped over the railing onto the deck. They wore no armor, were dressed in the loose-fitting rags that had marked sailors from the beginning of time. Joining them were Merovee, his unarmored honor guard and good old Cutha and the Saxons, all of whom had apparently dived into the ocean and swum to the boat, bypassing the Jutes altogether.

"Rowmen, tae your posts!" bellowed an old, fat sailor who looked every yard a ship's captain, rags or no. "Make free the lines, gi' me speed and sea room on this beast!"

A blow from behind staggered Mark. Merovee clapped him on the back. "Brilliantly executed, Medraut! I could not have planned it better myself, Brother!" The king smiled, winked, as the rest of the men congratulated Mark on his crafty battle plan.

The *trireme* lurched and rolled as the leeward oarsmen pushed her away from the blazing galleys.

CHAPTER 30

*T*HE HELL? PETER PONDERED. WHAT HAPPENED TO ME? *Must have been a cock-up at the—at the* . . . The words would not form in his head. He remembered a windowless room, a glowing engine, a deadly woman.

Sell—Selly! Selly Corwin. A cock-up in the lab, Blundell, Willks, the whole crew. Mother Mary, something's happening to my mind; can't remember the simplest things. He shuddered, frightened by the thought of being "lost in time" in A.D. 450, real memory gone, unable to stand firm against invasion by the Lancelot-mind.

The only saving grace was that, according to Willks and Blundell, the absolute worst that could happen, if Peter lost the struggle and was cast out of Lancelot's mind, was that he would fall back into his own body fifteen centuries into the future. *Then all I need do is try again, and again if necessary.*

Not like Londonderry; not like Gunnery Sergeant Conway.

Cei tugged at his elbow. "Prince," he said, his voice particularly insolent, "we're to just abandon Gormant, rightful ruler of Harlech, to his fate?"

"Well, that is . . ." Peter had no chance to formulate a diplomatic response, for Anlawdd interrupted.

"Leave the bastard. He betrayed us." Her face looked so pale, grim, yet so vulnerable that had Cors Cant not been standing right beside her, Peter might have slipped his arm around her shoulders. He almost did anyway, but realized it would have been a deliberate attempt to hurt the boy— pay him back a little for the deaths his bloody "honor" had cost.

Cei did not take the accusations well, but he said nothing. Peter's long experience warned him that the concatenation of recent circumstances were too much for the porter. Betrayal, scuttling, battle, and murder, sometime in the past twenty-four hours, Cei and presumably Bedwyr had "crossed over." Artus's carefully wrought alliance was breaking up . . . and in some measure, every event was Peter's fault.

It's Derry all over again. I mean Londonderry! I've balled up another assignment.

Peter closed his eyes. It had been a good career, all told, but perhaps time had come to retire. Too many mistakes, too much blood, too many friends blown apart on cold, Provie streets.

He smiled, felt a weight he had never noticed before lift from his shoulders. *That's it, as soon as this assignment is history, so am I. To hell with Colonel Crapper, and the SAS can stuff it up their royal backside.*

> Come all you young rebels,
> And list' while I sing;
> For the love of one's country
> Is a terrible thing.

Fuck all of them, the royal, bloody bastards. Medraut is Selly Corwin? Fine, he dies on the ship tonight. Bugger Artus and Blundell and Cors Bloody Cant Ewin and bugger that royal seamstress butcher, all in a bunch!

> *It banishes fear with*
> *The speed of a flame,*
> *And makes us all part of*
> *The Patriot Game.*

Peter led his assassins into a hard run up the mound-wall, which sloped gently enough to facilitate easy manning of the scaffold. A small mob of Jutes charged toward them, but as the team set and prepared for battle, the Jutes dodged past them toward the gate, apparently intent upon another battle, another war.

"Play your patriot games, you bastards!" yelled Peter after them. He continued more quietly. "Maybe you'll win in the long run—trouble is, in the long run, everyone dies."

"A harsh sentiment, my Prince, like not leaving on a trip because in the long run you're just going to come home again."

"Everyone does die, Anlawdd."

"But what a glorious trip we can make in the meanwhile."

Peter furrowed his brows at the girl. "Are you going back on your vow? I hear a distinct note of caring in your voice."

She looked back toward Harlech, calmer than she had been since they first realized the city was razed. The wind whipped auburn tresses across her face, made her head look like a burning tree. "My soul has been restored, Lancelot. I thought it was ripped away from me, like a child from his mother. But now I know it never can be, it's always attached, like my shadow. I'm not afraid of truth anymore, Lance; not even about me. I think that's what Merovee is always on about."

She looked into Peter's eyes, and he felt his groin stir.

She's grown. Not a little girl anymore. He smiled, noticed she had dropped the honorific from his name. *And why not? She's a bleedin' princess, like every other person here. Or at least, she thinks she is, which is good enough for me.*

Suddenly, Anlawdd's beauty compelled Peter almost as much as Gwynhwfyr's. *They both "understand"; that's what it is. They* see *themselves, and I'm still groping for my own mirror.*

"Speaking of Merovee," said Cors Cant, pointing westward, toward the docks. Peter jumped; he had nearly forgotten that anyone besides himself and Anlawdd was present.

Two vessels were merrily in flames, while a third frantically rowed southward. Deep in the harbor, a fourth galley moved to intercept the escaping craft.

"Gods," whispered Anlawdd. "Is one of those the king?"

"I'd say so," said Cei, squinting and tilting his head back. "See the fleeing *trireme?* She flies Merovee's colors."

"Bollocks," said Cei's brother; but Peter saw it too: a white-and-silver pennant, undoubtedly improvised from Merovee's tabard.

"Move!" commanded Peter, shoving Cors Cant toward the edge of the wall. "Over the side, drop to the ground! If we're going to get the bloody hell out of this bleeding place, that's our swan."

CHAPTER 31

HE CAN'T BE PETER, THOUGHT MARK BLUNDELL, STARING at King Merovee. *He's too much a part of this world—the men know him, you can't fake that.*

The Roman *trireme* lurched, skipped a trough, and slapped hard against the next wave, hurling Mark to his knees. Most of the battle-weary soldiers lay flat on the deck, desperately clutching any mast, stanchion, any ratline they could reach. The sailors danced barefoot about the deckplanks, never pausing long enough to lose their balance. Captain Naw bellowed them fore and aft, getting the feel of his new vessel.

At the stern Merovee stood wrapped in his cloak, staring at the pursuing Jutic galley. With more oarsmen, the Jutes gained, would overtake in a few minutes.

The king stood tall, doomed as Siegfried, faint, sardonic smile chiseled in his face. Mark shuddered, could not look away. Merovee stood taller than a man, colder than stone.

Freezing wind whipped the sails, which luffed ineffectually while the crew struggled them into place; the *trireme* slowed again, waves of bitter, cold salt water washing her decks.

Mark took a lungful of seawater as the spray caught him in the face. He choked, gripped a spar tighter.

"Give me speed," said Merovee, quiet voice cutting across wind's howl and seafoam scream. "I need more speed."

The captain shouted something, but the wind swallowed his words. The crew knew what to do anyway. The steersman leaned against the tiller, the few oarsmen below strained against their timber, and the galley bore closer to the wind. The sails caught like an airplane wing, and the *Sacred Blood,* newly named, shot forward.

Yet the Jutes gained still, for their sails were larger, their oarbanks full of men who had not swum a quarter mile through heavy surf or fought a battle on the docks.

Now the enemy galley was close enough to see the soldiers crowding the deck, nearly close enough for the Jutes to fire a shot at the *Sacred Blood.*

Merovee reached out a hand, gently touched Naw's sleeve. The men huddled, and when they separated, the captain's face was white. He swallowed, nodded. "Aye, me lord," he said, bluster entirely lost from his voice.

"But not yet," clarified the king. He held up his hand, as if ready to drop the starter's flag.

The crew froze, waited for an order. Nothing could be done until Captain Naw spoke. The Jute closed from four o'clock position.

The first catapult shot missed the *Sacred Blood* astern, but the Jutic gunner learned from his mistake: the next shot lacerated the topsail, partially fraying the mainstay. Had the shot actually cut the mainstay, the mainmast would have collapsed, bringing the *Sacred Blood* to a quick halt.

Merovee stared at the Jutes, raised his hand higher. He bowed his head, watched the deck . . . then sliced his hand down decisively.

"Hard tae starboard!" shouted Naw. The helmsman threw the tiller to the left, and the ship veered right, wallowed for a moment. "Now pull, ye bastards!" yelled the captain down the groove to the oarsmen.

In a moment, the crew adjusted the sails to the new bearing, while the oars bit deeply into the churning ocean.

If the Jutic captain held his course or turned to port, the two ships would pull almost directly apart from one another; by the time the Jutes turned 180 degrees about, the *Sacred Blood* would be a mile away.

But if the Jutic captain cut too sharply starboard, his top-heavy galley would capsize.

His only option was to cut an open, loose curve to starboard and pray he crossed in front of the *Sacred Blood.*

For one moment, however, the Jutes would be exposed, Captain Naw at their eight o'clock, picking up speed.

The Jutic captain was good; he reacted almost immediately. But fast though his giant galley was, it could not maneuver like the smaller *trireme.*

The *Sacred Blood* was light, her maneuver planned, her crew in the gravest extreme of desperation. Mark tried to close his eyes, but a force within compelled him to watch as death loomed.

The two galleys crisscrossed, and now it was the *Sacred Blood* that bore down upon the Jutes from their eight o'clock. "Come now," urged Naw, "just a wee, tiny faster . . . *got 'em!*"

The *Blood* hit a wave, jumped, skipped across the next crest, then shuddered and exploded as the metal-bound ram bit deep into the stern of the larger galley.

The *trireme* rolled hard to starboard, dipped her planks below the waterline. Men were swept off the deck, cast into the boiling water. Mark ground his teeth in agony at the horrible screech of ripping metal, splintering wood. The shock tore the railing from his grasp, flung him across the deck like a billiard ball.

He crashed against the mainmast, caught hold, and stayed with the ship. His head still rang from the horrific thundersound of the collision, but at last he could focus his eyes again.

The *Sacred Blood* and the Jutes parted company. Miraculously, the Roman *trireme* had suffered only minor damage, having perfectly rammed the enemy vessel.

The Jutic galley was not so lucky. Her entire stern, rudder and all, was sheared from the rest of the vessel, and she shipped badly astern. As Mark watched in horrified fascination, the galley groaned, rolled onto her side, capsized in exaggerated slow motion.

Nobody cheered. The *Sacred Blood* loosed her sails, shipped her oars, and drifted to an eerily silent halt. Sicambrians and Britons alike watched the armored Jutic soldiers tread water for a few moments, then sink one by one as their strength gave out.

Some of the enemy sailors caught hold of floating spars and splinters. They, too, silently watched the *Sacred Blood*, watched King Merovee, certain they would receive swift, merciless judgment.

"Lower a boat," said the king. "Pick up those of our men who fell overboard."

"Aye, me lord. An' what of *them?*" Naw indicated the Jutes.

Merovee shrugged, turned away.

Collecting the three Sicambrians and two Britons who were still alive took the better part of an hour, by Mark's estimate. At last, the *Sacred Blood* pulled away from the wreck of the Jutic galley. The enemy sailors still floated in the water, too frightened to make for the shore, too proud to beg for their rescue.

"Put to about a league south the wreck," ordered the king, "and let us wait there for Lancelot and his men. Pray God and His Son that they are all right, and let us give thanks for our fortune in battle."

King Merovee knelt, led the soldiers and crew in a long prayer of thanksgiving for their salvation. Then the oarsmen were sent to the cabin to rest, and the *Sacred Blood* continued toward her hoped-for rendezvous on wind power alone.

CHAPTER 32

PETER LED THE STRIKE TEAM ALONG THE BEACH, A SENSE OF urgency spurring him into a jog-trot that left both the bard and Anlawdd gasping for air. Cei and his brother Bedwyr had no difficulty keeping up.

The company took but an hour to travel four or five miles in the rock-strewn sand. During this time, the *trireme* ventured close to shore. At last, Peter called a halt, then waved at the galley.

Merovee waved back, beckoned them into the ocean.

"Can anybody *not* swim?" Peter asked. Cors Cant, Anlawdd, Cei, and Bedwyr snuck peeks at each other, but no one wanted to admit not knowing how to swim. The bard looked quite nervous until Anlawdd squeezed his shoulder.

"We can all make it so far as the boat," she said. But Peter heard a slight temblor beneath her veneer of calm certainty.

"It's only a few hundred yards," he said. "You can probably get a third of the way out before your feet even leave the seafloor."

Cei volunteered to go first. Peter picked Bedwyr second, then Cors Cant and Anlawdd at the same time. Peter himself would follow last.

Cei dived into the water with gusto, Australian-crawled to the boat using picture-perfect side breathing. Bedwyr swam as powerfully as his brother, though not as cleanly.

Cors Cant set out in a determined dog paddle, his breathing hampered by the metal cylinder clamped in his teeth. He still refused to let Peter see the cylinder, and Smythe was unwilling to make a scene, at least until they were all aboard the ship.

Then, of course, Peter would have the pressing matter of the killing of Selly "Medraut" Corwin. That would have to wait until dark, however.

He entered the chilly water, breaststroked toward the boat. He caught up with Cors Cant and Anlawdd, stayed behind them in case she lost the lad. They all made the boat, though the bard seemed more tired than anyone.

As they reached the *trireme,* sailors reached down, hauled them over the gunwales onto the deck. Merovee met Peter, embraced him warmly. "My brother, you *are* a sight! Dry clothes, all five!" The king pounded Peter on the back and pumped his arm until Peter, embarrassed by the open affection, shooed Merovee away so he could change clothes (and plot the "hit").

The galley, appropriately called the *Sacred Blood,* crawled south toward the Severn, though at a much slower pace than the *Blodewwedd* had sailed north: fire and blood had taken a toll among the oarsmen.

Peter sat on a rail on the bridge-tower, brooding across the *Blood,* toward the fo'c'sle, where Cutha and his traitor Saxons sat in misery, looking as if they expected to be thrown to the sharks at any moment. *Betrayers,* thought Peter, *I hate them all. Selly, Cutha, Gormant, Cors Cant, and Anlawdd—even Cei and Bedwyr, in all probability. Should all be shot, all be hanged.* His eye roved, caught the autumn-haired seamstress–princess staring at him. Their eyes locked for a moment; then he quickly turned away, felt his face flush with shame. *Hang the lot of us. Of them.*

At least I can take care of one of you bastards. Peter scanned the visible deck, located Medraut "supervising" some sailors, whose jobs would be easier if the boy could just manage to find a railing and tumble over.

But how to do the bitch without destroying Lancelot's life? He would have to be careful, leave no evidence proving Lancelot guilty of Peter's murder of Selly Corwin.

But what about the real Medraut, buried beneath the Selly? Peter buried the thought. *Can't make an omelet without breaking a few eggs,* he thought.

Later, alone inside the aft (captain's) cabin, he wrote a brief note in his investigative log, the Day-Twelve entry. While writing, he blocked on no fewer than five words that should have been on the tip of his forebrain. By the time Peter finished the entry, his hand shook so violently he could barely read his own writing, and sweat soaked his forehead. His subjective past—objectively fifteen hundred years yet to come—his "real time" was slipping away from him so quickly he knew something was dreadfully wrong.

The slipping had been happening all along, but it shifted into high gear right after he collapsed back in Harlech, when his *Einsatzgruppe* swore that he had died for a few minutes. *My God, did something happen back in the "real time," something that is affecting my mind?* The thought shivered a chill up his spine.

Hurry, finish the assignment, let them pull me back. The sooner I'm back in my own body, the better.

The *Sacred Blood* pitched and rolled as it cut the ocean swells at an angle. Peter leaned back against the cabin wall, let the gentle rocking of the Roman *trireme* lull him to sleep. Time enough to wake when the sun set, and all good murderers came out to play.

Peter–Lancelot jerked awake. He blinked, realized he could not remember who he was, could not remember whether he was supposed to be Peter in Lancelot's body or vice versa. The two souls warred within his head, pushed and shoved each other down, vying for supremacy.

He gasped, gripped something hard, a table. *Table,* he thought, turned his gaze downward. *Deck—bulkhead—cabin door. . . .*

A murderous rage flooded Lancelot as he thought of Gormant the betrayer. *I will personally lead the expedition to cut off his head, bring it back to Camlann on a pole!* More traitors, Cei and Bedwyr. Artus's champion considered their strengths, decided to bide his time, quietly replace Cei's honor guard with Lancelot's own, picked men, men who would look away at the crucial moment. . . .

"GET OUT OF MY HEAD!" Peter screamed, shoved hands against his temples as hard as he could until his agonized head pounded like a bass drum.

The world greyed, collapsed to a point. The table drifted upward, struck Peter on the chin. He shook his head, woke again as if for the first time, his mind again a blank.

Like a computer slowly rebooting, Peter fell back into himself. For an instant, he remembered who he was— Major Peter Smythe, 22-SAS. Then the pain struck, as if some devil had put Peter's head in a vise and twisted the handle all the way. He groaned, pulled into a tight, fetal ball.

At last, the pain subsided, and he was himself again. His entire head pounded, his bruised jaw especially sore.

Peter stood, shaken, walked the length of the cabin, five paces up, five back, while his heart pounded. *Anxious . . . hyperventilating . . . pulse supersonic. Jesus, Mary, what's happening to me? Am I dying, am I falling back to my real body?*

After a few moments, his metabolic rate returned to normal. He summoned up his courage, strode out on the deck to find "Medraut."

The sun was low. It burned a red road across the black-dark ocean swells, lit the sky afire with dusty orange. Peter watched the sun sink into the sea, drowning itself at last in deepest, burnt umber. Cold metal tingled in his palm: his knife—Lancelot's knife. *When did I draw it? Did anyone see?* He slid it back into its sheath but could not let go the hilt.

Sailors scurried around him, their shouts muted, like a telly with the volume turned down. The soldiers stayed out of the way, out of the sailors' way, out of Peter's way. Cei caught his eye, turned his face away, and busied himself with Captain Naw.

Peter walked the deck from stern to bow, each footfall echoing around his head like a funeral drum. They melted from his path, soldiers and sailors, all but one.

"Prince Lancelot," said Medraut, startled from his reverie. The young man stood alone at the bow, staring across the velvet sea at the bright spot where once the sun had set. "I didn't hear you approach. Sir. I mean Sire."

"Cold night."

"It was warm, but now a wind has picked up. You're right, Sire."

"The spray is cold. It numbs your face."

"Can't feel anything after a while, what?"

"Nothing but the ocean spray. Burns like hot oil."

Medraut turned back to the bow, fingered the shaft of

the ram. "Did, ah, King Merovee tell you what happened? With Cutha, I mean."

"I guess things like that will happen. Nothing to fret about." *Why did she bring that up? Something's wrong, something I can't quite remember.*

"I didn't mean to let the plan slip out like that. Of course, Merovee guessed I would, um, fall from grace. Somehow. How did he know that? The plan would have failed horribly if I hadn't."

"But I did, and even though I know he meant me to, I still feel like a . . ."

"There's no need to—"

"No, please, sir, let me finish. Sire. Ever since we— ended up in the water, I've been at sea. Ah, no pun intended. I mean, I've been struggling to keep my head above water, figure out what I'm supposed to be doing. What I mean is, is there any chance, Sire, we could, you know, just start over? As if we were just meeting for the first time? I'm sure it would be better for you, and I know it would be better for me if we just forgot this little expedition and, ah, how I, well, botched it up. A bit. Will that work, sir?"

Peter scanned the area; they were alone. *I told the lad we would have to tell Artus about what happened. I turned around, and before I could turn back, he had thrown himself into the sea, racked with remorse. . . .* "Hm? New beginning, yes, probably a grand idea."

"I'll be a new Medraut! You'll see, Prince."

I guess I just terribly miscalculated. I had just walked away when I heard a splash. He told me to turn my back, he had a . . . I turned my back, trying to think of what to say, and . . . No, I had just walked away when I heard a splash. Poor chap, I guess he just couldn't face his failure to check the second cart—no!—his failure in battle. It happens sometimes, Lord knows I've seen enough of it, people coming back from Derry—from LONDONderry with su-su-suicidal feelings.

The cold metal pressed against Peter's palm again, the

knife had leapt back into his hand. He hid it behind his
leg, smiled at Medraut.

The boy—the girl, Selly turned her back. Peter stood,
shifted his weight from left foot to right, back again. The
knife grew heavy, weighed at least ten pounds, twenty
pounds, weighed a hundred pounds. His muscles knotted,
heart lurched.

*Wait! Wait, did you check the second lorry? There's al-
ways a second exp—explo—expedition.*

Peter felt the boy, Cors Cant, creeping up behind him.
He looked quickly back over his shoulder: no one. They
were alone, Peter, Selly, and the ghost of Gunny Conway,
all waiting for the second lorry to explode.

He shifted his weight again; the knife pulled his arm
down with its massive force.

He dropped the blade. It fell to the deck with a clatter.

Medraut jumped, looked down in surprise. "Oh, sir, let
me get that for you." The boy stopped, picked up the murder weapon and handed it back to the murderer.

"Oh. Thank you, son." Peter stared at the knife. Never
saw one before in his life. Damned peculiar things. He
coughed, pushed it back in its sheath. He turned his back,
had just walked away when he heard, not a splash, but a
footstep. Not Cors Cant; Anlawdd.

"Oh," she said, stopping quickly upon observing the
tableau. "I can come back when you're not busy."

"No no," said Medraut, "that's quite all right, Miss. I'm
off. Just taking the air, don't'cha know. Heh heh." Medraut
smiled hesitantly at Peter—*do we have a deal?*—squared
himself away and stepped nimbly away amidships.

*What stopped me? Mother Mary, why in God's name did
I let the murdering savage just walk away?*

But Anlawdd had her own agenda, and she launched
into it straightaway.

"Prince Lancelot? I wonder if I might ask a favor. I
know that you know I'm really a princess, Prince
Gormant's daughter . . . and if you haven't figured it out
by now, which I'm pretty sure you have, being at least as
bright as That Boy, that was I in the *Dux Bellorum*'s room.

"But though I came close to striking the blow, I had already decided against it when you entered! I know I can't prove that to you; it's like trying to prove it was already going to rain before the Druid cast his spell! But that's my word, the word of a princess, and you'll just have to take it as read.

"I know you have to tell Artus about Gormant's treason; but is it really necessary to tell the *Dux Bellorum* the part about me being Gormant's daughter and a princess and all? For if Artus finds that out, he's sure to ship me off to some ally or relative of his where I can be held under house arrest, and that's worse than being sent to bed without supper or even dessert! After all, *I* wasn't the one who betrayed the *Dux Bellorum* . . . all right, well maybe a little by not telling him the minute I arrived and by sneaking into his room with a weapon; but I was completely mixed-up, like when you play Old Blind Homer and they put the cloth over your eyes and spin you around three times. So . . . is that okay?"

Peter stared, uncomprehending but still angry—she would have killed him! "Anlawdd, what was the bloody question?"

"Oh. Can you not tell Artus I almost murdered him, nor that I'm Gormant's daughter?" Now it was Anlawdd's turn to hop from one foot to the other.

Peter shook his head. *I'm paid by Defense, not Interior; but I'm still a cop for all that. I can't let her just walk away. Let her be damned by her own words!*

He opened his mouth to refuse curtly. Instead, the words were those spoken a long time ago by another and much greater judge: "Father, forgive her; she knew not what she did."

Anlawdd pursed her lips. "Um, I don't mean to be ungrateful, but is that a Yes or a No? I feel like a horse given right reins and left knee."

"I saw nothing and heard only silence. Can't speak for Cei or Bedwyr—or your bard, for that matter."

What the hell, he thought; *she can't pick her father, and she* did *pull back from the brink in Artus's room.* Anlawdd

was right: there was no way ever to tell whether she had
already decided not to strike when Peter scared her away.

"I know. Thank you, lord." She started to leave, turned
back. "Lancelot? You didn't feel anything in the tunnel, either." It was a statement, not a question.

"Nothing. It was all a nightmare."

"Good, I didn't see it either." She looked quickly left
and right, then stood on her tiptoes and kissed his lips.
"I'll find you at Camlann . . . I have something I—want to
discuss. Bye-e." She bolted away, light as a fairy on her
bare feet.

Jesus, God, that's what it was! Peter felt weak, grabbed
the railing for support. He suddenly realized *why* he had
been unable to kill Medraut. Selly Corwin was a cold-
blooded IRA terrorist: there was no possible way she
would accidentally leak a battle plan to, of all people,
Cutha the *Saxon.*

There was simply no way that Medraut could be Selly.
The lad's very act of criminal stupidity had cleared his
name.

For an instant, Peter felt relief, both that he had not
killed the boy and that Medraut was not Selly Corwin. He
was too likable, that young man. Then a wave of helpless
frustration washed through Peter.

*I'm back where I started! If not Medraut, who? Cors
Cant? Morgawse? Gwynhwfyr?*

Peter inhaled sharply. Gwynhwfyr! It was days since he
had thought seriously of the golden-haired princess of
Camlann, his own, his best girl, who just happened to be
his commander-in-chief's wife. What was he going to do
about Gwynhwfyr?

Their love brought down Camelot, he remembered. *But
Camelot* must *fall.* For in the real history, there had been
no Celtic–Roman Empire . . . Rome fell and plunged western Europe into a thousand-year Dark Age. *I love her, and
I know my love will bring about the ruin of Artus's whole
world . . . yet I consciously, willfully, march on into sin
and spiritual death, wearing "Conservation of Reality" to
mask my own animal lust.*

Peter put his face in his hands, terrified; he could not remember what Gwynhwfyr looked like.

CHAPTER 33

THE SEA ROSE AND FELL, SWELLED AND FLOODED, DIPPED AND ebbed, driven by wind and current and the tidal drag of the moon. Barometric pressure dropped—Peter felt it as an ache in his knees—and grey clouds rushed into the void to dim the world, throw back the sun, and weight Peter's heart like stones piled upon a corpse to make it sink into Llyr's watery arms.

The rest of the journey back from Harlech passed like a ghost train, quiet and steel grey, muted whistle crying in the iron mist. The *Sacred Blood* hugged the shore, but no one saw it; she shunned the open depths, but the "vasty deep" crept to the very gunwales. Sea met sky at a featureless, invisible horizon that Peter had to take on faith.

The men marched round the deck like the Damned *en route* to Judgment Day, eyes downcast, coughing moisture from their lungs until they were as dry as mummies. Three men vanished—over the side? into the air? Captain Naw consigned their souls, if located, to Llyr Neptune, and the burial detail threw bottles of brandied wine overboard in lieu of bodies never found.

Three days, four days, on the fifth day, the Severn swallowed them whole, and they docked long enough to retrieve the horses, then crossed the river once more to disembark. Without his log, Peter would have quickly lost count, but seventeen days had passed since he fell down the wabbit hole.

"The Lord has turned His face away from us," said a

Sicambrian sergeant, and Peter's force was more downcast than ever. Only Merovee seemed unaffected, imperturbable as always.

"I don't know about the Lord," said Cei. "The heart and purpose of Mithras lies hidden from men by the veil of death. But surely the *Dux Bellorum*'s sun has set, by the Grace of God, until and unless we return and drive those incubi from Harlech."

"You preach to the choir," said Peter.

"We need three legions. We must crush the buggers, may it please the Lord."

"Tell Artus. I'll back you all the way."

The force, reduced now to twenty-three, straggled back to Camlann. A mist rose up from the ground, thick with the odor of dank, rotting vegetation; it echoed around their feet as they waded through mud from a recent rain. Not a man spoke, save the religious Sicambrian sergeant, who prayed fervently in a stuporous whisper with every step.

At last they dragged across the city wall, slipped like thieves into Caer Camlann long after midnight. Peter dispersed the men, roused a stableboy, dropped Merovee in the *triclinium*, and made a one-minute report to Artus, Cei at Peter's side to nod and grunt agreement. Peter staggered up to his sleeping mat amid promises of a detailed debriefing in the morning.

He pushed aside the curtain to his—to Lancelot's quarters, collapsed onto hands and knees on the crinkly, straw mat. Sharp blades and needles pricked his palms, prodded his kneecaps. He was too tired to care. He sprawled face first into the sour-smelling pad.

"There's no place like home," he said. "There's no place like home. There's no place like home."

Peter clicked his heels together, tumbled into a deep, trancelike sleep. *Nineteen days on a dead man's quest,* he remembered thinking just before drifting off to dream of Jim Hawkins firing a machine gun at Long John Silver.

CHAPTER 34

I SLEPT ALL NIGHT AND HALF THE DAY, RISING AT THE CRACK of noon and staggering about Princess Gwynhwfyr's apartments like that dead Greek girl, Eurydice, that That Boy is always singing about. I think she's his favorite song, though I like the other ones best, the ones he won't sing around Artus because they're too daring, usually about love conquering all and lovers risking eternal damnation and even loss of their station by touching each other outside of marriage. Romans are big on marriage.

I still could not believe such death! Harlech, Canastyr, my father and his honor, my own illusions. Before tumbling out of bed, I woke myriad times, and each time for a few moments it was all a dream. Harlech stood, buildings unburned, people bravely resisting the invaders, their prince a stalwart general in the *Dux Bellorum*'s great empire.

Once, I sat up into the sunlight streaming through the window, dazzling my eyes and warming my cheeks, and I was *in* Harlech still; I even knew right were I was: it was ten years ago and I was in my father's room the day after my mother died. But it was all right because I knew it was just a dream . . . Mother was really still alive. Then I woke more fully, and the weight of memory fell across me like a winding sheet, and I remembered that my mother had died of childbed fever, taking what would have been my baby sister with her. I cried, wishing Father would talk to me, hold me, put his arm around my shoulder the way Uncle Leary does.

Then I blinked. Ten years rushed out of me like a heavy

breath of night air. I was eighteen, not eight, sitting up in the princess's bed in Caer Camlann, dreaming about my true love, my Orpheus, who is as bold as the sun on a cloudy day. And my city was gone, the dear old sod. Not the buildings; most of them still stood. But Harlech had no more soul . . . she sold it to the Jutes for another breath, another candle of life, the span of days between the waxing and waning moon.

Oh, Hades. I sat up, made sure I was alone, and let my chemise fall to the floor. I stood shivering in the cold sun and touched myself in prayer, letting Gwynhwfyr's wild-woman goddess enter me, wash the tears away. Crying for people who sold liberty for life is like feeling sorry for your husband when he loses your last *solidus* at dice and can't pay the rent. He knows exactly what he wants—and he deserves to get it, good and hard.

Artus gave us a banquet that night. I'm not sure whether he celebrated our return or hoped we'd get drunk and forget our failure. I nicked Gwynhwfyr's coral pink chemise and crimson tunic, upon which I had embroidered a hawk with a harp in his beak (I didn't tell her whom it represented); this time I asked her permission.

I needn't have bothered. I could have strolled into the *triclinium* starkers for all the attention That Boy gave me! I'll try it sometime, just to prove how inattentive he is.

He hovered over Artus and Lancelot like a message-pigeon. The *Dux Bellorum* didn't ask me for information, even though I had been everywhere the rest had, except that queer part That Boy told us about, with the fuzzy Orcas, that I'll bet he didn't mention to Artus.

I didn't know what to do. That Boy wouldn't even look at me. So I began to . . .

Prince Lancelot looked at me. He smiled, raised his cup. I felt my face get hot; I knew what was going on. Gwynhwfyr had been to see Queen Morgawse, who told her if she wanted to snare Lancelot, she must ignore him; and like a ninny, she took to heart the schemes of a woman who hasn't had a decent lover since she married King Morg. That is, Morgawse married Morg, not Gwynhwfyr. Princesses can be such jackasses, present company excepted, of course.

Lancelot knew he was being deliberately ignored, not being as stupid these days as he had been up until three weeks ago, so like a dog that is pushed off one bone only to start chewing on another, he flirted outrageously with me whenever Gwynhwfyr was peeking, which was constantly.

I didn't care. That Boy wouldn't look at me fairly, just kept sneaking glances over his harp. So I made sure to return Lancelot's affections whenever I caught That Boy eyeing me, and, I don't know how to say this, I began to feel something stir within me that I'd never felt before.

It wasn't like I feel about That Boy, though of course I'm not in love with That Boy or anything; Lancelot heated my blood, but not my heart. I wanted to know nothing about him. I just wanted his body on top of me, crushing me beneath those muscles and all that hair on his breast.

I told myself sternly to stop, but of course that was a mistake, for I always do the opposite of what anyone orders me. I found myself sitting in Lancelot's lap, don't know how I got there, whispering sweet who-knows-what in his ear as he cleared his throat, turned red, and fidgeted.

I was desperate to stop! I knew I was hurting That Boy, and even though he deserves everything he gets (good and hard), I felt so sorry for him, like a neglected dog when you have a new baby. But my fingers touched Lancelot's chest, hard as a Roman breastplate, and I felt his appreciation pressing stiffly against my thigh, and of a sudden, all I could imagine was finally becoming a woman.

I felt comfortable, for I understood what was happening: That Boy never fooled me; I knew he was pure, as was I. And I knew why I was so afraid that night so long ago when we stood together in Gwynhwfyr's apartments.

I wanted my first time with That Boy to be perfect; I wanted a bold rogue to seize me in his arms, rip off my chemise, and punish me severely for being so bad—either for sneaking into the *Dux Bellorum*'s room to slay him or

for turning nerveless as a young lad spying on
Gwynhwfyr's bath, I'm still not sure which.

(Mental note, I'll have to pinch a riding crop when he
finally gets bold enough to take what I'll always offer him
freely.)

But how could it be anything but a disaster if *both* of us
were still unbroken colts?

Lancelot was a man. He had experience. He could
awaken me, show me who I was, make me a woman without me having to be the general.

Then, when I was a worldly woman with experience, I
could take That Boy with calm detachment and make sure
it was perfect.

At least, that's what I kept telling myself.

Alas, I also told Lancelot. At least, I tried. I talked a lot
of nonsense about wanting a steady hand on the tiller so
I'd learn how to plow the field myself and teaching me to
fish so I'd never have to drop an unbaited line in the pond
again, and depending on how bright is the new Lancelot, he
either understood what I was babbling about or he
thinks I want to give up my crown for a rustic life as a forest warden.

My body burned, inside with desire, outside with the
gaze of a hundred eyes. Everyone watched me, it seemed,
Gwynhwfyr, Artus, Lancelot, and That Boy. I know they
all wanted me to stop, Lancelot most of all (for he
watched the princess), and that was like a command, and
you know what I do about commands. I boldly put my
hand between his legs and touched, held his lance tightly.
A shiver thrilled along my spine. I had never touched one
in peacetime before, and this one was so huge! Not quite
as large as I imagine That Boy's to be, though I've never
seen it full, but still large enough to frighten me. Would it
even fit? I would be mortified if I gave myself over to a
man, not even my true love, and I was so small he
couldn't even get inside. That would be like knitting a tunic for a present that he can't get over his shoulders.

"What's—what's—what's all this, then?" he whispered,
eloquent words of love.

"Do you want to, um?" I offered, articulate, poetic.

"You mean, you-know?"

"Well maybe not you-know, but, um, you know."

He shrugged, face red, heart pounding. "Yeah, all right."

And that was it, my first seduction. I got up, made sure That Boy saw me as I sauntered out of the hall, *away* from the stairs leading up to Lancelot's room. I doubled back around behind the palace, dashed upstairs without being spotted. I pushed aside his curtain, sat gingerly on his mat, chin on my knees.

Eleven hundred and three rabbity heartbeats later (I counted them), the prince joined me.

ℭHAPTER 35

ℭORS CANT TOYED WITH THE STRINGS ON HIS NEW HARP, given him by Artus himself upon the expedition's return. He tried not to look at Anlawdd making Venus-eyes at Lancelot. His gaze was drawn thither despite a desperate act of will, hooked like a fish on a line.

Is she punishing me for guessing who was under the black hood? he wondered bitterly.

She finally tired of twisting the knife, got up and left . . . out the front door, Cors Cant was relieved to see. The prince, apparently frustrated, headed up toward his room. *And I hope he's run out of pleasure ointment, too,* thought the bard bitterly.

As Cors Cant brooded, an extraordinarily heavy spider fell from the ceiling and landed on his shoulder, clutching at his flesh with its iron legs. He yelped, half flew into the air before realizing it was the *Dux Bellorum*'s iron hand clapping his shoulder.

"Sir," acknowledged Cors Cant, when he could breathe again.

"There is yet one point to discuss. Lancelot and Cei were not present, and you seemed to omit it from your report."

The spider was not on the bard's shoulder; it nested in his stomach, spun its web around and around. Cors Cant felt a terrible reluctance to discuss the Shibbols with anyone, especially not Artus *Dux Bellorum,* War Leader, builder of empires, defender of Britain.

Artus rose, gestured Cors Cant to follow. Merovee closed in behind the bard, calm, grey eyes and enigmatic smile preventing escape. They crossed the *triclinium,* ducked behind a tapestry into a hallway that Cors Cant never even knew existed.

Left, right, through a wooden door, then a hanging curtain; the passage snaked between the other rooms of the palace, terminated in a small office stocked floor to plastered ceiling with scrolls, bound manuscripts, maps, and military and engineering studies of obscure, geographical features. Cors Cant saw a proposed pontoon bridge across the River Blaiddllwyd, an oddly curved dam, a study of an "amphibious legion," whatever that was. Artus sat at the mahogany desk, made no attempt to hide or cover his projects.

"I will not tear your secrets from you," he said.

"I tego arcana Dei," said Merovee, almost too softly to hear.

"But I must have one piece of the puzzle only."

"Yes?" Cors Cant shrank from his *Dux Bellorum,* strangely reluctant to yield any of the treasures from his magical journey through the underground.

Artus pressed his hands together like a tent, rested his smooth-shaven chin on his fingertips. "I must see the scroll you recovered from the depths of Harlech. It may be . . . a holy relic."

Cors Cant gasped. *The scroll!* After carrying it through war and water, across the ocean and through the gates of mystical Caer Camlann, it fell out of his mind until the moment the *Dux Bellorum* resurrected it, as if, having accomplished its purpose by driving the bard to bring it from darkness to light, it stepped back into its own shadow to await unveiling before the two lords of this world.

Frightened by the image, which hung between them like the air of a thunderstorm just before lightning struck, the bard fumbled in his leine sleeve. After a moment's panic, he found the cylinder, uncorked it, and with trembling hand, poured the scroll out on Artus's desk.

Artus untied the scroll, held the edge steady while Merovee unrolled it matter-of-factly. The king read over Artus's shoulder, pursing his lips. At one point, Merovee's eyebrows arched for a moment. Artus remained impassive.

Cors Cant strained, could not quite make out the writing, upside down from his perspective. It seemed to be some sort of chart, with vertical and horizontal lines connecting words, like the scorecard of an elimination tourney. Like a family tree.

The bard looked up from the document, saw Merovee watching him, amused to death, as usual.

Cors Cant blushed. "I'm sorry, Majesty. I must not pry."

"The scroll is your property, son. We only need the information. I'm afraid . . ." Merovee trailed into silence, eyes narrowing.

He drifted away, perhaps to a battlefield a thousand leagues distant in Jerusalem, perhaps to Armageddon, many years hence. His mouth set hard, cruel. Cors Cant shivered, had never seen the king so grim, so merciless.

Merovee lowered his head. His long black hair fell across his smoldering eyes, masked the glint of raw lust for power. He reached forth his left hand, pressed fingers protectively against the vellum.

The voice, thought Cors Cant, *his damned voice in my head! Mine, mine, he says, but he can't have it. I found it. It was given to me by a dead prince, cold in his stone tomb!*

Cors Cant took a step toward the pair. Sensing danger, Artus looked up, impassive but ready.

Suddenly, Merovee smiled, shook his head. He stepped

back, eyes closed, and raised his hand, allowing the scroll to roll itself up again.

"I was right to so fear!" he exclaimed. "The revelation is not for me. It was given to you, my son, by whose hand I shall never know. Unroll it, study it, and tell me what you see."

Cors Cant expelled his lungful of air. He suddenly realized he was slightly aroused, casually shifted his hands downward to cover his leine. He moved forward, turned the scroll about and unrolled it, face red. *Hope they didn't see . . . especially the* Dux Bellorum; *wouldn't want him to get the wrong impression.*

Scroll. Concentrate on the scroll, as a Druid. . . .

The words were indeed names, connected by generational lines. The bard counted twenty-one rows of names, getting wider as they approached the top of the scroll. Some lines ended abruptly, whether because the person in question died childless, or because the line did not interest the author, Cors Cant could not tell.

Authors, thought the bard. He detected either three or four different handwritings. The lower names were Latinate, while the upper were in the tongue of the Languedoc, sometimes with Latin versions as well.

Cors Cant found the name "merovee -merovius-" in the top, right corner. It was boxed, as were all the male names of that line for seven previous generations. Prior to the Merovee line, a different line contained many boxed names, most male but some female.

"Is this you, Sire?" asked Cors Cant.

"My father's name was Morus, and his wife Julietta," said Merovee, without looking at the chart.

"Hm. We have a Morus directly below you, but your mother is shown as Jolie. Was she ever called that?"

The king shrugged. "Alas, I never had the pleasure of meeting her. She died moments before I was pulled from the womb."

"Who were your grandfathers?"

"Robert d'Alpine was my father's father, while my maternal grandfather was Robert Grand-Nez, called Rupertus

Fidelus after driving Alaric and his Visigoths out of Austrasia. Alas, Grandfather did not kill Alaric, and ten years later, the Visigoths pillaged and sacked Rome herself for three days."

"Sire, this is you. Your bloodline." Cors Cant looked at Merovee, was startled to see the king's face drained of blood, his white knuckles clutching Artus's desk. The *Dux Bellorum* looked neither at the bard nor the king.

Merovee spoke, voice thick, vibrating like a heavy table scraped across a tiled floor. "Master Bard, pray read down the list of my ancestors, those marked as monarchs . . . and tell me who is writ at the beginning."

Cors Cant cleared his throat, squinted to decipher the crabbed writing. "Morus, Robert D-A, Etienne D-Alpine. . . ." The lower he got on the chart, the harder it became to read the names, the ink more and more stained, spread, smudged. At last he came to the end: "Simonus Minor, Simonus Major, and—" The bard paused, held the vellum close to the lamp, disbelieving his vision.

"And?" prodded Merovee.

"And Jesu, by his wife Maria Magdalena." Cors Cant stared first at Merovee, face impassive yet betraying hidden triumph, then at Artus.

The *Dux Bellorum* stared at the king, mouth open, eyes wide. "Your—Your Majesty, you never warned me."

"Faithful bear, until this moment I knew only a fanciful rumor told me by my grandfather as he talked me to sleep at night."

"Jesus, Lord, Merovee, do you know what this *is?*" Artus stood, fingers gently, reverently touching the page. "This is the evidence, the proof! The holy grail, *san graal.*"

"*Sang Raal,*" corrected Merovee.

"The Blood Royal," repeated Cors Cant. The words held power, frightened him though he did not know why.

Artus smiled ferociously, pulling his lips away from his teeth like a dire wolf. "The rock of Peter is washed away by the blood of Jesus."

Cors Cant stared again at the genealogy, felt his stomach tighten as he realized what it showed. "But—how could Jesus father a child if he died unmarried?"

"Did he?" asked Merovee. "Whose word do we have that he actually died on the cross?"

"Well, the first saints, Matthew, Mark, Luke, and John. And Paul in his epistles."

"Paul was not present," said Artus, still the lawyer he had been in Rome before accepting a command in Merovee's Jerusalem legion. "He is hardly a credible witness, able to speak only hearsay."

"All right," Cors Cant retorted, angry and frightened at the implications. "But what about the four gospels?"

"Each gospel, each book was judged at the Council of Nicaea, but a century ago," said Attorney Artus, "at a time when the cult of Paul, the Catholic Church, through the Bishop of Rome, completely dominated the followers of Jesus the Christ. Valentinians, Marcionites, and especially the hated Basilidians had been thoroughly purged. There were Paullites and Paullites, and nobody but Paullites to judge which books were gospel, which blasphemy.

"Is it a wonder that the gospels of Thomas, of the Apostle Mary Magdalene, and most particularly the teachings of Basilides were declared anathema, apocryphal, heretical?"

"Basilides," said Merovee. "The old man was right all along."

"Basilides taught that Jesus did not die on the cross," explained the *Dux Bellorum.*

"Why did I never hear of this?" demanded Cors Cant, forgetting his station in his anxiety. "Why was this kept from me when I studied our Master's life and works?"

"Instead," said Merovee, "a substitute, Rome's own Simon of Cyrene, took the Lord's place on the cross . . . according to Basilides.

"The Lord fled first to Greece, to *Arcadia* in Greece, then up the very boot of Rome herself, to my own land of Sicambria, or Gaul as it is known to the Romans. Gallia Transalpina. There, he and his companion, his wife, Mary

Magdalene settled; there they obeyed the commandments of God. They were fruitful, multiplied.

"There was my bloodline begun. Even in Arcadia, I . . . *et in Arcadia ego.*" He bowed his head.

Cors Cant blinked. Surely, the glow that suffused Merovee's flowing black locks was merely the brilliance of the steady-burning lamp. The power that burst forth from the man was nought but the divine, kingly awe that bathes all monarchs in glory, anointed as they were by God Almighty. The healing touch in Merovee's hands was but a trick of the Builders of the Temple, alchemical medicine that even Cors Cant, failed bard, could sometimes find!

But the boy knelt, unable to stop himself. He slowly sank to his knees, interlaced his fingers, and bowed his own head.

A gentle hand touched his crown, and the shock of divine blessing shook Cors Cant, making every cable in his body jerk in a single seizure, a lightning shock. Merovee's hand remained; the king spoke in an unearthly, distant voice, as he had after Anlawdd cast her spell over him in the Harlech forest.

"Fear not the flesh, nor love it. If you fear it, it will gain mastery over you. If you love it, it will swallow and paralyze you."

Then the king lifted his hand, and Cors Cant looked up, tears upon his cheek. The *Dux Bellorum,* too, knelt before the Blood Royal.

The scroll had rolled itself up when the bard let go of it. Now Merovee picked it up, handed it back to Cors Cant. "Safeguard this relic, Bard. It was given unto you, not me."

Cors Cant took the scroll, his hand trembling violently. He clutched it tightly. *I knew, but did not know! I held it so tight through the underground, the swim, the flight in the* Sacred Blood. *I kept it safe from prying eyes . . . did I know what it was? Did it call to me, warn me of its urgency?*

"It shall never fall into the enemy's hands, Lord. It shall be ready when you call for it, to prove your claim."

Merovee sighed. "I do not know that I ever shall. It may not be given unto me to rule my city once again as King of Jerusalem. But this I know: you will be called upon to produce the scroll, Cors Cant Ewin, bard of Caer Camlann, when the All-Dragon's bones are cold."

Artus inhaled sharply, catching the apparent reference to his own death. He said nothing, however.

"Now I must leave," said Merovee. "I have urgent business with a close friend." He turned, left without another word or backward glance.

Artus rose, grunting with the strain, looking more tired and old than Cors Cant ever remembered. "I, too, have urgent business," said the *Pan-Draconis,* grim-lipped. "Do you know where my wife is?"

"I saw her last in the *triclinium,* sir," said the bard, rising lithely.

"Find her. Send her to me, here in my office."

"Yes, sir."

Cors Cant started to leave, but stopped at the door. Again, his duty warred with his oath to the woman he loved. *How can I not tell the defender of Britain that his wife's seamstress stood over his sleeping form with a blade—and is the daughter of the prince who betrayed him? But how can I betray Anlawdd myself?*

Pressure built inside him like a toy air bladder blown many breaths too large. Artus said nothing, but Cors Cant felt the *Dux Bellorum*'s gaze upon his back, the black eyes waiting.

Lancelot said nothing. But should he have? And I, too, said not a word about her!

He stared at his feet, wondered whether they guided his head when he walked or the other way around.

She is my princess. My goddess. My duty is to her—but he is the Dux Bellorum, *the all-father of Britain! My duty . . .*

"Something, Bard?"

She is my—my love.

"Nothing. Sir." *Screw duty . . . my first loyalty is to Her, as it should be!*

Cors Cant Ewin strode boldly out of the office, aware that he crossed more than one threshold.

He found his way back through the labyrinth without need of a ball of twine; it had been child's play to memorize the route. Back in the *triclinium,* he immediately located Princess Gwynhwfyr, surrounded (as usual) by a coterie of admirers. She sat on the lap of one knight, while the son of a senator known for his fulminations in the Senate against vice and corruption fondled her thigh.

"My lady," said Cors Cant, "the *Dux Bellorum* requests the exquisite pleasure of your always-faithful company in his office, where he works late." He was marginally successful at keeping judgment out of his voice.

If she noticed, she ignored it. "Thank you, little bard," she said, smiling mischievously. "As always, I enjoy the exquisite pleasure of the marshal and his great staff of office."

Cors Cant flushed vermilion, again the loser in the word tourney with Gwynhwfyr. He hurried away, praying that his body would obey his conscious will and not respond to the sight of the half-naked princess.

Just before he escaped the hall, a meaty hand caught his bicep, clutched so tight the bard yelped in pain.

Bedwyr thrust his bristle-bearded face into Cors Cant's, grinned nastily. One of his teeth was decayed, shifted forward and back with every word, and his breath stank of Pluto's underworld.

The monster hugged Cors Cant to his chest, put his lips next to the bard's ear, and whispered a vile blasphemy.

"She left from the front," he said, cruel humor in his voice, "but she circled around, like the song, and there you shall find her . . . in *his* room. *Fucking* him."

Bedwyr let the bard go, and Cors Cant fell to the floor, shaking. Cei's brother laughed, ugly and grating, turned and strolled off.

Cold, dead, black-dark in his heart, Cors Cant jumped to his feet, fled without a word toward the stairs.

CHAPTER 36

PETER WAITED ON HIS STOOL. HIS STOMACH TIGHTENED, forced bile up his throat, where it burned like American bathtub gin.

I should wait on the sleeping mat for her, he thought, stared at the rush-filled, flattened sack. He did not move from his perch.

The curtain-door rustled. He watched, feigning nonchalance, as Anlawdd slipped through the minimal opening, tugged the curtain back across the doorframe. Her chemise swished against her thighs as she strode into the room like a general among the ranks. She tried to look businesslike but could not stop her lower lip from trembling slightly.

"Well, Lancelot," she said, raised her arms, and dropped them.

"Well?"

Her cheeks reddened. "Well let's do it quickly, before That Boy misses me. I've told you why, let's not get ovary—*overly* romantic. That would be like sending flowers to a mule to thank it for pulling your plow." She gasped, put her hand to her mouth. "N-not that I meant to call you a mule!" she said, face as red as Selly Corwin's lipstick, "or to imply that—to compare what you're, what we're about to do with pulling my plow! Oh dear, I knew my tongue would run away with my head if I let it. I'm chattering like a Barbary ape, aren't I?"

Distance. Far away, you're not really here, are you? Back in Frankenstein's laboratory. You can do this, God knows you want to. It's not really fornication, is it? I mean, we're not really here.

"What do you mean, you told me why? Why you want to do this?"

"Yes," she said, scowling. "Didn't you listen to all that guff about plowing fishes?"

What on earth did all that mean? Was she actually a virgin at the advanced age of eighteen or nineteen?

Peter rose, standing a foot and a half behind himself, watching himself on a movie screen.

The beast beat upon his cage; Lancelot pounded at the portcullis. The pressure had built ever since the incident in Harlech, until Peter Smythe could scarcely hold back the flood of Lancelot's personality, feelings, thoughts— Lancelot's soul.

Peter gritted his teeth, smiled coldly. "Take off the tunic, Anlawdd."

She hesitated; then she, too, unfocused. Her eyes found a spot on the wall over his left shoulder, her body drifted as if caught between sleep and wake in the twilit limbo from which sprang the most horrific, demented dreams.

She undressed . . . for bed. For a bath. No sensuousness; she just unfastened her tunic at the shoulders, let it fall; untied her chemise, pulled it over her head.

Her breasts were small, but stood up so firm he almost asked her whether they were natural, realized it was a stupid question. The nipples were tiny, unlike Gwynhwfyr's ripe strawberries.

Gwynhwfyr! The name sent an electric shock through his body like a hospital crash cart; but nothing could stop the forward momentum. All Peter's energy was squandered against the tide of Lancelot; his moral wall of righteousness had fallen over, unsupported, uncemented, a sand castle against the wave of lust.

From behind himself, he observed, took notes. *Destruction imminent. Self-immolation. How quaint, throwing your life away like this.*

But on the other hand, is it really possible to "cheat" on another man's wife? Abstractly considered, of course . . .

Anlawdd unlaced her breeks; she wore nothing else. Her

nipples were only slightly redder than her pale skin, the same color as her auburn hair.

She squeezed her eyes shut, grimaced, and pulled off her last garment. She stood naked before him.

Ah, a natural redhead. Strangely, her pubic hair was much brighter than the hair on her head, almost orange.

Peter felt pressure in his groin, his penis pressing against his trousers. He stripped as matter-of-factly as she, within a minute stood before her as bare as Adam, fully engorged.

She tried to find her spot on the wall, but her gaze was drawn irresistibly to his cock. She stared, fixated, as if she had never even seen one before. Peter felt his own neck and buttocks flush in embarrassment, though if anything, the increased blood flow magnified the problem.

Jesus and the Magdalene, it's not as if I'm Long Dong Silver. I mean Lancelot isn't! If anything, he's—it's short and stumpy. What's she on about?

He tried to speak, order her to the bed, but he stammered so hard the words caught in his throat. He swallowed them back down; Anlawdd did not even notice he had spoken.

She crept forward, line-walking, edged past him. As she slipped by, she steeled herself to touch Peter with her fingers. He gasped, twitched as if jolted a second time by the resuscitator.

Resuscitator? What resuscitator?

She sat uncomfortably on the bed, seemed to recover her wits. "Well, Galahadus, are you going to show me why they dubbed you Lance?" She forced her legs apart, smiling artificially through the terror.

Peter fell heavily onto the mat, pricking his knees against the sharp, pointed rush stems. He crawled forward, hand over hand, resisted the impulse to throw himself on her like a mad fencer thrusting at a target still guarded.

He leaned across Anlawdd, his hairy chest against her tiny, erect nipples, and bit her throat—hard.

"Teeth!" she yelped in surprise, flinched for a moment then leaned her head back, exposing her soft, white neck.

Peter chewed on the side of her neck, worked to her nape, ran his tongue from trapezius to just behind her ear.

Anlawdd exhaled heavily, the faintest sound escaping her lips—not quite a moan, which implied too much loss of control, but a sound. He kissed her throat, her collarbone, the side of her breast. Touching so gently she almost could not feel it, he swirled his tongue around her right nipple. He watched himself as a cinema star, critiqued the performance, nodded in approval as his tongue successfully negotiated a particularly adroit maneuver *(hold Anlawdd's nipple gently between teeth, bite just hard enough for her to feel a tinge of fear, rub tip of tongue behind teeth against front of nipple).*

His body—*Lancelot's* body responded perfectly, a consummate incubus; but his inner vision matted *Her* face over Anlawdd's. *Her* body squirmed beneath his, *She* moaned with pleasure, screamed aloud, thrust herself up against him and begged for harder-deeper-faster, not teenage Anlawdd.

In fact, the soldier-seamstress passively let him take her, seemed even farther away than was Peter, even while her body, too, responded on the animal level. She was wet, not overly tight. When the first full thrust came, she sucked in a breath but did not cry out as Peter broke her hymen. For a few moments, her legs and vaginal muscles tightened, and he could not move. Then she made herself relax, allowed him to continue his pneumatic pumping.

Anlawdd began to hum, a song with no tune, but rhythmic beats in cadence with his thrusts. He stole a glance at her face, saw a single tear on her cheek. He looked back down at her body, feeling like a thief for stealing her privacy, sneaking a peek beneath Catwoman's mask.

Peter began to grow soft. He had not orgasmed. The detachment diminished sensation, painted the scene surreal; he exerted more effort keeping The Beast away from his heart than he did inaugurating "Princess" Anlawdd's sexual existence.

His penis grew so soft he feared to thrust, afraid that he would slip out on the upstroke and be unable to reenter.

Anlawdd did not seem to notice. Perhaps she did not care; maybe it was the thought that counted tonight, and that first, breaching thrust. Did she have what she wanted yet?

No, who cares if that bitch is done? I'm not! Peter locked his arms around her bum, pulled her onto him savagely. He refused to allow his equipment to retire without consummating.

He brought his knees up, careful not to pull out of her, then levered her up and leaned back. She waved her arms, trying to catch her balance. "Lance! What are you trying to . . . ?" Anlawdd trailed into silence, figured out that he wanted her to straddle him.

Peter was still inside the seamstress, just barely. He thrust slowly upward, excruciatingly slowly, pulling her just a fraction of an inch off of his penis, letting her slide back down.

She kept trying to speed up, but he kept a consistent pace. After a few moments, she fell into the rhythm. He started to tumesce.

Never fails, thought Peter, grimly kept up the grind.

At last he returned to the stiffness with which he had begun the exercise. Anlawdd had been carried away despite herself, despite any resolutions not to lose control. Even though it was her first time, she closed her eyes, leaned her head back, and gripped his chest hair with an angry, passionate, painful grasp. She slid herself up and down now, no longer needing Peter's help.

Anlawdd's lips moved, talking to herself; Peter could not make out whether she chanted his own name or Cors Cant's; neither did he care. Faintly, but aloud, he whispered "I love you, Gwynhwfyr." Anlawdd did not hear, or else cared as little as he.

He pumped, came closer and closer to the peak, but it receded like the horizon no matter how close he approached, like an asymptotic curve that crept closer and closer to the vertical but never quite reached it. Sweat soaked his body, his abdominal muscles cramped. Drilling Anlawdd was harder work than beating a pell or fighting Jutes in beach sand.

He closed his eyes, visualized beautiful, blond Gwynhwfyr. He realized it was unfair to Anlawdd, but the important thing now was to orgasm so she could honestly claim she was no longer a virgin.

He saw the point, the release, consummation; it rose, glistened like a greased Maypole in starlight. He stretched, *almost* reached it, stretched harder, fingers, arms straining, striving to touch it, grip it, get it over with and end the nightmare. *Who's this girl again? Oh yes, Anlawdd: princess, seamstress, soldier, spy. . . .*

CHAPTER 37

SLOW-STEP, ONE UP, TWO UP, DREADING WHAT HE MIGHT SEE at the top, Cors Cant Ewin climbed the stairs from the *triclinium,* worse than the endless rope in the underdwell beneath Harlech whose end was its own beginning.

Feet pounding like a stone troll, he hoped, prayed they would hear (one or the other), hoped that whatever was happening now, when he found Lancelot's room they would be engaged in nought but a brutal game of fox and hounds.

He cornered into the hall, plodded along to the curtain. It was shut, carefully closed so that not even a crack opened into the room; but no hanging cloth could disguise the animal grunts from the general, the sweet moan from—*no, can't be sure it is she, can I? And as I dare not interrupt the prince when he's with a—a woman, I must turn about and run downstairs.*

A voice whispered in his head. Memory, or a spirit guide? *Fear not the flesh, nor love it.* He reached out, touched the curtain, fingers icy, unresponsive.

If you fear it, it will gain mastery over you.

"Soul of a woman," he whispered, recalling Lancelot's hideous, prophetic verse. *Soul of a woman, soul of a woman, soul of a woman created in Pluto's blood-dark underdepths. . . .*

He took a deep breath, set his mouth in an ugly, determined sneer. *I don't care. Who cares? Not me! She can rut with the barbarian bastard for all I care, not that she even cares about me.* "After all," he said aloud, uncaring whether they heard, "you're a princess and I'm just a b-b-ard, and we can't marry or be together as you're so fond of telling me." His lip trembled; he bit it until it hurt sharply, stilled.

If you love it, it will swallow and paralyze you. Ready or un, here I come.

Cors Cant slid the curtain back silently, stared through the doorway at the drama.

Anlawdd sat naked atop Lancelot the legate, taking him, taking him inside her, inside her secret, crystal cave that she promised only to . . .

No. She never promised me anything but the love of a Sister for a Brother in the Builders of the Temple.

He was still silent, but Anlawdd opened her eyes suddenly as if he had spoken aloud. Her lips parted, her eyes widened *(eyes as big as saucers, eyes as big as millstones),* and she froze in mid—

She watched him, unspeaking, blinking rapidly. She betrayed no guilt, no remorse or shame; but her face whitened in panic. Lancelot still thrust against her, not yet realizing he performed at the center of the Circus Maximus.

She spoke at last, strangled out the words. "No, of course not!"

"Do you love him?" asked Cors Cant, dazed.

Lancelot froze at the sound of the bard's voice, swiveled his head to stare in shock.

"No, of course not. You know who I love, Cors Cant Ewin."

He stared. Nothing more to say.

"God, Cors," she begged, "you always knew I wasn't a

Roman." She looked him in the face. Slowly, as if against her will, her eyes were drawn to his hands . . . *the hands that brought Lancelot back from Arawn's realm.*

He lowered his gaze, stared at the hardwood floor.

Another woman gasped behind him. Cors Cant turned his head, bewildered by the new audience. Princess Gwynhwfyr stood on her toes to stare over Cors Cant's shoulder at the pair. Lancelot was alerted by some sixth sense. He stared back, also paralyzed. His face reddened with embarrassment as he realized his sex life was as popular as a Greek tragedy.

Gwynhwfyr thrust Cors Cant aside as easily as he had flung wide the curtain, breezed past him into the room, staring in shock. "Lancelot!" she cried. "You remembered my naming day!"

While the rest of the crew stood rooted like oaks, Gwynhwfyr efficiently unclasped the pins that held up her chemise, let it drop to the floor. Naked save for her sandals, alluringly laced right up to her knees, she bounded across the room and bounced into bed with Lancelot and Anlawdd.

She locked an arm around each, looked back at Cors Cant. "Come along, Bard," she cried, excited. "Drop that leine and show me what the boys whisper about each time you visit the baths!"

Anlawdd shrieked as if she had seen a snake, bolted out of the bed over the top of Gwynhwfyr. The Princess of Camlann grabbed at her legs, roped one. Off-balance, Anlawdd windmilled her arms, crashed to the floor face first. " 'Et go 'et go 'et go!" she shouted, a small river of blood dribbling out her mouth.

Mithras, thought Cors Cant, feeling himself begin to disassociate, as he had on the sandy beach battlefield, *she's knocked out a tooth, or split her lip open.*

"Where are you going?" demanded Gwynhwfyr, still lost in her illusions of a name-day orgy arranged just for her. "Anlawdd, you don't know how long I've dreamt of—" She might have said more, but Lancelot's meaty hand clapped over her mouth. He whispered frantically in her ear, entreaties of love that embarrassed Cors Cant even to hear, especially from the lips of the bloodthirsty champion of Mons Badonicus.

"Ow!" cried Anlawdd, suddenly realizing the blood on the floor was her own. She gripped her own mouth, doubled over, grimacing. "My 'ip!"

Stunned, the bard turned his back, walked slowly away, wondering dully who would betray him next ... Artus? Myrddin?

"Corth!" she cried behind him, trying to drag him back to an empty life of bedlust and bloodplay. "Corth!"

He staggered back down the stairs, dry-eyed but feeling as if he had been struck full in the face by Hephaestus's hammer. Anlawdd ran after him, uncaring about her nudity, her bloody mouth. *"Thtop,* you bathtard!" she shouted, attracting no little attention and not a few wolf whistles.

Cors Cant refused to even turn and look at her. As he shuffled through the *triclinium,* shaking with an emotion he could not even name, he spied Bedwyr. The foul, stinking giant smirked at him.

Without pausing, Cors Cant lifted a pewter mug from a table, hurled it at the general, brother of Cei. Bedwyr swatted it out of the air, laughing derisively. The still-feasting crowd cheered lustily.

"She's *his* and he's *hers,"* he bellowed, clearly referring to Lancelot and Gwynhwfyr, "and never be any different!"

At last, the tears fell. *Fucking bastard didn't even care about me and Anlawdd. Just didn't want Lancelot fucking around on Gwynhwfyr.*

Bedwyr edged closer, leaned against the table between them like a man dancing on a grave, terrified that a hand will rise up and grab his foot. "Tell your whore to stay away from Lancelot. Insect! Insect!"

On cruel whim, Cors Cant slid his own hand forward suddenly and touched Bedwyr's finger. The giant jerked his hand back as if burned, jumped back a pace. "Touch me not with your sorcerated hands!" he cried, both angry and frightened.

"Why?" asked the bard. "Are you afraid I'll raise you from the dead?"

With a final "insect!" shouted over his shoulder, Bedwyr pushed through the throng and vanished.

I am dead. I am no one. They all know. . . . Blinking back a salty ocean, Cors Cant Ewin stumbled toward the front of the *triclinium.* The great-hall mob were absorbed into the ground like water on beach sand, melting from the bard's touch.

Blind, he found the great doors and ran into the night.

CHAPTER 38

"SO IT WAS ALL A JOKE?" DEMANDED GWYNHWFYR, HER mouth curling grimly. "You heat me in the forge until I soften, then toss me in the water to cool without even pounding me?" The words were her usual banter, but this time they betrayed an undercurrent of real hurt.

"No, my love!" protested Peter. "I—I was just t-teaching Anlawdd how to—"

"But you *sent* for me! I came, saw you, that cute bard, and my seamstress in bed and naturally assumed it was my present."

"I never sent for you." *Whoops—that mightn't have been the most intelligent gambit, matey.*

Gwynhwfyr's impossibly white eyebrows lowered dangerously. Blond as Jean Harlow, she was nevertheless as intelligent as Marilyn Monroe. She understood the implication immediately.

"My husband told me you asked to see me. I see that perhaps he was looking out for my best interest, letting me see what you do the night you return, when I am yours for the taking."

"You wouldn't even talk to me at the feast!"

"You? Talk to a knight with a limp lance made of steamed asparagus who obviously prefers a-a-a *seamstress* to a princess? You *are* joking, Senator Galahadus." She looked away, her face freezing into a mask that showed none of the tempestuous emotion locked within. In a moment, Gwynhwfyr had become—regal. A *grande dame.*

Damage control. For God's sake, mate, don't let it end like this over a stupid, foolish peccadillo.

"I was, ah, frustrated, beloved. I was thinking of you the whole time. Honest." *It's even true!*

"Honestly!"

"Honest!"

She looked back at Peter, her lip curling in disgust. "You were thinking of *me* while you dallied with a lowborn, uncivilized *seamstress?* And while she wore one of *my* dresses!"

"She's not ..." *Was I supposed to keep this a secret? Can't remember, and who cares anyway?* "My only love, she's—she's not a seamstress."

Gwynhwfyr glared silently, waiting for Peter to drop the other shoe.

"Anlawdd is—she's the daughter of Prince Gormant of Harlech." *There, it's out. Now can't you understand that I love you, you royal pain in the arse?*

"She's a princess."

"Every inch. Ah, that is to say, every bit."

"The seamstress."

"Yes."

"My seamstress, Anlawdd of Harlech."

"Righto."

"Is Princess Anlawdd, daughter of Gormant."

"Got it in one, my love."

"So she's the same station as you and I."

"Indeed."

"So you can mar—marry her?"

"Yes—" Peter gasped, recoiled from Gwynhwfyr. "Beloved! I don't want to marry Anlawdd! I want to marry ..." He trailed off, feeling stupid. *I want to marry you, my pet, the wife of the* Dux Bellorum!

Gwynhwfyr gently let her face fall into her folded arms, said nothing for a long time.

At last, she spoke, but her voice was tiny, distant. "You cannot wed me, my true love, for I am already married. Yet you must marry; someone must look after your household. Perhaps your lance guided you true, Lancelot, in revealing your destiny, linked to Princess Anlawdd and Harlech."

"But I don't love Anlawdd. I love you."

She looked up, incredulous. "Love? Think you I married Artus for love? 'Twas statecraft; he leaves me alone to pursue my pleasures, and I leave him to his soldier-boys. A fine arrangement.

"But if he sent me here to discover you *flagrante,* then he is sending me a message: cool it down. I have embarrassed him, perhaps hurt his plans with Merovee; the king is quite the moralist, you must remember."

"Maybe it's time for you to decide, Gwynhwfyr." *Mother Mary, what am I saying? What am I doing? I'm here to find Selly Corwin, not woo a princess.*

Yet an answer followed close upon the accusation. All Peter's life he had believed that each man and each woman had one true love somewhere in the world, one true love that they would meet once in their lives. They might meet and never recognize each other; that would be a tragedy. They might meet when each was ready and fall into each other's arms ... triumph.

They might meet when one was already involved in a relationship. Then what? Would she choose love or choose duty?

Such a fate would be agony, waiting for your true love to decide whether you shall live forever spiritually or die for the rest of your life.

Gwynhwfyr nodded. "That's what I fear most. Beloved. I don't know which I shall choose."

Peter felt such an explosive pressure in his gut that he

thought Lancelot was breaking free at last, erupting through his entire body, about to seize Gwynhwfyr and take her by force. He crossed his fists across his chest like a corpse, squeezed with such force that he was unable to breathe, and his heart pounded like a cluster bomb.

It was not Lancelot. It was the emotion he had never before felt, not even with his erstwhile wife, love turned to panic and imminent loss.

The feeling waned; yet it lurked just below the surface like the Loch Ness monster.

Gwynhwfyr shook her head. "I don't know, Lance. I won't know for a few days. It's a big step ... might kill us both, depending how Artus feels about the threat." She discussed their possible deaths at the hand of the *Dux Bellorum;* yet her voice was flat, emotionless.

She rose. He caught her hand. She tarried a moment, back to Peter; then she squeezed his hand and slipped from his grasp.

She left, not bothering to dress, not looking back, lest she turn to salt like Lot's wife.

An infinite number of minutes later, the squire Gwyn came to the door: Artus urgently desired Peter's presence at council. Misty, predawn light filtered through the window hole as Peter rose like the living dead, stumbled belowstairs to smile and wear the mask for the *Dux Bellorum. Twenty days in the hole,* he thought dully, watching the dismal dawn through the upper-story windows as he passed.

CHAPTER 39

MARK BLUNDELL SAT IN MEDRAUT'S CRAMPED APARTMENTS, staring at the note the wily, old Druid Myrddin had slipped into his hand at the feast. "Come to Druid chamber abaft the palace next to basilica at mid o' the night," it read. *I wonder what language it's really written in?* thought Mark. *Could be ancient Welsh, Brithonic, or even Latin. If Medraut knew Latin, would I be able to tell which language I read?*

He mentally rearranged the words, and the sentence became gibberish. *Probably not Latin, then; word order should make no difference.*

Blundell paced the tiny room, waiting for the *cymbalum* that would mark midnight. The watchman usually struck it gently at night; Mark worried that he had somehow missed it while clumping up and down the room.

He had stuffed his ravenous belly at the supper feast. Now he worried how much fat and cholesterol he had consumed, making a piggie out of another man's body.

At last, he heard a faint tinkle, surely the midnight *cymbalum.* He found the stairs, turned left at the bottom and scuttled quickly through the chapel (*lalarium,* he remembered), pausing to cross himself after making sure he was alone. Then he double-timed through another great hall, as large as the *triclinium* but inhabited only by a dozen soldiers well into their cups playing an odd game with cast-metal dice.

Passing through a great set of gilded double doors, bedecked with a grillwork of volcanic glass and mother of pearl, Mark entered the *basilica,* or throne room. Artus

was not present. In fact, even during the day, the *Dux
Bellorum* spent little time sitting on his throne dispensing
"justice," if Mark could trust Rabirius Galbinius Galba, a
thoroughly Romanized Briton he had met on the ill-fated
Harlech expedition. Even so, a full platoon guarded the
throne. They looked as sharp as razors, every one, though
Blundell's head lolled and his eyelids drooped in the late
hour following the feast.

A single, brilliant lamp lit the *basilica,* throwing monstrous shadows on the wall behind the troopers. Heart in
his throat, feeling like a burglar, though he clutched his
note from Myrddin like an exculpatory hall pass, Mark
strolled through the throne room as nonchalantly as he
could manage. The *custodes* ignored him.

At last, he slipped through the opposite door of the *basilica* and mounted the stairs to Myrddin's room. Queen
Morgawse had been kind enough to give him directions
when he showed her the note at the feast.

The ancient greybeard waited impatiently, looking like
Walt Whitman, the American poet. "You're late," snapped
Myrddin. "I said mid o' the night."

Mark glanced down at his bare wrist, looking for the
wristwatch that was not there. Angry that he still could not
shake the habit, he silently cursed himself for a five-hatted
fool.

But when he looked back up at Myrddin, the Druid
grinned broadly. "Sorry, old man," he said, "but I had to
be sure it was you."

Mark's eyes widened. *Is it . . . have I finally found him?*
"Um, Peter?" he asked. He jumped as he bit his cheek.

"Mark?" Myrddin sighed in exaggerated relief.

Blundell extended his hand. "We meet on the level," he
said with a face-splitting grin.

"And we part on the square," said Myrddin, shaking
hands and gently probing against Mark's third knuckle.
The physicist returned the pressure.

"Thank God it's you, Mark," said the "Druid." "I was
afraid it might be—you know."

"Selly?"

"Herself. All I can say is thank Jesus I landed in the body of a true eccentric . . . nobody noticed anything weird about me because Myrddin was so weird to begin with!"

"Have you found her?" demanded Mark, his voice betraying his own eagerness.

Myrddin looked grim. "Indeed I have, lad, and you're not going to like it. Mark, I've studied everyone here at Camelot, and there is only one person who could possibly be that terrorist bitch. . . ."

"Who?"

"Someone you would never suspect, not in a fifteen hundred years. Someone who could single-handedly change history, for good or ill."

"Yes?" Mark wondered how long Peter would drag it out. The physicist remembered a television episode where a spy lay dying, and another spy asked who killed him. "Pity," gasped the dying spy, "don't think—I'll have time—to tell you—the name." Then he expired.

Myrddin took a deep breath. "Mark, Selly Corwin is in Artus's body."

"Artus! The *Dux Bellorum?*"

"That is he," affirmed Myrddin. "And you know what you must do, Mark."

"Me! Why not you?" Mark knew all too well what a military man like Peter would think was "necessary" to remove Selly's soul from this world.

"Law of Conservation of Reality, Mark. Sometimes, it needs a booster shot. Mark, we all know what happened to Arthur—Artus at the end, right?"

"He was killed," said Mark, straining to remember, trying to distinguish between textbook articles on Arthur and his Camelot he had read and torrid, late-night movies shown just after the news signed off.

Myrddin looked grave. "He was killed by Mordred . . . by Medraut, Mark."

Blundell scuffled his feet, tugged at the tight collar on the Sicambrian tunic he wore. Nothing comfortable resided in Medraut's chest of clothing, no flowing Roman togas or

Scottish kilts. Everything the boy owned clutched and grabbed and squeezed Mark's bodily parts. *A very repressed person,* he concluded.

"It's not like killing, really," coaxed Myrddin.

"It's *just* like killing! It *is* killing."

"You're not looking at it from the right perspective. You may kill Artus's body, but it's not really you, for *this*"— Myrddin thumped Mark on the chest—"belongs to Medraut . . . who plans to kill Artus anyway."

Blundell chewed a nail, tried to follow the clear, moral thread that the Masons taught always existed. *Somewhere here there is a left-hand path and a right-hand path, but damned if I can tell my left from my right these days.* He remembered the real-unreal forest coexisting with Willks's laboratory, the florid Colonel Cooper, Brother Smythe. *I took an oath always to help a fellow Mason in need,* he remembered.

But Myrddin continued, oblivious to Mark's turmoil: "While Selly, on the other hand, shan't die."

"She shan't? I mean, she won't?"

"Of course not. When you, um, terminate Artus, Selly returns to her real body on the floor of the lab."

"Then she just returns here and tries again!"

Myrddin rolled his eyes. "Then you arrest her, you dolt! Get that SAS chap, you know, the one who came to investigate after I used the machine myself . . ."

"Colonel Cooper?"

"Yes, good old Coop. Get Cooper to chuck her into the Maze as soon as she returns."

"But we have no proof! Nothing that would stand up in court, at least."

"Who needs proof? Who needs evidence? The SAS can just lock her up and swallow the key, evidence or not, guilty or innocent. Remember the Birmingham Seven?

"You see, we're in a state of martial law over that little scrap of rocks and trees and windy coastline, and we've suspended all rights heretofore enjoyed by us Englishmen."

"Oh."

"Just tell, ah, Cooper that she's IRA; that should be plenty enough evidence to lock her away for the rest of her life."

"Um, Peter, I, uh, have some very bad news for you."

"Yes?"

"Well . . . maybe not *very* bad, just—"

"Yes?"

"Just *mostly* very bad."

"Yes?"

God, how can I tell him? There's no gentle way to put it. "You're, um, becoming quite repetitive."

"Oi and it's you what's driving me there!"

"You, ah . . ."

"Yes?"

"Died."

Myrddin raised his bushy, white eyebrows. *Wonder whether Peter likes his new beard, wild fringe of hair, and bald pate? Well, he'll have plenty of time to get used to them.* "Something happened when Selly went through—a surge in the microcircuitry."

"What subsystem?"

"Oh, a microleakage on circuit pack twenty-three. Does that mean anything to you?"

Myrddin looked reflective for a moment, then answered. "No, no, can't say that it does. Did you say I died?"

Mark took a deep breath, tried to calm his heart. He once had to tell a mother that her son, his roommate at Oxford, had died in a boating accident. He went rowing while stone-drunk, fell out of the boat, and was so polluted that he could not swim to the bank, only a hundred feet away.

The memory of having to tell Neril's mother that he drowned was so traumatic, Blundell deliberately forced himself to forget it; but it returned to haunt him in his dreams at least once a month.

What Mark had to say to Myrddin gave him the same feeling, a pit in his stomach. *Now I know what a doctor feels like telling a patient he has AIDS.*

"Peter," he said, voice soft but determined, "the containment field powered down when we sent you back. It contracted, touched your body, and, well, electrocuted you.

"You died, Peter. Your body is dead. You—you can't ever come back. Ever."

Myrddin took the news surprisingly well. The old magician stroked his beard, blew out a long, slow breath. His twitching eye was the only indication of great emotion beneath the mask.

"Dead, hey?"

"As a clam."

Myrddin stood silent for a few moments, finally spoke. "This changes nothing, Mark. You still have to do it; Artus must still die by Medraut's hand. Selly's soul still has to be sent back to her real body so she can be arrested."

"Of course," added Mark, "I have to return at nearly the same instant, lest she arrive before me and escape, or even kill *my* body."

Myrddin smiled. "Well, my Romeo, you know what to do about that problem."

Mark winced. Killing Artus—Selly—would be bad enough; suicide would be a thousand times harder, even though he knew, intellectually, that he would just reawaken back in his own body. *Assuming I didn't die exactly the way Peter did,* he added.

"Mark, your . . . your father is really counting on you to do well on this project, make a name, hey?"

Father! Why did Peter have to dig the old man up? Blundell still returned home every fortnight to bask in the warm pleasure of the paternal iron fist. If Mark, the "boy," did not make the scrum, Daddy-Sir would be *dreadfully* disappointed.

At least Mother only whipped me. Father gave me long, excruciating lectures on honor, integrity, and following the lead, doing my part for the team.

"Weakness," he muttered, turning away from those piercing, grey eyes of Myrddin (*Myrddin's body,* he corrected himself). "My father despised weakness, indecision, dilly-dallying more than anything else in the world."

"Make a decision, Mark. Make it fast. It doesn't have to

be right, so long as it's *right now.* Are you with me or
against me ... Brother?"

"Brother?"

Myrddin raised his arms. "My God, my God, is there no
help for the widow's son?"

Blundell stared at the floor, fists alternately clenching
and releasing. *Father. Brother. Queen and country. Chap
really knows how to grind my face in it.*

He looked up at last, face grim. "I'll do it ... for all of
you. Not for me."

Myrddin nodded. "So long as you *do* it."

"W-when?" *My God, I can't believe this. I'm actually
conspiring to commit a murder-suicide!*

"Wait for my order. I'll tell you when, Mark. Now
you'd better leave ... I may be Peter Smythe, dashing,
young SAS agent; but my body is fifty-going-on-eighty-
year-old Myrddin, the court humbug. I need my beauty
sleep." Myrddin put his hand on Mark's back, propelled
him toward the door. "Sleep well," the magician added.
"Pleasant dreams."

The door closed behind Mark Blundell. "I will," he answered, late and unconvincingly.

ℂHAPTER 40

ℭORS CANT SAW NOTHING BUT A BLUR, HEARD ONLY HIS OWN
feet on the crushed-stone walkway as he pelted into the
night. The moon hid behind a cloud, painting the palace
black-dark. The cold stones grabbed at his feet like skele-
tal hands reaching up from their graves as the bard floundered through a cenotaph.

Then a stone shifted, his foot slid from under him, and

Cors Cant saw an ugly, jagged rock rushing toward his forehead.

At once, a huge arm wrapped around him, yanked him to a halt a handsbreadth above the killer rock. The arm plopped Cors Cant back on his feet, where he staggered, still dizzy from the acrobatics, still confused by the horrific vision in Lancelot's apartment.

"Yer almost bowled me over, ye wine-soaked, sheep-brained imbecile," said King Leary, grinning so wide Cors Cant could count every tooth.

"Sire," grumbled the bard, nodding his head curtly, freezingly. This bumpkin from Eire had no right to laugh at Cors Cant's troubles, even if he were the high king of the Emerald Isle.

"An ye took a header into yon rock garden, ye'd have crackit that noggin sure. I save yer life, lad; ye sould mak' a bit sang o't!"

"What?" What tongue did Leary speak?

"A sang . . . put the hale ting doon in a sang. Sure an' ye've got the knack o't."

"Thank you, I'm sure," said Cors Cant with all the dignity he could muster. *And I meant that to sting, by God.*

He stared awkwardly at the monarch. Leary was not the tallest man Cors Cant had seen, nor the biggest. He had not the quiet authority of Artus, nor the regal bearing of Merovee. He was not as much a warrior as Lancelot, nor as learned as Myrddin, nor yet as pragmatic as Cei (it was said that Leary, as Archdruid of Eire, started the practice of sacrificing a pregnant bull and eating rooster eggs to celebrate May Day, a tradition still followed even as Patrick's religion swept the island).

But something about the white-haired man with the crooked, knowing grin and the wild, white beard arrested Cors Cant, made him stop and explain himself.

"I . . . I saw Her."

"Her?" asked Leary, eyes wide. "You mean—She?"

"She, her, I mean Anlawdd, my—well, once my own."

"Yer own what, laddie?"

The bard flapped his arms in annoyance. "You know, or

at least you should remember back when you were young! My own, um, my intended." Cors Cant realized his cheeks were streaked with tears. *Please, God, don't let him see my weakness.*

"Jaysus, boy, yer intentions only lasted till ye saw her? Did ye nae notice her blud-hair?"

"No, you old—I mean, no, Your Highness! I mean I *saw* her with Lan—Lan. . . ." The bard abruptly fell silent, clenched his fists, and pressed them against his temples.

Leary led Cors Cant away from the door, along a windowless wall of the palace, sat them both down on a chilly, stone bench whose back was carved as a triangle, a glaring eye at the peak. "There, lad, spak' yer woes. Tell me a' that's happened."

The bard opened his mouth to protest indignantly; instead, a torrent of words rained out. Cors Cant told the king everything about Anlawdd, from the day they went riding to find the crystal caverns and found Saxons instead, to the moment he found the princess with Lancelot's *flagrante* in her *delicto*.

The cold, rough stone caught at Cors Cant's legs. He leaned forward, rubbed his eyes, trying to rub away the vision of Anlawdd finally naked, but with . . . *him.*

"What am I to do?" he asked the king. "I've lost her. She's not . . ."

"Nae princess nae more?"

"No, I mean she's not—"

"Nae more the warrior?"

"No! Stop interrupting. She's not—"

"She's nae more Anlawdd?"

Cors Cant choked back his rude reply, rationality gaining control. It was not wise to insult the high king of Eire, no matter what the provocation.

"Sure but that's what yer saying, is't not? That since sweet Anlawdd sat still an' reluctantly allowed the champeen o'Caer Camlann tae tak' her, she's nae more adored, nae more loo'ed, nae more what mad' ye fall to love wi' her in the first place."

Cors Cant sat on the bench, shivering. His flesh felt as

cold as the snows that whispered on the wind, though autumn had not yet retreated.

"She is who she is," he said. "She told me that, long ago. I should have listened."

"Mayhap ye did."

The bard smiled grimly. "The question is, who am I?"

"Isn't it always?"

"I could say I am who I am."

"Oi, but I'd ask ye who *that* is, and we're back tae the beginning o' the hunt."

Cors Cant leaned forward, stared at the ground, looking for one sign of life. The grass was dead; brown tendrils of ivy looped in swirls of death at his feet. Even the ants had fled underground—too cold. "I don't even know whether I can trust her. She said she was a princess, daughter of Prince Gormant the traitor! But Cei said Gormant didn't know her.

"How can I believe anything she says or does if I can't even believe that she is who she says she is?"

Leary chuckled. "Oh, sure and she's a princess. Very highborn, she is. Sometimes when a king or prince gang waulkin', among those what still practice the Guest-Right, he laves a wee, tiny piece o' himself behind."

Cors Cant looked up. "Your Highness . . . are you saying Anlawdd was sired by a royal visitor to the court of Harlech? Gotten by a king or prince upon Gormant's wife, may her soul rest in peace?"

"I say what I say."

"Hm. It would explain Gormant's reaction. And his favoritism. I ask again, Majesty, say you this is so?"

"I say I *know* she be highborn, her father o' the blood most royal."

"Most royal?" He turned to look at the king, but Leary, eyes closed, smiled enigmatically, always the trickster Gwydion. "Jesus, Lord," whispered Cors Cant, "is she *your* daughter?"

"She was raised as Gormant's daughter, princess o' Harlech, an' that's all I be permitted tae say. She's right, an' he's right too, depending on which angle ye view the sang . . . sure, but that's e'en the case, ye'll have seen yoursel'."

"So all you've really said," observed the bard with some annoyance, "is that she is who she is."

"Aye, it does seem tae come back tae that more oft than not. But it's deeper, laddie. Ye know who she is, who ye are yoursel'; but can she live in your world, or you in hers?"

"She's not going to change, is she?"

"Aye, but sure she will! An' so shall you, though whether left nae right, forward nae back, it disna suit guessin'. I'm not asking you aboot tomorrow, hidden behind the closed eye o' the gods. Just today: can your warp cleave tae her woof *today,* richt noo?"

"Yes," answered Cors Cant before he could even think about his decision. "Wait . . . I mean maybe if she—"

"Nae, ye spoke the clear thought once. Dinna muddle it wi' muckle hesitations an' backtrails. Ye told her once ye loved her, but 'twas lust for the flesh, nae?"

The night Merovee arrived, in Gwynhwfyr's room! "How—how did you know about that?"

"An' since then, ye've built her idols, first as *princess,* then *Builder,* then *goddess,* ha' ye nae? An' where in a' that architecture is she to simply be She?"

Cors Cant stirred up the dirt, pushed dead stems of ivy aside as he drew a Druid sigil. *Peace,* it meant. *None in my heart . . . perhaps that's been the problem all along. She's the warrior, yet I make war upon myself!*

"Yes," he said again, "I can live with that. With her."

The king put his hand on the bard's shoulder. "Seek her. She is your chalice, your holy grail. She pours life into you, fills ye tae the brim. *Seek her an' tell her.* Sang it tae she, bard! Sing nae the songs o' the feasthall, nae the songs o' battle, but sing aye the songs o' the heart. Sing of love, ae fond kiss, a warm partin' and merrily met once again."

She is who she is—Anlawdd. Not princess, goddess, seamstress, assassin; just . . . Anlawdd. Such a simple solution. Yet had King Leary or Merovee or a leaping gnome bounced up to Cors Cant a week before and told him this simple solution, he would have stared dumbly, shaking his head, uncomprehending.

That's the secret, the final secret of the Builders ... you can't reveal their secrets, for they mean nothing until you learn them for yourself! That's the final secret of all initiations.

The Shibbols laughed, one left, one right.

"At last, he's learned to see *the light!*"

Seen it, touched it, felt its heat; felt its pulse, followed its beat. *No more sucking at the teat of pedantry and reason fleet, a dancer born with two left feet.*

"Drain the cup. The wine is sweet!" Shibbols squeaked, pressed him tight, drained his soul of hurt and fright.

"The message that your future sends: initiation *never* ends."

"But Shibbols are forever-friends."

"Come wi' me," said King Leary. " 'Tis time to become a true *Fellow* o' the Craft. Dana knows, but ye've risen *fast!* Noo, all has been mad' ready for th' high degree." Leary extended his hand, which Cors Cant took. As brothers in a dream, they crossed back under the great arch of Caer Camlann, across the tiny courtyard beside the *triclinium,* where a pine tree stood still green, a vibrant sigil of life among autumn's death. They entered the Old Hall that was already standing when the divine Julius sent the first legions to Prydein. Leary led Cors Cant Ewin to an old stair that led down into an ancient, black-dark cellar used only to store wine and spirits.

In a trice, rough hands grabbed the bard from behind, and he was hoodwinked. Cors Cant did not resist as they dragged him across the floor, did not struggle against the iron grip of his assailant. *What I will must be,* he thought, *thus whatever is, is my will. . . .*

During the struggle, the familiar voice of a seamstress he once knew whispered in his ear. "Now you *daren't* call me 'Your Highness' ever again, Boy!"

He laughed aloud as unseen hands tore away his right

sandal and rent his leine, exposing his right breast and
right arm to the chilly, musty, cellar air.

CHAPTER 41

PETER RECLINED ON A COUCH AT THE COUNCIL TABLE, WHICH
was set as low as a table in a Japanese restaurant. He listened to the *Dux Bellorum* with only half his attention, the
rest spent keeping The Beast down.

Lancelot had broken out four times since returning from
Harlech. Ever since Peter's collapse in that town, The
Beast seemed stronger, seized control with frightening
suddenness. *What's happened to me?* wondered Peter.
What's happened? Am I losing my soul?

He decided he must complete his mission as quickly as
possible, hoping that when The Beast finally regained control of Lancelot's body, Peter's mind would drift back to
his own body, fifteen centuries ahead.

*Selly. Must focus on Selly bloody Corwin. Forget about
the bleeding battle, forget Artus, forget the boy and his
princess! Selly. . . .*

But still the *Dux Bellorum* spoke, Artus *Pan-Draconis,*
his arresting, hypnotic voice impossible to ignore.

"An empire is not like the white, southern cliffs; it
stands not upon its own, weathering buffets by wind and
wave with stately imperturbability.

"No, an empire is like unto a great palace. It is built by
men, and must be braced and supported, ever maintained,
or it collapses with the sound of thunder into stone blocks
and wooden boards.

"Cei, Porter to Caer Camlann: what holds my empire
together?"

"Eh?" Cei blinked, unprepared for the question. "Er, the benevolent rule of the *Dux Bellorum.*"

Artus smiled sardonically. "Lancelot?"

Peter was ready. "The army, sir. Sword and spear hold your, ah, empire together."

"A close answer, my friend, but let me ask your countryman the question."

King Merovee did not stir, did not look up from his steepled hands, which he studied with the intensity of meditation. "Faith," he proclaimed.

"Rem acu tetigisti," said Artus. "You have touched it with a needle, Your Majesty.

"Faith, gentles, knights; faith holds the legionnaire to his centurion, the citizen to the Senate, even the slave to his master. Cei! I order you to strike my head from my body this instant!"

Cei stared, then lowered his brow, a faint smirk on his lips. He made no move toward a weapon.

"You see, my friends?" asked the *Dux Bellorum.* "I have no magic to bind you to my words. Every command I utter sparks a new decision in your minds: follow the wise old man, or ignore the doddering fool?

"Understand . . . there is no king, no prince—*there is no governor anywhere.* Every man is his own king, decides for himself when he will obey, when rebel. Thus, my empire, every empire, is held together solely by *faith:* the faith of the people, from prince to slave, in the justice, fairness, and ultimate strength of the sovereign—his ability to protect and nurture the *populi.*"

The generals, princes, and knights around the council table stared blankly, not comprehending the philosophical treatise. They worshiped the voice, however, could listen for hours as his voice caressed them like a courtesan's hands.

Even Peter was lost, though he guessed it had to do with Harlech and would eventually lead to rationale for a war of liberation. Only Merovee smiled, but still did not raise his head.

"This faith is shattered," declared the *Dux Bellorum.*

"Surely not shattered?" asked Bedwyr, pushing away from the table. As usual, he refused to recline, perching on the couch as if it were a proper, British stool.

Artus raised his voice, allowed sorrowing anger to reverberate through the hall.

"How long until every barbarian north of Londinium hears about the fall of Harlech, the betrayal by Gormant? After the legions withdrew from Britain, how long until Rome herself fell to Alaric and his Visigoths? *Three years.* Now Attila the Hun stalks Gaul, and Flavius Placidius Valentinianus can only shake his fist and beg Pope Leo for an army."

Artus spread his hands on the table. "We cannot afford to suffer *any* defeat, withdraw from *any* province; for if we do, every Saxon, Jute, Hun, and Gael with two legs and an axe-arm will swarm across us like a plague of locusts ... for the *populi,* soldier and citizen alike, will lose faith in the *Pax Britannicus.*

"And without faith, my commands are but the rantings of an old lawyer." He lay back on his couch, raised his hand, and marked the sign of the cross upon the assemblage, blessing them.

Peter jerked at bit at the blasphemy, not expecting it from the *Dux Bellorum.* Then he wondered, was it truly blasphemous? Ordained or not, was Artus not father confessor to them all, in a sense?

"Restore my empire," said Artus. "Give me back Harlech, my children.

"Four legions will I take, and I shall take personal command of the expedition. I shall captain the Dragon legion myself; Cei and Lancelot shall each command his own legion. Lancelot shall of course be First General of the entire army.

"Now Cei, recite for me the details of logistics, support, and provisioning for this expedition."

As the porter droned, Peter thought quickly. Whatever Selly planned, she would probably strike during the action; wartime engagement provided perfect cover for anything her black heart might plot.

But Peter was to be separated from the most likely
target—Artus *Dux Bellorum* himself. As well, Cei and
Bedwyr were ready to declare open rebellion—Peter
writhed guiltily, believing their state to be in large part his
own fault, suddenly breaking whatever agreements the real
Lancelot, The Beast, had made with them—yet Cei had
been given an entire legion!

Everything had fallen apart. Peter had failed to discover
Selly, lost Harlech, alienated Cei and Bedwyr, and was
even now losing control to The Beast within. He felt a
mad desire to run to Merovee, confess his shortcomings,
and beg the king to tell him what to do. But Peter could
no more do that than he could have ducked out of
Sandhurst during the Horrible Year and begged his father
for advice.

It's Medraut. It must be.

*No, it cannot be Medraut . . . the boy is not an IRA
killer!*

Peter clenched his teeth in fury at his own, Hamlet-like
indecision.

Cei rattled on about logistics, supply lines, foraging,
dart and arrow supplies—everything Peter had always
hated about command. He listened as attentively as he
could, but his mind calculated like one of Professor . . .
Professor . . .

Once again, simple knowledge from his real time escaped Peter's mind, drifted away like dreams in daylight.
He pounded his thigh hard with a ringing smack, forced
the name *Willks* back into his head.

Cei stopped in mid-lecture. The assemblage turned to
stare at Peter, whose ears flushed. "Er—flea bite," he explained.

*My mind calculates like one of Willks's Macintosh neu-
ral nets,* thought Peter precisely, enunciating each word in
his head, branding the elusive terms on his cerebrum. *The
problem: how to separate A (Artus) from B and C (Bedwyr
and Cei) so that proposition P for Peter can interact upon
A, P(A), in private, let A know that he cannot trust either
B or C?*

Cei finally finished, and Artus formally broke up the assembly. Each went his separate way—except for Bedwyr and Cei, who stuck to Peter and Artus like barnacles on a whale's belly. Twice, Peter tried to lead Artus off for a quiet chat; both times, Cei hustled up with new details, suggestions, questions. The second time, when Artus glanced down at the map, the porter curled his lip at Peter as if to say *no, matey, you won't get even a moment alone with the DB . . . not if my brother or I can stop you!*

Artus resisted efforts at conversation, immersed in the minutiae of strategic planning. At last, frustrated and concerned, Peter made polite good-evens and chugged off to his room.

With the curtain closed and his back to the doorway, he carefully read through his entire investigative log, skimpy though it was. When he finished, he shook his head, dismayed at the amount of useless wheel-spinning. As quietly as he could, he began to write.

Twenty-one days.

The solution to the puzzle is—that there is no solution. I cannot smoke Selly out by waiting for her to make a mistake.

Fencing—try to anticipate your opponent's attack—he'll draw you into his blade feinting left right left until you jump and he holds the line, cuts into your open side. No you must wait watchful, when he attacks he opens himself. Sun-tzu: invincibility is in yourself, vulnerability is in your opponent—skillful warriors can be invincible but they cannot force their opponents to be vulnerable.

When she attacks she must move off her center, lose invincibility and become vulnerable, like saber fencing. Withdraw, withdraw and when she cuts wait till the last second, parry and riposte.

I'll find her when she chooses to show herself . . . if she never does, I win by default.

Peter laid down his charcoal pencil, hid the journal, and sat up half the night futilely trying to penetrate Selly Corwin's mask, ignoring his own wise advice.

At last, just before dawn, he started awake from a comfortless doze, banged his head against the wall, cracking it and dislodging a large piece of plaster. An explosion echoed round his skull, like the blast that killed Gunnery Sergeant Conway.

Peter listened, wondering whether he could hear a sound over his own kettledrum heartbeat.

The explosion repeated, two tiny raps against his door-frame, booming through the villa like an especially heavy mouse tread.

Slowly, like a ghostly phantom opening a door in a horror movie, an unseen hand drew back the curtain. Peter stared, still paralyzed from the hypnopompic state of dream-sleep, an invisible claw cold as the abyss of space squeezing his heart, which beat wildly, out of control.

Bigfoot leaned into the room, a seven-foot humanoid covered from head to foot by matted hair. Peter raised his fist, felt rather than saw the axe clutched in his hand.

Then he blinked—saw that old pederast, Myrddin the Mummer, a frail, old man with a Walt Whitman beard and cataract-clouded eyes. Peter gasped, tried to quiet his tap-dancing heart.

"Sorry to disturb you," said the mountebank, "but I, um, that is, it's jolly important. Have you a minute, Sir Lance-lot?"

"What the hell do *you* want, you bloody rude bastard?"

Myrddin hemmed, shuffled his feet. He tugged at his collar. "Say," he said with no preamble, "is this Harlech expedition really *on the level?*"

Mary Mother of God! thought Peter, *yet another bloody, damned Mason!*

"Go away, Myrddin. Just go away. If you stick your filthy monkey's paw out to show me a funny handshake, I'll break it off."

The Druid fell silent, but he did not withdraw. After a suitable interval, he tried another gambit.

"Still, ah, defending the sheep, Sir Lancelot?"

"I'll *feed you* to the goddamned sheep if you don't—" Peter stopped in mid-rant. He had had a conversation about defending sheep earlier, quite recently. Three weeks ago, in fact. He struggled to drag it to the fore, found it after a long search.

Peter asked, "have you ever read the three gospels—Matthew, Luke, and John?"

Myrddin slowly smiled. "Don't tell me you've forgotten old *Mark,* have you? What would the rock of Christ say?"

"Good old Peter. Jesus and Mary, Mark, is that really *you?*"

The old magician sighed in relief, sank to his knees. "Thank God I found you, Peter!" he exclaimed.

"Jesus, what's happened? Why are you here? Where's Selly, have you got a fix on her?"

"Well, you were gone for so long, and then your superior arrived, um, Cooper."

"Colonel Cooper?"

"The very one. He arrived and seemed to think it was all Willks's fault."

"Yes, the old fart never did like scientists much. Or anyone who attended university, to be honest."

"So I talked the Old Man into letting me go back to help you. And Peter—I've found her!"

"Her? *Selly?*" Peter leaned forward, almost grabbed the ancient, doddering young man by his shoulders and shook him like a suspect in the Maze.

"Well, actually I don't *quite* know whose body she's in, but I know the next best thing: I know what she's plotting to do."

Peter clenched his fists, while Myrddin licked his lips, took a deep breath. "Mind you," he said, "it's somewhat speculative . . . but I'm almost positive Selly is planning to kill King Arthur during this campaign."

Peter stared, incredulous. "What makes you think that? What possible advantage could she have for—"

"Peter," interrupted Myrddin, "we—well, Cooper, actually—found Selly's orders, straight from the Belfast division of the Provisional IRA. It was coded, of course, and partially burned. She'd thrown it in the fireplace in her room, but it fell beneath the grate and didn't burn all the way. We won't know the full text until it gets back from

decoding, but Cooper was able to pick out some words—
enough to make it clear that Arthur himself, or Artus, or
whatever he's calling himself here, is the intended target."

"Artus? She's going to kill Artus?"

"Well, that's what her orders said. I'm sure she'll obey
her orders . . . you know what those IRA chaps are like."

Peter scratched his chin. Something was not right,
something peculiar in the "old magician's" words.
"But . . . didn't Artus—Arthur—die anyway in the old
stories? In battle, I mean, with Morgawse and Mordred?"
*Or was history already changed? Did Arthur originally
live, but now I remember him having died because Selly
succeeded in changing the past?*

Myrddin scowled, tugged at his beard. "Hm. You're
right, he did. At least, that's how I remember it *now.*"

"You're thinking what I'm thinking?"

"That she may have already changed the past? It's possible. But we needn't look that far for our own purpose.

"Peter, Arthur *must win this war.* If he does not, history
will be changed—and not for the better."

"So . . . you think Selly plans to strike and slay Artus
before he drives the Jutes out of Harlech."

Myrddin nodded. "Almost certainly. She must! Otherwise, her whole trip was useless . . . after all, it would do
no good to kill him afterward. As you pointed out, he's
going to die soon anyway."

Peter was not sure how much of the conversation he
bought, but he wanted to keep it moving, not analyze it
until later.

"When will she try it?"

Myrddin shrugged. "Your guess, my guess. As the um,
ahem, court Druid, I am privy to a lot of inside information . . . even things that Sir Lancelot doesn't hear."

Peter bristled at being demoted to knight. "Prince.
Prince Lancelot. Ah, not that it really matters."

"Prince," he agreed. "I might hear about the impending
attack even before you do. If so, I'll alert you immediately,
Brother Smythe."

"Thank you," said Peter. "And now, I must get at least

a bit more sleep before they blow the pipes and crash the cymbals for another frozen daybreak." He gestured Myrddin away, and the mountebank took the hint. In a moment, Peter was alone with his thoughts. At last, he began to analyze.

By the time day "officially" began, he had come to a conclusion: he had absolutely no way of telling whether Myrddin really was Mark Blundell, or if he had just spent a pleasant, few moments chatting with Selly Corwin herself. He shivered at the thought.

So I'm back to where I was, he thought. *I must wait patiently for the blow, a week or more before we march, then be ready to parry and riposte like a* Blitzkrieg.

Groaning with exhaustion, he climbed out of the bed to begin drilling his new, green troops all over again.

CHAPTER 42

CORS CANT SHIFTED UNCOMFORTABLY ON HIS RENTED PONY, clutching its shaggy hair whenever he felt ready to slide off left or right onto a sharp pile of rocks or into an icy, autumn stream. His backside had ached for a week after returning from Harlech, and here he was, back on a horse again!

She's right about one thought. I was definitely not born for heroism.

He sighed. "She"—Anlawdd—had been assigned to another legion by Artus himself. Worse, the girlfriend of the niece of the slave who cleaned Morgawse's apartments the day that Artus spoke with his half sister for nearly a whole day said that the slave of the wife of one of Morgawse's Sarmatian Amazon honor guards told her that Anlawdd, who was still playing the role of Gwynhwfyr's seamstress, had specifically *requested* she be assigned to a different legion than Cors Cant.

The bard rode in silence, except when ordered by the *Dux Bellorum* to honor him with a song or tale. *He probably wonders whether I'm about to dash myself off the nearest cliff,* thought Cors Cant, *for every selection I have given cries out in pain and despair like a thousand Trojan women.*

In seven days, Cors Cant had not found a way to talk to Anlawdd. He knew what he had to say, but his pride would not allow him to apologize for acting like what he was: a civilized Roman.

For her part, Anlawdd was not speaking to him—for real, this time.

He accosted the princess once. She told him that love did not always mean acceptance. "We live each in our own world, Cors Cant, and they might not touch on enough borders." Then she added the vilest phrase ever spoken: "Maybe we should just be friends."

Two days later, he summoned a slave and pressed a note ("I love you" in Cymric) into her hand for the princess-seamstress; but later, the slave girl could not remember whether she had given the note to Anlawdd, and if so, what Anlawdd said. There was no reply, and Cors Cant took to eating his meals in his apartment, unless Artus specifically demanded his presence.

When the expedition finally departed, after a week of preparation, Anlawdd did not even wish him hard luck.

As he rode, Cors Cant sang of the despair of Penelope, waiting so many years for Ulysses to return from Troy. He sang of the death of Orion at the hands of his beloved goddess, Artemis. He sang of Persephone, eating six pomegranate seeds in the realm of Hades, thus being torn from her mother Demeter six months of the year. He sang of Aeneas's sorrow at the destruction of Troy.

Of course, he sang of Orpheus (twice), the Greek harpist who could not trust the shade of his true love, Eurydice, to follow him out of the halls of the dead; Orpheus turned at

the last moment, as he had sworn not to do, only to see
Eurydice torn from his grasp and dragged back into Hades,
there to remain forever a shade.

Do I share his hubris? thought Cors Cant. *Is it* hubris
even to compare my hubris *to that of the divine Orpheus?*
The bard shivered at the similarity; they even shared sim-
ilar mysteries: the Builders of the Temple and Orphism.

The jolting pony shook Cors Cant awake in the middle
of his song. He had been riding, playing, and singing, eyes
closed, oblivious to the surrounding legion. Now awake,
he almost tumbled from his horse once again.

A tear rolled down his cheek. He continued the song
without any telltale pause.

Cors Cant rode near Artus in the legion that the *Dux
Bellorum* himself commanded. Good King Merovee rode
alongside, as did Grinning King Leary. The Irish archking
always seemed to be sharing a joke that nobody else got;
either that, or he was drunk all the time.

Lancelot commanded his own legion, as did Cei, with
Bedwyr as his general of brigades.

By sheer, wretched luck—or perhaps because of another
direct request—Artus seeded Anlawdd into *Lancelot's* legion, of all places. Horrible, agonizing images flashed
through Cors Cant's mind unbidden, terrible Greek paint-
ings, sacred to Eros, of the prince and princess together in
myriad different ways, each more athletic than the last.

I can't keep this inside, thought the bard. *Have to talk to
someone—anyone.* He contemplated Merovee.

*No, he is not the one. If I had to confess my own sin and
inadequacy, I'd tackle him this moment, make him listen.
But this is deeper . . . what's between us? Love, infatua-
tion?* He shook his head, guided his pony toward Leary. *I
need a real father, not a holy one.*

The problem was, Leary might be *her* real father. But
even that might not be so bad, he decided. At least he
would not be so detached and mystical, like Merovee;
Anlawdd's happiness should mean at least as much to her
father as it did to her (possible) lover.

Cors Cant inhaled, opened his mouth for a witty conversation opener, to lull the archking into a mellow mood before springing the heavy questions. But Leary spoke first.

"She's nae Roman, ye know."

"What? Who?"

"Who? Who were we just talkin' aboot? Anlawdd, ye stew-headed warbler."

Cors Cant's mouth remained open. He could recall no earlier conversation in the past week with Leary about Anlawdd. The archking was remembering forward in time again.

"She's nae Roman, an' ye're daft an' ye try to paint her as one."

"How am I painting her as a Roman?"

"Expectin' her to obey Augustan marriage rites, for one. She canna do as ye'd like, cleavin' unto one an' only one from vows to the funeral bier."

Cors Cant craned his neck to look Leary in the eyes. "That's not a problem! Well, all right, it's *a* problem, but not *the* problem." He paused, but Leary waited for the bard to continue. The archking rode a great draft stallion, certainly war-trained, with such grace and artistry that by comparison the bard felt like a clumsy child on his pony.

"Sire, I fear she might love only the romance of my songs, the mysteries I've been taught and continue to be taught, in love with the thought of love herself. When I offered—Sire, I beg forgiveness if you are her father!— when we stood alone together in Princess Gwynhwfyr's bedchamber ... ah, the princess was out, of course ... when the starlight illumined Anlawdd like a thousand candles, she stood clad only in a sheer chemise—and *nothing happened.*

"Yet here, when that foul beast Lan—when Prince Lancelot offers her nothing more than animal rutting such as he does with the *Dux Bellorum*'s wife (I hope you already knew that), she casts aside the chemise and d-does every foul, immoral thing he asks!"

Cors Cant suddenly gasped, realized to whom he spoke. If Leary really *were* Anlawdd's father, he might be justified in striking the bard's head from his shoulders for such an offensive description. Worse, the aging monarch might challenge the champion Lancelot himself, destroying himself and the potential alliance with Artus and Merovee.

But Leary did neither. He laughed out loud. "Fear not, Cors Cant! Any father o' such a lass as she, sure he already knows not tae fence her like a prize-winnin' sow!

"An' that's good advice for ye too, laddie. Such a lass as she, ye catch her by lying on your belly, arms outstretched as a cross, lettin' her tak' ye or lave ye as she pleaseth."

"Lie on my belly?"

"A figure o' metaphor, child."

"But . . . will she come? Or do I just get a face full of dirt?"

Leary shook his head. With the wild hair and shaggy beard, he reminded Cors Cant of the bard's own pony. "It disna suit tae guess," he said, an expression he liked.

"But sure if ye try tae reel her in like a fish, she'll swim off the hook. But if I had tae guess, I'd guess she'll be gang tae ye. At this harbor, she's lookin' to drop anchor, I reckon, an' ye're a handy stanchion to moor her lines an' make fast her ship."

"Could she be testing me?"

"Let her test ye, lad. Show her ye dinna plan tae trap her in the harbor. Show her she can sail free whene'er she needs, an' she'll tak' heart. I guess."

"Don't you know?"

"Wi' *her?* Dinna be daft, Bard! She's as much a mystery as anything that young Myrddin has taught ye."

Young Myrddin? Leary must be as old as the Dux Bellorum'*s father!* Somehow the words did comfort Cors Cant, however, and he made formal good-byes and drifted back through the pack to ride again next to Artus.

The legion walked briskly all day, camped with great efficiency at night. With each passing night, Merovee drifted farther and farther from the main encampment, until finally he was hidden behind a great throw of boulders, as alone in the midst of a war as Cors Cant felt in the midst of his crisis of doubt.

They crossed the great river where Lancelot and his
crew had taken ship, but remained on foot, being far too
numerous to sail to Harlech, even with a hundred ships.
They marched along the great Northern Road, which did
not live up to Cors Cant's expectations after all that Artus
had told him about Roman roads—for one difference, it
never ran true-straight for more than half a league before
bending.

Along the route, the legion raised levies as numerous as
their original numbers, swelling their ranks to nearly three
thousand foot and seventy horse.

They scavenged food, harvesting the fourth-part of any
field and slaughtering one out of every six swine, kine, or
yeanlings they encountered. The farmers stood tight-lipped
and grim-faced, presumably grateful to the benevolence of
the mighty *Dux Bellorum* that the legion did not scythe
and slaughter them all.

Lancelot's legion tracked a different route, east of Artus,
raising its own levies and ravaging a slightly different
countryside. Farther east, Cei's troops tramped brown, dry
hills and rolling woodlands. By the time they reached Harlech, said Artus, they would be spread by about a league
apiece, Cei's legion to be held in reserve in case the Jutes
opportunistically fortified the High Place, Eryri, and Harlech City against recapture.

Cors Cant slapped at yet another flea bite. "God, for a
bath," he moaned. "I'm beginning to feel like a Saxon."
The *Dux Bellorum* paid no mind, riding silently as he
played and replayed the upcoming battle in all its permu-
tations.

At night, the bard lay upon his stomach, an extra blanket folded over his head to block out some of the noise of
three thousand human bodies, at least five hundred of
whom restlessly wandered about at any hour of the night.
No matter where Cors Cant threw his bedroll, he found
himself blocking a major thoroughfare from the guard
post, to the water trough, to the cookfire, to the blade
grinder. He lay rigid, lightly dozing then starting awake,

occasionally weeping with frustration, loneliness, and exhaustion.

Days passed, a week. Cors Cant began to wonder whether he had ever known Anlawdd at all. Was she merely a fire-haired vision, the product of some potent, magical spoor he had swallowed? But no, she was the one who gave him the spoor cantrip. He shook his head, confused, all the higher brain-souls burned out by the horrific march.

The soldiers seemed to enjoy marching, or at least grumbling about marching. They laughed and joked and collapsed into sleep immediately when not trudging, eating, or pontificating. A dozen different religious rites were observed, none well attended.

Aside from Merovee and Artus, the only souls that Cors Cant knew well were Centurion Cacamwri, now captain of the Praetorian Guard, being groomed for general, and Archking Leary. Cacamwri seemed no longer to remember his grudge against Cors Cant, now too far beneath the newly promoted captain—which suited the bard fine. He had disliked Cacamwri since the man was a lance-sergeant, nearly as arrogant then as now.

Cors Cant spent more and more time with Leary, who never turned away. "I'm bright," said the bard one noon, as he picked at a meat pie allegedly "straight out of Apicius," according to the cook, but which tasted more like sloppicus.

"An interestin' opening line," mused Leary. "Does it work wi' the lasses?"

"Bright, loyal, honorable, faithful in my devotions. Yet I cannot stand the thought of blood and I have no head for intrigue."

Leary grinned. "Aye, that lets oot civil service an' the priesthood."

"But if I could not sing and compose, what would I do? Would I clean stables, hoe a row from dawn to midnight, starve?"

The archking turned serious for a moment, stroking his beard. He stared into the sky, eyes bluer than the heavens.

"Sure an' one purpose of civilization," he ventured, "is to nurture e'en the apple that falls farthest frae the tree."

"Hunh?"

"The Huns, the Visigoths, e'en the Jutes and Saxons dare not support a useless, parasitic class—exceptin' the priests, of course. They live too close to the wind, where every breath may blow them over.

"But an empire, now, sure and that's something! Athens, Rome, Alexandria, Constantinople ... such places gather so many resources and distribute them so efficiently that they can afford tae throw awa' good food on a mere tale-spinner."

"Thank you, Your Highness," said Cors Cant, stiffening.

"O, smooth yer hackles, laddie! Artus says it disna well suit tae starve a bard, so tak' whate'er is offered. But where would ye be withoot that voice? The same hole ye'd inhabit among the Saxons, or other Barbary apes: ye'd be a slave."

"A slave! But I'm highborn, or at least a citizen. . . ."

"Citizen? Think ye the Saxons gather in a Senate and vote upon which Irish village to raid? D'ye think they even ken the rule of law, or worry muckle much about accounts or commerce? They recognize no citizens, lad, an' ye'd be lucky indeed, weak as ye are in the strengths of war, tae be recognized as useful in other ways.

"As an empire expands, it finds more and more room for the pegs that stand up. Another time, another place an' ye'd be hammered doon, lad. Dinna forget it."

After a fortnight, Cors Cant's longing for his autumn goddess cooled to a dull ache, a fist pressing against his diaphragm. He sketched her in the dirt, on scraps of paper, in the sky.

And the next morning, he awoke to discover he understood her.

Not goddess, princess, warrior, or even seamstress ... she was a mortal woman, stumbling through life as confused and frightened as he. Her tongue tied itself in knots when she stood before him, as did his own; but in

Anlawdd's case, her knotted tongue spewed nonstop babble rather than awkward silence.

He even understood why she lay with Prince Lancelot: she clutched at certainty, needed an "edge" to give her the confidence to take the next step, and the next.

Great. Now what do I do with this great revelation? Will I ever see her again? The bard resolved that if they ever met again, he would simply tell her that he loved her and wanted her . . . on any terms she desired. Cors Cant realized, to his surprise, that it was the truth; he would not even mind sharing her with every traveling guest who knocked upon their door, if she insisted, so long as he, himself, was not left needing.

He looked back upon his older self, dead now these many weeks, and laughed aloud, understanding Leary's perpetual amusement as well. *How small I was, and how much taller I've grown!*

He slept well that night for the first time since the march began.

In the morning of the fifteenth day out from Caer Camlann, Cors Cant was startled out of a deep slumber by a light kick in his side. He cautiously lifted the blanket from his head, saw one of Merovee's Sicambrians standing in an incredibly formal "at ease" position.

The bard sat up groggily, and the soldier crisply handed him a summons from the king. Merovee "requested" the pleasure of Cors Cant's company that night at middle-night . . . alone, "for the widow's son."

As the sun crawled across the sky and the legion crawled up the coastline, Cors Cant's stomach squeezed tighter and tighter in anticipation. It was such an excruciatingly polite, formal command; he knew it meant an extraordinary encounter.

He remembered Merovee's prophecy the last time they saw Harlech, nearly a month before. *Is this the toast to Death?* he wondered. *Merovee himself is the emperor, and surely I am the fool. But which of us shall lose himself in Scots-Land?*

They marched all morning, then suddenly bivouacked

around noon on the plain of Dinas Emrys. Rumors spread through the camp of a huge army of Jutes ahead, though heavy fog obscured the plain.

Cors Cant waited impatiently for sunset, then for the full moon to rise to its apex.

At last, nearly bursting with nervous eagerness and trepidation, he threaded a path through the warhounds, sons of Mars and Mithras. Their japes died as he passed; conversations fell silent until the bard was gone. Cors Cant was not one of *Them*. And all had heard of his "mystic hands." They feared him, then hated him for frightening them.

He struggled up a steep hill, stumbling as he stepped into a field mouse hole. The tents and bedrolls thinned. At last, he crossed a barren zone, the buffer between Artus's legion and the increasingly reclusive Merovee. On the other side was the king's low, sloping tent, diagonal edge set against the slight wind, guarded on all four corners of the square by giant Sicambrian warriors, bare axes in hand.

Cors Cant stopped, watched the canvas door flap for many, many heartbeats. He noted every detail: white canvas with runes and sigils of power embroidered and painted along the sides, intricate patterns of astrological signs, endlessly repeating patterns of spirals, swastikas, a huge, golden eagle upon a staff (sign of a Roman governor, which Merovee was before Rome withdrew and he crowned himself king).

Surrounding the door flap was a figure Cors Cant recognized from a scroll rescued from the library at Alexandria: Nuit, Egyptian goddess of the night. She bent impossibly around the hole in the tent, supporting the entire heavens upon her long, lean back.

Swallowing, Cors Cant strode forward as self-confidently as he could fake. The guards did not move until the instant he stepped within range of a good flèche attack. Then, they raised their axes to "port arms" and stepped to block his passage.

Without a word, Cors Cant handed over the note. The first bodyguard read it, handed it to the second. When both silently agreed, they stepped far enough apart that the bard could barely squeeze through.

He ducked his head, skulked along a "corridor" whose walls and ceiling were fashioned out of the tent fabric. Despite the chilly, night air, braziers inside the tent kept it hot enough to drench the boy in sweat. Smoke rasped his throat.

Pushing through a last diaphragm, Cors Cant reached the center of the tent, where Merovee held court to an empty chamber upon a make-do throne, a wooden saddle sewn with cushions.

King Merovee's head was bent forward, as if staring at his own sandals, and his ink black hair cascaded down his back and across his face, making him look like a man-wolf caught in the act of changing from one to the other. The brilliant tunic, white as a toga but uniquely cut, was stained by days of travel.

Cors Cant bowed formally, remained bent at the waist, praying the king noticed and returned the salute so that the bard could straighten up again. When Merovee did not move, Cors Cant loudly cleared his throat.

The noise startled the king, who jerked his head up, declaring, "God's love forsworn! Are you my assassin come at last?"

"No, Sire, I am Cors Cant, court bard to Caer Camlann." The boy hesitantly straightened; Merovee did not object.

Merovee blinked, cleared his head. He had been asleep when Cors Cant made the noise. He brushed the wild mane from his face, pulled the mask of the emperor across his features once again.

Cors Cant noticed two glasses of elixir upon a low table before the king, accompanied by a bottle . . . *the* bottle, the one that had been in Lancelot's room and which the champion vainly tried to hide. Upon the left-hand grail was an image of a blade; upon the right, the image of a cup.

The fool and the emperor drink a toast to Death, and the bigger fool drops his cup. Which of us is the bigger

*fool, he who pretends he is a governor, or he who follows
though he knows there is no governor anywhere?*

Merovee smiled up at Cors Cant. The king's face was
white as the snows on Eryri, the High Place overlooking
Harlech . . . white as the shrouded corpse in Cors Cant's
vision aboard the *Blodewwedd.* His hands shook. For the
first time, the bard saw Merovee as an old man, patrician
governor of Gallia Transalpina until his patrons withdrew,
appointing him "king" in their place.

"Yes, son," said Merovee. "Saturn has caught up to me.
I feel his icy breath upon the nape of my neck, his blue
hands clutching my heart. This is winter; 'twill be winter
until the sun sets."

"Sire, may the sun not set for many years now."

Merove looked down at the table, at his pale, wrinkled
hands. He turned them palm-up. "Many times I have laid
them upon a terrible wound, felt the *blood royal* flow
through my hands into the rupture and seal it. But even I
have never called a man back from Pluto's demesnes.
They all talk about you, you realize."

Cors Cant nodded. "Your Majesty, I was, um, initiated
into the third degree before we left Caer Camlann."

Merovee nodded. "You rise remarkably fast. You have a
patron of great rank and quality." A cryptic remark: did he
mean himself? Leary? Even Lancelot, who was obviously
a Builder, though one would never have thought it to talk
to the old Lancelot, who seemed to return more and more
as the expedition progressed. "You realize you and
Anlawdd are now of the same degree."

"I'm surprised you're telling me this. Isn't it . . . secret?"

Merovee gently touched the bottle. "As winter creeps
along, I find more beauty in blazing illumination than sub-
tle, indirect lighting.

"But the Builders are all brothers and sisters, as were
the Basilidians of old from whom we descend. What matters secular rank and privilege? Faugh, the concerns of the
Lord of This World! When Satan offered Our Lord all the
lands of the earth as His kingdom, the Savior rejected

them. Thus do we all as Builders reject any rank but our own degrees, which mark nought but learning and initiation, not control."

"I find that very seductive, Your Majesty." Cors Cant edged closer to the table. The liquid in each cup seemed identical: thick wine that looked amber in the brass vessels by candlelight.

Merovee waved his hand impatiently. "I'm not attempting to seduce you with tales of a classless heaven! Merely to point out that I am only King Merovee when other ears are flapping. Today, this moment, I am Brother Galbanius Merovius, you are Brother Corus Cantus. Do you understand, child? *Rank hath no meaning* within the Builders."

Cors Cant stared. What was the king really trying to tell him? The bard struggled, aware it was a test . . . and he was failing.

"King and queen," continued the king, "prince and princess, knight and citizen, priest and even slave . . . all are as one in the eyes of the Lord. Can we Builders be less tolerant than the Great Architect Himself?"

Cors Cant looked down at his sandaled feet, felt so utterly stupid. The moving finger writes, but what it wrote may as well have been Egyptian pictographs for all Cors Cant could cipher.

Whom can I ask? Who can explain it? Leary's explanations often left him more confused than before the archking started "explaining," and of course Lancelot was out. Not that he blamed the champion; who could possibly resist Anlawdd when she reached out, opened her heart?

A crazy thought occurred to the bard. Perhaps he could turn for help to Anlawdd herself? It would be a good approach, getting them back on speaking terms without discussing the Incident. *Yes,* he decided, *I'll cut across to Lancelot's legion and ask Sister Anlawdd to interpret Merovee's lesson.*

At that instant, Cors Cant was illuminated.

"Anlawdd!" he cried, was rewarded by a genuine smile from the king. "She's the same—we're the same . . ."

The grandmother of all illusions, cast by the Prince of Lies himself! The peculiar madness by which one woman is greater than another, and untouchable, merely because of her father's rank and status before her. "O Lord my God," whispered Cors Cant, "we are equals, she and I."

He finally understood. Communication is only possible between equals; all else is but orders and reports, demands and flattery.

Love is the ultimate communication. Thus, logic compels that love is only possible between equals.

"Jesus Lord and Mithras, is *that* why she never let me into her heart? Because I always sought it from below?"

Merovee smiled enigmatically, said nothing, leaving the bard to grade his own lesson, as usual.

"Even Lancelot," continued Cors Cant, speaking aloud his own amazed thoughts as if he were alone. "Even the Incident—she was trying to tell me even then that she could only give herself to an equal, to a prince!"

"Every man and woman a star," said the king. "Do you love her?"

The bard blinked, remembered where he was. "Yes," he said, and truly felt it for the first time.

"Do you understand what that means?"

"Yes." Cors Cant did not hesitate. If loving Anlawdd meant loving a wild she-wolf that chased her own prey and lay with whom she chose, then so be it. "I love her for who she is, for Anlawdd. I would love no other."

Merovee laughed, pounding the table like the great king of the Sicambrians once again. "Then choose, son, while the spirit fills your heart and brain!"

"Choose, Sire?"

Merovee indicated the two vessels, the amber wine. Cors Cant stared at the bottle, the same bottle he smelled in Lancelot's apartment . . . the bottle full of deadly nightshade or thorn apple venom. *Oh God,* thought the bard, *one of the cups is poisoned!*

"Ch-choose?"

Merovee carefully placed one hand next to each cup. "I have known for many years that I would be shown the promised land, yet never allowed to enter. I shall never be emperor, Cors Cant Ewin. That honor falls to my son ... the son whose future is foretold by his past."

The king rose, pressed both cups forward simultaneously. "I know I must someday step aside," he said, voice almost too low to hear. "So long as I live, my son lives in my shadow. Yet it is he, not I, who must rule. But is that time now, or years in the future? We shall see." He indicated the cups. "Choose one, Cors Cant Ewin, and let us drink a toast to Fortuna. One draught contains nectar from the Tree of Understanding, the other from the Tree of Eternity. Choose, Bard, and don't bollix it up."

Translation, thought Cors Cant; *one draught contains merely wine—the Tree of Understanding;* in vino veritas ... *"in wine is truth." The other cup, the Tree of Eternity, contains eternal sleep.*

He stared sickly at the cups. One was emblazoned with a blade that bore an uncanny resemblance to the phantom sword that had extended itself to him outside Lancelot's window, preventing him from tumbling heels over head to dash out his brains on the cobbles below. The other was decorated with a near-perfect replica of the cup he had seized in the caverns below Harlech when the sword dangled above his face.

Both were essential parts of the human nature, both necessary. But which meant life, and which death, *today?*

Did even Merovee know which cup was poisoned?

"The fool and the emperor drink a toast to Death," said Merovee.

Cup or sword. Sword or cup. Reason against sympathy ... which do I lack?

The bard stared from one to the other, reached out a hand toward the chalice—hesitated, then moved to touch the blade. He withdrew his fingers, having taken neither.

Then clarity struck, his second epiphany of the night. "I lack neither sword nor cup," he said, "and surely not the staff of intuition. What I most lack—what I have *always* lacked—is the pentacle of valor.

"I lack *courage,* Sire. I have always run away from ev-

ery choice not thrust upon me by God. I ran from
Londinium when Vortigern's Saxon mercenaries sacked
her, then cheered from afar as the tyrant fell, his grand
tower at Dinas Emrys (this very plain) knocked over by
the red-and-white dragons fighting beneath the earth, if
Myrddin can be believed.

"I ran from my duty to Artus, to Lancelot, even ran
from my beloved when she offered me love as an equal. I
painted her first as princess, then murderess, then goddess,
all to avoid opening my breast and pulling out my bleeding heart, as our Lord taught."

Merovee held up a hand, produced a single *milliarense*,
smallest true coin of the empire. "I give you courage,
Brother Corus Cantus. Take this pentacle and harden your
resolve." He dropped the coin on the table, where it rang
and spun exactly between the two cups.

Cors Cant watched the coin until it stopped; then he
shrugged. "So in the end, it doesn't matter which I
choose . . . only that I have the courage to choose. All
right, then I choose the cup, you barmy bastard, because
I've always *hated* the God-damned sword! Um, begging
your pardon, Your Majesty. Didn't mean to call you a
name."

With no hesitation this time, Cors Cant reached out and
picked up the vessel imprinted with the sword.

Merovee cocked an eyebrow. "All right," said Cors
Cant, "so I changed my mind." He clutched the sword-cup
with both hands, stared in horrified fascination at the possibly deadly liquid within. *Can I really bring myself to
drink it?* he wondered.

Merovee breathed a great sigh of relief, picked up the
alternate cup. He raised it high, and the bard touched his
own grail to the *Blood Royal*'s. "*In vino veritas,*" said the
king.

"*Cave canem,*" responded Cors Cant. With one motion,
the two men drank their wine. All the way up and down
again, the bard wondered whether he would have the courage to swallow.

The terrible, burning fluid flowed down Cors Cant's

throat like liquid fire. He gagged, coughed, but held it down. When he could breathe again, he realized he was gripping his testicles tightly. He dropped them like hot coals.

Merovee seemed similarly affected, though not as severely. "Not the best quality wine," whispered the king, hoarsely. "Present from Lancelot through Cei."

The bard sat across from the king, and they played "ask me a question" as two brothers.

"Do you love her?" asked the king.

"Yes," said Cors Cant. "The scroll is an official, legal genealogy, admissible as evidence in an ecclesiastical trial, Sire . . . right?"

"Yes." Merovee narrowed his eyes, smiled. "Do you *want* to love her?"

"Jesus, I don't know!"

"I get a point; answer the question this time."

The bard stared at the empty cup in his hand, wondered whether this was the last game he would ever play. "No. I have to be honest, I wish I didn't—you know, feel this way about her. All right, what do you intend to do with it?"

"That's not a Yes-or-No question, son. Lose one question for cheating."

"Sorry."

"Not as sorry as you're going to be when you end up with a score of less than nothing."

"Um. . . ." *Jesus . . . it shows he's descended from Jesus.* "Do you mean to—force the Church to recognize you as . . ." *Can't be king; he's already a king, and no one disputes that.* "As emperor?"

"Yes." Merovee smiled. "Good thrust. This scroll proves I can legitimately lay claim to the imperial throne, more so than that usurper Flavius Valentinianus, certes. Now . . . can you love her after what she's done and *nearly* done?"

"Yes." Cors Cant blinked. It was the first time anyone asked him such a question, and he was surprised he an-

swered so quickly. But the answer was true; he was finally
Anlawdd's equal, and could truly love her.

But how did Merovee know what Anlawdd had *nearly*
done? Or was he just fishing?

Cors Cant carefully considered his next question. "Emperor is not enough. You could take that throne by force;
you have many friends among the legions, even among
Valentinian's Praetorian Guard." The bard waited, watched
the king's reaction.

"I won't make it easy, son," said the king. "Search not
my face for confirmation. Ask your question."

*What had Artus once called him? King of . . . of Jerusa-
lem?* Cors Cant gasped. "You intend to make them accept
you as the true King of Jerusalem, successor to Jesus!"

"Yes," said Merovee, obviously pleased with the bard's
reasoning ability. "Have you realized yet you can never
marry?"

Cors Cant slumped back onto his stool, nearly falling
backward. "Oh Lord, then he knows! Artus knows she's a
princess."

Merovee smiled, triumphant. "Yes. Alas, that must
count as one of your questions."

"Did Lancelot tell him after all?"

"You're getting ahead of me. It's my turn for a question.
But I'll show a kingly benevolence and give you a square
answer.

"No, Lancelot said nothing, and neither did Leary or
Anlawdd herself. *I* told Artus that Anlawdd was princess
of Harlech."

"You!"

"Understand, boy; she's too valuable a commodity to let
her galavant all over the countryside without precautions.
She is the heir to Gormant's throne *and* his perfidy."

"Oh God, you wouldn't hold that against Anlawdd,
would you? She had nothing to do with Gormant's treason!"

"She committed her own treason. Cors Cant Ewin, I'm
sorry, but Anlawdd will either be exiled or put under
house arrest; I'm sure that Artus will exact no harsher sen-

tence. But he can issue no lesser punishment. Her crime was terrible." Merovee lowered his gaze, seemed almost embarrassed. "I will not apologize for alerting Artus, naturally."

"Naturally." The bard could not keep the bitterness from his voice.

"But I am sad. I liked her, and understand her dilemma."

"Exile or imprisonment—for how long?"

"As long as Artus is *Dux Bellorum*. At least."

"She doesn't deserve that."

The king shrugged. "Neither one of us deserves to be illuminated tonight . . . but both shall be, by the left-hand or right-hand path. Now it is my turn to ask my next question. I suggest you get back to the tack you sailed before. Is the question, 'how can Cors Cant and Anlawdd marry?' *really* the question you should be asking?"

The bard pondered the seemingly innocent query. A glimmer of light touched his mind. "No?"

"Answer me, don't riddle me."

"No. No, it's not." Cors Cant brightened, suddenly catching the king's cast. "No, what I *really* want to ask is, 'how can we be together forever?' " He grinned like a loon. "Jove's blood, I never thought of that! Lancelot and Gwynhwfyr aren't married, yet they're together constantly, and Artus turns a blind eye. But who would be willing to marry her and let us be together?"

"Not a legal question. You've lost three points now."

Cors Cant looked the old king in his grey eyes. "You're trying to take over the Church itself, aren't you?"

Merovee hesitated.

"Come on," said the boy, "don't make me penalize you."

The king shook his head, chuckled. "Well, I have only myself to blame. I opened Pandora's box. Yes, Bard, those are my plans. That scroll you found is sufficient precedent to demand I be invested . . . as Bishop of Jerusalem, supreme authority in the Faith, above even Pope Leo.

"After Jesus' death, his twin brother, James, ran the unbroken Church from the temple at Jerusalem. Then Paul gained power and moved the center of the Faith to Rome.

"Paul's power flowed from Peter, the rock upon whom the Lord built his house. After all, James was only the brother of Jesus, not his heir."

"But if Jesus *did* have a son and heir," demanded Cors Cant, "that would be a more powerful connection than Paul's . . . wouldn't it?"

Merovee held up a warning finger. "First, my last question: when Anlawdd marries a king or prince, to remain with her you must become her servant, her subject. Can you live with that?"

It was a horrifying thought, to be under the orders of the woman you love. Would she abuse her authority? Would bedchamber arguments become public punishments?

Did Cors Cant *really* trust his Anlawdd with that much real power over his life, his freedom, and his future?

"Yes," he said in a strong voice, knowing it was the truest answer either had given that night. "She won't betray me. She will never jeopardize our love. I put myself into Princess Anlawdd's hands."

Merovee leaned his head back, looked suddenly wearied. It was near dawn. Cors Cant blinked, felt strangely dizzy.

Merovee whispered, too softly to hear. "I am directly descended from Jesus and Mary. The scroll proves it. But it is not enough . . . not even that is enough.

"The Church is too powerful; I know that now. I will not succeed in establishing my claim, for I have too often thwarted Leo's policies and supported his enemies."

He leaned forward, caught the bard in an iron gaze. "Ah, but those enemies! It's a new idea, this Church Militant, and Leo will not last long as Bishop of Rome. He's no Damasus.

"Too late for me; too late for Merovius Rex . . . but there is yet *Merovius Minor,* my son." The king pressed his lips together, stared into the future with a grim, determined look. "You must safeguard my son's lineage, Cors Cant Ewin. Sicambria falls, and even the mighty All-

Dragon, Artus *Pan-Draconis* stands close to Death, holding Death's hand.

"Guard the evidence well, lad. Keep it safe; Merovius Minor shall one day call upon you to prove his claim."

Cors Cant's heart suddenly lurched, pounded violently. He suddenly remembered the wine, the drained cup. *No! Not now! Don't let me die for such a senseless purpose!*

He half rose. Panic flooded his body as his stomach contracted violently. "Oh God," he sobbed, "I'm dying!"

Merovee almost smiled, the corners of his mouth barely twitching. "We're all dying," he said.

"The wine!"

"Poisoned," agreed the monarch.

"O Lord my God," said the boy. "I'm only nineteen!"

Now Merovee did smile. "And you, at least, shall live to see twenty." His face suddenly turned grey as ash, and he clamped his teeth together in a spasm of pain.

"You?" asked Cors Cant. "But I thought—I felt . . ." Pity flooded Cors Cant's mind. He reached out, took one of Merovee's hands. Nightshade and thorn apple both produced nightmare visions (or ultimate insights) before killing. *How in God's name did he hold himself together for so long, retain enough rationality to play "ask me a question"?* The bard marveled; the dying king must be very, very familiar with the effects of the cantrip, have taken it many times in the past . . . and he was still sane.

King Merovee was not listening. *"Mors ultima ratio. Death is the final accounting. Our Father, Which art in heaven, hallowed be Thy name . . . oh God, it hurts! I didn't know it would hurt so much.*

"Thy kingdom come. Take me now, Lord God. Thy will be done in earth, as it is in heaven. Give us this day our daily . . .

"The foolish emperor drinks a toast to death, the final accountant. Mother . . ." Merovee fell forward, his face against the wooden table. "Cors—Cors Cant, will you tell me where is hid my lineage?"

"No, Lord. I cannot." He would never betray Anlawdd's crystal cave. The days of divided loyalty were past. Cors

Cant would pledge fealty to one and only one woman in all corners of the empire.

"But it hurts!" Merovee sat bolt upright, arms wrapped tightly around his belly. His face was as wan as a sunrise moon, his eyes wild and unfocused. "Give us this d-day our daily bread, and for . . . forgive us . . . forgive me. . . .

"They told us we could eat anybody once. A time to rend, and a time to sew. Beware of the dog! A living dog beats a dead lion."

"I returned, and saw under the sun," quoted Cors Cant, catching the reference, "that the race is not to the swift, nor the battle to the strong, neither yet bread to the wise, nor yet riches to men of understanding, nor yet favor to men of skill; but time and chance happeneth to them all." It was his favorite passage from the Christian book of the Preacher.

Merovee continued, oblivious. "Forgive us our debts, as we forgive who so neglect learning in his youth, loses the past and is dead for the future." Then the king awoke, stared directly at Cors Cant. "Waste not fresh tears over old griefs," he quoted.

"When good men die," responded the bard, "their goodness does not perish, but lives though they are gone."

Merovee sighed, smiled peacefully, then slumped back in his chair, silent at last.

Cors Cant reached out, gently stroked that kingly brow. Then he backed slowly out of the presence of the Blood Royal, ducked out of the tent. He stood blinking at the sun as it burst over the horizon, a brighter patch of overcast.

He looked back at the two Sicambrian guards, frightened that they would think he murdered the king. They wept, heads bowed, as they closed and tied the door flap of Merovee's tent. Finished, they stood at attention, axes crossed to bar the entrance to Thanatos, god of death, as tears rolled unchecked down their cheeks. *How did they know? How did they know?* thought the bard. He ran back to the main body of Artus's legions through the foggy cocklight.

Soldiers scurried about their tasks, grim and efficient.

Something important had happened. Cors Cant grabbed the arm of a centurion he did not know. Not Cacamwri.

"Sir," cried the bard, "what is it? What's happening?"

The centurion yanked his arm free, studied Cors Cant for a moment. "Jutes," he said at last. "The scouts report a huge, Jutic army less than a league distant. Don't know how the bastards could've missed them." He dodged the bard and faded into the mob.

Wonderful. A great battle on the very day that Artus's ally and co-emperor kills himself! Cors Cant staggered away as quickly as he could, fear shaking the vestiges of exhaustion from his eyes. He sought for Artus, afraid to tell him that the king was dead, but more afraid *not* to tell.

A twisted thought lodged in Cors Cant's head: as one died, another was reborn. Face red with guilt, he buried the image of Anlawdd. *Please don't let her fall in battle,* he prayed; *now that the light has finally dawned, please God, give me just one day of real love!*

He ran toward the *Dux Bellorum*'s tent, grateful beyond words that he had no sword to tempt, no harp to distract.

CHAPTER 43

PETER SLOWLY RODE ACROSS THE DESOLATE PLAIN, ALMOST A moonscape. Faster than a walk, and his giant war-horse (Eponimius, he remembered) would surely manage to find a snake hole and break his leg.

The girl beside him kept her face down, hidden by a mass of hair turned the color of dried blood by night and the moon. Peter watched her sympathetically, wondering whether she were as wracked by guilt as he.

"Are you all right with this, Anlawdd?" he asked. She

grunted noncommittally, but he persevered. "It's normal to feel a little guilt when you've cheated—"

She sighed. "For three weeks you've asked, and for three weeks I've said I don't feel guilty, I'm just thinking, a bad habit I picked up from my Uncle Leary, who's always saying he can hear gears and water clocks spinning in my head like a field of windmills."

Leary again. That gnomic Irishman was turning up more often than a vicar's bottom in a knacking shop. *First he turns Artus on to a gram of hash, then he gets a jolly one off on the blessed Saint Patrick, and now he's teaching his little niece how to cheat on her fiancé!*

Peter tugged guiltily on his tunic, feeling flushed and overly hot in the chilly breeze. *For three weeks, I'm the one who's felt like a louse.*

But Anlawdd had only stopped to draw in a breath. "I'm not sorry for what I did, and it's not cheating since That Boy and I aren't even speaking, and anyway we haven't made anything official, but I *am* sorry at how he took it." She raised her head, shook back her hair. "But I guess it's my fault. I should have known he'd take it hard after I refused him, then he prances in and finds me with *you,* of all people . . . no offense, Lancelot."

"None taken," said Peter stuffily; but if he entertained illusions of becoming a more active conversationalist, Anlawdd dashed them.

"But my first time with That Boy has got to mean something, not like lying with you, which is like cooking yourself supper in an empty house."

"Really!"

"I mean, who cares how it comes out? But with That Boy, I want it to be like a twelve-course meal for a house full of senators, every detail perfect from broth to brisket to bread pudding."

She fell silent, gasping for air. Peter pounced on the opening. "I had hoped you planned to apologize to Cors Cant . . . hence you decided to accompany me across this wasteland to Artus's legions." At least once, sometimes twice a day, Peter found occasion to cross the divide and check on Myrddin. The wizard still seemed to be Mark Blundell, but the more he pondered, the less confident he was that he could tell Blundell from Selly.

Myrddin fell into none of the traps Peter set—which either meant Myrddin was Mark, or Myrddin was Selly and she was smarter than Peter (which was old news). Whoever Myrddin really was, he or she had certainly pegged "Lancelot of the Languedoc" as Mayor Peter Smythe ... a deadly disadvantage if Myrddin did turn out to be Selly.

Shortly after the legions left Caer Camlann, Peter set his squire (and apparently son) Gwyn to spy on Myrddin whenever Peter himself could not be present.

As Peter and Anlawdd rode across the foggy plain, a huge force suddenly exploded inside him. Lancelot, The Beast, still struggled to free himself from his Promethean chains. The world faded. . . .

Peter shook himself. Anlawdd was saying something.

"Lancelot? Prince, are you still with me?"

"Y-yes," he answered, struggled to remember what he was doing on this barren plain with Cors Cant's girl. Some time had elapsed, but he did not know how much.

The Beast was becoming more powerful by the day, was regaining control again and again.

He looked at the height of the bright spot in the overcast that marked the full moon. Lancelot had been in control of his own body again for an hour.

"To sum up," she said, concluding a long oration he had missed, "we've got to work *something* out. We can't leave it like this."

Anlawdd suddenly reined in Merillwyn, stared at Peter. "Pardon my directness, Lancelot, but are you really Lancelot?"

Peter stared back, nonplussed. "What in the world do you mean?"

"You know perfectly well what I mean, unless I'm wrong, in which case you don't have the slightest idea what I'm talking about. But I'm not wrong. I'm never wrong. I thought I was, once, but I was mistaken." Following one of Anlawdd's soliloquies was like actually listening to the words of an American rap song.

But Peter caught the gist. The idea that a twenty-first century schizoid man could successfully impersonate a fifth-century Roman knight for several weeks without detection had been addlepated at best. If Mark Blundell (or Selly Corwin) had so quickly caught on to Peter's impersonation of Lancelot of the Languedoc, what about those who actually knew the real prince?

I could lie like a rug, talk my way out of it, he thought. *Plausible deniability, that's all I need.* It was true; who would want to believe that the champion of Caer Camlann had been replaced by an identical, evil twin?

"What made you ask that?" he parried, stalling.

"Lancelot, in the last month, you've suddenly become so reasonable I'd have guessed you grew an extra head. Would the old Lancelot have tolerated That Boy bursting in on his lovemaking? Granted I only knew him for a quarter year, I think it's a safe gamble he would have split Cors Cant—I mean, That Boy, in twain with a single blow of his axe.

"Of course," she added, leaning on her saddle and staring Peter in the eyes, "if you *had* tried such a stunt, I would have killed you before you half crossed the room.

"So I ask again: are you really Lancelot of Caer Camlann?"

Peter opened his mouth to chide the girl for her disrespect toward a legate and consul when, abruptly, the truth spilled out. After all, Anlawdd had confessed to him first.

"No," he said, his voice shrinking from bombast to breathy whisper in a single sentence, "I'm not Lancelot, not champion, not even a . . . a Sicambrian."

Too many lies, he told himself. *Too many trips to the Fountain of Perpetual Disinformation. I'll tell her, then I'll kill her.* But as the mask fell, his control over his own self-loathing, always loose, ready to slip, fell to the ground beside him.

Peter realized he had spent the last eighteen years of his life as a stick, an inert piece of wood that only came alive when swung in the hands of a sadistic gaoler—when it became a truncheon. "I do it all for queen and country," he told himself again and again until he could close his eyes at night without seeing the faces that The Stick had smashed.

Now he was caught in such a web of lies and deceit that he could barely tell whether he was Peter Smythe dreaming he was Lancelot, or The Beast dreaming that the demon Peter Smythe possessed his body . . . and the difference between the two worldviews was rapidly becoming moot as The Beast slowly drove him from control of Lancelot's body.

Peter Smythe spilled everything. He watched as if from afar, unable to stopper his mouth, as, in relentless monotone, he told Anlawdd who he was, where he was from, why he was sent back. Every last secret.

When he finished, Anlawdd stood utterly silent for two whole minutes . . . probably a "personal best." Three times, she opened her mouth, closed it again, like a sea bass. At last, she mustered strength to say something.

"A magnificent tale, Lancelot, or Peter, if you prefer. Have you ever thought of testing for the Druid College? You could add 'bard' to your list of titles."

"Anlawdd," he said, "the sooner I find Selly, the quicker I'll be out of your life, out of your time. You can have the old Lancelot back. Might not be an improvement, but at least you'll know where you stand."

Anlawdd stared at Peter. "Lancelot—or Peter, if you now prefer—from where I'm sitting, on Merillwyn, the most likely (and charitable) conclusion I can draw is that the full moon has touched you, despite being hidden behind clouds tonight.

"Ah ah! Don't interrupt, Prince, a bad habit you share with That Boy. Lan—, ah, Peter, I have known for some time that there was something wrong with you. I even set spies to check you out, and they told me interesting tales indeed. No, no names, I'd never betray their confidence."

Gee, thought Peter, *I can't imagine who you might mean. If I ever find out for sure that that bard did a bag-*

job on my quarters, you'll be a widow before you're a wife.

Unstoppable as always, Anlawdd continued. "But I do have to admit I like the new Lancelot better than the old, and I don't just mean in bed. That was a one-time, special, Circus Maximus event; don't expect an encore performance.

"I'm going to do what Uncle Leary and King Merovee always teach: make an executive decision. For now, at least, I'm going to trust that whether you're a *very* minor godling possessing Lancelot, or just barmy as an alchemist, house odds are better betting on you than on Cei, Bedwyr, the Paullites, the Romans, or even Artus, whom I don't know all that well and have never doted on the way That Boy does. After all, I nearly slew him once, and that doesn't bode well for his staying power ... plunging a dagger in the *Dux Bellorum* seems to be like plunging another kind of blade into Princess Gwynhwfyr—I mean, if *anyone* can do it, where's the sport?"

Peter understood the subtext. No matter what else, Peter did care about Anlawdd, and she knew it. She knew he intended her no harm ... something she could not necessarily say for any of the other powers in Camlann except Merovee, who was probably the only other potentate in Britain besides Peter who would never betray her, never blab her secrets to the *Dux Bellorum*.

The silence was, of course, temporary. After she replenished her oxygen supply, she opened fire again. "But what can *I* do? I'm not a necromanceress, you know. I can't summon up King Bran and ask him to finger your she-demon for you.

"And I'll tell you right now, I don't trust you as far as I can heave a cat or swing a brick. I will *not* hit anyone with my axe for you, so don't even bother asking. And don't try to tell me that Sally Corwind is Cors Cant, because I guarantee you I would know the difference."

She momentarily lost her place in her mental notes, fell silent. Peter seized the initiative. "Anlawdd, all I need are your eyes and ears. Look, love, you found *me* out! You said yourself you knew there was something strange for weeks. All I want to know is, who *else* has acted kind of funny recently? Anyone?"

While she pondered, Peter noticed that she never stopped watching him, and her hand never strayed far from the savage (single-bladed, British) battle-axe she carried, though he'd never actually seen her use it.

"Well, there is one person who seemed to change pretty abruptly; but he's not your Sally Conner, I can almost guarantee it."

"Well? Who?"

She arched an eyebrow. "Peter Lancelot, you should know! You spotted the change yourself."

"You don't mean that young lad Medraut?"

"Brother Prince, the old Medraut might have abandoned his troops to charge the enemy single-handed, but he would *not* have stood waist deep in Llyr's piss blubbering with fright."

"Good point."

"But whoever he is, he's not Sally."

"Selly."

"He's not even a woman. I can tell. For one thing, according to his men, he devised a tricky battle plan that fooled the Jutes ... and women just don't have a head for war and battle. And who would have trained a woman in battlefield strategy in the first place? That's like building a wall with gold bricks, the very thing you're trying to defend."

Peter stared at her, amused. "Um, Anlawdd, I don't like to point out the obvious, but ..."

"Pig dung. I'm unique, one-of-a-breed. Apart from me, Queen Boudicca, and Queen Artemisia of Halicarnassus, I can't think of a single, other warrior maiden. And trust me, it's the sort of thing I would follow."

Peter did trust the princess ... to a point. He agreed there was something strange about Medraut, but was not prepared to rule out the scenario where Medraut was really Selly, who of course could have received training in battlefield tactics in the IRA. For that matter, he could not rule out the scenario where Medraut was nothing more than a braggart; and when blades flew, he was revealed as a frightened kid. All the same, Anlawdd's testimony made Peter even more suspicious of Myrddin.

She said nothing more, and Peter was only too happy to spur Eponimius across the deserted plain toward Artus. Silently, he decided his only sane course of action: wait until Myrddin, "Mark Blundell," points out "Selly Corwin" to him, then kill them both. For Selly, a quick trip fifteen hundred years back to tomorrow and the waiting arms of Colonel Cooper and the 22-SAS. For Mark, no harm, no foul.

That done, he would fall upon his own sword, return to his own body (he hoped) fifteen centuries hence.

They rode another mile when suddenly Anlawdd hissed, reined in her mount. Ahead, a lone figure stood atop a slight rise, leaned on an improvised staff. At first, Peter thought it was Myrddin the Humbug (or possibly, Irish terrorist); then he realized it was the sorcerer's apprentice.

Cors Cant watched them approach. it was not until they were nearly upon him in the blackness that Peter saw how stricken the boy's face was. A great tragedy had occurred, driving Cors Cant into the desolation of Dinas Emrys.

CHAPTER 44

THE BARD WATCHED THE BETRAYERS APPROACH, STARTLED BY his own lack of rancor. The weeks apart from Anlawdd had washed away his anger that Lancelot had been her first, rather than Cors Cant himself.

Truthfully, it relieved him of the terrible fear that he would prove as inept at love as doddering old Emperor

Claudius the Half-wit at statesmanship. Now the burden fell upon Anlawdd to teach *him* how it all worked.

Cors Cant closed his eyes. They were betrayers, but not because of one night or a score of nights futtering each other. Both had betrayed Artus, thus the entire empire: Anlawdd betrayed Artus by not telling him of her father's treachery, and Lancelot betrayed him by leading a rebellion and poisoning Merovee.

Or did he? Suddenly, the bard was not sure. Did the prince know what was in the bottle in his own apartment? Before carrying tales to Artus, Cors Cant decided he had better make sure, lest he, too, betray an innocent.

The riders had nearly arrived. Cors Cant shuddered, remembering that the cursed plain of Dinas Emrys was where Vortigern and his monstrous giant, Rhita Fawr, were finally defeated and captured by Artus and Merovee.

Vortigern, the murdering bastard who had pillaged Lludd-Dun, Londinium, allowing his foot soldiers to rape and execute Cors Cant's parents and sister, later tore off huge pieces of Prydein and gave them to his Saxon lickspittles, Hengist and Horsa, as East-Saxony and South-Saxony.

After Artus finally captured Vortigern, he bound him hands to feet and threw him to Vortigern's own slaves, who hacked their master to pieces with kitchen knives and gardening tools.

Rhita Fawr, too large to be slain by ordinary means (he had survived a spear thrust entirely through his body six years earlier), was chained by each limb to four teams of horses and pulled apart.

Where the blood of the two inhuman monsters spilled, witnesses claimed it was black and tacky to the touch, like tar. It blackened the ground, where now nothing grew, not a single blade of grass, not a weed or shoot. A horrible odor permeated the air, so thick Cors Cant could taste it— though some ancients claimed the smell had preceded Vortigern's death and was nothing more sinister than sulfurous essence escaping from Pluto's realm through cracks in the earth.

Cors Cant had braved the fen to confront Lancelot on his own ground, surrounded by his own legions. It seemed like a good idea at the time; but now it struck him as pretty stupid, as he stood on unhallowed ground in cold, black night, surrounded by the shades of traitors who allied with Saxon devils for personal gain. But the real reason still held: confronting Lancelot was the only way to prove to Anlawdd that Cors Cant was not a coward, not afraid of dying . . . only of dealing death himself. And he needed her to relent, let him show that his love was stronger than his moral outrage.

The pair's unexpected approach on horseback made the rest of Cors Cant's trip unnecessary. He left his pony to nose bootlessly for something to graze, climbed the biggest hill on the plain (all of seven fathoms elevation), and made sure they saw him.

Anlawdd suddenly reined in, let Lancelot proceed alone. She watched the bard from twenty strides distance, unreadable expression on her face.

He recognized the expression. She wore it when confronted by an enemy, waiting with what the Druid war philosophers called "perfect invulnerability" for him to make the first move, move off his own invulnerable spot, and open himself to counterattack. She had worn the same expression when she watched the Saxons who tried to kidnap her near Camlann—just before she killed them.

Lancelot seemed not to care about Anlawdd's presence. His face was contorted, as if struggling against unbearable agony. For an instant, he was the old Lancelot again, and Cors Cant took an involuntary step backward. Then the new Lancelot returned, mastered himself.

"Ho, Bard. What brings you out here in this desolate landscape? And you'd better not answer 'my horse.' "

"Tragic news, my Prince. The king—Merovius Rex—is dead."

"What?" Lancelot seemed genuinely shocked, and the bard felt a wave of uncertainty about his earlier accusatory thoughts. "Dead? Merovee is dead? What in God's name happened?"

Cors Cant said nothing. Lancelot urged Eponimius closer, leaned over until he was directly above the bard. "Answer me, boy: *what happened to Merovee?*"

"It seems he was poisoned," said Cors Cant, slowly and distinctly, "either by his food or perhaps his wine."

Lancelot sat up straight, pulled the reins a little tighter to his body. "God," he whispered, "it never ends. His wine? Jesus, he's gone?"

Cors Cant closed his eyes, slowed his breathing. *Myrddin, if you ever loved your pupil, ride with me now!* The bard had few Druid talents yet . . . only the heightened sense of smell and hearing that comes from hours of silent meditation, hearing his own heart, his breath, the rustle of insects crawling over his bare feet, the breath, heartbeat, slight, involuntary movements of his fellow students at the college.

He extended those senses now, cast them out like a net upon Prince Lancelot of the Languedoc, champion of Caer Camlann.

He listened to Lancelot's heartbeat: it pounded rapidly, the pulse nearly doubling and the heart beating so loud that even Anlawdd might have been able to hear it.

He listened to the breath: suddenly rapid and shallow, frequency rising to match the elevated heartbeat. He heard Lancelot lick his suddenly dry lips.

Cors Cant smelled the sweat dripping down the prince's chest and back, felt rather than saw Lancelot shrink slightly in the saddle.

He had every physical symptom of a man wracked by sudden guilt.

Cors Cant opened his eyes again. Now he could carry the tale of the poisoned wine to Artus *Dux Bellorum* with a clear conscience. Lancelot was surely guilty, or at least complicit, in Merovee's murder.

The boy looked at the champion, felt a rush of fear. The new Lancelot stared back, not stupid like the old. In the instant of full eye contact, Cors Cant realized that the prince had deduced how much he knew from his own reactions.

Jesus and Mithras . . . I guess I'm not the only trained observer here.

His stomach fluttered, and his knees grew suddenly weak. The planned confrontation that he earlier thought was stupid but necessary, now seemed insane and foolhardy. He was the only witness to Merovee's death . . . and here he stood, leine to breastplate, with the murderer, who *knew* he had been discovered with the bloody, metaphorical dagger in his hand.

Lancelot spoke in a low, menacing voice, sounding much more like the Lancelot of old. "Boy, what *do* you know about that bottle of wine?"

A metallic scrape caught both their attentions. Cors Cant craned for a look, Lancelot actually half turned in his saddle to stare back at Anlawdd.

She held a well-balanced axe in her hand, the same neutral expression on her face. "Remember what I told you earlier?" she asked cryptically. "Maybe you can get one of us, but if I escape, you-know-what gets buried you-know-where, and if That Boy escapes, he'll run you all the way back to the *Dux Bellorum*'s pickets, and you'll be arrested."

Lancelot passed his hand over his eyes. When he uncovered his face, the new Lancelot was back in evidence. He smiled, a weary, resigned smile, no longer full of menace. "I guess you can run on and on," he said, "but great God A'mighty gonna pull you down."

Lancelot nudged Eponimius around the boy, kneed the horse on toward Artus's encampment. "Pack your trash, son," he said, "we have a date with the *Dux Bellorum.*"

Cors Cant did not mount, walking his shaggy pony instead. After a moment, Anlawdd rode up and dismounted beside him.

"Don't be ridiculous," she said, sounding stricken.

"Well is it true?" he asked. "Does he wear that damned scale-mail even to bed?"

"Don't be ridiculous, Cors Cant Ewin. You know why I did it, or you should, which is about the same." Her voice shook, and she, too, sounded like a soul caught by grief's torment. "Mary, Mother of God, you'd think we were both Romans, the way you're carrying on about a single bed-sharing! That's like a child who cries with jealousy when his mother stops to pet a dog on the road."

"I'm not a child, you're surely not my mother, he's not a dog, and I'm not jealous, Anlawdd. My mother died in Londinium after being raped by three soldiers, then beaten with spear butts. She was slain by a traitor who sold out Prydein for Saxon gold.

"The question is," he continued, staring meaningfully at her, "who turns traitor for the Church's gold?"

"Cors Cant Ewin, what *are* you talking about? I can't make heads nor eagles out of it."

Anlawdd looked legitimately confused, and Cors Cant's heart softened immediately. *God, how could I think her a treasoner? And how long would I have kept secret my own father's betrayal, had he been the man who opened the gates of Londinium to Vortigern, instead of the captain of the first cohort to be butchered?*

Would I have obeyed Father had he set me to slay instead of serve the Dux Bellorum?

Ashamed, he stared down at his sandaled feet, carefully placed one foot in front of the other. He realized he could never tell her his suspicions about Lancelot. She might think it merely the concoction of a jealous, irrational mind . . . and the bard could not live with Anlawdd thinking he lied to her, accusing an innocent man, just to get rid of a potential rival for her affections.

No, he had to win her honestly, which meant he had to finally swallow his medicine, keep his promise first to sainted Merovee, then to Archking Leary.

He had to finally Tell Her.

You've done everything but, said the familiar voice in his head. It was Merovee's voice, even though the king was dead—long live the king. With a lump in his throat, the bard understood that it had been his own words all along, merely using Merovee's authoritative tones to tell himself what he needed to hear. It was his higher soul, the master who made the grass green and the sky blue, trying to lead him away from the abyss ... the yapping dog on Cei's tarot trump, the Fool.

"Anlawdd ..." he began, faded to silence. She squeezed his hand hard; he did not even remember her taking it. His ears, still preternaturally tuned, heard her own heartbeat and breathing speed up. Her palms were slippery with sweat.

By Jupiter and Jesus, this time I am really going to say it! "Anlawdd," he began again, taking a deep breath to steady his balance, "I have loved you from—well, from a month or so after I met you. I—I love you now. I'll love you tomorrow."

She trembled, sniffed. He realized she wept as they walked. "That's the first time you've said it without meaning something entirely different, Boy."

"I know," he said.

"Cors Cant Ewin, even though I'm not speaking to you ... Oh to hell with it, I'm tired of games. I love you too. So there."

"I know," he repeated.

"How long?"

Cors Cant shrugged, invisible in the dark. "I guess I figured it out when I found you two together. I saw the expression on your face before you saw me, while he was inside you, then after."

"What did it look like before?"

"The same way you look when you're washing Gwynhwfyr's chemise. And after, you looked like you'd just discovered you'd *torn* her favorite chemise."

He stopped, pulled her to a halt beside him. Quickly, before he could think about what he was doing, Cors Cant caught her head with a hand on each side, gently but firmly pulled her face to his, and kissed her hard. After a few seconds, they had to break to gasp for air.

"I—I don't want our first time to be on Dinas Emrys," she whispered, voice cracking.

"Screw screwing," he said. "I just want to kiss you, Mistress."

"My wish is your command, Master." She wrapped her

arms around the bard, who entwined her body with his own limbs, and they locked their open mouths together again. He smiled through the kiss, amused at the titles, which referred to their equal degrees as Master Builders . . . the only ranking system either of them recognized.

This time Cors Cant waited until he was ready to pass out before finally breaking. They clutched each other, dizzy, seeing stars in the overcast sky.

"Cors Cant Ewin, there has *got* to be a better technique."

"We need a love philosopher."

"Is there such a person?"

"Not in this civilized, Roman hell," he admitted.

She suddenly pushed him to arm's length, held him tight. "You finally did it," she declared.

"Won you?"

She raised her eyebrows, looked impressed. "You've grown, Cors. Taller than I, maybe. You're learning to trust your spirit guide, as I'm sure it was he who told you to kiss me.

"Yes, my prince, you've discovered the key to winning your princess. But remember, Cors Cant. Don't you dare forget that you must win me every day for the rest of our lives together. You can't ever get complacent and decide I'm conquered territory."

"I say the same to you, Anlawdd. I can't scry the future . . . not my personal future, in any case. That's beyond the powers of any but the most learned Druids like Myrddin and Cynddylig Cyfarwydd the Guider. Anlawdd, I can't promise I won't ever, you know, leave. I just don't know."

"Nor I. I believe in love, Cors, but all that 'prince and princess' rot is fine for bedtime tales, but we're both going to grow, and God knows we might not grow in the same direction, though if we're good and lucky, maybe we'll grow closely enough that we don't have to take different roads."

"I'd rather be lucky than good."

"You're both, Cors Cant; you got me." She smiled, enigmatic as the Sphinx. "Love isn't enough, at least according to Uncle Leary, who's usually right on this sort of thing, having lived three hundred summers, he says. You need love, you need lust, you need friendship and respect."

"We've each shown the other three of the four," responded the bard, with a faintly lascivious smile.

"And you need to keep secrets from each other."

"What? Why?"

"You have to be whole people separately before you can unite, and you never become as one. That's another bedtime tale. You still have separate lives, things the other doesn't share. Hence the secrets . . . it's like having one room in your house that's all your own, where you keep the things from before, beneath, and around your love."

"Oh."

They walked after Lancelot, trailing far behind, Anlawdd's arm around Cors Cant's shoulder and his around her waist.

"Yes," he said, "I've thought about that."

"The problem is, how do we stay together, given the difference in our secular ranks?"

"I've thought of that. We can't jolly well get married."

"Not unless we bolt, say to Africa."

"You have to marry a king or a prince, or at least a general . . . and what man, having attained such high rank, should allow a half-trained bard to claim privileges upon his wife?"

"I'm getting old, Cors. I'll be nineteen next summer . . . I must marry soon, choosy or not. I've managed to ward off the blow for several years now, but it will fall shortly."

"Anlawdd, I don't mean to hurt you with unpleasant memories, but—would any man of quality marry you at all, given your father's, um, disgrace?" Cors Cant noted with relief that she held him tighter, did not push him away.

"Yes, I have thought about that, too, Cors. I don't know. We should ask someone, Merovee. Oh! I didn't mean that!"

"Hard to believe he's dead, isn't it? He foresaw it . . . remember, in the grove below Harlech?"

"Not really. I remember he said something about you being a mouse and meeting Death."

"The fool and the emperor drink a toast to Death, and the bigger fool drops his cup," quoted the bard. "Remember now?"

She shrugged. "Never thought portents were very importent."

"Leary," stated Cors Cant forcefully.

"You can't be serious."

"He's the one to ask."

"Oh, to *ask*. For a minute I thought you meant—"

"He's a Builder, isn't he. And he gave me good advice when Merovee was, um, not available."

"I don't know. I've never trusted Uncle Leary. He's too clever by half."

"Well too clever by half sure beats being half-clever. Isn't that what we need now, too much cleverness?" He leaned close to her ear, whispered, "And Princess, are you sure he's only your uncle? He nearly admitted that his relationship with you was much closer."

"Ah, yes, well there has been that rumor. It would sure make a better lineage than daughter of a traitor, wouldn't it?" She sighed. "All right, Cors Cant Ewin, Boy Bard, lead on. I'll put up with asking that hairy Barbary ape if you'll tell me what in the world you meant about Lancelot a while back there. Leaving that hanging is like dropping only one boot."

He shook his head, then realized she could not see a headshake any better than a shrug. "Sorry, Anlawdd. I'm afraid that will have to be my first secret."

"Bastard," she said, pulling him closer.

CHAPTER 45

DEAD. GONE, CROSSED THE STYX, JOINED THE DARK KING Arawn in Anufyn ... the thought rolled round and round my brain with every step back toward the *Dux Bellorum*'s camp, like a loose cart wheel spinning down to a stop.

How could Merovee have allowed himself to die, when he *knew* I still had a confession burning a hole in my stomach?

He had responsibilities! He was no mere king with the right to cast his life away on trivial quests, wars, or assorted adventures. He was the heir to— the distant son of—well, the Blood Royal ran strong in his veins.

It was all I could do, as I walked alongside That Boy, not to fall to the ground weeping ... not just for my inability to confess, of course, but for Merovee himself, and what we had lost by his death. True, I heard he had a son; but what if the son was like Claudius to Drusus, a terrible disappointment? Or worse, what if Merovius Minor were like Canastyr!

It was a long walk, and I wished I could simply mount Merillwyn; but That Boy seemed as afraid of horses as ever, and remained afoot beside his shaggy beast.

With every step, however, I breathed as Uncle Leary had taught me, calmed myself. I needed a clear head, not a heart full of grief, to confront Artus *Dux Bellorum*.

I stopped so suddenly that Merillwyn actually bumped into me, nearly bowled me over.

When did I decide to confess to Artus?

Cors Cant—I mean, That Boy—noticed he was alone,

glanced back once; but he was wise enough to realize I had to wrestle with my own demons. He waited, looking the way we would go, toward Artus's pavilion, rather than back at me.

Confessing to That Boy must have finally cured me of sick fear, I reasoned. The thought rang true: I knew the punishment would be horrible, but eventually, I must tell Artus himself what Gormant did . . . and what I had nearly done.

There would be punishment, exile, perhaps even prison. But no longer would I hide my light beneath a bushel . . . let them all see me for who I really was! What was it that That Boy had quoted me once, after Artus decreed that a philanthropist should have his hand stricken from his arm for some petty fraud? Oh, yes: *fiat justitia ruat coelum.* "Let justice be done though heaven should fall."

Confessing to anyone else, even to Merovee, was like bandaging an arrow wound without removing the arrow. So long as Merovee were alive, I would *never* have confessed to the person I had actually wounded: Artus *Dux Bellorum.* It took the king's death to wake the somnambulant princess.

I grinned. "You sly wolf," I said aloud. "You died for *my* sins, didn't you?"

"Who?" asked That Boy.

I shook my head, gestured him to continue. Suddenly, I was eager to get the whole sordid mess behind me and take my punishment . . . like a warrior.

CHAPTER 46

PETER STOOD BEFORE ARTUS, IMPATIENT BUT IMPASSIVE. THE *Dux Bellorum* ignored his champion, studying a hastily scribbled force allocation map as if trying to burn a hole through it.

"Intelligence," he muttered for the fifth time. "Where's my intelligence?" Artus sounded distinctly rattled.

"Sir," began Peter a third time. This time, the *Dux Bellorum* looked up wearily. His ashen face caused Peter's annoyance to dissipate. Would Artus even last out the night? *Coronary occlusion,* thought Peter.

"Where is Cei?" demanded the War-Leader. "Where are my outriders?"

"Cei commands his own legions, sir."

"Or Bedwyr?"

"With his brother's legions."

"But I must *know* where they are! How am I to fight an entire Jutic army without knowing their disposition?"

"Whom did you send to scout, sir?"

Artus thought for a moment, trying to recapture here-and-now. "Cacamwri. I sent Cacamwri with a cohort of the Praetorian Guard."

"The Guard? Sir, that leaves you unprotected."

"Who'd want to kill me? Anyway, that blackguard's probably joyriding, running down unattached Jutic units for the fun of killing." The bitterness in his voice took Peter by surprise.

"I'm sure Cacamwri is scouting as well as he is able, if he hasn't been killed or captured himself. Sir, I have terrible news. I don't know how to soften the blow, but . . . King Merovee is dead."

Artus nodded. "Yes."

"You were very close."

The *Dux Bellorum* sat on his folding stool, hands clasped between his knees. "He was my All-Dragon, I was his lance." His eyes were dead grey, but dry. "He was to be emperor. Did you know?"

"Artus . . . sir, my news is not finished."

"More? Would you kill me with words before I strike a blow?" He smiled, a wan attempt at humor that quickly died.

"Merovee was poisoned. He drank wine given him by, ah, by Cei and Bedwyr. Poisoned wine."

Artus watched Peter dispassionately. "Some say Merovee deliberately drank poisoned wine. Some say he committed suicide. I wish he had fallen upon his sword; it's more classical."

Peter vigorously shook his head. "The poison came from Cei. God help me, I know, for Cei approached me to join in a rebellion against you."

"No."

"And Bedwyr is a part. They plan to desert you, take their legions back to their own principality. Don't count on them."

"No, Galahadus. If Cei said that, he was but testing your own loyalty. Cei would never desert me; not old Cei, my porter and first champion of my claim."

"Sir, there is another threat to your life. A—witch from far away, farther than Sicambria or Rome, plans to murder you. She is a shape-shifter and has taken the form of one of your court; I'm not sure which one."

"Myrddin protects me from all such magic. Else I'd already be dead a hundred times over."

How in the name of all that's holy can I convince him? "Sir, do me a favor? Just don't turn your back on Myrddin. I don't trust him . . . don't trust any of these priests and conjurers."

"First Cei, then Bedwyr, and now Myrddin! Galahadus,

my lance, what spirit has possessed you? You see ghosts behind every tent flap."

Artus's eyes strayed back to the map. Peter began to speak, realized it was hopeless. He would have to handle it himself; he would get no cooperation from the *Dux Bellorum.*

Not surprising, he thought. *His empire is crumbling around him like a mud hut in a rainstorm. With Merovee dead, the best he could hope for is to rule Britain—and even that's in jeopardy now.*

Head low, Peter saluted, left the *Dux Bellorum*'s tent.

He stood for a moment in the lantern light outside the command tent, cloak wrapped tightly against the biting cold. Winter was coming, the snow and storms putting an end to campaigning. Artus had one shot to drive the Jutes from Harlech, after which they would have a whole season to fortify the city and create permanent supply lines.

Peter shivered, more from the sense of inevitability than from the wind. Camelot was ending, though only Peter— and Artus—knew it.

He blew on his hands, wondered whether he should seek out a troopers' fire to warm himself before returning to his own legion, wondering what to do about Myrddin, wondering whether Myrddin was Mark, Selly, or some unknown third party.

"The kid," he suddenly said aloud. It took him a few moments to consciously understand what he meant by the remark. He had to check with Gwyn, find out what Myrddin was up to.

He found the blond boy with his hand down his pants, lazily playing with himself in the empty tent. Peter cleared his throat with a deep rumble.

Gwyn whipped his hand out guiltily, stood at an angle to hide the evidence of his recent activity. "S-Sire! Prince Lancelot! I—I didn't expect you here." His face turned crimson in the lamplight, looking, with his yellow hair, like a tomato with a banana-peel helmet.

"Well?" demanded Peter.

"Hunh? Oh, Myrddin. He hasn't done anything, Sire."

"Nothing? Hasn't eaten or slept, urinated against a tree, talked to anyone?"

"Oh. Certes, he's had a couple of long conversations with Artus, one with Cei, and one with Medraut."

"What! Alone?"

"Well yes, now that you ask, Sire."

"You chowderheaded leprechaun, that's *exactly* what I wanted you to tell me about! Jesus, Mary, and Joseph, don't you know what a spy *does?*"

Gwyn looked so abashed that Peter relented, softened. "Look, son, keep your pants laced, all right?"

Gwyn nodded vigorously, flushing again.

"Tell me the moment *anything* happens involving Myrddin . . . especially anything unusual."

It took Peter less than an hour to ride back to his own legion. He walked the pickets yet again, silently cursed the nighttime fog, and wished his own scout, Hir Amren, would return with intelligence.

"Probably out sodding-off with Cacamwri," he muttered.

CHAPTER 47

"CORS," SAID ANLAWDD, GRIPPING HIS HAND TIGHTLY, "I'M afraid."

"You?" He stared in amazement. The princess-warrior who had stared down three armed Saxons and watched her hometown gutted by a Jutic holocaust was afraid to talk to the *Dux Bellorum*.

She hung her head, clenched her teeth. "I've . . . I've always had a hard time with celebrated kings and war-

leaders. My tongue ties itself in knots like a drunken
snake."

"But you're a princess yourself!"

"Of a backward little town in a cantref way off in the
sticks, Cors Cant Ewin."

"And your fa—I mean, your uncle is the archking of all
Eire!"

"What? Don't be silly, he's just Uncle Leary. Cors Cant,
you've attached yourself to this court like a barnacle for
ten years—of course, talking to Artus means nothing to
you!"

He shook his head. "No, I can't."

"Cors . . . is it possible for you to speak for me?"

"No I can't. That's one thing Artus absolutely hates, a
Philadelphia lawyer, orating his client's cause while the
client stands mute and smirks at the *Dux Bellorum.*"

"I never smirk!"

"Well, that's how he would see it, anyway. You have to
plead your own case, my love. But I'll tell you this. . . ."

"Don't say it, Cors. You may regret it."

"Whatever fate he decrees for you, for your father's
treason and your own—"

"Don't make promises, darling."

The bard stubbornly pushed on. "Whatever fate he decrees, I'll share it with you. On my honor I shall."

"Great. Now in addition to getting my own head lopped
off, I can be responsible for *your* death as well."

"No," he contradicted, emboldened by discovering that
Anlawdd requited his love. "If I die or go into exile, it's
because *I* chose to join you. My life is my responsibility,
no one else's. That's Merovee's most important lesson."

She looked up, raised her eyebrows. "If you learned that
much, you learned more than most, Cors Cant. Personally,
I think *my* life is all the responsibility of that old pederast,
Leary . . . but I haven't quite put my finger on how he did
it. But you are right about one thing . . . I can't allow anyone to speak for me. I must stand up like a man and catch
the consequences of my own folly." She smiled weakly,
gestured toward the *Dux Bellorum*'s command tent.

Moments later, they stood side by side before Artus *Pan-Draconis,* the *Dux Bellorum* of the Holy Celto-Romantic Empire, what was left of it after Merovee's suicide.

Artus waited patiently while Anlawdd opened her mouth, took a deep breath, then let it out, too embarrassed and ashamed to say anything.

"Speak, Princess," he said, gently urging her on. He hated lawyers but had infinite patience for a person honestly trying to speak her mind, no matter how long it took her.

A tear rolled down Anlawdd's cheek, but her pride would not let her wipe it or otherwise acknowledge its existence. Finally, she choked out the words.

"Artus *Dux Bellorum,* my family is shamed by treachery, and I'm here to apologize for my dad being a right bastard and plotting with the Saxons and Jutes against you, and for my own near miss at throwing in with them, sneaking into your room, dagger in hand, like a child out to slay her nightmare, even though I'd never have done that myself if I'd known who was involved. And I also feel really bad about not telling you about it, like a little girl who breaks her mother's favorite vase and hides the pieces so she won't get caught." She paused to gulp air.

"Princess Anlawdd, your silence carried a great cost . . . much greater than your own near treason."

"I know, you don't have to tell—"

As patient as Artus could be to let a person speak her mind, he would not be stopped from speaking his own, no matter how much the words hurt. "Lancelot lost half a *maniple* because he walked into a trap he didn't know existed, a trap you could have warned him about."

Anlawdd stared at the ground, rubbed a line in the dirt with her boot toe. "I'm sorry," she said. "I have no excuse. I was confused and stupid. I'll . . . I'll give you my title if I must."

Artus turned suddenly to Cors Cant. "Don't feel superior, Bard. You, too, cost many lives by your foolishness and inaction."

"What! How?" Cors Cant staggered, not expecting the sudden accusation.

"Whom did you tell about Cutha's signaling Harlech the night before Lancelot's attack?"

"No one, I just . . ." His voice faded into silence as he realized the truth of the *Dux Bellorum*'s condemnation. A horrible feeling of helpless grief gripped him; he suddenly understood the pain Anlawdd felt, moved a little closer to her.

Artus stood, stared into nothingness a thousand miles beyond the tent wall. "Actions have consequences," he said. *"Cave canem*, beware of the dog. You both allowed your dog-soul to overrule your rational soul. And you're still doing it; that's the part that pains me the most."

Cors Cant stared at Artus, hoping he was not talking about what it sounded like. Artus confirmed the bard's worst fears, saying, "This blasphemous relationship between you two cannot continue. Oh, you try to hide it, but I hear the rumors, I see how you look at each other when you think no one's watching. I know what the young people get into nowadays, and it's a damned sight more improper than in my youth."

At once, Anlawdd lost all her shyness and fear of celebrity, indignantly putting fists on hips and lecturing Artus. "Now you listen, Artus All-Dragon, we've been perfectly proper about this from the first day to today, like a child the month before Yule! We've done nothing, haven't even touched each other. We've kissed one time, out on the moors with only Lancelot as witness. How can you say we—"

It was a tactical error to mention the man who had stolen the *Dux Bellorum*'s wife. Cors Cant could have warned Anlawdd, save he had no idea she would bring up Lancelot. Anlawdd's defense sparked a five-minute lecture on proper, Roman morality including total abstinence from sex between unmarried persons, and an even more savage denunciation of the "Greek disease" as Artus called it.

During this talk, the *Dux Bellorum* had moved closer to the pair. Now he stood right next to Cors Cant, talked as if only to the bard. "Surely you understand what I mean," he said, putting his hand on the small of Cors Cant's back. "We just can't have it here; this is a proper, Roman household, and we're going to be a proper, Roman family."

The bard squirmed away, edged toward Anlawdd. Prometheanism did not bother him; it was a fine, old Greek tradition. Very classical. Everyone knew about Artus and young men, though no one said anything aloud.

But the *combination* of such desire with scathing denunciations of anyone who felt them gave Cors Cant the creeps. *He's under terrible stress,* thought the bard. *He's lost all sense of discretion!*

"And you know," continued Artus, "that marriage would be an even greater blasphemy. Anlawdd is of the highest caste, but you, my boy, although a wonderful bard, wise and gentle, are but a priest. No, no I cannot allow this to go on. Son, do you know what God holds in store for fornicators and adulterers?"

Cors Cant shook his head, frightened.

"Hell. Eternal damnation, forever and ever. Cut off from the spirit of God, made to suffer unimaginable torments . . . and all for such a short moment of small pleasure."

Anlawdd said nothing, her expression occult. Cors Cant felt himself flush, both with fear and shame at entertaining arrogant and ungodly ambitions.

The Builders, what were they? Fat, old, greybearded men playing at blasphemy and heresy. There *were* differences between the quality, the merchants, artisans, yeomen, slaves. Was there literally *no distinction* between a citizen and a barbarian? Or between Gwynhwfyr and one of her own slaves?

I live in a civilized society, he thought. *This society has rules. All rules are arbitrary—if I throw the entire Roman baby out the window with the bathwater, don't I have to replace it with yet another set of rules, equally arbitrary? Where does it end, total anarchy?*

"Now I don't mean you two can't be friends," continued Artus in a more forgiving tone. "I think it's a fine idea

when royalty fraternize with citizens, so long as a certain
distance is kept." He punctuated this point by putting an
arm around each of them in a friendly, fatherly way, a
"let's-all-be-friends" gesture. "Use my friendship with the
beloved Merovius Rex as your guide, may he rest in peace
in the arms of the Lord, and my friendship with Prince
Lancelot. We share many good times together, but always
remember where the invisible line is drawn between a
prince and a mere general."

"Excuse me, General," said Anlawdd; Cors Cant winced
when she called the *Dux Bellorum* by the title he had just
used in a self-deprecating way. The bard understood
Anlawdd was trying to use her advantage of royalty, but it
was another bad move; he felt Artus stiffen at the familiarity as Anlawdd continued. "Aren't you *married* to a princess?"

After a frosty silence, Artus recovered control of his
temper. In ten years, Cors Cant had only twice before seen
him so close to exploding in anger.

*God, can I really share my love's fate if she brings
death or imprisonment upon herself?* The answer rose
immediately: *yes.*

"Princess Anlawdd"—Artus avoided the obvious tit-for-
tat by *not* overemphasizing her title—"that is entirely different. We married for political reasons, to cement an
alliance. I'm sure you understand that in a very personal
way." He pointedly looked at her.

"I assure you that when the time comes, I shall find a
suitable match for you. And I will take your own wishes
very much into account." Artus smiled warmly. "I won't
marry you off to a doddering old general, I promise."

"Um, you say *you* will find me a match? That would
mean . . ."

"Yes, Princess. I have decided to allow you to keep legal title to Harlech, despite Prince Gormant's treason
against the State. But in practice, Harlech will be admin-
istered by a governor. Bedwyr, perhaps, unless you have a
strong objection."

"I have a strong objection to anyone but *me* governing *my* city, and that brainless Barbary ape in particular!"

"Perhaps another governor then. But Princess Anlawdd, I will appoint a governor for Harlech. You will stay here as my honored guest."

"Hostage."

Artus shrugged. "Guarantee for your citizens' continued loyalty. You may make supervised visits to Harlech; in fact, I think it's a good idea. Let the people see their monarch, that's what I've always said. I constantly tell Cei and Lancelot they should return now and again to their principalities, take a more active role in their people's lives. Particularly judging citizen disputes," Artus added, rambling far from the point.

He's losing all control, thought Cors Cant. Artus had completely forgotten where he was, the battle that lay ahead tomorrow or the next day with a huge Jutic army. "Nothing assures and satisfies a citizen more than to know that his governor or monarch takes a personal interest in settling lawsuits and criminal cases fairly and impartially. *Fiat justitia ruat coelum!* That's what I always say."

Artus blinked, realized he held both Cors Cant and Anlawdd by their shoulders in a death grip. He let go, patted them both on the back. "Thank you for visiting me, my children. Princess, did I tell you you're to remain here, and I'll send a governor to administer Harlech? Good, I see that I did. If you have nothing else, you are dismissed." He plodded wearily back to his chair, stared into space.

"My love," whispered the bard to Anlawdd, "can you wait for me outside? I have something I must say to the *Dux Bellorum* . . . then something I must say to you."

Her face paled slightly in the lamplight. "Is it about us?"

"Yes."

"Will I like it?"

"I honestly don't know. Wait for me? I won't be a minute."

She opened her mouth to probe further, realized he was

not going to tell her before he told her. Mastering herself, she said "I'll wait, dear heart, but I've made a decision of my own."

"What?"

"I'll show you mine if you show me yours." A weak jest.

"I won't be a minute." Cors Cant waited until Anlawdd left the tent. Then he approached the *Dux Bellorum,* waited until Artus noticed him.

"Eh? Are you still here, Bard? Is there something else?"

"Yes, sir." He hesitated, uncertain how to begin, afraid of the consequences.

"Say it, Cors Cant. I will not punish you for speaking your mind; you know that."

"You haven't in the past," agreed the bard. "All right. Sir, it's Lancelot. I saw . . ." *And how exactly am I going to explain breaking into the legate's apartment?*

With a hole in the pit of his stomach, Cors Cant told Artus everything, from his own surreptitious entry into Lancelot's apartment to the bottle of poisoned wine to having seen Cei give the bottle back to Lancelot on the Harlech beach to Merovee saying the wine came from Lancelot by way of Cei.

Artus seemed genuinely surprised. "You were *with* Merovius when he died?"

"Yes, sir."

"Why wasn't I told this?" His mouth set grimly, the closest he normally came to pique.

"By whom?"

"The captain of Merovius's House Division, General Pius Britannicus, personally informed me of His Majesty's death by poison. He said Merovius drank the poison willingly . . . but he said nothing about *you* being present."

Cors Cant started to tell Artus about being forced to choose which glass to drain, but a voice warned him to keep that to himself. "I was summoned by His Majesty," he said instead. "Maybe he told the captain to keep quiet about it to avoid implicating me if there were an inquest. In any case, he didn't tell me to keep quiet, and I won't.

Sir, Merovius got that wine from Lancelot and Cei. They killed him, and I think they're plotting to kill you, too."

"Don't be ridiculous, my boy. I have known Galahadus for many years, during which he's always shown utter loyalty. And Cei! My own porter, captain of my household! Bard, do you know Cei was the first to uphold my claim to the combined armies of Britain? Even Rome was dubious that I could hold together this motley gaggle of a hundred local kings, princes, generals, knights and citizens, professional soldiers and political appointees! But Cei pledged me his own men, and they became my first legion.

"Do you now ask me to believe that Cei, my wife's cousin, turns against me, plotting with my Lance to bring me down?"

"Sir," said Cors Cant, rattling the dice and hoping for a double-Jupiter, "there is another piece of evidence. I had a—a vision."

"A vision?" Artus looked skeptical, but waited for the bard to continue.

"On the field, during the tournament, when Lancelot fought Cutha. I looked at the stands afterward and saw you struck by a mortal blow, struck by Lancelot!"

Artus dropped into lawyer mode, cross-examined the bard's account. "Did you *actually* see Lancelot strike me?"

"Well . . . no sir. But your breast was soaked with blood. The blow was mortal, it must have been."

"What made you think Lancelot struck it?"

"Sir, blood drenched his two hands as it would do if he had struck you with a dagger."

Artus smiled. "There, you see? Perhaps his hands became bloody trying to pluck the dagger from me after another struck the blow." He shook his head vigorously. "Cors Cant Ewin, you've let your imagination run wild. I don't blame you; it's all that bard nonsense they teach you up at the Druid College. I never should have let you go there . . . you're suited to be a top administrator, or a priest, not a tale-singer."

Cors Cant silently debated telling him the rest of the vision: Gwynhwfyr, too, was soaked with blood, decided against it. Artus was not to be convinced. "I, uh, had another vision, Sir. On the ship. A shrouded body . . ." He faded into silence; even he could not say that the body he saw was Artus, and not, for example, Merovee.

Artus waved his hand. "Enough of these signs and portents. I never pay attention to them anyway. They're always so open to interpretation. A red bird falls out of the sky, and a priest of Mithras says it's a good omen that I'll win the battle against the redheaded Saxons, while a priest of the Church says it's an ill portent that I'll be struck down in my prime.

"Cors Cant, a battle looms, and you have preparations to make. Go see if Myrddin needs help with his spells against the Jutes. I must study the plans once more."

Dismissed, Cors Cant left, knowing he had failed to persuade the *Dux Bellorum*. His vision would now surely come to pass, and Artus would be slain by the hand of the man he loved and trusted most, his lance, his spear, Galahad, called Lancelot.

Anlawdd was sitting on a rock outside the tent, arms folded across her chest. She looked very, very scared. She rose and approached the moment he passed the Praetorian Guard, but stopped more than a stride away. "What did you want to tell me?" she asked, voice steady.

He held out his hand. Reluctantly, she took it. "My love," he said, "I've made a decision about us. About me, actually."

"Yes?" she asked, voice neutral.

"I can't . . . Anlawdd, we can't stay. With Artus, I mean. If we stay, he'll never let us be together, and I couldn't live with that restriction."

She exhaled heavily, stepped forward and took both his hands in hers. "Thank Jesus and the Magdalene," she said, softly enough that the guard could not hear. "I was afraid you wanted to tell me we couldn't see each other again. That would be like—I don't even know what it would be like. Horrible, I guess, but understandable."

"Better not call on the Lord and Lady, my love. I'm afraid we're going to see them soon enough, and when we do it, it won't be a pleasant meeting." He led her away from the tent, threaded through the tents of the legionnaires. Anlawdd held his hand tightly, kept silence as they passed the nervous, joking soldiers.

Leary's pavilion was set apart from the more soldierly, Roman tents of the legion. He had his own guards, but they were unarmed save for ceremonial daggers, to underscore his role as observer only in the upcoming battle. Cors Cant hoped the Jutes would not be so crazy as to murder Eire. They must know it would call upon them the wrath of every man and woman on the Small Island.

They approached the guards. "Is the Ard-Ri at home?" asked the bard in Gaelic.

"Eire is absent, and we mourn until he returns," said the guard by formula.

"May we enter to await him?"

"No," said the guard succinctly.

Anlawdd tried. "Can we wait inside for Leary?"

"Of course," said the guard. "Enter freely. I'll send a messenger to His High Majesty telling him you wait his pleasure, Your Grace." He drew back the tent flap, gestured them both inside.

Anlawdd nudged Cors Cant in the ribs. "Rank hath its privileges," she said. He grunted, annoyed.

Inside, she grew more serious. "Cors Cant, what did you mean about meeting Jesus and not liking it?"

"Artus was right, my love. What we're doing is blasphemous, denying the sanctity of marriage ordained by God Himself."

"But that's ridiculous! You don't really believe all that enternal damnation stuff, do you?" But he did, and she saw immediately that he did. "Well," she admitted after a moment, "truth be told, I guess I do too. I guess."

"We have a decision to make," said the bard. "We can stay and follow God's will, which made one of us a princess and the other a bard . . . rank hath its privileges, as you say."

"Don't throw that back at me. I only meant it as a joke."

"I'm sorry, I didn't mean it like that. Or, we can . . ."
He faded to silence.

"Run away? Live together as fornicators and be damned
forever?"

"Basically, those are our only choices."

For long moments, both were silent, digesting the stark
duality. At last, Cors Cant spoke. "My heart, I made my
decision some time ago."

"Yes?" she asked, cautiously.

"If the Lord says I must go to hell for loving you, then
in the name of God, *I will go to hell.*"

Anlawdd closed her eyes, tensed, then relaxed, at peace.
"And if God sends you to hell, Cors Cant Ewin, then I
surely would spurn heaven."

"Then it's done. We've thrown the dice. We're conscious heretics with no one to blame but ourselves."

"Thrown," she agreed. They embraced, held each other
tight; but it was not rejoicing. Cors Cant buried his face in
her neck, and she stroked the back of his head, staring into
tomorrow and weeping for lost yesterday.

Leary entered the pavilion at that moment, stood in re-
spectful silence until Anlawdd whispered his arrival to the
bard. They separated, stood hand in hand before the
archking.

Leary grinned wholeheartedly. Soon the lovers smiled
also; it was impossible to remain grave around Archking
Leary. "Sure an ye hold each other closer, ye'll be wearing
each the ayther's troosers," he observed. "I've given your
problem muckle consideration. An' damn me an I think
I've got the answer."

CHAPTER 48

PETER PACED IN HIS OWN COMMAND TENT, JAW CLENCHED against the tidal flood of Lancelot of the Languedoc.

Man wants his body back. No blame. Do the same. Get out, get out, get OUT!

He put his hands over his ears, squeezed tight. The aching subsided slightly, but in a very short order of time, probably within two or three days, Peter would lose all control. Lancelot would reclaim his body, and Peter would return to his own, back in Willks's laboratory.

Already, it took tremendous concentration to even remember the real world—modern words and concepts slipped away, temporal aphasia. It took Peter an hour earlier that night to remember the word "gun" and what the things did.

He paced up, back. Five steps to the front of the tent; turn, five steps back. He allowed his head to brush the roof each time, rather than ducking; contact with the cool, cotton interior fabric soothed him for some reason.

Think think think. . . .

The most frustrating, anxious part of an operation was when the commander had done all that he could and simply waited for the enemy to make a move. Again, he tried to think of a man or woman he could trust enough to spy upon Medraut; again he failed.

Gwyn was more urgently needed to spy on Myrddin. Cors Cant was out . . . apparently, he had figured out where Merovee's poisoned bottle of wine came from and had certainly resigned as "Lancelot's" spy. In any case, both he and Anlawdd, otherwise a good candidate herself

for the job, had both vanished shortly after he left them in
Artus's bivouac. The soldiers he sent to find them returned
empty-handed.

Cei and Bedwyr were a bit too busy plotting to murder
Lancelot and rebel against Artus to do any favors.

Merovee was dead. Gwynhwfyr and Morgawse were
presumably still back at Camlann, three weeks march behind, and neither would make a good spy in any event.

Peter had set Hir Amren to watch the boy. Medraut had
been Hir Amren's CO under Merovee when they liberated
the *trireme*. Now, Peter had promoted Hir Amren to horse-
captain, the equivalent of a colonel, and given him the
two-cohort House Division (the personal guard for a general or legate). But he had no firm idea of Hir Amren's
loyalty, whether he had simply set a fox pup to watch the
fox.

*Damn it, he did try to look at his bloody watch . . . I
know he did!* Peter silently cursed himself, paced up and
down the tent, five steps forward, five steps back. *Why
didn't I listen to my instincts, kill Medraut when I had the
opportunity?*

Because there's been too much killing already.

*Almost. Not quite enough. Two more to go: just kill both
of them, Myrddin and Medraut, and have done with it!*

Putting himself in Selly's boots, Peter realized she undoubtedly had someone spying on *him;* someone loyal to
her who would faithfully report anything Peter did. If he
decided to simply kill both Myrddin and Medraut, and he
picked the wrong person to die first, Selly would hear
about it immediately and would fade before Peter could
find her (whichever one she was). She would hurry to do
her dirty business, and Peter would be stuck without a
partner, waiting for the knife in his own back.

It made no difference. Peter could not bring himself to
do it. When all was said, he was *not* Lancelot of the
Languedoc. Human life held too much value for Peter to
simply kill a boy because he *thought* the boy had looked
for a nonexistent watch when he asked him the time.

Myrddin was unquestionably either Selly Corwin or

Mark Blundell ... but even so, whichever modern scientist inhabited that body, *Myrddin himself* was still in there as well ... Peter more than anyone else knew that was true. To kill Myrddin's body meant to kill Myrddin, an innocent, old mountebank.

That was murder, not justice; a mortal sin.

If Selly Corwin inhabited Myrddin's body, then Peter could rationalize killing him as necessary to prevent greater evil: whatever Selly "would have done," it caused Peter's entire world to fade out of existence in favor of Treeland, seemingly uninhabited. No cities, no industrial revolution, no technology.

No wars, no crime, no suffering.

Bullshit, I don't know that. Maybe starvation and epidemic disease are commonplace.

Really? You mean like in the "real" world?

He paced, let the cool fabric brush across his head. It smelled like smoked cheese from years of warm fires sending smoke to crawl across the ceiling toward the ventilation hole in the center.

If Myrddin is Selly, I will kill him. He felt better making a decision, any decision. But what if Myrddin were Blundell? And what about Medraut?

Peter reached the back of the tent, turned, paced five steps toward the front. The most anxious moment: he had done all that he could do, simply waited for Selly bloody Corwin to make her move.

Footsteps, hurrying toward Peter's tent. He paused, facing the tent flap, heart pounding. Every muscle in his body twitched faintly, causing him to tremble all over.

If it's to happen, it'll be NOW.

A burly sergeant-at-arms opened the tent flap, saluted Peter, who nodded in acknowledgment, not trusting himself to return the salute with steady hand. "Your pardon, Prince Legate, your s— I mean, your squire, Galahadus Minor, to see you, with guest."

Gwyn the Stainless pushed the man aside, barged into the tent. He dragged the old humbug (or IRA terrorist) Myrddin by the arm.

"Tell my old man what you told me," said Gwyn.

"It's happening, Peter," said Myrddin. "She's striking now! We must stop her!"

Icy calm washed over Peter. Clearly, the wait was over. One way or another, the final round had begun.

"Leave us," Peter said to Lancelot's son.

"Sire, I was watching him like you said, but he saw me and came to tell—" Gwyn shut up as Peter stared expectantly at him. Looking hurt, he let go his suspect, reluctantly quit the tent.

Myrddin waited, hopping from one foot to another, while Gwyn slowly left. "It's happening," he repeated, voice cracking with urgency. "She's making her move!"

"Really? So now you know who she is?"

Myrddin took a deep breath, licked his lips. "It's Arthur, I mean Artus's own son. Medraut."

Of course. But which is which?

"I set spies to watch Artus," said Myrddin, "reasoning that was where the attack was most likely to come. You remember Selly's orders? Thank God I was right. Medraut has been quietly replacing Artus's normal guard with Medraut's own handpicked men all night, and he just had a secret meeting with Cei. It's happening, it's, what do you chaps say, going down right now!"

"And I suppose you want me to stop it. For the widow's son, eh Mark?"

"What?"

"Who is the widow's son?"

"What are you—? Oh, I get it." Myrddin looked conspiratorially left and right, stuck out a wizened paw. They shook, Myrddin giving the proper Masonic sign for third degree. He leaned forward, whispered into Peter's ear. "At this degree, I am authorized to tell you the widow's son is Hiram Abiff, the king who built Solomon's temple."

Damn, thought Peter. If Myrddin had not known the answer, it would have positively identified "him" as Selly Corwin. But *knowing* the answer still left the question open; after all, if Peter could learn Masonic secrets by studying, so could Selly. Maybe she was a Mason-buff;

maybe her father had secretly been a Mason. Or maybe Blundell talked too much drunken pillow talk.

Peter had run out of delays. The moment arrived to do what he did best but hated most: let the snake strike and hope to catch the blow in time. He nodded to Myrddin. "Lead on, Macduff," he said.

As they exited the tent, Myrddin grumbled "That's *lay on,* not lead on. Didn't you go to school, Peter?"

Peter clenched his teeth. Another lost opportunity. Either Myrddin was Blundell or Selly was better educated in the classics than he hoped. They stepped out into the chilly night.

"Where's your horse?" Peter asked.

Myrddin shrugged. "Don't have one. That Gwyn fellow mounted me on the back of his nag. I'll ride with you."

Peter started to say "like bloody hell you will," stopped himself in time. *Play the role,* he thought. *If you really thought he were Mark, you'd have no qualms.* He swallowed, called for Eponimius.

So that's the plan, is it? Ride all the way across that shattered plain with Myrddin at my back, giving him every opportunity to show his colors by sticking a dagger in my back?

A stable slave brought the massive draft horse, kept loosely saddled in case of just such an emergency. The boy cinched the girth, then dropped to hands and knees, making himself into a step stool. Embarrassed, Peter quickly stepped upon the boy, thence into the saddle. A legionnaire groom handed him the reins.

Myrddin hesitated, looking worried. Peter extended his hand, and the wizard climbed unsteadily onto the slave's back, then gingerly eased onto the giant war-horse behind Peter.

The slave, apparently none the worse for wear, stood and bowed deeply.

The pair set off across the moor toward Artus's encampment. Thick fog shrouded the land, swirled around Eponimius's hooves and drifted like ocean waves across their path. Looking up, Peter could see no stars and only a faint brightness that marked the full moon, close to setting; dawn was not distant. He would have gotten lost in a moment, but Eponimius knew the path.

Myrddin said nothing, only gripped Peter's sides tightly. Peter held himself stiffly, trying to make as little contact as possible. Phantom ants crawled up and down his spine. *Will she do it? When?* His heart, once calm, started to pound again as he waited for the inevitable dagger blow.

He hoped he would have enough warning from Selly's body language to slip the blow, survive long enough to kill her . . . *if* Myrddin were Selly Corwin, and *if* she decided not to pass up the golden opportunity to eliminate her foe.

The furlongs crawled past, though Eponimius walked briskly. In his head, Peter intoned the Lord's Prayer again and again, interspersed with the Our Fathers and Hail Marys he could remember from catechism class. Twice, he caught himself sliding his axe from its sheath . . . *Do these thoughts of murder come from Lancelot or me?* he wondered, let the axe slide back into place on Eponimius's right flank.

The damp fog soaked his clothes, freezing him. But Myrddin felt hellishly cold, like the ninth circle of Dante's Inferno, the lake of ice. Was it natural for a human being to so thoroughly suck all the heat out of a body? Pressed against Peter's back, the ancient mystic felt like a window onto the abyss, the frozen limbo of lost souls. His frigid, spiritless body radiated evil.

Peter shook his head. *Letting my imagination gallop from one end of the fen to the other.* The charlatan was quite cold, but was not an eldritch, "ancient one," out of a Lovecraft story. He was not a *lloigor.*

His body is just an old man's, with old-man circulation, Peter told himself over and over.

Suddenly, Peter tensed. He felt Myrddin's hand move slyly off his hip. Major Peter Smythe held his breath, wondering whether to bat the old wizard off the horse immediately. *But I have to know! I have to know for sure!*

He clenched his teeth, narrowed his eyes. The blow would come any second now, any moment. . . .

A minute passed, then another. Stealing a look down at his side, he saw that Myrddin had merely wrapped his cloak around his hand.

When the Druid spoke, Peter nearly leapt out of his skin. "Wish I had my old arctic overcoat and thermal knickers," he said. "This chap's body has no blood."

Peter could not help himself, laughed much too loud, too long for such a feeble joke.

"Maybe I ought to quit physics," Myrddin continued, "and write for 'Red Dwarf.'" Peter was unfamiliar with the reference, apparently a television show, and he maintained a dignified silence as Myrddin "entertained" him for the rest of the way with impenetrable routines about a hologrammatic "Felix Unger" and his adventures with a brain-damaged computer.

Just as they crested a slope, finding themselves overlooking a blurry glow of lights—Artus's bivouac— Myrddin suddenly grabbed Peter's shoulder with clammy hand. Peter's heart leapt; there had been no warning, no "body language."

He realized the risk he had taken. Peter's plan to "slip the blow" was wishful thinking; had it come, it would have come like a .30-06 bullet in the night, outflying the sound waves of its own firing. Had Myrddin been Selly, and had she wanted Peter dead, he would be dead.

"Now's the time," said Myrddin, "for all good men, and all that."

Peter grunted, leaned forward. Eponimius obediently broke into a trot. Peter rose in the saddle, trying to post without stirrups, but it was almost impossible. Myrddin bounced behind him like a paddleball.

They pulled up far short of Artus's tent, dismounted quickly. A slave boy ran up, took the horse. Peter sternly warned the boy to say nothing about their being present and not to let anyone else see Eponimius if at all possible.

At least Medraut won't know we're here yet, thought Peter. No other rider could have crossed the plain any faster than Peter and Myrddin. With luck, they might be able to

get to Artus's tent before Medraut struck (if he were really
Selly Corwin) and without detection by Selly's spies.

They crept from shadow to shadow, using tents as concealment and avoiding the occasional nightwalker. The
pickets had presented no difficulty; as soon as they recognized Lancelot and Myrddin, they waved them through. At
last, Peter and the wizard lay prone, hidden by fog, shadows, and scrubby bracken, watching the giant command
tent of the *Dux Bellorum.*

(HAPTER 49

PETER SMYTHE AND MYRDDIN THE MAGICIAN LAY IN ABSO-
lute silence. Once, Myrddin started to whisper something, but Peter turned to look at him with such ferocity
that he shrank back and said nothing further. They lay,
watched, and waited.

Time crawled. It was nearly dawn, according to Peter's
internal clock; but the foggy, overcast sky was no brighter
than it had been at midnight. Peter expected a generalized
brightening, but zero-zero visibility continued long after
the sun was theoretically up.

A stealthy movement caught his attention. He watched,
licked his lips, a wolf watching a rabbit.

It moved again, and now Peter was able to pick out the
outlines of a person creeping exquisitely slowly toward
Artus's command tent.

The person walked erect, but kept to the shadows of tent
and clotheslines as Peter and Myrddin had. *Oh Lord,*
thought Peter, stomach twisting sickeningly; it was the
same furtive figure that he had seen creeping in the *Dux
Bellorum*'s apartment.

Anlawdd had returned to finish the job—the putative princess had come to slay Artus after all!

He almost called her name in fury and befuddlement, nearly rose from his concealment and ruined the stakeout, perhaps intentionally.

Just then, the assassin looked back over the shoulder then stepped into the open. Lantern light that surrounded the *Dux Bellorum*'s quarters illuminated the footpad's face: it was Medraut.

I'm sorry it's the boy, Peter thought; *but thank Jesus and Mary it's not Anlawdd.*

Myrddin annoyingly tapped Peter's shoulder, pointed unnecessarily at the lad. Peter said nothing. As Medraut approached the front of the tent, Peter saw someone behind the boy. It was one of the Praetorian Guard. They, too, had apparently spotted Medraut while he slunk through the shadows.

Five soldiers surrounded him, like points of a pentagram. As soon as they realized who he was, however, they brought him to the front of the tent. One guardsman went inside, came out after a moment. They held the flap open as Medraut entered.

"Get up," said Peter, rising to his feet, "it's show time."

As Peter approached, the soldiers snapped to attention, saluted. Peter returned the salute, headed for the flap. "Um, Sire," began one of the guardsmen, hesitant, "the *Dux Bellorum* asked not to be disturbed."

"Then see that we're not disturbed, soldier," answered Peter as gruffly as he could.

"But he's in there with that kid, the one what, you know." He motioned with his head toward the tent.

"Medraut's here? Good, saves me having to send for him. Back to your post, legionnaire."

Still dubious, Cacamwri's Guard backed away, allowed the Executive Officer of the army to enter Artus's tent unmolested and unheralded.

Myrddin followed, lagging behind. Peter moved briskly through the outer antechamber of the pavilion, found the door to Artus's command center. He heard the *Dux*

Bellorum and Medraut talking inside. Peter pushed the hanging curtain aside a crack so he could see.

"Gwynhwfyr's um, here? In the camp?" asked Medraut.

Artus nodded. "At my suggestion, they joined the camp followers the day after we left. They caught up some time after we stopped yesternoon. This will be the most glorious battle of my career, and I want my wife at my side . . . and my son."

Medraut watched quizzically.

"Yes, you heard right," said Artus. "When we break the back of King Hrundal and drive the Jutes from our northern lands, I shall finally acknowledge you as my son and heir, as I should have done many years ago. I cannot give you the legions, my boy. You must earn those by rising up the ranks, as I did. They are not mine to give. I suppose I could simply dub you the next *Dux Bellorum,* but as they say, *cucullus non facit monachum.* The cowl does not make the monk. They would not follow you, my son.

"But I have much wealth, land, many houses and villas, and all of these will be shared by you and Gwynhwfyr when I die . . . which will be soon, I fear." He put his hand to his heart, smiled ruefully.

His face is so ashen! marveled Peter. Clearly, Artus had a serious heart problem, probably a circulatory problem. His skin was much greyer than it had been in Caer Camlann. During their interview earlier that evening, Peter had thought it was just the lamplight. But there was no question: Artus's heart was not pumping enough blood to warm his body.

Medraut stared at the *Dux Bellorum,* his biological father. But his mind was a million miles away . . . or fifteen hundred years.

The "boy" was terrified, trembling with anxious excitement. *My God,* thought Peter, *Medraut is steeling himself for some dreadful task.*

"But I have much to do before I pass on," said the *Dux Bellorum,* "and I want you to help me. Merovee is dead; I'm sure you heard. After a great crisis of conscience, he took his own life. I don't know why.

"But that leaves me up a tree without a ladder, as they like to say. I *must* extend the New Roman Empire from Britain to Sicambria, and from there across Europa, lest the light fail when the legions withdraw and men fall back into bestial savagery and Paulism."

My God, thought Peter, *the man is prophetic.* Of course, Peter believed it was the Church that *prevented* the final collapse into barbarism during the Dark Ages, but he supposed it was a matter of interpretation.

The image affected Medraut sorely. He gasped, retreated a step toward Peter, into the shadows. His breath was ragged, getting faster. *She's going to do it—the bitch is really going to do it!* Mark had been right after all.

Medraut slipped his hand behind his back, began to slowly draw a dagger from his belt-sheath, but hesitated. Artus was not paying close enough attention; Peter saw that the *Dux Bellorum* was oblivious to his peril.

At once, everything clicked. Naturally, Selly would *want* the "New Roman Empire" of Artus to collapse and the Church to take over ... for Selly Corwin, or whatever her real name was, was a fanatical *Catholic.*

Selly's plan from Day-One to Day-Forty-nine had been to murder King Arthur prematurely, before he could win this final battle and establish England as a great nation.

That was why everything had disappeared in Peter's time, slowly fading into a forest world ... because England never even got its first foothold of greatness under its legendary father-king, Arthur Pendragon!

The world slowed to a stop. Artus stood in mid-oratory, gesturing grandly toward what would someday become "England's green and pleasant land." Medraut froze, dagger fully drawn, still hidden behind his back. For some reason, he still hesitated, unable or unwilling to strike, like the Danish prince.

Peter had a clean shot at Medraut's—Selly Corwin's back; and unlike the terrorist, he had no moment of indecision, no remorse or uncertainty this time.

Without conscious thought, he stepped forward briskly,

drew his own knife, not bothering to conceal it. Neither person saw him yet.

Emotionless, just as in Londonderry, Harlech, and a dozen other robotic missions, Peter Smythe caught Medraut around the throat with his left arm, pulled him back. Medraut flailed his arms and arched his back, exactly what Peter was waiting for. As soon as Medraut bent backward, Peter rotated his right hip back to open a clear line of fire, then drove his commando knife—dagger—into Medraut's kidney.

He held the boy tight, pushed the blade to the hilt. Then he pulled it out, let Medraut collapse to the ground.

Artus was still befuddled, did not comprehend what had just happened. "Lancelot," he said, "how come you're here? Lance, help the boy, I think he's fallen!"

The *Dux Bellorum* rushed forward, gently touched Medraut's cheek. The lad blinked, looked down at his right arm, covered with blood. His hand still held his own dagger, now also bloody.

"You stabbed yourself," said Artus, voice on the verge of breaking. "Don't move, we'll get a surgeon. It's just a cut, you'll be all right. Don't move."

He cradled his son's head in his arms, stroked the boy's hair. "Lancelot!" He ordered. "Call a surgeon!"

Almost, Peter obeyed, so powerful was the *Dux Bellorum*'s hold on his loyalty. Shaking, he put his hand on Artus's shoulder. "The wound is mortal, General."

"Lance, what are you doing? Get a surgeon!"

"Sir. . . ." Peter pointed at the widening pool of blood beneath them. Artus stared, enough a soldier to know a death wound when he finally saw it. He hugged his son, whispered "I'm sorry . . . I'm sorry, son . . . I should have—years ago, I should have acknowledged . . ."

Medraut looked up at Artus. "Selly?" he said. "Did you kill me?"

Selly?

"It's all right, son," said Artus, kissing Medraut's forehead. "It wasn't intentional. You won't go to hell. It was a terrible, terrible accident."

"Selly? I thought we were-were . . ." Medraut's breath failed for a moment. As he inhaled, Peter, watching Medraut's back, saw bubbles in the wound. *Punctured lung,* he thought dully.

"Mark?" he asked the dying boy.

"Selly?" Medraut looked from Artus to Peter. "Who . . . ?"

"I'm Peter."

Medraut shook his head, coughed horribly. Blood now flecked his lips. "Peter . . . magician . . ."

"Myrddin is Peter?" Medraut nodded. "And Artus is Selly?"

The boy looked at Artus, opened his mouth. A stream of blood mixed with saliva dribbled out. He looked back at Peter.

"I b-bollixed it up, didn't I?" said Medraut. Peter said nothing. "Pete . . . Peter, is that P-Peter?"

"Yes, I'm here, Mark."

"Do me some . . . something?"

"All right."

"For the w-w . . ." Medraut coughed again, then seemed to gain strength. He struggled somewhat upright.

"Son!" cried Artus. "Are you all right?" If he had been mystified by the previous conversation, he did not show it.

"For the widow's son," concluded Medraut.

"All right. What?"

"Burr . . . bury something."

"Bury what?"

"Anything. Writing. Note. Here."

"Bury a note?" What was Blundell talking about? "Here, at Dinas Emrys?"

"Bury note." Medraut's breaths came raggedly; he gasped for air, fell back into Artus's arms. "Sealed . . . earthen jar . . . sealed with clay . . . wax . . . airtight. Bury note . . . who you are . . . Peter. Find it . . . later."

Light dawned on Peter Smythe. "You want me to bury a note so you can dig it up in modern times, prove we were back here?"

Medraut smiled, nodded. His eyes were closed.

"Sealed," he repeated, "like . . . Dead Sea . . . scrolls." Suddenly he opened his eyes. "Selly!" he exclaimed. Then he settled back, voice fading to nothingness as he said, "Sorry . . . don't think . . . I'll have . . . time . . . to tell you . . . who she . . . is."

Medraut lay still. Artus held the body, wept softly.

"You don't need to, Brother Mark," said Peter. He looked around; Myrddin—Selly Corwin—had absented herself.

Major Peter Smythe stood. He had little control over Lancelot's body now; it lurched as he walked. The Beast had grown strong, gnawed at the Promethean chains by which Peter had bound the Sicambrian's spirit. His vision faded, jerked left and right as he fought Lancelot for control of his eyeballs.

He looked down, covered with blood from head to toe. *Had it all wrong, you useless sod,* he told himself.

Selly Corwin never wanted to kill Artus.

Why bother? He died anyway. But in the real history, Artus *Dux Bellorum* died *never having established his* Romano-Celtic *empire.*

"Jesus, God, I am a bloody, damned fool!"

Arthur, Artus, was not an English king.

He was Welsh. A Celt. In Selly Corwin's twisted mind, he was a hero for fighting *against* the Angles and Saxons—Anglo-Saxons—who gave England its people, its culture, even its very name: Angle-Land.

But Arthur fought them. He beat them back, kept the land mostly free of Saxon domain. The Saxons had established a foothold, obviously in West-Saxony, East-Saxony, South-Saxony. Wessex, Essex, and Sussex, of course. And now their allies, the Jutes, pushed in on Arthur's domain from the north.

But would they prevail? In the original history, the job was easy because *Arthur died* before defeating them . . . slain by his bastard son Mordred, Medraut.

The same Medraut that Peter had just killed, preventing the assassination.

"God, Selly," he breathed, "you're *beautiful,* you bird."

She had wielded him like a cricket bat, stopping Medraut from bowling over Artus, her team's wicket.

Apparently, Artus now survives long enough to drive the Jutes out of Gwynedd, Peter realized. *Once the north is free, he can concentrate on the Saxons in the south, if not this year, then the next.*

And somehow, he succeeds—he's Arthur! Britain never becomes England. The industrial revolution never happens—at least not here. My entire world ceases to exist.

No, worse: it never even was!

Peter stared at Artus *Pan-Draconis, Dux Bellorum.* Father-king of England, Welsh Celt. Artus held his dead son's body, silent, no longer weeping. He seemed stricken, stared vacantly at the tent.

Where the hell is Cacamwri's Praetorian Guard? wondered Peter. Then he realized he had been too expert, made hardly any noise. Artus was too stunned to call out, had begged Peter "Lancelot," to call for the surgeon.

"Lancelot," champion of Caer Camlann, consul, legate of the silver and black, had stood mute, watching two innocent men die in a single body, Medraut's.

As yet, nobody was even aware of the murder.

He looked at Artus, his general. His father. *Sent me to Sandhurst. Sent me into the army. Father, did you ever do what I do? Were you just an army colonel, fighting Jerrys and North Koreans ... or did you spend days and nights hunting Irish snakes like Saint Patrick did, waiting for the bullet in the back of the head, the bomb in the boot?*

He watched Artus, whose life he had just saved, obligating him to perpetual protection. The man who was supposed to die in the original timeline.

"I have no time," said Peter. He blinked; tears wetted his cheeks. "I have no time. No time."

He knelt, seized the *Dux Bellorum's* hair, and drew his head back, exposing his throat. With a quick swipe of his sharp, not-quite-sharp-enough knife, Peter opened King Arthur's carotid artery.

A nasty line paraded around Peter's head like the narrator at the end of an army training film: *Thus is the world redeemed from Smythe's selfish act of personal love by holy murder.*

I've become an agent for the Law of Conservation of Reality, thought Peter as his gorge rose.

Arthur stared at Peter, pawed at his neck. He collapsed forward onto the dead body of his bastard son, Mordred. His mouth opened and closed, his eyes castigating his best friend mildly, as if correcting a minor fault of etiquette. "Gwynhwfyr ..." he said, "don't—don't let her see ... don't let her hate you."

He laid his head heavily on Medraut's back, closed his eyes.

"I have no time," repeated Peter, chest aching, "for king or country.

"I am merely a Special Branchman for the Law of Conservation of Reality."

For fifteen hundred years, Peter stared at two dead bodies, barely even comprehending what he had just done.

Then he stood. His hands dripped with Artus's blood.

"Jesus," said a voice behind him. He turned: Gwynhwfyr stood in the doorway, skin pale as moonlight, golden hair bound back by a net of sapphire stars. She wore a furry, yellow tunic trimmed with cloth-of-gold.

Gwynhwfyr stepped forward, eyes riveted to the tableau, father holding son, both dead and gore soaked. She crouched down, ruining her costly tunic, and expertly felt first Artus's wrist pulse, then Medraut's carotid.

She stood, stared at her calfskin-gloved hands, now almost as red as Peter's, as if she'd never seen them before. Her voice was weak, reedy. But she controlled herself, only hunted eyes betraying her panic at the lifeless, bloody body of her husband.

"Looks bad, Lance. Bad. Really bad. I'd say you did it, and I bet *they* will, too." She nodded toward the soldiers outside the tent.

"I did," he said, still in shock himself.

"I know. Brigit's love, I pray you didn't do it for me."

She watched Peter, eyes blinking rapidly. She stumbled, sat suddenly on Artus's empty throne.

"No."

"Thank the Lord and Lady." Gwynhwfyr covered her face with her hands.

She's losing it, thought Peter dully. "My love," he said, "I didn't even think of you while I . . . when I did it."

The princess dropped her hands to her lap, back in control. Terrible sadness frosted her face, innocent no more.

She would never fully recover. How could she? Already, she was a different, colder Gwynhwfyr; she knew they would never see each other again after the inquest showed that Lancelot murdered Artus.

"Can I ask *why* you did it?"

Peter shook his head sadly. How could he possibly explain?

The princess frowned, almost touched her hand to her lips, remembered the blood and hastily dropped her hands to her side. Pain forced a tear down her cheek. "Well, my bold fish, this poses a few problems. How can I ever get you *out* of this?"

He stared at her, aghast. "You'd do that after I admitted murdering your husband? Didn't you even love him?"

"Terribly. But he's gone, Galahad. I don't have him anymore. I only have you . . . whom I also love."

"Gwynhwfyr, I—I don't know how long you're going to have me."

"Oh?" Her voice sounded thin, frightened. Would she lose both the men in her life on the same day?

Would she? Peter considered. What did he have to go back to? Would a few days make any difference at all? "Gwynhwfyr . . . please, it's important that you know I did *not* do this out of jealousy. I didn't do it to take you away from him . . . I loved him."

"I know."

"But—I do love you. And I will stay as long as I'm able. I won't leave voluntarily. When did you decide you loved me?"

She looked at Peter, seemed to understand. "A few

weeks back, when you, when you became a different person. I just can't describe ... oh God, Lance, he's still dead!"

Peter took a deep breath, let it out. "Gwynnie, I am not Lancelot of the Languedoc."

She bowed her head, nodded. "I wondered. Which god are you?"

Peter shrugged. "Any god you want. I'm not a god, sweetness. A, uh, a magician from far away sent my spirit here. I took over Lancelot's body ... but he's too strong, and I'll be driven out again.

"In any case, it wouldn't be right, holding on to his body. I've done too much damage already."

Gwynhwfyr looked up, hopeful for the first moment since she saw her husband and his son. "How far?"

Peter tried to answer; the words would not come. It was not temporal aphasia; he could not bring himself to tear her heart out a second time. Finally, he answered. "My only love Gwynhwfyr, you cannot get there from here. Ever."

"Can't you return? Maybe, into another body? What if someone volunteered to give you his body permanently?"

"Who would do that?"

"But what if someone did! Could you return?"

Peter shook his head. "It doesn't work like that. I can't specifically target someone ... it's more or less random whom I end up in."

"I don't care! I love *you,* whoever you are, not the body you're in."

"Could be a woman."

"That's fine with me."

"Could be a slave, or an ugly, old crone, or a little boy." Her gaze did not waver.

"And it could be months in the future ... or the past. We can't control the time dimension that well."

She bit her lip, began to weep for the first time. "Can't you at least *try?* Lance—oh God, what is your name?"

"Peter. Peter Smythe."

"Peter the smith, I'll wait for you ... I'll wait forever,

if need be. Give me a sign that I'll know you when you come, no matter who you are."

"I'll say ..." He thought for a moment, nodded. "I'll say I'm the widow's son."

"Are you really? Descended from Jesus?"

Peter shook his head. "No one is! He died on the cross and never married the Magdalene. It's just a damnable heresy, and a tidal wave of blood sweeps across the land, all because of that stupid, evil myth!"

It was true. Had it not been for the Basilidian Heresy, Artus might never have hatched dreams of empire, Merovee would still be alive, and Peter's hands would not drip blood.

"So, so what do we tell the Praetorian Guard?" Gwynhwfyr paced, perspired, pulled at her clothes. Her eyes sought left, right. A classic anxiety attack.

"Tell them Medraut murdered Artus, and I killed Medraut."

She nodded. "That's—that's—that's what I saw. Ready? Here comes the scream."

True to her word, Gwynhwfyr let out a shriek that nearly split Peter's eardrums and brought a dozen soldiers, all frightened out of their wits by the human air-raid siren. She cringed in a corner of the tent like Lady Macbeth, gory hands over her face, screaming and convulsing so convincingly that Peter almost shook her and told her to stop it.

For his part, Peter stood in the middle of the tent, bloody dagger in hand, looking stupid and shellshocked ... an easy role to play.

Cacamwri interrogated him for an hour. The guard released word that Medraut had died but said not a word to the troops about Artus.

After the preliminary questioning, Cacamwri tentatively accepted Peter's and Gwynhwfyr's account, though he warned that there would definitely be an inquest at which they would be compelled to testify under the most sacred oaths.

A surgeon arrived, measured Peter's knife blade and

Medraut's wound, announced that Medraut was probably
killed by that dagger. He could say nothing about Artus's
slit throat, of course, beyond the fact that it was cut by a
relatively sharp but not razor-sharp implement (there was
tearing). Both Peter's and Medraut's knife were likely can-
didates, since both were caked with drying blood.

Gwynhwfyr, who had "fainted" early in the interroga-
tion, was carried from the tent by the barber-surgeon's
assistants. Peter was eventually set loose to wander the
compound under the special circumstances that there was
a war to be won and Peter, "Lancelot," commanded his
own legion a league away.

Peter returned to the stable where Eponimius was
boarded, discovered Myrddin, Selly Corwin, sitting on an
anvil waiting for him.

"Congratulations," she smirked. "I hear you slew that
murderous assassin Medraut before he had a chance to kill
the *Dux Bellorum.*"

The Beast surged and retreated inside Peter's head, Lancelot's head, again and again. The night of the knife had
taken its toll; not even a day remained for Peter to maintain control of this body.

"Why, Selly?" asked Peter, not expecting a straight answer.

She surprised him. "Arthur died, and we Saxons overran
this beautiful island. Now we won't." Selly smiled,
shrugged, looking grotesque in her old-man body.

We *Saxons?*

"But with Artus—Arthur alive," he argued, "the Holy
Roman Catholic Church will never gain a foothold
here ... Celtic Artus may be, but an apostate! How can
you so arbitrarily deny salvation to all of your people?"

She looked surprised, stroked her beard. "The Church?
What the bloody hell gave you the idea that I was *Catholic?*"

Peter was stunned.

"If I'm anything," she continued, "I'm Anglican, dear."

"But ... but the Irish Republican Army—"

"Has nothing whatsoever to do with me, love. Oh I

don't deny buying their bombs; they're excellent trading partners, actually. Always pay promptly, never ask embarrassing questions."

Peter staggered as Lancelot burst his bonds. The right half of his body lurched uncontrollably for a moment, groped wildly for an axe where none dangled. Then Peter regained some slight control, pushed The Beast aside, for at least a moment.

"Do you feel him there?" she asked, honestly curious. "Does Lancelot push at your brain the way Myrddin pushes at mine? I guess it's a damned sight harder for you, holding back such a savage warrior. Myrddin's just a frightened, feeble, old stage magician."

"Selly Corwin . . . is that your real name?" She nodded. "You're—English?"

"As English as Frank Kitz and H.B.Samuels."

Anarchists. "You're an anarchist?"

"I guess. No, not really."

"Then *why,* Selly? God. Jesus, why? I really, really want to understand."

She grinned like a feeding shark, showing Myrddin's rotten teeth. "Because I *hate to death* all you bloody, Saxon bastards!"

He stared at her, loathing rising up his throat like bile. "Selly, you *are* one of us bloody, Saxon bastards."

"So? Like John Quail, if I'd known what a barmy business life was, I wouldn't have bothered to be born. I didn't ask for it, you know."

"You don't even know why you did it, do you?"

She smiled, leaned back. "It's enough that I destroyed you, your land, your people, your country, your culture. All of you. That's enough, Peter fucking Smythe, isn't it? I did it because I *could,* you murdering bastard.

"And what of you, Peter Bloody-Handed Smythe? Have you ever looked in a mirror? Do you actually throw a reflection, or a shadow at noon?

"You killed him, killed the boy, Medraut, for no better reason than *you thought he was me!*

"Do you see now why I had to . . . had to do it?"

She grinned like a loon. Stared. The "thousand-yard stare," just like Charlie Manson.

Peter Smythe said nothing to disabuse her delusion of success. He slid his dagger from its sheath, the same knife that had claimed two lives an hour before. What was one more?

Come out, come out, wherever you are, he beckoned The Beast.

Selly saw the naked blade, grinned as wide as the ancient gaffer could do without cracking his face. She spread her arms wide, said, "Take me, I'm yours! Send me back! I shall return, you know, to help the *Dux Bellorum* in the hour of his greatest need."

"From a forest-world with no time machine?"

"Eh?"

"I saw part of that world before I left, Selly. There's no technology, not even an auto." *Kill her, take her now!* For once, the cagey Sicambrian refused to bite.

"Oh well. Good thing I've spent months studying the history of science," she said, batting eyelids beneath immense, busy brows. "It may take a few years to rebuild the toroid, but I'll just recalculate the time and return to Camlann a few weeks from now.

"Oh," she added as afterthought, "did I remember to tell you? When we talked, Mark—that oh-so-charming Medraut—let slip that your body died back in the real time there, Petey-bird.

"You're dead. When you die here, when Lancelot finally pushes you out, that's it. You're history. *Adios,* you're a ghost." She laughed scornfully.

Peter realized he had an audience. A number of legionnaires surrounded the pair, staring openmouthed. Excited whispers reached Peter's ears: *return in our hour of greatest need.*

"*Mors ultima ratio,*" said Peter. He stepped forward and plunged the knife into Myrddin. The Druid convulsed once, died without fuss.

Gosh, thought Peter, *I guess I forgot to tell you that*

poor Artus did *die after all. The world is safe for us Saxons, you and me . . . old crow.*

Vaya con dios, Selly bloody Corwin. I hope you enjoy an extended holiday at the Crum.

The mob of soldiers panicked, surged back away from the battle-maddened Lancelot, now thoroughly in control. For a few moments, Peter watched passively from his new prison behind the eyes of The Beast.

Then he let himself drift, drift on the wings of death, thinking one last, loving good-bye to Gwynhwfyr, the only woman he had ever truly loved.

Cave Canem, he thought; *beware of the dog.*

CHAPTER 50

Cors Cant kissed Anlawdd gently as she snuggled deeper into his arms. Hours had passed, yet he still could not sleep. *I have an answer,* the old archking had said, but refused to elaborate. He beetled off, leaving them in his own pavilion with strict instructions not to leave or make too much noise.

"Um, Anlawdd," began Cors Cant.

"Yes, darling?"

"We, um, both finally admit we love each other, don't we?"

"Yes."

"And as we can never wed, mutual love is as much as we'll ever have between us . . . isn't it?"

"Yes . . . ?" She lowered her brows suspiciously. "Cors Cant Ewin, I hope you're not going to suggest rutting like a pair of wild boars, are you?"

"No! No," he amended hastily.

"Because you know very well that I eventually *will* marry *someone,* and if that someone happens to be civilized, he'll surely expect me not to have any previous progeny, especially those that resemble a certain bard. So unless you have one of those lambskin sacks that the Romans slip over their you-know-whats, we shall abstain."

"But—but you and Lancelot. . . ."

"Peter, he's taken to calling himself these days. And that was my first. You can't get pregnant the first time."

Cors Cant looked at her with a strange expression. "Yes you can," he said.

"No."

"Yes. My mother and father conceived *me* with but a single go."

Anlawdd's eyebrows shot upward. "Indeed? Oh well . . . whoops. I guess we'll just have to ride that wave if it crests."

"'And in any event," continued the bard, "what if you wed a wild, pagan Celt, like Gwynhwfyr, who would *welcome* a brood as proof of fertility?"

"I'd actually prefer a man, Cors Cant."

"You know what I mean!"

"Well, then we'll burn that bridge as well when we come to it." She reached up, stroked his face. "Cors, I do want you. Please understand. Just don't put me in that quandary just yet, not until we know what boots and cloak to wear from one moment to the next. That would be like setting both a bowl of food and a baying hound right in front of a starving fox!"

"All I wanted to do was hold you," he lied, crossing his legs.

"Of course," she said, curled up against him. Within moments, Anlawdd was asleep and snoring to wake the shades in Hades. Even had the bard not been anxious about their situation and Leary's "solution," his ladylove's bullfrog impersonation would have kept him awake.

I guess I'm going to have to learn to live with it, he thought ruefully. *Maybe I can fill my ears with wax?* It worked for Ulysses, preventing his crew from hearing the deadly song of the Sirens.

He dozed fitfully, dreaming of auburn-haired Sirens blowing on rams' horns.

Cors Cant was shaken awake by Archking Leary, returned from his secret mission. "Get up," commanded Leary, kicking Anlawdd repeatedly until she grudgingly opened her dazed eyes. "There's been a wee bit of an accident."

"Accident?"

"Medraut is dead, slain by Lancelot, an' some be sayin' that the *Dux Bellorum* too has met his end."

"What!" Cors Cant bolted upright, and even Anlawdd struggled to a sitting position. The bard was paralyzed by indecision, like Anlawdd's starving fox, aware that his rightful duty was to stand by his lord's side, yet knowing that his beloved needed him now more than ever before.

"Stand ye still," said Leary, cheerful voice replaced by a command tone that brought instant, unthinking obedience. *A Builder trick,* thought the bard wildly; *both Anlawdd and Merovee had used it.*

He gasped, remembering that the Long-Haired King, half-fish they said (and now he knew what they meant, exactly which ancestor of his was represented by the fish), was forever dead . . . and remembering too that Cors Cant alone held the key to the succession of Merovius Minor.

You will be called upon to produce the scroll when the All-Dragon's bones are cold. . . . The words burned in Cors Cant's brain, Merovee's prophecy in Artus's office when both were thoroughly alive.

"Artus is *dead?"* demanded Anlawdd, still groggily trying to make sense of the last few moments.

"Na, na, we dinna know that. An' he is dead, this whole place will erupt into chaos. In any case, Lancelot slew Myrddin, an'—"

Cors Cant cried aloud, fell heavily onto his backside. "Oh God, no! Not Myrddin and Artus both!" Tears streaked his cheeks.

Anlawdd crawled over next to him, held him tight, pulling the boy over to cradle his head in her lap. "It's all right," she cooed. "I won't let you go. I won't ever die, we'll be together forever, like two constellations side by side."

Too stunned to speak, Cors Cant rested his head against her leg, wept silently.

"My children, this is all touching, but sure an' we've got to move fast. We've but a few moments left before we must fly this beehive, an' much tae do. Meet my very great friend, Father Fidelus Damasus, one o' the chaplains of Lancelot's legions an' a representative o' the Roman Paulists. I'd hae gotten Patrick himsel', but he's rather busy now, convertin' me whole, bludy kingdom tae the Church Militant."

Anlawdd reluctantly shook the priest's hand, mumbled greetings. She stroked her love's hair.

"The good father," said Leary, "is here tae perform a marriage ceremony acceptable tae the Church."

"I can't get married," explained Anlawdd sadly, "because Cors Cant was born a mere citizen, not even a knight, let alone the quality." Her voice was flat, leaden.

Leary grinned, infecting the princess with a tiny piece of his perpetual good humor. "Not tae him, lass. Tae *me.*"

This roused the bard from his lethargy. "What?" he demanded. "You? You're going to marry Anlawdd? *That's* your God-damned solution?"

Anlawdd gasped, then hushed the babbling bard. "It's *inspired,* Cors Can Ewin! If you can't see that, then you're as thickheaded as Bedwyr! Surely Uncle Leary won't mind if you and I—"

"Ah ah ah!" cautioned Leary, holding up his hand and flicking a glance at the Catholic priest.

Anlawdd instantly clamped her mouth shut, swallowed the rest of whatever she was going to say.

"You be th' witness, lad," said Leary to Cors Cant.

Dumbly, still wondering what had happened to the world in the last few minutes (did Eris take over, Greek goddess of chaos and confusion?), the bard stood where the priest pointed. Cors Cant even managed to contain himself and shake his head when he was asked if he knew any reason that Anlawdd could not marry Archking Leary . . . her father.

Either no one's told the priest, thought the boy, *or the Paulists are much more liberal than I've been led to believe.*

The moment Father Damasus finished, Leary grabbed their cloaks, threw them at the pair, and pushed them toward the door, leaving the priest behind to finish the paperwork.

"But Sire!" complained Damasus, "it's customary to hold a reception. . . ."

"Nae time, nae time," countered Leary, cheerfully. "I'll be late already tae me own weddin' night!" So saying, the three bounded off into the night.

Leary let Cors Cant and Anlawdd get far enough ahead for some privacy, if they spoke quietly.

"My love, my only love," she said, "it's best this way. It's the perfect solution. As I started to say before Leary reminded me that walls and priests have ears, he surely will leave us alone together after, well, you know. You can be my court bard, since I'm now archqueen of Eire, and we'll be together forever!"

"After 'I know' *what?* Jesus and Mithras, is the old goat really going to demand a wedding night?"

"Wouldn't be a legal wedding without one, now would it? Besides, what's the problem? Didn't you once say you'd take me as I am, no matter how many other men—or women, I thought I heard you say—I wanted? This way, if there's a child (by Lancelot, Leary, or even you, dear heart), Leary can raise her as a true princess.

"Besides," continued Anlawdd, "I'm sure one night with Leary will teach me everything I need to know to please you in bed . . . or so I've heard." She looked at Cors Cant, smiled faintly. "No, I think it's very Romantic," she answered.

"But my heart . . . *he's your father!* Or he might be your father. Don't you think it's kind of . . . creepy?"

"No, dear heart, I think it's very Romantic, sacrificing himself for the good of his daughter."

Cors Cant shivered, imagining the ghastly wedding night. "God, hell was bad enough. But now I have to have *him* as my lord as well? That uncivilized, pagan Eirelander?"

"Watch your tongue, Cors Cant Ewin! That's my husband you're cutting." Throwing her head back, Anlawdd dropped back to walk beside Archking Leary.

They scurried through the swirling mob, dodging the crush of bodies as well as they could. When the *Dux Bellorum* had not appeared, the mob of legionnaires under his command leapt to the conclusion that he had, in fact, been slain. At last, the Praetorian Guard admitted this was true.

Nobody knew what to do, what was next. Would they still fight the Jutes? Withdraw? What of Lancelot, what of Cei?

The latter two questions were quickly answered, at least, when Lancelot's legion suddenly arrived at Artus's bivouac, marching in battle formation, led by Hir Amren. They demanded the release of the legate, who was not in custody, as it happened. As Artus's legions were not even formed into ranks, they complained to their generals about undue intimidation by the silver and black.

Then Cei and his own legion arrived, and it quickly became obvious that Cei was joining with Lancelot, whenever the latter could be found, and both legions were breaking from the empire in the wake of the *Dux Bellorum*'s death.

At last, the Dragon and Eagle legions were roused to action. Battle formation notwithstanding, they still outnumbered the combined forces of the rebels, and were better trained to boot. A brief civil war erupted, quickly stanched by the respective legates and generals, who drove their troops apart.

It was through this swirling chaos that Leary, Cors Cant, and Anlawdd made good their escape, Anlawdd atop Merillwyn, the bard on his shaggy pony, and the archking of Eire riding an obstinate donkey, which Cors Cant thought suited him perfectly.

CHAPTER 51

LANCELOT OF THE LANGUEDOC, FINALLY RECOVERED FROM his long illness, having at last cast out the demon that prisoned his very soul and stole his body, puzzled over the cryptic scratchings on sheets of vellum. He recognized the letters as belonging to the language used by the power-mad Paulists, but could make no sense of the words.

He briefly considered asking Cei to translate, decided it might not be a good idea: the old porter, true friend though he was, did not quite seem to believe Lancelot's account of being bound by a demon. The legate could not take the chance that something in the journal, obviously written by the devil over the past month and a half, might incriminate Lancelot in Cei's eyes.

The Sicambrian needed his ally . . . at least for now.

So what to do with the scratchings? Lancelot was afraid to burn them; the wise women always said that setting devil words to flame released their full potential rather than destroying it. The gods of his fathers alone knew what evil cantrips were contained therein.

A little voice inside him, a dim memory he could not quite drag out into the light kept repeating *bury it, bury it, bury it.* It seemed a reasonable suggestion.

He left the Treaty Pavilion, where he, Cei, and General Cacamwri, once captain of the Praetorian Guard, now legate (by fiat) of the *Dux Bellorum*'s personal Dragon and Eagle legions, had just finished signing a winter peace accord. Lancelot slowly walked to the command tent of his erstwhile best friend, his dead commander, Artus *Pan-Draconis,* the once and never again *Dux Bellorum.*

He dimly remembered the scene, the knife in his hands, *somebody's* blood on his soul. *No! Stop those thoughts. Not safe to remember that yet. Maybe later.*

Maybe never.

Here, he decided. This was the right spot. Here he would bury the evil, demonic writing.

Seal it, said the memory; *protect it, don't let it decay with age!*

Lancelot looked around, found a small but sturdy wooden box, banded with steel. He dumped from the box the battle plans for the Jutic campaign, now useless, and quickly filled it with the damned words. Closing the chest, he wound cords torn from the curtains around it again and again, tying it very tight. Feeling dissatisfied, the legate tied an intricate Celtic knot he had learned from Artus himself.

Lancelot looked at the tightly wrapped strongbox, nodded satisfaction at last. No piece of paper, no matter how magicked, was going to escape from *that* prison!

He paced off the exact center of Artus's tent, dug a hole using his dagger. He dropped in the box, covered up the hole again.

Lancelot tamped the dirt down, spent much time scattering and scuffing the dirt to make it look exactly like the rest of the tent floor. Tomorrow or the next day, the troops would sadly strike the great man's tent, cart it away ... and no one would ever know what foulness had been left behind, cleansed from their worthless, British souls.

Lancelot smiled—a job well-done—and finding Eponimius (kicking the slave who had failed to curry the war-horse), he returned to his own legion with all deliberate speed.

CHAPTER 52

THE SUN WAS UP. IT HAD BURNED AWAY THE OVERCAST AND the fog, leaving a clear but cloudy day. Looking northwest, Cors Cant saw a distant dust cloud.

"It's the Jutes retreating," sighed Anlawdd wearily. "I'd hoped they would attack and unite the remnants of Artus's forces, but no such luck. They're withdrawing, waiting to see the outcome of the civil war."

Cors Cant dismounted, stood beside her. "Do you really care?" he asked.

She leaned against him, let him put his arms around her. Leary pretended not to see, busied himself with adjusting the saddle-sacks on his donkey.

"Not anymore," she said, quiet but determined.

"Where?"

"I just want to get the hell out of here, Cors Cant, go somewhere else."

"Where?" he repeated.

"Would you please wait until I answer your questions before you ask them? Anywhere, dear heart. Anywhere they haven't even heard of Artus or Lancelot, Cei or Caer Camlann."

"That's a tall order, my Princess. You'd probably have to journey all the way to Africa, south of Egypt and across the desert."

She sighed again. "A wonderful dream, Cors. But of course, we're actually going to Eire. I have duties, my love."

Cors Cant spit on his left shoulder. "Duty can go to hell!"

337

"Don't remind me," said Anlawdd, troubled. Then she brightened. "Africa . . . isn't that where Cei's elephants are?"

"Supposedly. If you can believe anything Cei says. Big as a house, nose like a snake," he mocked. "If there really is any such a beast, I'll eat my harp."

"You haven't got a harp," she pointed out. "And in any case, I'd prefer you ate something else. Me, for instance."

"Eat you? What do you mean?"

Anlawdd glanced at Leary, grinned back at the erstwhile bard. "Oh, just wait till I show you, Cors Cant Ewin!"

Laughing inanely at her nonexistent joke, she led Merillwyn down a slope to the east, away from both Jutes and Britons, leaving a puzzled young innocent to follow in her wake.

CHAPTER 53

So that's about it. My tale is sung. I wish I could say that Cors Cant Ewin and I lived happily forevermore in Leary's palace at Tara, but I don't know that part yet. Here we are, picking our way down a steep hill covered by yellow grass that brushes against my knees, even atop Merillwyn, so steep that for once, I envy That Boy his shaggy, highland pony, and I'm as dark about tomorrow as the next fellow—except that the next fellow is Uncle Leary, and he probably sees tomorrow as easily as I see yesterday; but he's a tight-lipped bastard behind that beard, and he won't rat out the future.

At least I've learned to love, which is something, I guess; and I've learned to hate, to fear, and to overcome fear. I'm surely more a warrior now than I was before, and even more a princess! But I think I'm somewhat less the Anlawdd I had been, and that saddens me.

I didn't want to leave her behind, lost in the ruins of Harlech. Perhaps That Boy met her when he wandered the bowels of the city; I don't know, for he still won't tell me whom he *did* meet.

I didn't want to leave Harlech herself, either: the palace, the stadium, the baths and fountains, even though no water ran and the baths were cold with nobody left to light the *hypocaust.*

But I mean, *really,* Anlawdd! You have to grow up sometime, you know. I'm sure you didn't want to leave Mother that first time, either . . . but you can't live in the womb forever.

Can I?

Oh, Hell. Bugger all. Weighing what I've gained against all that I lost, I'd say I still got a bargain. I've That Boy, Cors Cant; and I've a grander kingdom to replace my sacked and stolen city.

I squeeze my eyes shut and feel His arms around me, His breath on my throat. Then I open them, blink at the sudden illumination. Golden sunlight spills across the island, across Prydein, catches against my hair and burns it red (no longer auburn).

Wait, I wonder . . . *do I mean him, or Him? Does it matter?*

I blink in surprise. I guess it really doesn't.

CHAPTER 54

MARK BLUNDELL STOOD AT THE CENTER OF A FIFTY-FOOT-wide, grave-hole deep excavation. *Please God,* he thought, *don't let Peter forget to bury that blasted note!*

For two days, the expedition had dug up the countryside north of Llyn Dinas, Lake Dinas, starting from the center of the triangle that Mark Blundell had sighted fifteen hundred years earlier, working outward. For two days, they had found nothing.

Roundhaven was getting impatient. Mark had lured him out to the excavation site by vivid accounts of his adventure and promises of confirmatory evidence that the temporal toroid actually worked. If they did not find something substantial soon, the minister, always far too busy for even his normal duties, would have to leave, friend or no friend.

To date, they had not even found evidence of a great battle, such as the one that surely must have taken place between Jutes and Britons the day after Mark had been killed. All the expedition had turned up so far was a double-denarius stamped with a picture of Tiberius and the inscription "IMPERATOR TIBERIVS CLAVDIVS PRINCEPS" on one side, "ANNO DOMINI XXVII" on the other.

I should try to find out when Selly is allowed visitors, Mark thought. She had been so stunned when she returned, staring at the laboratory, Willks, and Blundell and repeating "You're gone, you *must* be gone," that Cooper and the two sergeants had had no trouble at all carting her away. If they had given her a trial, it was some secret, star-chamber proceeding, because Blundell never heard a word and was not called to testify.

He had, however, been asked to say a few words at Peter Smythe's funeral. A few words is exactly what he said, for he discovered that most of what he knew about Peter had been classified as an "official secret." The scores of men who attended the service were obviously military, but they were dressed in civilian clothes and refused to give their names, even when directly asked. Mark ground his teeth, chalked it up to the SAS's obsession with secrecy.

Blundell closed his eyes, prayed for the thousandth time in two days. This time, at last, God answered his prayers.

One of the graduate students from Cardiff shouted in glee that she had found something. Mark ran across the broken ground, tripped and fell sprawling, turning his ankle.

Refusing to give in to mere pain when important scientific confirmation was at stake, he staggered back to one foot, hopped across to the excited students, who were pawing at the dirt with hands and brushes.

Even before he joined the group, Mark felt his heart sink. Whatever they had found, it was clearly not a sealed, earthenware jar, such as the one in which the Dead Sea scrolls were found.

It was the remains of a box. Blundell limped closer, leaned over the find. He was not an archaeologist, but even he could tell the box was immensely old. It had once been made of strong wood; now all that remained was dessicated, crumbled fragments and the rusted, steel framework.

The students gingerly brushed away some of the dirt atop the box. "Definitely Roman," declared one, pointing at the Latinate inscription stamped on each hinge. "FV III" it said.

"Flavius Placidius Valentinianus," suggested Mark breathlessly. "Valentinian the third. This is it, this has to be it!"

The student who had found the box leaned very close, inspecting it. "Whatever this box contained," she said at last, "it's long since crumbled into dust, sir." She looked up at Mark. "I'm sorry, sir, you won't get much out of this box except very old dirt." She shrugged apologetically.

Mark sat back, wincing at the pain in his ankle. *No blame,* he said, wondering how long it would take him to forgive Brother Smythe for forgetting about the earthenware jar. Whatever note he had buried, fifteen centuries had been plenty of time for it to crumble, decay, be attacked by worms and turned into topsoil.

"I'm sorry, Mark," said Roundhaven, looking over the physicist's shoulder. "I've invested all the time I have in this time travel project, and nothing to show for it. I know how much this means to you, but . . . well, Colonel Cooper's got a lot of pull with the PM.

"I'm afraid I'm going to have to pull the plug." He gripped Mark's shoulder for a moment. "Come on over to the house in a few days. Bring your father. I can't make it up to you, but at least I can feed you a good supper.

"Will you tell Willks? He'll get formal notification before the next Royal Academy meeting, but I'd like him to hear it from you, first."

"Of course," said Mark automatically, his voice mechanical, uninflected.

Roundhaven nodded, walked back toward his MG. Mark turned back to the ancient, wooden strongbox. "We met on the level, Peter," he said, a lump in his throat, "and parted on the square. But if I ever get my hands on you in heaven, Smythe, you're going to be one fallen angel."

Mark Blundell stood, took a last look at the first place he had ever died, then limped slowly toward his own four-wheel drive, wondering how he was going to shift without putting any weight on his foot.

THE ABSOLUTE, FINAL, HONEST-TO-GOD END

Afterword to Far Beyond the Wave

Most weary seemed the sea, weary the oar,
Weary the wandering fields of barren foam.
Then some one said, "We will return no more";
And all at once they sang, "Our island home
Is far beyond the wave; we will no longer roam."

ALFRED, LORD TENNYSON, *The Lotos-Eaters*

THIS IS, IN FACT, A *FOREWORD* THAT CAN STILL BE READ BEfore reading the fine novel that precedes it. I promise to write carefully to not ruin the suspense or spoil your enjoyment (excepting those soreheads who insist *any* writing of mine spoils their enjoyment!).

Despite the trappings of fantasy, *Arthur War Lord* is actually a science fiction book. There is no element of magic that cannot be satisfactorily explained by science, though the characters don't always know that.

I always love science fiction masquerading as fantasy, such as in Jack Vance's *Planet of Adventure* series, and fantasy masquerading as science fiction, à la Randall Garrett's "Lord D'Arcy" stories; so I am delighted to actually have a chance to write such a crossover.

An ideal example of this sort of melding is found in Mark Twain's *Connecticutt Yankee in King Arthur's Court,* a brilliant novel to which *Arthur War Lord* evidently owes its basic idea (a modern chap going back to Arthurian times).

However, I deliberately avoided any closer correspondence to that book—first, because the idea of a modern-

day man reinventing today's technology in the past has
been so thoroughly covered by Twain, L. Sprague de
Camp, and other authors; second, because "rewriting Mark
Twain is like arm-wrestling Hercules," as Princess
Anlawdd might say in the pages that follow. Er, precede.

Regarding Anlawdd, you might notice intriguing similarities to the Princess Eilonwy from Lloyd Alexander's
Newbery-Award-winning pentology *The Chronicles of
Taran.* The parallel is deliberate; I absolutely fell in love
with that red-haired princess, and I'm still furious with
Lloyd for giving her to that little weasel Taran instead of
saving her for me.

You can think of Anlawdd, if you wish, as a somewhat
more mystical (and bloodthirsty) version of Princess
Eilonwy (and you might note that both Lloyd and I shame-
lessly stole character names from the Welsh-Arthurian epic
"Culhwch and Olwen").

For the world of *Arthur War Lord,* I looked first to what
is known *historically* about Arthur—or Artus *Dux
Bellorum* ("war leader," or "war lord")—and only second-
arily to the romantic, troubador versions that became popular in 12th century France and were compiled by Thomas
Malory three centuries later as *Le Morte D'Arthur.* Thus,
my "Artus" considers himself a Roman, doesn't wear plate
armor, isn't a king, and doesn't go questing for any holy
grails.

However, I never allowed faithful adherence to the mess
of history or the mythic "matter of Britain" to interfere
with a good plot-bit. Hence, I shifted everybody backward
about fifty years in time so I could have Artus and King
Merovee of Sicambria monkeying around Europe together;
and I allowed Lancelot to creep into the story, despite the
fact that he doesn't even appear in the original Welsh versions.

The *mileau* is as historically accurate as I could make it:
the Romans really did have concrete apartment buildings;
they really did have plumbing that brought water to your
doorstep (and they charged water rates for the service);

and Artus's palace of "Caer Camlann" is based exactly on the floor plan of the Flavian Palace in Rome.

Of course, in reality, the few such astonishing buildings in Britain in A.D. 450 left truly stunning ruins, and we know where they all were. So if you're looking for amazingly accurate historical fiction, read Harry Turtledove or Judy Tarr!

Speaking of Tarr, she is responsible for all the wonderful Latin translations in this book . . . so if any closet classicists out there quibble with the Latin, be advised that Tarr is a professor of Mediaeval Studies and that Latin literature is her field.

A word about the pronounciation of Welsh names: don't even bother. It's not worth the *tsouris*. Just pronounce them any way that seems natural to you. If you want to call Anlawdd "Annie," go ahead; she won't mind.

By the way, the fellow on the covers of the two books in this series, *Arthur War Lord* and *Far Beyond the Wave,* is Lancelot; Arthur, or "Artus," looks like a typical Roman governor. Think of *I, Claudius* on PBS.

If you wish to refresh your memory of the first book, please read the synopsis at the beginning of this volume; I included everything important.

Have a good read, and remember to buy early, buy often!

AVONOVA PRESENTS
AWARD-WINNING NOVELS
FROM MASTERS OF SCIENCE FICTION